CATCHING THE FLY

PLAYING FOR KEEPS SERIES

LAUREN FRASER

CONTENTS

Blurb   V

BEFORE YOU READ   VI

1. Chapter One   1

2. Chapter Two   13

3. Chapter Three   20

4. Chapter Four   30

5. Chapter Five   42

6. Chapter Six   51

7. Chapter Seven   59

8. Chapter Eight   77

9. Chapter Nine   91

10. Chapter Ten   110

11. Chapter Eleven   121

12. Chapter Twelve   146

13. Chapter Thirteen   163

14. Chapter Fourteen   176

15.	Chapter Fifteen	187
16.	Chapter Sixteen	198
17.	Chapter Seventeen	211
18.	Chapter Eighteen	227
19.	Chapter Nineteen	244
20.	Chapter Twenty	252
21.	Chapter Twenty-One	263
22.	Chapter Twenty-Two	274
23.	Chapter Twenty-Three	287
24.	Chapter Twenty-Four	302
25.	Chapter Twenty-Five	316
26.	Chapter Twenty-Six	326
27.	Chapter Twenty-Seven	335
28.	Chapter Twenty-Eight	343
29.	Chapter Twenty-Nine	356
30.	Epilogue	366
	About Lauren Fraser	385
	Also by Lauren Fraser	387

BLURB

Arrogant Ball Player? No thanks. Broody grump who rescues dogs? Yes please. Too bad he's both.

When Annie Wright met Brandon Sims, she thought he was just an arrogant baseball player, self-absorbed and only out for #1. And who needs that? Not this girl.

But when the gruff athlete walks into her veterinary clinic with a wounded dog he's rescued, she sees a totally unexpected side of him. Beneath his tough exterior is a guy who's more cinnamon roll than he lets on—too bad he's terrified of showing it.

She's always been a sucker for an underdog. And what's more underdog than a guy who doesn't realize how great he is?

Grab this steamy wounded hero stand-alone about a veterinarian who can't help but fall for a grumpy pro baller and his adorable dog.

BEFORE YOU READ

This book contains content that may be triggering for some readers.

If you would like to learn more about the content warnings for this book please visit Lauren's website: https://www.laurenfraser.com/catching-the-fly

CHAPTER ONE

What a shitty way to end the season. Brandon Sim's stared into his half empty beer. There wasn't enough alcohol in the world to drown out what he was feeling. The season had looked so promising early on. How the hell could they get knocked out in the first round of playoffs?

"Another round?" Lou Hernandez asked.

Brandon blinked and looked up from his glass at the first baseman, then at the rest of the table. His teammates looked just as dejected and pathetic as he felt.

"Yeah, may as well," he replied. Just because there wasn't enough beer to make him forget, it didn't mean he wasn't going to try.

Scanning the bar, his sight lingered on a sexy brunette at a table of women. While beer might not work, a woman like that would go a long way toward turning the night around. The brunette threw her head back and let out a loud, full-bodied laugh he could hear from across the room. People from the neighboring tables all turned to look at her, but she seemed oblivious to the stares. Or maybe she just didn't care.

He took a sip of beer as he watched her. He'd always had a thing for brunettes and judging from her laughter, she'd be exactly what he was looking for in bed. Loud and uninhibited.

She glanced over at him and their gaze met. The woman watched him longer than was polite. He knew interest when he saw it. Hell yeah, this night just got a lot better. He drained the last of his beer. "If you'll excuse me, gentleman, I think I've found a better offer."

"What? The brunette that just gave you the cold shoulder?" Lou asked.

"She didn't give me the cold shoulder. She was eyeing me up. She's interested."

Lou snorted. "There's zero chance she's going home with you tonight."

"Yeah, you want to bet?"

Lou turned and looked at the table of women. The redhead nudged the brunette, who shook her head, refusing to look their way. "Oh definitely. It's on. Zero chance with that one."

"What do you want to bet?"

"All right, let's see." Lou tapped his nose with his finger like it would help him think.

"My god, you two are pathetic. You'll bet on anything," Pete said.

"Come on, Pete, look at that woman. There's no way she'd go home with cocky McGee here?" Lou flicked his thumb toward Brandon.

Brandon glanced over at the woman again. She still hadn't looked back at him. A little niggle of doubt stirred in his chest. Maybe she wasn't such a sure thing. But no, he knew interest when he saw it, and she had definitely been interested. She might play it coy now, but she was attracted to him.

"Yeah, I don't think she's in the market for a hookup, man. The blonde at her table maybe, but not the brunette," Pete agreed.

"Okay, so when you lose, you can do my laundry for a month," Lou said.

"And when I win?" Brandon asked.

Lou smirked. "Not happening, but I'd do yours."

"Nah, I want my car fully detailed, inside and out."

"Fuck that, that shit's expensive," Lou groaned.

"What? Not feeling so cocky now, Lourdes?" Brandon said, using his teammate's full name. "We both know your housekeeper would be doing my laundry if you lost. This way you gotta put up some cold, hard cash," Brandon taunted.

Lourdes Hernandez hated losing. It was one of the things that made him such a great first baseman.

Lou stuck out his hand. "Deal."

Brandon shook his hand. "My car is going to look so good."

"You two are idiots," Ryan Graves said.

"Yeah, but I'm going to be an idiot with a pretty car and a hot woman in my bed," Brandon said.

"We'll see," Lou mocked.

Brandon pushed away from the table and walked toward the group of women. The brunette flicked a glance his way, then back to her friends.

He stopped at the edge of the round table beside the brunette. "Hi ladies."

The sexy brunette gave him a small smile. Unfortunately, her redheaded friend glanced at him and rolled her eyes, hard. He flicked a look back at his friends, who all watched him raptly.

Okay shit, maybe this was going to be a lot harder than he'd expected, but he liked a challenge. He turned to the sexy brunette. "Hi, I'm Brandon."

She looked at him, then at his friends, then back at him. "Okay," she replied.

Okay, that was it? That was all she was going to give him? "What's your name?" he asked.

Crickets.

The blonde beside her seemed to take pity on him. "Her name is Annie and I'm Jen." She pointed to the redhead. "This is Patrice and Carla," she said, indicating the other brunette at the table.

"Nice to meet you all. Can I buy you ladies a round of drinks?"

"No," the redhead replied.

"Absolutely," Carla said at the same time. The redhead glared at her friend.

"Have I offended you in some way?" Brandon asked the redhead, Patrice. What was the woman's problem? He hadn't even come over to talk to her, so why was she hitting him so hard with the cold shoulder?

Patrice glanced at him, then looked over at his friends. "Let me guess, you have some kind of wager with your friends that you can bag one of us for the night?"

He winced, then tried to recover so she didn't see it. How the hell did she know that and why did it sound so bad when she said it?

When he'd been talking with Lou, it hadn't sounded that awful. It was just something they did. A friendly wager to up the thrill of the chase a little bit.

Ignoring the grumpy redhead, he turned to Annie. "Look, I noticed you, obviously, and thought you were gorgeous and would kick myself if I didn't come over."

"So the wager is to bang Annie, then?" Patrice asked.

The table rattled and shook. "Ouch, I just kicked the post," Carla groaned.

Patrice narrowed her eyes at her friend and Brandon bit back a laugh. He was pretty sure if that post hadn't gotten in the way Carla would have kicked her friend under the table.

He knew redheads could be fiery, but this lady took the prize. Patrice sure as hell was not on board with him being there, but so far, Annie hadn't shut him down and her other friends weren't completely opposed to him hitting on her. So that was good.

"So how come people keep coming up to your table tonight? Who are you guys?" Jen asked.

"We play for the Hawks," Brandon replied, keeping his eyes on Annie the entire time to see if she had any reaction. Unfortunately, she didn't.

"Like the baseball team?" Jen said.

"Yeah." He scanned the room. Several of his teammates played pool in the back corner. "This is kind of a known Hawks hangout."

"Known. Meaning if we're here, we must have known that you guys would be here after your game?" Patrice asked.

He shrugged. In his experience on a game night, the only people in the place were Hawks fans.

"My god," the redhead mumbled.

What was with this woman? He didn't stand a hope in hell of getting anywhere with Annie if this woman didn't let up a little.

"How come you're so prickly?" he asked.

"I just think it's a bit ridiculous that you think just because you're some big shot ballplayer we'll all drop our panties the second you ask."

"Hey now, that's not fair. I don't expect all of you to drop your panties." The only panties he cared about were Annie's. He flashed her what he hoped was a charming smile.

Annie rolled her eyes, but two of her friends giggled at least. So he still had hope. She hadn't shot him down yet, but she wasn't giving him the green light either. And for some reason, it kind of turned him on. Normally women fawned all over themselves with him and that wasn't being egotistical, it was just the facts.

He stared at the woman in front of him. She really was beautiful. He could just imagine what her thick, wavy brown hair would feel like against his fingers. The way her green eyes sparked with a hint of interest made him wonder what they would look like during the heat of passion.

"Look, why don't we try this again?" He shifted his body so he was looking down at her. "Hi, I'm Brandon. I was sitting over there with my friends and couldn't help but notice how beautiful you are, and I was wondering if I could buy you a drink."

Her eyes softened, and she smirked slightly. "Does that usually work?"

He shifted uncomfortably. "Usually yeah?"

Annie laughed and shook her head. "Wow, okay, that's not saying much about my gender." She looked around at her friends. "Would that work on any of you?"

Oh shit, please don't ask the redhead that. Brandon watched the other women expectantly, knowing full well their answers could either help him or kill him dead in the water.

"Definitely not," the redhead grumbled.

That was not surprising. Of course she would say that.

"He's pretty cute, so—" Jen shrugged.

"I'm not ashamed to admit I'd go home with him." Carla winked at him.

"Umm thanks, I think."

Carla's gaze ran up and down his body and he had to fight to stand still. God, was that what women felt like when he did that? Shit, he sure hoped not because he felt like he needed a shower.

He glanced over at Annie. The right side of her mouth curved up slightly. He was pretty sure she was enjoying his discomfort. And fair enough, he maybe deserved that.

Annie shifted in her chair and faced him. "So what's the bet?"

"Pardon?" he replied.

Picking up where Patrice had left off, she asked, "What's the bet? You take me home and what do you win?"

"I get to go home with you." He let his gaze roam down her body suggestively. "I think what I'm winning is pretty obvious."

"Right." She snickered. "Besides the obvious."

She glanced over at his friends who were pretending to be in conversation but were still very obviously paying attention to what was happening with the ladies.

"What was the wager?" she asked.

"How come you're so sure we made a wager?"

"Because we all know guys like you. There's no chance you and your buddy with the hat don't have some kind of bet going on. So spill it."

He rubbed the back of his neck. "You make it sound like me coming over here was just some kind of game. It wasn't. At all."

"Mmm-hmm."

He should just leave. There was zero chance this woman was going home with him. Why did he feel the need to stick around and talk to her? To explain himself. Why did he even care? "Okay, yes, we made a bet, but I was coming over here regardless."

"So, what was the bet?"

"Get my car fully detailed," he mumbled.

"Nice. That's better than I thought it was going to be. I was expecting you'd owe him a beer or something. But car detailing is good, that's worth winning over."

She looked him up and down. "So what, you wanted to just fuck here in the bathroom?"

He stepped back. "God, no, I'm not that big of a dick."

"Oh, so you have to go home with me to win?"

"Fuck, no, i...it's not," he stammered. "Look, forget it. I'm sorry I bothered you."

"It's all good." Annie laughed. "You're a good-looking guy. I'm sure you'll find some other woman who's willing to go home with you."

Annie turned to her friends. "And on that note, I'm going to head out."

"Already?" Carla whined.

"Yeah, I have an early morning."

"Okay, we love you." Jen blew her a kiss across the table.

Annie stood up and he knew he should step back, but he couldn't help himself. The impression she had of him cut. Sure he could be an asshole, but he wasn't the guy she thought he was. Or at least he hoped he wasn't. Okay, making a wager on sex was kind of douche thing to do but...He took a deep breath.

"Look Annie, I'm really sorry if I offended you. Honestly, when I saw you the only thought on my brain was I have to meet her. Yeah, maybe I went about it the wrong way, but I had to take my shot. I would have regretted it if I hadn't come over."

"I appreciate your apology," Annie replied.

"Can I at least walk you to your car?"

"What? So your friends think you won the bet? You walk me to my car, then head home and they are none the wiser?"

"Jesus. What the fuck kind of men have you met before? No, I don't cheat. That's not winning."

"Then why do you want to walk me to my car? I think I've made it pretty clear we aren't going home together."

"Oh, believe me, I'm very aware," he muttered. "But I don't like the idea of you walking to your car alone. It's late, it's not the best area. I'd just feel better if you let me walk you to your car, so I know you got there safely."

She stared at him, assessing him. "And I'd be safe with you?"

"Yeah, of course."

"How do I know that?"

"You don't I guess." He looked around the bar. "Most of the people in here know who I am. Fans wouldn't like me if I was known to be sleazy."

"He's right, Annie," Jen said. "Just let him walk you to your car. We'd all feel better knowing you were safe."

"Fine," she agreed begrudgingly.

Of course this was how his evening was going to play out. The team had been destroyed on the field and now he was striking out with a woman. Perfect.

He didn't even bother looking over at his friends as he walked out of the bar with Annie. Let them think what they wanted. The moment he walked back into the bar they'd realize he'd lost the bet.

"I'm just down here," Annie said when they exited the bar.

He kept pace with her as they walked down the street. At the corner, a group of intoxicated men watched as they walked toward them. Instinctively, he stepped closer to Annie, minimizing the distance between them, leaving no question that they were together.

Once they were past the group, Annie spoke. "Thanks for walking me to my car. I appreciate it." She glanced over her shoulder at the group of men.

"No problem."

"So you're really going to go back to the bar and admit to your friend you lost the bet?"

"Yeah, of course." Out of the corner of his eye, he could see her sneaking little glances at him. "Why do you sound so surprised?"

"I don't know. Your friends already think you won. It'd be pretty easy to just head home. In my experience, that's what most people would do."

He stuck his hands in his pockets. "I'm not most people."

"This is me," she said, stopping beside a newer looking SUV.

"Any chance I could get your number? I meant what I said about regretting it if I didn't take my shot."

"I don't think that's a good idea," she replied.

"Why's that?"

"I just don't think we have much in common."

"How do you know? We just met."

"Call it a hunch," she said.

He dug his hands deeper into his pockets and exhaled. "That's too bad. If you change your mind, my last name's Sims. I can be reached through the team."

"I won't, but thanks." She smiled, softening the blow.

He couldn't remember the last time a woman had shot him down. Just because it didn't happen very often didn't mean it didn't suck when it did.

"Thanks for walking me to my car and for proving me wrong about what kind of guy you are."

"Anytime."

What was he doing with his life? Was she wrong about what kind of guy he was? Not really. He'd gone up to her thinking she was a sure thing. Believing he was going to go home with her.

The fact she proved him wrong didn't change the kind of person he was. It just said she wasn't the kind of person he'd thought she was. It said nothing about him.

When did he become that guy?

He waited while Annie got into her car, started it and drove away before slowly walking back toward the bar.

Back inside the bar, he nodded to Annie's friends as he walked past.

"What are you doing back here already?" Lou asked.

"Didn't work out," he muttered. Sliding into his vacant seat, he eyed his empty beer glass. May as well get drunk since he wasn't getting lucky. He picked up the jug from the middle of the table and refilled his mug.

"What happened? I thought that was a sure thing?" Lou pressed.

"Clearly it wasn't," he grumbled. "And maybe we shouldn't bet on things like women anymore."

"Ah, don't be all sour because you lost," Lou mocked.

"I'm not, I'm just saying, maybe that's kind of a dick thing to do."

"Whatever," Lou said. "You still lost. My car is going to look so pretty when she's all sparkly. This is so much better than laundry."

"Fuck you." He laughed.

CHAPTER TWO

B randon's heart pounded as he sprinted down the last hill. He flicked a glance at his watch, then kicked his speed up even faster. If he wanted to beat his best time, he needed to turn it up. Arms pumping, his legs burned as he rounded the last corner and past the giant rock marker he used to indicate the imaginary finish line. He glanced at his wrist again and smiled. Yes, he'd broken his personal best by three seconds. Not a lot, but he still beat it.

Slowly walking in circles, he let his heartbeat slow down. He paused when he heard a soft whimpering sound. What was that? Was that an animal?

Standing still, he strained to hear where the sound was coming from. He couldn't hear anything, then from off to the right he heard a soft whimper like a wounded animal.

Following the sound, he climbed up the hill toward the road. Cars zoomed down the freeway, making it hard to hear anything. This was stupid. Why was he even bothering? It was probably nothing.

He was just about to turn around when he saw movement in the bush at the top of the hill. It didn't hurt to check it out.

Carefully trudging through the brush, he could see what looked like possibly a furry leg sticking out of the bush. As he stepped closer to the bush, a low growl sounded.

Moving slowly so as not to scare the unknown animal, he stepped around the bush. As he rounded the side, a beaten and bloody dog raised its head slightly. The animal's face was shredded. Brandon sucked in a breath. There was no way that happened from a car.

The dog tried to lift its head more but could barely move. "Jesus, what happened to you?" Brandon muttered.

Holding out his hands to show the dog he wasn't going to harm it, he stepped closer. "It's okay, I just want to take a look at you and see if I can help," he told the dog.

Brandon bent down closer. God, how was this thing even still alive? He crept closer. The dog growled roughly, his massacred face distorting even further as the dog's lip curled. Brandon sat down on the ground. "It's okay, I'm not going to hurt you," he soothed.

How the hell had this dog gotten here? He looked up at the road, then back at the dog. Had someone thrown him out of their car? That was the only thing that made sense given the condition of the dog. There was no way he'd crawled down there.

He couldn't just leave him there. Brandon eyed the road again, then down the hill toward his running trail. It's not like he could carry the dog back to his car. But maybe he could swing back around and pick him up from the road.

Pushing himself up, he walked up to the road and looked down. He couldn't see the dog from up there. Shit. How was he going to know where to stop? Spotting loose garbage along the side of the road, he walked along and picked it up. He placed the garbage all in a pile at the edge of the meridian, dumped his water bottle out all over the cement and prayed it would stay wet long enough for him to get to his car and back so he could easily see his makeshift mile marker.

Taking note of the trees and surrounding area, he hopped back over the meridian and climbed back down to the dog. Taking off his shirt, he tied it around the bush so he could spot it from the road just in case his makeshift marker didn't work.

He bent down as close as he dared to the dog. "I'm just going to get my car and I'll be right back, buddy, okay?"

The dog simply watched him. It didn't growl at all. Whether that was because he trusted him or because he was too weak, he couldn't say. Brandon took one last look at the beaten dog and took off as fast as he dared toward his car.

He pushed his body. He was in good shape, but he'd already pushed it during his run and had planned to do the last mile as a walking cool down. Not adding in a hike up a steep hill followed by a one mile sprint. By the time he hit his car, his lungs burned.

Brandon pounded his other water bottle, then threw his car into gear. Where the hell was he supposed to take a wounded dog on a Sunday? First, he had to make sure the dog would survive getting into the car.

Keeping his eyes peeled, he spotted his makeshift marker on the side of the highway and pulled over. He looked over the edge. His shirt lay lifeless against the bush. God, he hoped that wasn't some bad omen of what he'd find when he got down there.

What could he use as a blanket? He spotted his hoodie on the floor of the backseat and grabbed it. Good enough.

Carefully trudging down the hill, he paused at the edge of the bush. The dog's low growl was the only indication it was still alive. "It's okay, buddy, it's just me. I'm going to take you some place and see if they can fix you up."

In order to give the dog some time to get used to him, he untied his shirt and put it back on, then sat down on the ground as close as he could to the dog. "I know this is going to hurt, but I have to pick you up and carry you. I'm sorry."

He moved his hand toward the dog, and it snarled. There wasn't a single place he could see that looked like it wouldn't hurt to touch. How the hell was he going to do this without getting bitten?

He moved closer to the dog. The animal watched him, wary. He stretched his hand out closer but avoided touching the dog. Hoping if he could get his scent, he'd sense he wasn't in danger. After several minutes, he crept closer again. "I'm gonna pick you up now. I'll try to be gentle." The dog eyed him but didn't move. Brandon held his hoodie out for the dog to sniff. "I just need to wrap you in this to keep you safe."

He eyed the sweatshirt, then the dog. How the hell was he going to do this without freaking the dog out?

Brandon took a deep breath. The moment the sweat-shirt wrapped around the dog, the wounded animal snapped and flailed. Brandon winced when the dog's teeth connected with his bare arm. Shit, that hurt.

"It's okay, it's okay," he tried to soothe the dog as he wrapped it safely in his hoodie. Once the dog was bundled, Brandon didn't move as he continued to speak calmly until the dog stopped fighting. Finally, the fight left the dog's body and the animal stopped squirming.

Not wanting to scare it, Brandon continued to stay put, talking to the dog. It was probably wishful thinking but after a few minutes Brandon could swear the dog started to trust him as it shifted its weight against his chest like it was trying to get more comfortable.

"That's it, buddy," he soothed. "I'm not gonna lie. The walk up the hill is gonna suck. I'm gonna try not to hurt you at all, but I can't promise. But we need to move so I can get you to a vet so they can help you."

Brandon looked at the dog's mangled face and into the one eye he thought might still be working. "Don't bite me again, okay, cuz that hurt. I don't blame you. I would have bitten me too. But let's not do it again because I don't want to accidentally drop you or anything and I might if you get me good." Brandon stared into the dog's eye. "I need you to trust me. I'm gonna try my best not to hurt you."

The dog closed its eye and dropped his head against Brandon's chest. Taking that as a sign of agreement, he began his assent up the steep terrain. At one particularly steep section, the dog growled slightly when Brandon had to adjust his body to push up the hill, but thankfully he didn't bite.

When Brandon made it to the top of the hill, he looked down at the bundle in his arms. Blood soaked through parts of his sweatshirt. Shit, some of the wounds had reopened as they came up the hill.

Brandon eyed the newly restored leather on the back-seat of his classic Bronco, then the bleeding dog. Oh well, he sighed and eased the dog into the backseat. The animal barely raised his head as he slid him further onto the seat. God, he hoped this dog made it.

Rushing around to the driver's side, he jumped into the car. He needed to find a vet. Fast. He punched the satellite search feature on his phone. "Find an emergency vet clinic," he said.

He called the first number, which listed an emergency vet number. He pushed one to be connected. No answer. He tried the next number on the list. Same thing. Fuck.

Four phone calls later, he finally got someone on the line. What the hell was the point of after hours service if no one answered the goddamn phone?

"I need a vet," he said the moment a real person answered the phone.

"Is this an emergency?"

"I wouldn't be calling the emergency number if it wasn't," he snapped.

"Sir, I'm gonna need you to calm down."

Brandon grit his teeth. In what world did telling someone to calm down ever work? "I found an injured dog and I need to bring him in."

"You found an injured dog?"

"Yes."

"How do you know it's injured?"

"Are you fucking kidding me?" he snarled.

"Sir. I understand you are stressed, but I will not be spoken to rudely."

"Then how about you don't ask stupid questions and just tell me where I can bring this dog. He's covered in blood, barely alive. I just need to bring him in to see a vet."

"You found him like this?"

"Jesus, yes, that's what I said." Did they not freaking train people on these call lines for how to respond to emergencies? What the hell?

"Sir."

From that tone, the woman was just one more swear word away from hanging up on him, regardless of the dog's injuries. "Sorry. I'm worried about this dog and I'd like to bring it in, please."

With directions to the vet's office, Brandon took off. He just hoped he got there in time.

CHAPTER THREE

"**I** need a vet," a male voice yelled from the clinic waiting room.

Annie turned her attention to the noise. She could dimly hear the muted voice of their receptionist, Dana, followed by the man's loud, agitated reply, "Get a fucking vet."

Damn. It was never a good thing when someone came into their office sounding like that.

Annie placed her hand on the quivering dog in front of her. She ran a soothing hand down its spine. "It's okay, Skittles." She looked at her veterinarian assistant, Janelle. "Give me a minute, and I'll be right back."

"Don't worry about it. Just send Terri in and we can do the blood draw and clip his nails since his owner wanted that done while he was here."

"Perfect, thanks."

Squaring her shoulders, she mentally prepared herself for what she might find when she stepped outside. The first thing she saw when she walked toward the waiting room was a huge male frame. The second was the large bundle in his arms. What looked like a bloody sweatshirt wrapped around something. Her chest tightened. Had he hit an animal with his car?

"Dr. Wright, thank goodness," Dana gushed.

The man turned toward her with the bundle is his arms. Her stomach flipped. Brandon Sims. The sexy baseball player from the bar.

"Are you the doctor?" he asked.

Annie stepped closer, trying to make out what kind of animal he had wrapped in the sweatshirt. "I'm the vet, yes."

"Help him. Please," he begged, holding his arms out toward her.

"What happened?"

"I don't know. Help him."

She moved to reach her hand out and the animal growled. "Okay, bring him in here." She gestured toward the exam room to the right of the entrance.

Brandon moved swiftly into the room, then looked at her like he was waiting for direction.

"Can you put him on the table?" From the size and the growl, she'd guess it was a dog in his arms, but the animal had curled its face into Brandon's chest and she couldn't make out much of anything.

He set the animal on the table, and it moaned in pain. "Shh, shh, it's okay," Brandon cooed. "This nice lady is going to help you."

He obviously didn't have a clue who she was. It stung a little, but what did she expect from a guy who made bets with his friends about picking up women?

Pushing back her annoyance, Annie eyed him. Despite solidifying her view of him as a player, at least he seemed to care about the dog. If she hadn't seen it for herself, she wouldn't have thought someone so big could be so gentle.

Brandon gently peeled back the sweatshirt, exposing the dog.

Oh Jesus.

Annie sucked in a breath. Stepping closer, she scanned the dog visually. The dog's body was shredded. There was so much blood she couldn't tell the extent of the damage, but what she could see it was bad. "This dog has been attacked."

"Yeah." Brandon moved his hand like he was going to touch the dog, then pulled it back and turned to her. His eyes were tortured as he looked at her. "Do something."

Annie moved closer to the table. The dog's lip curled in a snarl the closer she got. Damn it, she wasn't going to be able to do any kind of examination if she couldn't get close to it.

"Poor baby," she murmured. As she touched the edge of the table, the dog tried to move away from her.

"Shh, shh, it's okay, she's not going to hurt you," Brandon said.

"I'm just going to do a visual exam until he feels a little safer with me coming near." Annie watched as the dog tried to shift closer to Brandon. "Can you just keep talking to him? That seems to be helping."

Without being able to touch the dog, it was hard to see the full extent of the damage. It would help if she knew for sure what had attacked him. Living in the city, the only thing she could think of that would do this kind of damage was another dog. But if they'd been camping or something, it could have been a different animal.

"What happened to him?" she asked.

"I don't know."

"What do you mean you don't know? Did he get loose or where was he when it happened?"

"I don't know," Brandon muttered.

Her gut clenched. "What do you mean, you don't know?"

"I mean, I don't know," he snapped. Brandon straightened to his full height and glared at her. "Why does it matter what happened? He's hurt, help him, that's your fucking job."

Annie's spine snapped. "Whoa. I'm going to need you to take a breath." Trying to give him the benefit of the doubt, she paused so she remained calm. His dog was injured, and people didn't always behave well when they were scared. "I get that you're scared, but I'm trying to help."

"Are you?" he snarled. "Look at him." He gestured toward the dog. "He's hurting. His fucking leg is barely attached. Jesus, fucking help him."

"I can see his leg is barely attached. He's obviously lost his eye as well. I'm just trying to figure out what happened." She took a breath. "Okay, let's start with his name."

"I don't know. He's not my dog."

Okay, she had not seen that coming. "Who's dog is he?"

"I have no idea. I found him when I was out running."

That didn't make any sense. The dog clearly trusted him, but every time she got close, he looked ready to fight. "When did you find him?"

Brandon glanced at his watch. "About forty-five minutes ago." He pushed his hand through his brown hair. "I had to leave him and go get my car. My..." He cleared his throat. "My hoodie was the only thing I had to carry him in. Did I hurt him by moving him?"

"I don't know." She eyed the wounded animal. It was amazing the dog was even alive from the looks of him. He was clearly in a lot of pain. "You can just leave him with us and we'll take care of him."

Brandon's eyes narrowed. "What do you mean take care of him?"

She looked at the dog again. "Unfortunately, given the situation, I think the only humane thing to do is to help him let go and cross over."

"You want to kill him?"

"No, I want to ease his suffering."

"Right," he scoffed. "You're not giving up on him that easy."

Annie reared back. "Pardon me?"

"I'll pay. Whatever it costs for you to give him a chance, I'll pay it."

"Brandon." She sighed.

His head snapped up at the use of his name, and she winced. Crap, she hadn't wanted to admit she knew who he was when he clearly didn't remember her. Hoping to avoid any explanation, she focused on the dog. "We're talking thousands of dollars of surgery and even then I don't know if he will make it."

"But you could at least try." He glared at her.

"And then what? Try to get him adopted?"

"Sure, why not?"

She looked over at the mangled dog on her table. "On a good day, a Pitbull is hard to adopt. He won't let me near him, and I don't know if that's his injuries speaking or something else. We don't know anything about this dog. He could be unadoptable." She pointedly looked at the obvious bite mark on Brandon's arm.

"He at least deserves the chance to find out."

"Brandon, I don't even know if he will survive the surgery."

"He'll survive."

"We don't know that."

"He'll survive. He didn't fight this fucking hard to live just to die now." He stared at the dog. "He's a fighter."

"That's kind of the problem. He might be so used to fighting he doesn't know how not to." She stepped toward the table and the dog snarled. If she had to guess, she'd say even before the injury this dog hadn't had an easy life. "Abused dogs are hard to adopt."

Brandon's entire posture changed. It was like a darkness overtook the entire room. "You think he was abused?" He hadn't raised his voice, but somehow it felt like the walls shook as he spoke.

"If I had to guess, yes," she said softly.

"You need to fix him, Doc."

"And then what? Who is going to look after him? It's just cruel to make him go through with all the surgery and recovery to not have a home to go to."

"He'll have a home," Brandon declared.

"Right. Are you going to keep him with your schedule?"

His back stiffened. Emotion clouded his eyes, but when he raised his head to look at her, he'd masked his face, and she could no longer read him. "You worry about your job. I'll worry about mine."

"I'm not going to do surgery on a dog just to see him have to be put down."

"He won't be getting put down," Brandon snarled. "You know who I am. I've got millions of followers. He'll get adopted. He won't be getting put down."

Arrogant prick. Just because he's some famous ass-hole doesn't mean he can find someone to look after a high-needs dog. Annie looked at the dog on the table. Shit. The dog deserved a chance.

"Fine. But there are no guarantee's he's going to make it through surgery. Despite how he's acting, this dog is seriously injured."

"Yeah, I'd have to be a fucking idiot not to see that."

Annie closed her eyes and counted to ten. It wasn't good business practice to swear at a paying client. "Give your number to Dana at the front desk and she'll call you with an update later today."

"I'm not just leaving him here."

Lord, this man was trying her patience. She took another deep breath. "He's in good hands."

"He won't even let you near him. How the fuck are you supposed to sedate him?"

The man had a point. It would be a lot easier to give the dog something to calm him down with him in the room. "This isn't my first time around an injured animal. They often don't want to let anyone near them."

Granted, most of the dogs she saw weren't in this condition. "I promise to do everything in my power to give him the best possible chance."

She looked down at the wounded dog. The sooner she was able to help him, the better chance he'd have. "Just give me a minute and I'll be right back."

Annie rushed out of the room. She popped her head into Skittles' exam room. "Change of plans. I need to do emergency surgery on this dog that just came in. Terri, can you wrap up things with Skittles and ask Dr. Main to do his vaccination for me? Janelle, I need you to prep the OR for an amputation, leg and eye and we'll see what else needs done once we get in there."

"Oh my god," Terri cried.

"Yeah, it's a bad one."

"I'm on it," Janelle said, and hastily followed Annie out of the room and down the hall.

Her vet tech, Sarah, stepped out of the breakroom. "Sarah, perfect. I'm gonna need your help to move a dog into the exam room once I get him settled."

"Sure."

"Exam room 2. I'll buzz you when I'm ready," she called as she proceeded to the pharmacy.

After grabbing what she needed, she hurried back to the room. Both man and dog watched her as she approached. Even as injured as he was, the dog assessed her every move like he was ready to attack. What had this dog been through that he was like this? Poor thing.

Brandon stepped closer to the dog. "All right, Leo, the doc's going to fix you up."

Leo? "I thought you didn't know his name?"

"I don't. But he's a fighter. He's got the heart of a lion, so it seemed fitting."

Annie looked down at the wounded animal. "Yeah, it does."

It was going to take all of her skill to give this dog a fighting chance. She looked over at the giant baseball player across the table. He seemed to care about Leo now, but would he still in a couple weeks when the dog was ready to go home if he made it? Only time would tell.

She pulled a needle out of her coat pocket. "I'm just going to give him something to help with the pain and help him relax so we can move him."

Leo growled when she stepped closer. Brandon slowly reached out and touched an exposed spot on the dog's good front leg. Surprisingly, the dog let him. Annie eyed Brandon. "You really just met this dog?"

"Yeah."

It was remarkable how much the dog seemed to trust a stranger. While Brandon continued to gently stroke the dog's foot, cooing and talking to keep the dog calm, she quickly went to work, finding a vein in his back leg. In record time, she was done.

While she waited for the medicine to kick in, she rested her hip against the edge of the table. "It was good of you to bring him in."

"Didn't really have much choice. I wasn't going to leave him there."

"A lot of people would have."

"Yeah, well, a lot of people suck."

Unfortunately, sometimes that was true, especially when it came to animals. "Once I have him sedated, I'll be able to get a better look at his injuries and we can call you with a quote or to discuss the next steps, depending on what I find."

Brandon raised his head and looked at her. His eyes narrowed. "I don't need a quote. I need you to do whatever you can to give him the best chance of survival."

"If you're sure, then we'll call you when he's out of surgery."

As Brandon looked down at the dog, sadness clouded his face before he sighed and nodded his head. "You keep fighting and I'll see you after surgery," he told the dog.

Okay, maybe the guy wasn't so bad after all. Clearly, he cared about animals, so he couldn't be all bad, despite how arrogant he'd seemed the first time they'd met and again today.

He pinned her with a stare. "Make sure that I do," he growled.

Or maybe he was that bad. "Give Dana your number and we'll call you when he's out."

With a grunt, Brandon turned on his heel and walked toward the door of the small exam room. The second he stepped out of the room, it instantly felt like it doubled in size and her nerves calmed.

She looked down at the dog on the table. Now the real work began.

CHAPTER FOUR

The following morning, Brandon nodded to a couple of his teammates as he wandered into the gym. During the off-season, they all kept their own hours. He preferred working out mid-day when the gym was virtually empty, but he wanted to head to the vet to check in on Leo as soon as possible.

Dr. Wright had called last night before she left for the evening and had said Leo was doing well, but he needed to see him for himself.

As he began doing his warmup, his mind wandered to the sexy vet. He hadn't recognized her at first. The sedate vet with the tight, low ponytail and glasses had barely resembled the knockout from the bar with the bawdy laugh. It was the slightly disdainful look in her eyes that he'd recognized more than anything.

The woman had already shot him down once and after yesterday's encounter, he was pretty sure her feelings about him being a dick had only solidified. His concern for Leo hadn't exactly softened his edges much. The fucking receptionist had practically hidden under her desk when she'd seen him.

"Brandon, can you spot me?" his teammate Smitty called.

Brandon glanced over at the bench where Smitty was setting up his weights. "Sure."

Smitty lay down on the bench and positioned himself under the barbell for his chest press. Brandon eyed the weights. "This your max?"

"Yeah."

"Cool, you mind if I work in?"

Smitty's eyes widened. "This is your warmup weight?"

Brandon looked at the weight. "It's a little heavier than what I normally warmup with, but it'll work."

"How much heavier?"

"About 10lbs."

"Fuck, my max is 10lbs heavier than your warmup. That's depressing."

Brandon shrugged. "Why? I've got like five or six inches on you."

"Still," Smitty muttered. "Kind of embarrassing."

"Eh. Do you lift more than you used to?"

"Yeah."

"All right then." Brandon rolled his shoulders and stepped up behind the bench to spot. "Let's go."

Smitty placed his hands on the bar and lifted. By the fifth rep, he was getting a little shaky. By the sixth, Brandon placed his hands on the bar in case he needed help. At seven, he rolled his eyes as Smitty attempted one more rep, while Brandon held most of the weight.

Even with his teammates, it still happened the moment he got around them. They felt the need to push it. He honestly couldn't give two fucks how much they lifted, but for whatever reason, they cared when he was the one spotting them.

Smitty jumped up and traded him places. He repped out a quick ten that had Smitty staring at him with his mouth open.

"What?"

Smitty shook his head. "Nothing, that's just impressive, man."

"Mmm," he grunted.

"So uh, Kia wanted me to ask you to dinner."

Over the past several months, he'd become good friends with Kia, much to his teammate's dismay. The woman seemed determined to bring him into their little fold. "Yeah, I saw the text yesterday."

Smitty glared at him. "Why didn't you respond then?"

He rubbed the back of his neck. "Sorry. I meant to. I had a thing and got busy."

"So tonight?"

"Umm." He was planning on forcing his way into the vet's office and spending the day with Leo.

"Tomorrow?"

It didn't seem like he was getting out of this. He'd never been one to do dinners and shit with friends. If they were doing something specific, they hung out. If they weren't, they didn't. Intimate dinners to get to know each other better was not his thing in the least. But it was Kia's and he had to admit once he got there it was usually kind of nice. Usually.

"What do you have tonight that you can't make dinner?"

Brandon shifted his body uncomfortably. "I don't know, stuff."

"What stuff?" Smitty pressed.

"Jesus, I don't know. Stuff."

"No, you need to do better than that, dude. There's no way I'm going home and telling Kia that you couldn't make it because you had stuff. She'll be all over my ass saying I didn't make her precious B feel welcome and shit. No. Unless you have a date with guaranteed sex, you're coming."

Getting laid made him think of the sexy vet. Unfortunately, that wasn't on the table. "Fine, tell Kia I'll be there."

"Cool." Smitty tapped the barbell. "You want me to spot you?"

"Let me do the next set and then yeah." He added another plate on each side and did a quick set then grabbed another plate. Smitty's eyes boggled as he watched him load his max weight.

"Jesus," Smitty mumbled.

Brandon lined up and hammered out his reps without help. Looked like he was upping his weight next time.

"What'd you do to your arm?" Smitty asked.

He glanced at the bandage on his arm. "Umm, I didn't take my time to properly introduce myself."

"To what?"

"A dog." He flexed his arm. "Speaking of, I gotta head out to check on him."

"To check on a dog?"

"Yeah."

"You?"

Brandon's shoulders stiffened. "Yeah me, why do you sound so surprised?

"I don't know. I just didn't know you liked dogs."

"Of course I like dogs. I'm not a psycho."

Smitty snorted. "That's the criteria? Like DSM5 definition?"

"Fuck you." He laughed. "I'm just saying, everyone likes dogs."

"I sure as hell don't like my neighbor's. Although I guess it's more my neighbor I don't like rather than the dog."

"What's wrong with the neighbor?"

"His fucking dog shits everywhere and he never picks it up. It doesn't matter how many times I talk to him. It's like he sends the fucking thing over to my yard to do his business."

"Probably does."

"You think?"

Brandon shrugged. "If he does it every time, yeah."

"Fucker," Smitty growled. "I keep threatening to throw it at his front door, but Kia won't let me."

"Bag it and put it on his doorstep. Eventually, he'll get the message."

Smitty narrowed his eyes like he was deep in thought. "Kia can't get mad at me for just returning his dog's shit to him in a bag, right?"

"I have no idea, man." How the hell was he supposed to know what would make her upset? He was single for a reason.

"What are you doing after this?" Smitty asked.

"Why?" Brandon eyed his teammate warily.

"If you came over, I could tell her you did it and then gage her response."

"Fuck that, man. I'm not taking that bullet for you."

"But we're teammates," Smitty complained.

"Yeah, and taking one on the field is a whole lot different from taking one with your woman. You're on your own, dude. Besides, I've got plans."

"Fine, but if I don't show up tomorrow for my workout, you know what happened to me."

"Got it. If you're a no show send the cadaver dog."

"Jesus, that got dark in a hurry. I just meant she'd maimed me, not killed me."

"Eh, you know Kia, it could go either way," Brandon snickered.

"True." Smitty shuddered.

"Good luck." Brandon slapped his teammate on the back. "I'm outta here. See you later."

Brandon threw his gear in his bag, nodded to a couple of teammates on his way out the door as he pulled his phone out of his bag. Swiping, he grinned at the text message from the vet with a photo of Leo.

> Good morning, Mr. Sims. Dr. Wright asked us to update you on Leo this morning.

> He is doing much better today, even ate some breakfast.

Photo of Leo eating.

Brandon winced as he looked at the dog's missing leg and eye. Poor guy.

> Thanks. I'm going to come by and see him shortly.

Sounds good.

Brandon tossed his bag into the back of his Bronco. On his way to the vet clinic, he swung into the coffee shop drive through. A cup of coffee was as good as an olive branch on any day. After yesterday's showing, he probably owed the vet and the receptionist at least that.

As he pulled up to order, he paused. What the hell did she drink? "Can I get a plain black coffee and, umm...What is your most popular coffee?"

"Excuse me?"

"What kind of coffee is ordered the most?" He paused. "Umm, by women." Kia and Rayne both drank foamy shit, but he had no idea what it was or if they even drank the same thing.

"Oh, umm, probably a latte. Although our flavored drinks are pretty popular as well."

"Great," he grumbled. "Can you give me whatever your two most popular drinks are as well?"

"You just want me to pick?" the voice asked.

"Yeah, please."

"Okay. Drive through."

He pulled up to the window and tapped his card. The woman handed him a drink. "This is a vanilla latte." She handed another drink over. "This is a caramel macchiato. I wrote the names on top. I picked two safe options that most people like."

"Perfect, thank you."

"No problem." She handed over the final takeout cup. "And that's your black coffee."

"Thanks. I appreciate the help. Have a good one." He set the coffee in the holder between the seats and threw it into gear. Several minutes later, he pulled up in front of Pacific Paws Animal Hospital. As much as he was looking forward to seeing Leo, part of him was also looking forward to seeing the sexy vet.

He scooped up the coffees and made his way inside. The receptionist from yesterday was sitting behind the counter. When she saw him, her eyes widened and he winced. That was never a good sign. He held out the coffee cups. "Peace offering?"

"Is that coffee?"

"Yeah?" Shit. Had coffee been the wrong choice?

"What kind?"

He set his black coffee down on the counter. "A latte and a caramel macchiato. I wasn't sure what you and the doc liked."

"You got one for me and one for Dr. Wright?" The woman beamed at him.

"Umm yeah." He rocked back on his heels. Why did he feel so fucking nervous?

"Let me just buzz her and let her know you're here."

A moment later, Dr. Wright walked out from the back. Today she was wearing jeans and a shirt instead of the scrubs she'd been in the day before. She glanced at him and smiled tightly. "Brandon."

"He brought us coffee," Dana said.

The doc raised an eyebrow. "Peace offering?" she asked.

"Yep."

She smiled. "Did you bring us fancy coffees?"

"Yes."

"What's yours?" she asked.

"Black."

"Can I have that one?"

"Umm." He eyed the fancy coffees. "Ugh, sure."

"Cool. As much as I like the fancy stuff, it doesn't love me."

He rocked back on his heels. "Right."

She chuckled. "Sorry to overshare, but it's true."

She picked up his coffee cup, leaving him with the caramel macchiato. Jesus that sounded disgusting.

"You want to take these out to the picnic area for a minute and chat?" she asked.

He glanced toward the door leading to the back where he knew Leo was then back at her. "Umm sure."

Following her outside, he waited to speak. The moment they sat down, he pinned her with a stare. "Your receptionist said he's doing better today, so what's up?"

"Physically he is doing a lot better. But I'm just going to be honest with you, Brandon. He's in bad shape more than just physically."

"What do you mean?"

"I mean he's obviously been badly abused. He won't let anyone near him. I honestly don't know how you will be able to find anyone to adopt him because I don't know that he's safe around people. My staff is all terrified of him."

Needing a moment to gather his thoughts, he took a sip of his coffee and grimaced when the sickly sweet liquid hit his tongue. "God, why would someone drink that?" he asked, eyeing the offensive cup.

The doc smiled. "Did you want your coffee back?"

"Nah, it's fine. Umm." He scrubbed a hand across his face. "How do you know he's been abused and not just reacting to his injuries?"

"Unfortunately experience. I've seen a lot of abused dogs and there are certain telltale indicators. Yes, some of Leo's problems are because he's in pain and scared, but I'm going to be honest with you, Brandon. Not all the scarring on his body is from an animal. I can't say for sure, but based on the injuries, both old and new, if I had to guess, I'd say he was chained up regularly and used in dogfighting."

"What?" he roared. "Like the fucking dog fights people go to jail for?"

She nodded sadly. "Yes, if I was guessing I'd say he lost the fight and they didn't think he'd recover."

Nausea rolled in his stomach. "So they threw him away?"

"Probably. Yes. There have been a few dogs found on that stretch of highway. Leo is the first one that's been found alive."

"Jesus." He covered his mouth. What kind of sick fuck would just throw away a dog like that? Images of the way his dad had treated him as a kid instantly swarmed into his mind. A man like his dad, that's who.

Well, there was no fucking way he wasn't making sure Leo had better than that. "But he's going to physically recover from his injuries."

"Yes, physically I think he'll be fine. Dogs are incredibly resilient. It won't take him long to get used to missing a leg. He's already getting up and around a bit."

"You said he lost his eye too?"

"He did, yes, and I can't tell how much he's seeing out of the remaining one. He's definitely seeing something, but I'm not sure how much."

"Okay, so most of the work needs to come around helping him to trust people." On that one he could completely relate to the dog. People sucked.

"Yes, and that won't be easy."

"It's off season. I've got time."

"Brandon, I don't mean to be rude, but what do you know about abused animals?"

Considering he'd been one, he knew a hell of a lot. He didn't imagine dogs were that much different from humans. There were still days when it took everything he had not to bite the hand that fed him. But he sure as hell wasn't going to tell the doc all that. "Good thing I've got lots of time to figure it out."

"Brandon, it's admirable that you want to take this on, but I just want to prepare you for the road ahead. He may never be able to be rehabilitated."

That's what the social worker had said about him too, and he was just fine. "Like I told you Saturday, Dr. Wright, Leo is a fighter and he deserves the chance. And if what you say is true, I'm even more determined to make sure he gets it."

Dr. Wright sighed. "Alright then, since it sounds like you'll be here a lot, you may as well call me Annie."

"I remember your name, Doc," he told her.

Annie's eyes widened. "You do? Yesterday it didn't seem like you remembered me."

It wasn't like he was likely to forget a woman like her. He'd approached her for a reason in the bar. The woman was gorgeous. And unfortunately, now that he knew what she did for a living, she was even more attractive. But definitely not the right woman for a guy like him. "Yesterday, I wasn't really thinking of anything but Leo."

"Understandable. It's just when I said your name you seemed confused."

"It took me a minute to remember where we'd met. You look a little different at work."

She snorted and gestured to her shirt covered in dog hair. "Yeah, weirdly enough my friends don't love vet chic, they prefer mohair rather than dog hair."

He shrugged. She looked pretty good to him. If he was being honest, he actually preferred this look, more girl next door. But if she'd looked like this in the bar, he never would have approached her. Siren he could do, girl next door he steered clear of. "It was more you look different with the hair up and glasses."

She absently touched her hair and snickered. "Yeah, it's a good look."

"I'm not complaining."

Annie's head snapped up and their eyes met. A shimmer of awareness flashed between them. This was a bad idea. He cleared his throat. "So, umm, any chance I can see Leo?"

She studied him a moment longer, then pushed away from the table. "Absolutely. Let's go."

CHAPTER FIVE

How the hell was she going to get this dog to trust her?

It had been three days and Leo still didn't want to let anyone but Brandon near his crate. Speaking of, where was he? He'd said he'd be by this morning and it was already almost eleven o'clock. And why did she care so damn much? He was just some grumpy ballplayer.

Dana popped her head into the back. "He's here," she hissed.

Annie raised her eyebrow. "Okay?"

Why did Dana say it like that? Brandon practically lived here the past few days. Besides going to the restroom, she didn't think he'd left his spot on the floor next to Leo's crate all day yesterday.

At the idea of seeing Brandon, her stomach flipped. The fact that it took everything in her not to fix her hair just made her mad. He was here to see the dog, not her.

"He brought a girl," Dana said.

Annie's stomach fell. "What?"

"He brought a woman with him. And of course she's gorgeous. I mean why wouldn't she be? Look at the guy."

"A woman?"

"Mmm-hmm," Dana peered through the little window on the door and looked out at the waiting area and sighed. "Guess there goes my chance of asking him for coffee."

"He seriously brought a woman with him." What the hell? Yesterday, he'd been flirting with her, acting like he was interested again. Was this all just some game to him?

"What's the matter?" Dana asked. Suddenly, her eyes widened. "Oh my god, you like him."

"What? No, I don't." Her gut clenched. Okay, maybe she did just a little. The past couple of days with Leo, she'd thought maybe she'd been wrong about him at first.

Obviously, she wasn't. Clearly her first impression of him as some playboy asshole had been bang on.

Without thinking, she stormed through the door. The moment her eyes landed on Brandon and his friend, she pulled up short. To call that woman gorgeous was such an understatement.

What the heck had she been thinking? She'd never stood a chance with him if this was the kind of woman he went for.

Brandon's eyes lit up when he saw her. "Hey Doc."

She would not be taken in by his big muscles and warm smile. "What can I do for you, Brandon?"

His forehead wrinkled as he studied her. "We just came by to see Leo." He held up a bag from the local bakery.

If he thought he was doing some kind of makeshift romantic date here, he was out of his mind. "This is a vet clinic, Brandon, not the farmer's market."

Brandon's eyes narrowed. "Excuse me."

She glanced at his friend and raised her eyebrow. "Leo is still recovering from his injuries. He's not really up for company."

He studied her for several seconds. Suddenly, it was like a mask slipped over his face. The warmth in his eyes from a second ago was gone. Now he looked cold and hard. Not at all like the man she'd seen the past couple of days.

"I know he's recovering. That's why we're here."

The woman placed her hand on Brandon's arm and the look on his face softened slightly. "B, it's okay," she said.

The familiarity in the way the other woman spoke to him made Annie's chest hurt. This wasn't some casual date he was trying to impress. God, she was such an idiot. She'd stupidly thought he was actually interested in her. What an idiot she'd been.

The other woman stepped forward and held out her hand toward Annie. "Hi, I'm Rayne."

Annie shook the woman's hand. "Dr. Wright."

Rayne looked at her like she knew exactly what Annie was doing. "Nice to meet you, Dr. Wright. Brandon has told me all about you."

"Really? He hasn't mentioned you." She couldn't keep the annoyance out of her tone.

Rayne's mouth curled up slightly in amusement before she turned to Brandon. "Seriously, B, you didn't tell her you wanted me to come?"

He shrugged like a petulant child.

Rayne squeezed his arm, then turned back to Annie. "Sorry about that. Brandon's got a big heart, but he's not a big talker." Rayne smiled. "Let's start again, shall we?"

Annie cocked her eyebrow at the other woman. This oughta be good.

"As I mentioned, I'm Rayne." Rayne glanced at Brandon, then back at her. "I do energy work, so Reiki, Jin Shin, that kind of thing, and Brandon was hoping I could help Leo."

"You do Reiki?"

"I do, yes. Are you familiar with it?"

"I am. I was at a conference last year and there was a speaker who had really good success in equine therapy with Reiki."

"Oh good, I'm glad you're familiar with it. Reiki works really well with animals. From what Brandon tells me, Leo probably won't let me near him to start, and that's fine. I can do distance healing and hopefully, over time, he will start to trust me enough to get close to him."

"So you're here to do energy healing on Leo?" Annie looked at Rayne, then Brandon. So this wasn't a date? He'd brought someone to help Leo?

Brandon rocked back on his heels and shoved his hands in his pocket. She wanted to wipe the cocky smirk off his face.

Rayne smiled kindly. "I am, if that's okay with you. I realize having an extra person in your space is an inconvenience. B said he's here all the time anyway, so I can just squish up next to him and stay out of the way."

The idea of this gorgeous woman snuggling up to Brandon had her jaw clenching. Damn it. She hated that she had this response to him. There was nothing between them. She had no right to be jealous. Unfortunately, that didn't stop it from happening.

"No, it's fine. We've had to move Leo's crate away from the other animals because it was too stressful for him to have them near, so there is plenty of room where he is. Why don't I show you?"

"I can take her, Doc," Brandon said.

"No, that's fine. I'd really like to see Rayne work if that's okay with you," she said, turning to the other woman.

After hearing the speaker last year, she was curious about the treatment and how it worked. She'd been meaning to look into it, but had never gotten around to it.

"No, I don't mind at all."

Annie led the way to the back of the clinic. They had a full house today for the spay/neuter clinic.

"Why are there so many animals here today?" Brandon asked.

"We do a spay/neuter clinic every couple of months for low income pet owners."

"How does that work?" Brandon asked.

"What do you mean?

"You said low income, so how does it work?"

"Oh, it's income tested, then we have a sliding scale for fees. If they can't afford to pay anything, it's free."

"Free?"

"Yes. The majority of people we see are free, although some pay a small fee of $50."

"Who subsidizes the program?"

Annie raised her eyebrow at the direct question. "I do."

"You do? So this isn't a government-funded program?"

Government funded? Yeah right. "No, we work closely with a couple of rescue organizations, but funding is very minimal and the need is high. So we do what we can."

"So you lose money doing this?" Brandon studied her closely.

"Yes, but it's a good cause." Just how much money they lost was a bit of a sore point with her partners. They were able to get a tax writeoff for some of the expenses, but it still lost them money each time they ran the clinic. Her partners thought they should stop running the clinic. They'd come to a compromise and Annie was the only one who did the surgeries now, which meant the number of animals they could help was smaller.

"Hmm," Brandon grunted.

Annie stopped at Leo's crate. The dog pressed up against the back of his crate and growled.

"It's okay, buddy," Brandon murmured. The moment the dog heard Brandon's voice, he stopped growling.

It was amazing to watch. She'd never seen a dog behave like that with a person they'd just met before. It was like Leo knew the gigantic man would protect him and he didn't have to worry. As much as Brandon said he wasn't adopting the dog, the bond between them was already so strong.

Brandon dropped onto the ground beside the crate and began speaking to the dog. After a couple minutes, he opened the crate door, moved out of the way, and leaned his back against the wall beside the crate.

"Are you sure we can take up as much space as we need?" Rayne asked.

"Of course."

"I think Leo would feel safer if I didn't get too close to him to start." Rayne sat down on the floor several feet away from Brandon and the dog. "I'm going to give him a few minutes to get used to me being here before I start."

Annie sat down beside Rayne. Leo eyed them, then slowly crawled out of the crate and lay beside Brandon.

"Oh, poor thing," Rayne spoke softly as Leo shifted his injured body to get comfortable.

Brandon looked over at them. "Jesus, Rayne," he muttered.

Tears streamed down Rayne's face as she looked at Annie. "He was a fighting dog, right?"

"I think so, yes. Judging by the extensive damage, old and new, Leo has not had an easy life. His reaction to both people and other animals indicates he was abused. Brandon is the only person he seems to trust at all."

Rayne watched the dog, then looked at Annie. "He's beginning to trust you," Rayne said.

"I'd like to think so. Being around him with Brandon helps I think. When I watch them together, it's like Leo knows Brandon will protect him."

"I will," Brandon replied. He slid his hand out onto the floor and rested it near the dog.

"Be careful Brandon," Annie said. Yes, the dog seemed to trust Brandon, but he was still a severely abused dog and that fight-or-flight instinct was strong.

"We're good, right, buddy?" Brandon asked.

Leo laid his head down on the ground and sighed as if to say, yeah, we're good.

"I'm going to get started," Rayne said.

Annie watched as Rayne prepared herself for the session. The woman raised her hands and held them palms up, facing Leo. The dog raised his head and looked at Rayne. After a few moments, he shifted closer to Brandon and laid his head down again. Leo was practically laying against Brandon.

Brandon raised his head and looked at her. His eyes filled with shock before he smiled. The display of emotion on the big man was like a fist to the gut. How as she supposed to stay immune to him when he cared so much for an injured dog.

"Annie?" She heard her assistant, Sarah's, voice call her name from down the hall. Annie glanced at her watch. Damn, she needed to get going on the surgeries. "If you'll excuse me," she murmured.

Not wanting anything to interrupt the Reiki session, she slowly left the room so as not to alarm the dog. When she was out of the room, she hurried to find Sarah.

"Sarah," Annie said as she walked into the surgery room.

"How are you doing?" Sarah asked.

"Fine, why?"

"I heard Brandon brought a woman with him."

"He did."

"That sucks. I thought for sure he was going to ask you on a date after the way you two have been making eyes at each other the past few days."

"We have not been making eyes at each other."

Sarah made a face. "Oh yes, you have. Big googly ones." Sarah sighed. "I can't believe he brought a date here. What an asshole."

"He didn't bring a date. Rayne is here to do Reiki on Leo."

Sarah's annoyance visibly melted right before her eyes. "He brought someone here to do Reiki on Leo. Oh my god, could the man be any sweeter?" Sarah held her hand over her heart. "Annie, how can you possibly resist that?"

"There's nothing to resist. He's here for Leo. This has nothing to do with me."

"Mmm-hmm, so if he asked you out what would you say?"

"He's not going to ask me out."

"But if he did?"

Her stomach fluttered at the idea of going on a date with Brandon. "He's not going to ask me out."

"How do you know?"

"If you saw the woman he brought with him today, you'd know why."

"I thought you said she was just here to do Reiki."

Annie pictured the connection between Rayne and Brandon. There was something between them. Maybe they were just friends, but if he could be friends with a woman who looked like that, what kind of women did he actually date, not just sleep with?

No, the idea he could possibly be interested in her for real was utterly ridiculous. "She is. Just trust me, Brandon is not interested in me. Now, can we please stop talking about this and focus on our work? Who do we have first?"

For the next several hours, Annie didn't have time to think about Brandon. Or at least not much anyway.

CHAPTER SIX

B randon's phone buzzed in his pocket. He glanced down at the screen and grinned when he saw his former teammate's name. He swiped to answer the call. "Carter, hey, what's up?"

"B, guess who's becoming a Hawk?"

"Holy shit. You got traded here?"

"Yep. Looks like we'll be playing together again."

"That's awesome, man. Happy for you."

"Thanks. So what do I need to know?"

"For the most part, really good guys, but you've got some big shoes to fill. This city loved Gonzo. There were some angry fans when he got traded."

"I can imagine."

Silence filled the air as Brandon waited for his friend to talk. He didn't. He remembered that feeling well. Coming to a new team, worrying about the dynamics and gelling with the guys. "It's gonna be great. The core guys are solid. You put the team first and you'll be fine. They're good guys."

"Cool. I'm looking forward to playing with Saunders at short. The guy can move."

"Yeah, it's a solid infield. You're gonna be a good addition." The guys had all been worried about who the team would bring in to fill Gonzo's spot. There'd been some speculation that it would be Davis from Seattle. He was a good ballplayer but had a reputation for stirring shit up, so the team had been stressing about what was going to happen to their flow. The last thing they needed was some showboat who thought he was more important than the team.

Thank god they'd signed Carter. No one was going to fill Gonzo's role completely, but if anyone could slide into his spot seamlessly and not piss off the team, it was him.

It had been a few years since they'd played together, but Carter was a lot like him. The kind of player who put his head down and played the fucking game. All the other shit was just a distraction.

"I was thinking of coming into town next week to look for a place. Any chance I can crash with you?"

"Umm."

Carter chuckled. "Dude, I'm not asking to move in. It's a couple of days."

Brandon rubbed the back of his neck. He liked having his own space. Growing up the way he had, he liked his privacy.

It was stupid after all this time that it still mattered, but it did. He'd never been one to make friends easily. But Carter was someone he considered a friend. That didn't mean they'd braided each other's hair and told each other their secrets, but they were friends. And in his experience, good friends didn't come along all that often.

Sure he hung out with the team and went out after the games with the guys, but in the offseason he mostly stuck to himself or he tried to. Since becoming friends with Kia that wasn't always easy. She'd made it her mission to make sure he was included in everything and somehow Rayne had jumped on board. Between the two of them, saying no to a social event wasn't an option. But it'd be nice to have Carter around. He'd been one of the few guys in the minors that he'd like hanging out with.

"I know, sorry, yeah maybe. But umm, depending on when you come I might have a dog."

"What do you mean you might have a dog?"

"I...uh...found a dog and looks like he needs a home."

Carter snickered. "Wow, look at you, B, getting all domesticated and shit."

"Fuck off," he muttered. "It's a dog, not a fucking kid." He shuddered. The very idea of having a kid gave him hives. There was no fucking way he was ever doing that. Not after the way he'd been raised. No kid deserved someone like him. Fuck, if he was being honest, no dog did either, but it didn't look like Leo had a lot of options.

"Still, I just never pictured you with a dog, but now that I think about it, it makes sense."

"Why's that?"

"I don't know. Probably be good company, but doesn't talk so you don't have to worry about being social."

"Fuck you, I can be social," he grumbled.

Carter chuckled. "Yeah, but you hate it."

"I don't hate it. I just don't see the point in talking constantly. I talk when I have something to say." The past couple of seasons, he'd actually been making an effort to get to know some of his teammates. Granted Gonzo had been one of the guys he hung out with the most and now that he was gone he'd started slipping back into his old ways but with Carter joining the team there was no way he'd let him not go out.

"So. Once I have my flight details, I'll let you know so you can pick me up."

"Jesus, I haven't even said you could stay and now I'm picking you up at the fucking airport? Not happening."

"Fine, the ride is negotiable. Staying isn't. We're in enough hotels during the season. I'm not doing it when I come house hunting if I don't have to."

"Umm, since I didn't say you could stay, you have to."

"Fuck off. I'm staying at your place. End of discussion. How many times did I save your ass when we were in Texas? You owe me."

He was right. Carter had always been one to jump in and take one for the team, whatever that looked like. Being the wingman to get girls and to get out of situations with them, and on more than one occasion he'd run interference so Brandon could get out of some social obligation. "Fine, but you keep your fucking mess contained. First time you leave dishes lying around, you're gone."

"Got it. I've lived with you, bro. I remember how anal you are about cleanliness."

"I'm not anal, I'm just not disgusting."

Carter snorted. "Dude, you're the fucking poster child for kitchen OCD."

He wasn't OCD, he just liked things how he liked them. If someone used something they should put it back where it belonged. "Yeah, and the one time I tried to not make you guys clean up, Sully gave us all fucking food poisoning. There's a reason there are food safety standards. Sticking to them doesn't make me weird."

"Nope, but washing the entire counter again when you spot a fly kind of does."

"Did you want to stay? Because keep it up asshole and your ass will be taking an Uber to a fucking hotel."

"Okay, okay, I'm just bugging ya." Carter made a weird sound on the other end of the line.

"What?" Brandon asked.

"Nothing, just wondering what kind of dog this is?"

"I don't know like a Pitbull."

"Don't they shed?"

"Probably."

Carter hooted. "Oh Jesus, this is going to be good to watch."

Brandon looked around his pristine house. Images of dog hair bunnies floating into the corners made him cringe. But then he pictured Leo and all the shit the dog had been through. How realistically he'd be put down if he didn't take him in and suddenly the dog hair didn't seem like it would be a problem. "That's why I've got a vacuum."

"We'll see, man."

"Just a heads up, Leo's been through some shit, and he doesn't really like people."

"You're adopting a dog that doesn't like people?" Carter paused and Brandon could practically picture the look on his friend's face.

"This just gets better and better. Sorry I can't have people over. My dog won't like it," Carter snickered.

"I'm going to socialize him, asshole. He's just had a rough go and at the moment he's not too trusting."

"Is he going to try to rip my arm off?"

"I don't know. Guess it depends if you leave your dishes lying around."

"Ha ha."

"Honestly, I don't know what he's going to be like in the house. He's come a long way already, but we've got some mountains to move still."

Rayne said she'd be with him when he brought Leo home to help him get settled and he'd spoken to a respected trainer about doing some 1:1. But fuck, he still cringed when he heard a glass shatter and the shit with his dad had been over a decade ago, so it's not like he could expect the dog to heal overnight. "Now that I think about it maybe having you stay here will be good."

"Just remember, I'm on the home team again, so we need your dog not to eat me."

"Got it. I'll see if I can rent one of those outfits they use to train attack dogs."

"Jesus, please tell me you're joking."

Unfortunately, he wasn't sure if he was. Leo was getting better about not snarling when the veterinarian staff came near, but he still wouldn't let them touch him. As long as Carter gave him space, it should be fine. "I don't think we'll need it. He's still healing from his injuries, so I think you can outrun him."

"Awesome," Carter mumbled. "Maybe I will stay in that hotel."

"Nah, I think this will be good for Leo. Just give me a few days to get him settled in here. So don't book till later next week?"

"Sure. Thanks, man."

"Yep."

He hung up the phone and looked around his apartment. Was having a dog like having a kid? Was there shit he needed to do to dog proof the place? Maybe he could sweet talk Annie into going shopping with him. If he played his cards right, maybe he could get her to come back to his place and dog proof things, maybe get some dinner or something.

Brandon looked around his house. As usual, nothing was out of place, so why did he feel the need to clean it?

Would she like his place? Or would she think he was anal like Carter did? He rarely brought anyone into his space. It was his. Only his. During his time in the minors, he'd always had roommates and while it was a lot better than living with his dad, it still hadn't felt entirely safe. This house was the first time he'd ever truly been able to relax in his home since before his mom died.

He wandered toward his bedroom. His eyes landed on the thick door and lock he'd installed the moment he moved in. A therapist would have a fucking field day with him if they saw it. He hadn't lived with his father for a decade and yet he still felt he needed it.

Fuck, maybe having Annie come back here with him was a mistake. He was trying to impress her, not give her a crash course into his dysfunction.

But as he eyed his bed, he pictured Annie in it. His dick twitched as he imagined her spread out naked on the mattress, begging him to fuck her. The only way that was going to happen was to let her in the front door.

His fingers itched to clean something.

Anything.

Fuck.

He clenched his fists. Maybe if he just changed the sheets. He took a step toward the bed then stopped. No. He rolled his shoulders and rocked his neck back and forth in little half circles as he breathed. He'd worked really fucking hard to control this tendency. This need to control every little thing. And he did a good job of it everywhere but in his home. Here shit was different. And a little part of him hated that he hadn't mastered it here.

What would Annie say if she could see him now, sweating as he fought the urge to clean his room like a fucking neurotic maid? Yep, she'd definitely want to sleep with him like this. Jesus.

He closed his eyes and took a breath. His hand flexed and released on its own before he shook out his fingers. Running his palm over the dark gray comforter, he smoothed it out, then turned on his heels and walked out of the bedroom. He smiled to himself. The need inside him hadn't won. The beast had been caged, at least for a little while.

With a little spring in his step, he grabbed his keys and wallet from the counter and headed to the vet clinic.

CHAPTER SEVEN

What was wrong with her? It was like she was back in high school again, but instead of crushing on the captain of the football team, she was lusting after a baseball player. Either way, it was ridiculous, and yet here she was watching Brandon through the window.

"Whatcha doing?"

Startled, Annie yelped. Spinning, she stared at Sarah. With a nervous laugh, Annie slapped her palm across her heart like that would keep it from beating out of her chest.

"My god, you scared me," she said. "Why are you sneaking up on me?"

"I didn't sneak, you were just zoned out. Whatcha doing?" Sarah peered past her. "Ah, I see what you're looking at. No wonder you didn't hear me come in."

Annie winced. Busted. Damn it. "Was there something you needed?"

Sarah leaned her hip against the breakroom table. "I think you've got a little crush on our resident grump," Sarah teased.

"What? No, I don't, and Brandon isn't grumpy."

Sarah made a scoffing sound. "Uh yeah, he is. The man barely speaks. He nods when he comes in, asks about Leo, then sits there for hours with his headphones in or reads a book and doesn't speak."

"He talks. He's trying to be respectful and stay out of the way so we can work. He's just following the rules I laid out when I agreed to let him be here all the time."

Sarah's eyes crinkled with amusement as she looked at her.

"What?" Annie asked.

"You really have it bad. I wouldn't have taken you for the kind of person who'd fall for the jock." Sarah looked through the breakroom window again. "But when a man looks that fine, I can't blame you in the least. Mmm, look at him in that plaid. He's like a sexy lumberjack. He can sling his wood at me anytime."

Annie shoved her coworker on the shoulder. "Stop it, he's a client."

"Yeah, a client you'd like to climb like a tree."

"Oh my god." Annie acted affronted, but in reality Sarah was bang on. She'd definitely had her fair share of impure thoughts about Brandon. Her traitorous body went on high alert whenever he was in the room and don't even get her started on the way his muscles rippled when he picked up Leo. Phew.

"You should ask him out," Sarah said.

"What?"

"Ask him out."

Annie snorted. "Yeah right. Did we not just finish talking about the way the man looks?"

"Mmm-hmm," Sarah said. "So you're admitting you were looking?"

"Well, I'm not dead so obviously—" She rolled her eyes. "But there's a big difference between appreciating the way a man looks and asking him out."

"He'd say yes."

"Yeah right," Annie scoffed. The man was like a walking advertisement for men's fitness. He could have any woman he wanted.

"He would. He watches you all the time."

"He does not."

"Yeah, he does. The minute you're around his body language changes."

"And you say I'm staring at him. How much are you watching him to know that?"

"When his body language changes, so does Leo's. I think that's why Leo trusts you more than the rest of us. Because Brandon does."

"Trusting me isn't the same thing as being interested in me."

"Trust me, Annie, the man is interested. He wouldn't stare at your ass as often as he does if he was just appreciating your vet skills."

Her stomach zipped. Brandon stared at her ass?

Uh, she did have it bad. She should be offended he was staring at her ass, instead she was flattered and a little excited. Ugh.

Enough. This wasn't getting her anywhere. "How's Leo?"

"Okay, I see how it is." Sarah smirked. "He seems to be doing okay. Little grumbly as usual, but he ate his breakfast, which is good."

"That's good. How do his incisions look?"

"From what I could tell, he was moving around the yard pretty well. Everything looks good from a distance. Maybe you can use that as an excuse to go talk to Brandon and you can get a better look."

"In what world is me caring about a dog just a ploy to talk to a man?"

Sarah winced. "Sorry. I know how much you care about Leo. We all do. That was out of line."

It was, but maybe if she wasn't also interested in the man, she wouldn't have been so offended. Unfortunately, it hit a little too close to home.

Annie's attention went back to the man and dog in question. As she watched Brandon and Leo, the dog stood up, did an awkward spin, and flopped down against Brandon.

"Holy shit," Sarah gasped. "Did you see that? He's laying against him." Sarah gripped Annie's arm in excitement.

Annie covered her mouth with her hand as emotion clogged her throat. There was genuine hope for Leo. Sure, he only let Brandon get near him so far, but the fact he was actively choosing to touch a human was huge.

Brandon stroked the top of Leo's foot. His hand looked huge against the paw. It was amazing to watch such a large man be so gentle. Even more astounding, given Brandon's size, was how Leo appeared to have no fear around him. Yet the dog was on guard with all of her staff.

"Oh my heart," Sarah said softly.

"Mine too," Annie said. It was truly a beautiful thing to see them together. She had no clue how someone with Brandon's schedule would be able to care for the dog, but witnessing this connection, they had to try.

She strolled toward the pair. Leo raised his head and growled as she got closer. Brandon placed his hand on the dog's back. "Relax, dude, it's just the doc, she's not going to hurt you," Brandon said.

Leo looked at Brandon, then eyed her warily.

"Brandon, can you see if Leo will let you shift him slightly toward you so I can see his incision a bit clearer? We don't want to traumatize him any more than necessary, so we've been giving him as much space as possible, but I need to check things a little. If he growls or doesn't like it, we can wait."

Brandon ran his hand down Leo's shoulder. "Okay, buddy, we're going to let the doc have a look at your stitches. But don't worry, I got you. I can take her if I need to." He winked at Annie and her heart fluttered.

Brandon shifted his weight. Leo didn't take his eyes off her, but he allowed Brandon to shift him onto his side. "Good boy," Brandon cooed.

Annie stepped closer and Leo growled.

"Dude, come on, that's no way to treat a lady," Brandon said. Leo looked at him, and Brandon laughed. "What's with the side-eye? It's true. Be nice."

With a grumble, Leo rolled, exposing his stitches more clearly. "That's it, buddy."

Annie crouched down several feet away and examined the area. The incision site looked really good. It was healing nicely. "Brandon, do you see anything that looks infected or angry at any of the marks?"

He examined the dog. Annie gaped in awe as Leo let Brandon touch him all around his incisions and the various other small stitched areas around his body. "Nah, everything looks really good. Nothing seems to be bugging him."

"I can't believe he lets you do that."

Brandon stroked the dog's shoulder again. "We've got an understanding, don't we, bud?"

Leo looked up, and Brandon grinned.

Annie's heart melted at the look of love on both the dog and the man's face. She sat down on the floor and eased a little closer to the pair. Leo eyed her, but didn't move.

"Progress," Brandon said.

"Absolutely." Annie grinned back at him. "So I hear you've officially decided to foster Leo. At least for the time being."

"Yeah. I've got a couple more months before the season starts, so we should be able to put a pretty good dent in some training. I've spoken to a bunch of trainers and found a couple that specialize in hard cases like Leo and they've agreed to work with us."

"You've hired trainers?" Who did that on their own? They'd had lots of fosters come in and out of their clinic, but she'd never had someone like Brandon.

"I don't know what the hell I'm doing. I need all the help I can get."

"You're willing to put that kind of time into him?"

He shrugged like it was no big deal. "It's the off season. Besides working out and fixing up my house, what else am I gonna do? Besides, he'll be good company." He scratched the dog's head. "Speaking of. Do you have like a list of supplies or something for me to buy?"

"We have a welcome package for new pet owners that Dana can give you," Annie said.

"Why doesn't Annie go shopping with you?" Sarah piped in.

Annie's head snapped toward her vet tech. What the hell?

"Really?" Brandon said, looking at her hopefully. "Would you do that?"

"Umm...uh," she stammered.

"Of course she would. Why don't you go now? Annie doesn't have any clients until her surgery at 2:00 pm."

She stared at the other woman. Just what did Sarah think she was doing?

"That would be amazing. I'll even make sure you get some food before you come back," Brandon agreed.

"She'll do it," Sarah chimed before Annie even had a chance to respond.

Brandon smirked at the other woman, then turned his attention back to her. "Seems Sarah thinks it's a good idea, so what do you say, Doc, you up for a little shopping trip this afternoon?"

He gently adjusted his body and bent down closer to Leo so the pair were almost head to head. "Please?" Brandon batted his eyes.

What a pair. She chuckled. "Fine, but I want a real lunch, not a hot dog from the street vendor outside the store."

"There's hotdogs?" Brandon perked up. "I could be all over a hot dog."

She rolled her eyes. "Not a chance. Real food or no deal."

"I could argue that a hotdog is real food, but deal. A sit down lunch seems like a good bargain."

"I'll let you two figure out the details." Sarah smiled and wiggled her fingers in a little wave as she walked away, obviously pleased with herself.

But since the result was she was spending time with Brandon, it was hard to be mad at the other woman for meddling.

"Do you have any supplies at home for Leo?" Annie asked.

Brandon looked down at his lap and rubbed the back of his neck. "Umm, I've never had a dog before, and I'm not saying I'm keeping him, but while he's staying with me, I want to make sure it's safe."

"Why wouldn't it be safe?"

"I don't know. Dogs eat shit and they lick stuff. They're like babies, right?"

"Sort of I guess. They aren't going to stick anything in a light socket, but they will eat your socks and potentially your couch."

"Why the fuck would he eat my couch?"

She shrugged. "Not saying he would, but some dogs are a bit funny."

"Jesus," he muttered and eyed the dog. "You better not eat my fucking couch."

Leo blinked up at him, and Brandon shook his head. "Fuck."

Annie chuckled. "You're going to love him even if he does eat your couch. But if you crate train him, the chances of that happening are a lot less."

"Crate train?"

"Mmm-hmm, like this one." She pointed at the crate. "And get him some toys, and work on the training."

"When can I bring him home?"

"I'd like to keep him for another few days still just to make sure everything is healing well and keep him calm until his stitches heal."

"I'm not going to take him running or anything."

"I know, but once he feels at home, it's going to be pretty hard to get him to stay still. Dogs are notorious for ripping stitches and doing things too soon if left to their own devices."

Brandon's phone buzzed and he pulled it out of his pocket. "You cool if Rayne comes by this afternoon and does another treatment."

Even though she knew they were just friends, she couldn't help the little stab of jealousy that flared through her at the mention of the other woman. "Sure no problem."

"Cool." Brandon typed a response, then shoved his phone back in his pocket. "You want to head out?"

"Sure. Let me just let Sarah know Rayne is coming. Did she say what time?"

"No, sometime this afternoon, but I'm not sure. You need me to ask?"

"It's fine."

"Want me to take him to the bathroom?" Brandon asked.

"Oh no, that's not really the easiest job, so I don't want to make you do that." Given the wide berth Leo required of the staff, getting him in and out of the crate and outside took a lot of strategic planning. It wasn't for the faint of heart.

"Why's it not easy?" Brandon looked down at the dog, then back at her. His forehead wrinkled with confusion.

"He's a bit temperamental about the process."

"Is that right?" Brandon eyed the dog. "I gotta learn sometime, so may as well do it now."

Annie couldn't help but stare as Brandon uncoiled his tall, muscular body from the floor. Someone as large as him shouldn't move so fluidly.

Brandon towered over the dog as he looked down. "All right, buddy, let's go pee."

This was not going to go well. Leo was skittish about the entire process. But maybe Brandon was right and he needed to know what he was signing on for.

He turned to her. "Where to, Doc?"

She pointed to the door off to the left of the crate. "Just out there."

"Come on, Leo, let's hit it."

"Wow!" Annie gasped as Leo pushed himself upright and hobbled after Brandon toward the door. She moved to follow and the dog growled.

"Leo," Brandon said firmly. "What did we talk about?"

Annie wasn't 100% sure but she thought she heard Brandon mumble, "How am I supposed to impress the doc if you keep growling at her?" as he walked out the door.

At least that's what she hoped he said. She leaned against the door frame and watched Brandon and Leo wander around the fenced-in yard while the dog figured out where to go. If she hadn't seen it for herself, she never would have believed it. Leo was like a different dog around Brandon. What was it about this man that a dog like Leo felt he could trust him?

If the dog could, then maybe she could as well.

Leo finished peeing and continued to sniff around the yard. For the first time that she'd seen, he was behaving like a normal dog in the yard. Not guarded and edgy, but finally relaxed and calm. She didn't want to make him come inside.

Brandon crouched down and called the dog to him. Leo hobbled over. "Look at you maneuvering on three wheels. We're gonna be playing fetch in no time." Brandon glanced up at her. "He'll be able to play fetch, right? That won't hurt him?"

"No, it won't hurt him once he heals. Dogs are remarkably resilient. He'll be running in no time."

"Cool." Brandon scratched the top of Leo's head and the dog's entire body wriggled with pleasure.

"I just can't believe it," she murmured.

"What's that?" Brandon asked.

"This." She waved her hand between the two of them. "Leo and you. It's amazing."

"Eh, like you said, it's probably just because I'm a big guy. He figures I can keep him safe."

"If anything, that normally has the opposite effect."

Brandon stood silently watching the dog for a few seconds. He absently rubbed his arm, then nodded. "Yeah, I guess that makes sense."

Annie watched as Brandon seemed lost in thought. Amazingly, Leo shifted and leaned against the man's leg. Brandon shook his head like he was clearing his thoughts, then looked down and rubbed Leo's ear. "All right, what do you say we get going?"

"You okay?" she asked.

"Yeah, course."

Annie studied him a moment, then nodded. "All right, let's get him back in the crate and head out."

Back inside, Brandon shut the crate door behind Leo, then turned to her. "Ready?"

"Yeah, you make that look so easy."

"What?"

"Taking him out, putting him in his crate. All of it. He trusts you. You clearly care about him. I can't imagine you not keeping him. Are you sure you're just going to foster?"

Brandon rubbed the back of his neck. "Ugh, yeah. I uh...I don't know. I want to keep him. I'm just not sure how that will work when I'm away. It's probably better for him if I just foster and then let him have a real family, a real life. He deserves that."

"I'm pretty sure he'd think being with you was a real life."

Brandon glanced down at the crate and sighed. "Yeah maybe. I'm just not sure how to make that work. But I can definitely commit to the next few months and getting him properly trained. I've interviewed a shit-ton of of trainers. I think I've narrowed it down to two, and now I just need to see which one Leo likes best."

God, could the man be sweeter. "You're gonna let Leo interview his trainer?"

"Well yeah, of course." Brandon looked at her like she was crazy for even asking.

She bit back a smile. "Of course."

"What? Leo doesn't trust most people. If he prefers one over the other that just makes things easier for him, so what do I care which one we chose?"

"Well, price is usually a factor."

"You can't really put a price on that kind of thing, can you?"

Spoken like someone with money. "Umm, not it if you can afford it, I guess."

"While he's with me, he's getting the best life he can have."

Annie linked her arm with his. "All right, Mr. Money-bags, let's go spend that hard earned money on setting Leo up at your place."

As they walked to the front door, she could feel her staff watching them. She glanced over at Sarah. The woman practically bounced with glee as she grinned back at her. Good lord, it wasn't that big a deal. She was helping Brandon shop, not running away for the weekend. Other than their first encounter, he hadn't given her any indication he particularly found her attractive even. Although given how she looked at work most of the time when he came in she couldn't blame him.

In the parking lot, Brandon paused. "You want to just come with me and I can bring you back here after?" He pointed at a truck in the middle of the parking lot.

Annie eyed the beat-up pickup that had seen better days. Interesting. Not at all what she'd pictured for a professional athlete. She'd assumed he'd have some luxury car or truck that cost more than she made in a year, not this.

Annie glanced over at Brandon and he raised a brow in question, almost like he expected her to say something about this car. She didn't.

"Sure." Her stomach jittered when he went around to the passenger side of his truck and opened the door for her. "Thanks."

Nerves danced in her belly. She was going shopping for dog supplies with Brandon, not going on a date, so why did she feel so excited? When she glanced at him, her stomach flipped. Lordy, she had it bad for this man.

Brandon nodded, but didn't say anything as he waited for her to get inside. When she was comfortably situated, he closed the door behind her and walked around the front of the truck.

The radio fired to life with the engine. Two men argued about Baltimore's defensive line and whether they would be able to hold off Buffalo this weekend.

"You like football?" she asked.

"Yeah, I like pretty much any sport, honestly. We can turn it off." He reached for the control.

"No, it's fine. It's not that far to the pet store I was thinking of. Just up a couple of blocks."

"You sure?"

"Absolutely. So, who are you cheering for?"

"Uh, I think Baltimore will win, but I don't necessarily cheer for either of those two teams."

"Who do you cheer for?"

"Come on now, we live in San Diego. Gotta cheer for the home team."

She chuckled. "Right, of course. I know. I just wasn't sure if you did."

"I do. It wouldn't be cool if I didn't." He pulled into the pet superstore parking lot. "You ever go to a game?"

"No, I haven't, but they look fun." No, they didn't. Why'd she say that?

"If you ever want to go, let me know." Brandon pulled the car into a parking stall and turned off the car.

Oh crap. Did he just suggest they go on a date? To a football game? She hated football. "Uh."

"Or not." Brandon mumbled as he pushed open the car door.

Shit, shit, shit. She wanted to go on a date with him. She'd love to. Crap. "Brandon," she called.

"It's all good, Doc."

She hopped out of the car and hurried to meet him around the front. "I didn't mean that how it sounded."

The corner of Brandon's mouth tipped up in a slightly sad smile. "You don't have to explain anything. I appreciate you coming here with me. Let's just get the stuff for Leo."

"I hate football," she blurted.

Brandon stopped in his tracks and turned to her. "What?"

"I hate football. I don't understand it. It makes no sense to me. It's just a bunch of grown men crashing into each other. And don't even get me started on the whole concussion protocol. I just..." She shrugged. "I hate it. I don't know why I said it would be fun."

Brandon smirked. "How do you feel about baseball?"

She winced. "Honestly? It's kind of boring."

Brandon slapped his hand across his chest. "Ouch."

"But I prefer boring to aggressive, so I'd much rather watch baseball."

"Well that's something I guess." He chuckled. "Shopping for dog stuff can't be boring, so let's go."

Annie linked her arm with Brandon's. "Shopping is definitely not boring."

"I'm gonna regret this aren't I?"

"Probably." She flashed him a toothy grin and waggled her eyebrows. "Grab one of those flat carts."

His eyes widened. "Why the hell do I need one of those? How much shit am I buying?"

"You need a crate and a bed and food and toys, so grab the flat one." She couldn't make out what Brandon muttered as he wandered toward the cart rack, but she could imagine.

Once inside the store, she rubbed her hands together. "Where do you want to start?"

Brandon glanced around like a deer in headlights. "Uh—" He looked to the right, then left. "In the dog section."

"Haha, funny guy. How about we look at crates first?"

"I don't think I need one of those."

Annie rolled her eyes so hard she almost pulled a muscle. How many times had she heard that before? "Yes, you do," she told him.

"Why? I'll be home most of the time and I'll bring him with me when I can, so he'll barely be alone."

"You might want to put him in there at night."

"I thought you said he needed a dog bed. Won't he sleep there?"

"He will when you are home and can keep an eye on him. And when you can't monitor him, he'll be in the crate."

Brandon's forehead wrinkled with obvious confusion. "Leo can barely move. It's not like he's gonna get into much trouble."

"You'd be surprised. Now come on." Assuming Brandon would follow, she started to walk toward the back of the store where she knew they kept the crates.

Forty-five minutes and an obscene amount of money later, they were done. "I think your credit card is smoking," she said as they loaded their supplies into the back of his truck.

Brandon shrugged. "Any place in particular you want to eat?"

"The pub just around the corner is decent and has an outdoor patio, so you can watch your stuff."

Her phone buzzed. Annie pulled it from her pocket and swiped to answer when she saw the clinic number. "Hello?"

"Sorry, Annie, we need you back here. We have a walk-in. The guy hit a dog with his car," Dana said.

"On my way." She hung up the phone and sighed. Damn. She'd been really looking forward to lunch with Brandon. "I'm sorry there's an emergency, so I have to get back."

"No problem."

"Sorry about this." In her experience, most guys hated when her job interfered with their plans. The last guy she'd dated had been such an asshole about it, she hadn't even considered dating anyone for the past few months.

"You got nothing to apologize for, Doc." He quickly shoved the bags into the truck bed and slammed it shut. "Let's go."

Was this guy for real? It was a little mindboggling. She couldn't reconcile the guy she'd met the first night at the bar with the guy she kept seeing. Which one was the real Brandon Sims? And was she brave enough to find out?

CHAPTER EIGHT

A week later, Brandon and Carter walked into the nightclub. The music pounded through the speakers so loud he could feel it in his bones. It was perfect. He closed his eyes and absorbed the feeling of the music.

Carter nudged him. "Did they say where they'd be?"

"VIP section." He glanced over the heads of the people around them. On the balcony above them, he saw his teammates and their partners. Spotting a set of stairs off to the left, he nodded in that direction for Carter to follow.

As much as he hated socializing and the niceties of going out with a group, he did love dancing. Not that he'd ever admit that to anyone if they asked.

Growing up, when his mom had still been alive, she loved to do these dance parties with just the two of them. When he'd had a tough day at school, she'd put on music and she'd start dancing around the living room.

She'd kept at it until eventually he'd dance along with her. By the time their party was over, his mood had lifted and his troubles forgotten.

After she died, it wasn't the same. His dad thought it was girly to dance around the house and mocked the idea, so it became something he locked away. Dancing around the house when he felt like shit wasn't an option when the other person in the house was the one making him need to dance. His father had made it painfully clear that dancing wasn't a safe way to let go. He couldn't remember the last time he'd done an actual dance party. But going to the club, having some beers with the boys and picking up women and dancing the night away was completely acceptable. Even encouraged. He'd quickly found that not only did a night of clubbing help him release any pent up anger, it also generally guaranteed he was going to end the night getting laid.

A bouncer stood at the bottom of the stairs. Brandon gave him their names and the guy let them through.

Kia jumped up when they got to the top of the stairs. "Brandon, you came," she squealed and threw her arms around him in a sloppy hug.

Brandon caught her as she launched herself at him. Raising his eyebrow at Smitty, he asked, "How much has she had to drink?"

Kia pushed against his chest. "Why are you asking him? I'm the one that's drunk."

"I'm aware. That's why I'm asking. You do a little pre-gaming before you left home?"

Smitty stepped up beside her and wrapped his arm around her waist. Kia melted against the other man.

"Mmm, we dropped off Max this afternoon at my sister's, and then we had margaritas on the beach."

"Some of us had more than others," Smitty muttered.

"I want to introduce you all to someone. This is Carter Daye. He just signed with the Hawks."

Pete stepped forward and held out his hand. "Third base?"

"Yeah," Carter agreed.

"Big shoes. You up for it?" Pete asked.

"Absolutely."

Pete snorted. "Don't get cocky, new guy. You're replacing a heavy metal player. It's not going to be that easy."

"I'm up for the challenge."

"Right, then how come I've never heard of you before?"

"What?" Carter's eyes widened and he looked at Brandon pleadingly for help.

Carter was on his own. If he wanted to fit in with these guys, he needed to do it without him jumping to the rescue.

"Never heard of you before. What about you Smitty?" Pete asked.

"No clue. Is he any good, B?"

"Eh, he's all right."

Carter gaped at him. "All right?"

"He's no Gonzo," Brandon added, trying not to laugh when the muscle in Carter's jaw ticked with annoyance.

"No one is," Smitty added.

Ryan Graves slapped Carter on the shoulder. "They're just fucking with you, man, relax. No need to stroke out. I'm Ryan."

Carter glared at Brandon when Pete and Smitty started to laugh. "What the hell?"

"What?" Brandon shrugged.

"You guys are real funny," Carter said.

"Come on, new guy, let's get you a drink." Pete put his arm around Carter's shoulder. "Brandon, beer?" Pete called when the server stopped to take their order.

"Whiskey, neat." He glanced at Carter, then left him to get to know his new teammates alone. Hernandez and Montgomery stood at the railing with a guy he didn't recognize. That was one thing he hated about the off season. There were always changes. Some he wanted, others like Gonzo leaving he didn't. But Carter would be a good addition. He knew his position and was solid on the sticks.

Brandon leaned on the railing beside Lourdes Hernandez.

"Hey Bran," his teammate said.

"Hey." Brandon nodded to Chase, then said, "Hey, I'm Brandon," to the new guy.

"Justin Clark."

"Nice to meet ya." Who the hell was Justin Clark? When the guys had done it to Carter, it had been funny because he'd already talked to them about Carter getting traded to their team, so they all knew who he was. But if Brandon did the same thing to Justin, it would look like he was a dick, but he honestly didn't have a clue who the guy was.

Lou leaned over to him. "He's Chase's date."

"Cool." He leaned around Lou to get a better look at the guy.

"Day-um." Lou nudged him in the ribs. "Brunette, two o'clock, black shirt. Mmm."

Brandon's head pivoted to see who Lou was talking about. He'd barely glanced down when he saw her.

Holy shit, Annie.

A second later, he realized she was the woman in the black shirt.

"Don't even fucking think about it," he growled.

"What?" Lou blinked at him.

"Don't even fucking think about it. She's off limits."

"You can't call dibs. I saw her first."

His teammate obviously didn't recognize Annie and there was no chance Brandon was letting the other man go after Doc. She was his. "I'm telling you, if you go near her. I'll rip your throat out."

Lou threw his hands up. "Jesus, relax. You don't need to be an asshole about it."

The server came up and handed him his whiskey. Brandon threw the liquid back in one gulp and set the glass on the table.

Annie was here.

Weaving his way toward the stairs, he ignored his friends as they tried to get his attention. He had one goal in mind. Getting to Annie.

He pushed his way through the crowd. As a big guy, he was used to drawing attention, so when Annie's friend grabbed her arm, he was confident it was about him. Annie turned. Her eyes widened when she saw him, then a smile split across her full lips.

"Hey," he said as he stepped into the space in front of her.

"Hi, what are you doing here?"

He nodded toward the VIP section. "Just out with some friends."

Annie's friend shoved herself closer to them and pressed her chest out. "Hi there."

Brandon nodded at the other woman, barely taking his eyes off Annie. She looked incredible. She'd done something to her lips. They looked fuller, poutier than normal, and he couldn't stop looking at them. As he stared at her mouth, she licked those lips and he bit back a groan.

"How do you two know each other?" Annie's friend asked.

"We met at the clinic," Annie said.

"Pretty sure we met when you shot me down."

"I didn't shoot you down."

He raised an eyebrow at her, and she laughed. "Okay yes, I shot you down, but that's because I thought you were a jerk."

He couldn't help but laugh at her honesty. "You thought I was a jerk? And now?"

She looked at her friend, then back at him. "Undecided."

"Ouch."

Annie grinned.

Her friend wrapped her arm around Annie's shoulder, then pinned him with a stare? "You know what might help her decide?"

"What's that?"

"Take us all up to the VIP section with you."

Annie scrunched up her face like she'd eaten something distasteful. Her friend smacked her. "Stop," the woman warned. "When else are we going to get the chance to go to the VIP section?"

Brandon watched Annie. The fact that she didn't seem to want to go made him considerably more inclined to offer. "We can go up if you want."

Annie eyed the dance floor, and her friend groaned. "No, if you go dance, I'll never get to go to the VIP area and you know it."

"Fine," Annie replied, then turned to Brandon. "It would be great if you'd take us to the VIP area."

He glanced around. "Just you two?"

The little brunette spitfire whipped around and grabbed two more women before Annie even had a chance to answer.

"No, there's four of us," Annie agreed.

"Did I hear VIP?" one of the newcomers asked. The blonde looked at Brandon. Her gaze slid slowly down his body. "Hi there, handsome. Who are you?"

Curious about what Annie would think of her friend blatantly checking him out, he looked at her. She just shrugged, as if to say he was on his own. Big help she was.

"I'm Brandon."

"Brandon?" The blonde whipped her head toward Annie. "Like your Brandon?"

Her Brandon? So Doc had been talking about him with her friends. He definitely didn't hate hearing that. "Your Brandon?" he asked.

The blonde slapped her hand over her mouth, but with the music he could barely make out what she said as she rambled in an attempt to take back what she'd just admitted.

He leaned in close to Annie. "Too late, Doc, I can't unhear that you've been talking about me."

"Shut up." She pushed his shoulder teasingly, then left her hand on his forearm.

"So VIP? Yes?" the brunette asked.

"Yeah," he replied, then leaned back into Annie. "What are your friends' names?"

Annie pointed to the blonde. "Sydney." Then the brunette. "Ashley and I think you already know, Jess."

Brandon looked at the third woman. He was supposed to know her? Shit. "Hey," he said, hoping to hide the fact that he had no idea who she was.

"Ouch." Jess winced. "You have no idea who I am, do you?"

Crap, so much for his poker face. "Sorry, no."

"I'm going to pretend it's because I look so different when I'm dressed up and not because you are oblivious to anyone but Annie when you are at the clinic."

He looked at the woman again. Was he really that big of a dick that he didn't recognize the people at the clinic? He didn't think so. He made an effort to talk to the staff every time he went in, well maybe not talk but at least acknowledge and he was pretty sure he'd never talked to this woman before in his life.

Annie leaned closer to him. "Jessica is one of the vets in the clinic."

"Shit, sorry," he said.

"You should be. Good thing you're taking us to the VIP section to make up for it," Jessica said. The little smirk on her face confused him. Clearly, he was missing something. He just didn't have a clue what.

"Yeah, I'm really sorry I'm not usually that oblivious. I guess I'm pretty focused on Leo when I'm there."

"From what I've seen you're pretty focused on Annie," Jessica smiled sweetly.

Annie gave her friend a little shove. "Oh my god, you were on vacation most of the time. You saw Brandon there like one time and you didn't even talk, so stop." Annie laughed.

"No point in me talking to him when he was clearly smitten with you," Jessica said, then turned to him. "Right?"

Nope, he wasn't answering that one. "So VIP?" He swept his arm toward the upper level.

"Absolutely," Annie agreed.

Leading the way, he wove his way through the crowd to the VIP section. He had no doubt he was about to be grilled by his teammates for going down and coming right back up with a group of women, especially when he'd been a dick to Lou about Annie.

The bouncer waved them through. They walked up to his group. Several of the guys who were single, including Carter, sat up as they approached. Brandon wove toward them, hoping to pawn off Annie's friends so he could get some alone time with her.

He stopped beside Carter, Lou and Tony. "Hey guys, wanted to introduce you to a couple of people." He turned to Annie's friends. "Ladies, these are some of my teammates. Carter, Lourdes, but we all call him Lou, and Tony." As expected, the guys puffed up with the arrival of the women. "Guys, this is Sydney, Jess, Ashley and this is Annie." He touched Annie's waist when he said her name.

"Annie, like Leo's vet?" Carter asked.

Her eyes widened slightly. "That's right," she replied, then glanced at him and smiled.

"B's talked about you a lot. I heard you did an amazing job with Leo. He still looks pretty rough, so I can't even imagine how bad he looked when B found him."

"It was touch and go at first," Annie agreed.

Shit. Carter started to get that stupid little smirk of his. That could only mean one thing. He was planning on stirring shit up. Brandon glared at his friend in warning.

Carter chuckled. "So Annie, you came upstairs with B, so that must mean your opinion on him has softened a little since you first met?"

Annie's eyes crinkled with amusement when she looked at him, then back at Carter. "He's growing on me."

"Wait, how'd you first meet?" Tony asked.

"Oh shit, you're the chick from the bar," Lou said with a laugh.

"I am. I hear you got your car detailed."

Lou let out a whooping laugh. "I sure did."

Annie's eyes crinkled with amusement as she looked at Brandon. She was getting way too much enjoyment out of this. Wanting to change the subject, he glanced around. "Where's Chase?"

"Dancing," Lou replied, then cringed and pretended to shudder.

Brandon eyed the dance floor and sighed. Wasn't the whole point of coming to a club to dance? Why were they all sitting around? With a sigh, he placed his hand on Annie's back. "You want a drink?"

She glanced at the dance floor below them, then back at him. "You probably need some drinks before you dance, right?"

"No, why would I need to drink first?"

"I don't know. Most guys I know need the liquid courage."

"I'm not most guys."

She licked her lips again, then bit the bottom one as she cocked her head to the side and studied him. "I'm beginning to see that."

She stepped closer to him. "So tell me Brandon, are you as nice as you seem?"

He could feel the heat from her body as she pressed against him, and he bit back a groan. Fuck, he wanted this woman. "No, I'm not."

"Good." She flashed him a naughty smile that made his dick perk up and take notice.

She flicked her hand toward the dance floor. "So you game?"

Needing to touch her, he rested his palm against her hip and leaned in close. "I'm down for anything you want, Doc."

"Anything?"

He held her stare. Awareness shimmered between them. "Anything."

"Interesting. Most guys wouldn't make such an open statement."

He leaned in close and smiled when she shivered. "I thought we'd established I'm not like most guys."

"That we did." She trailed her hand down the length of his arm, slowly, like she was enjoying the feel of his muscles. It took everything in him not to flex.

"How about we start with dancing and see where the night takes us?" he asked.

Annie nibbled her bottom lip, then smiled. "All right then, let's dance."

Brandon turned to the group and flicked his thumb toward the dance floor. "We're dancing."

"Already?" Tony asked. "Don't you want a drink first?"

Brandon looked at Annie and winked. "Nah, we're good."

Taking her hand, he led her out of the VIP area. Bodies bumped against them. Annie hooked her fingers in his waistband as he pushed his way through the thrum of bodies and created a space for them on the dance floor.

The music thumped through the speakers. Brandon let his body move to the beat. Annie didn't move. Her mouth gaped as she looked at him.

"What's the matter?" he asked.

"You can dance?"

"What? Of course I can dance."

"No, like, you can really dance," she said.

"It's not really that hard. You just move to the beat."

"But you can actually hear the beat. Most of the guys I know are dancing to a different song than I am."

He chuckled. "Well then, I guess it's a good thing you're here with me and not them, isn't it?"

Annie stepped closer to him. "I guess so."

The song changed and Annie let out a little squeal, then spun in a circle and threw her arms in the air as her hips moved to the rhythm of the music.

Now it was his turn to gape. Captivated, he watched her move. He couldn't take his eyes off her.

Annie smirked, then fisted her hand in his shirt and pulled. He willingly allowed her to pull him closer. "You gonna dance or you just gonna watch?" she asked.

"Is just watching an option?"

Annie's eyes darkened. "Not at the moment it's not, but it can be arranged."

Jesus. His dick twitched. Who was this woman? This wasn't the let's keep it professional woman he was so used to. "How much have you had to drink?"

"Just a couple of drinks. Why?" She stood on tiptoes and pressed her lips against his ear. "You trying to figure out if you can take advantage of me?" she teased as she rhythmically moved her body closer to his.

He placed his hand on the small of her back. "Just trying to figure out if I have a hope in hell of this going anywhere beyond the dance floor."

"Mmm, you hoping I'll go home with you tonight?"

"Definitely."

Annie raised her arms over her head and coyly danced away from him, then came back in. "You think it's gonna be that easy?"

His fingers itched to drag her against him. "I have no idea."

Annie turned and rubbed against his body as she moved to the music. Jesus, the woman was going to kill him.

"Show me what you got." She smirked at him over her shoulder.

When she moved away, he grabbed her hand and spun her back toward him. Grabbing her hip with his other hand as he perfectly moved with her body to the beat of the music.

Annie's eyes widened. "Damn, baller's got moves."

Her arms wrapped around his neck as she allowed him to move them to the beat.

He moved closer, allowing his breath to drag along her neck before he spoke in her ear. "I haven't even begun to show you my moves."

He felt her shiver against him, but she didn't say a word. She just threaded her fingers through his hair as he let the music take them where it wanted to go.

An hour later, sweat dripped down his back. The dance floor was so packed there wasn't an inch of Annie's body that hadn't rubbed up against him. Their clothing was the only thing preventing them from fucking right there on the dance floor. He didn't think his dick had ever been harder in his life.

Sweet Mother of God, he wanted her. His dick throbbed against his jeans, demanding he make his move.

Leaning in, he pressed his mouth against her ear. "You want to get out of here?"

Heat flared in her eyes when she looked at him. Without saying a word, she grabbed his hand and pulled him off the dance floor.

Thank fuck they were on the same page.

CHAPTER NINE

What was she doing? Brandon was a client. Albeit a very sexy client, but a client none the less. But he hadn't felt like a client when he'd been pressed up against her on the dance floor and he sure didn't look at her like a client.

Once they crossed this line, they couldn't uncross it. She bit her bottom lip and glanced over at him. "You sure this is a good idea?"

Brandon stopped walking and looked at her. "I am, are you not?"

"I don't know." Her tooth dug into her bottom lip again. "I don't sleep with clients."

Brandon's lip curled up slightly. "That's good, cuz I'm pretty sure that's illegal."

She rolled her eyes. "Not what I meant and you know it."

"Stop over thinking it, Doc. We are both single, consenting adults. We aren't doing anything wrong. But if you're uncomfortable, I can just drive you home and drop you off."

"Okay."

"Okay I'm dropping you off? Or okay let's do this?" he asked.

A group of drunk men stumbled toward them, raucously bouncing against each other. Brandon stepped closer to her and pulled her protectively against his side.

"Well, hello there," one of the guy's said, eyeing her lasciviously.

"No," Brandon growled at the guy.

"No?" One drunk guy pulled away from the herd.

Brandon's posture stiffened and he tucked her further behind him. "The lady's not interested."

She didn't feel the least bit worried, which was strange. Normally if she saw three drunk men on the street she'd be worried, no matter who she was with, but she wasn't. Everything about Brandon's posture said he could handle anything that came their way.

One of the drunk guy's friends wrapped his arm around the drunk one's neck. "Come on, let's go, plenty of other hot girls inside."

"You're not that hot anyway, bitch," the drunk guy slurred and allowed himself to be pulled away.

"That was rude," she muttered. No need to insult her just because she wasn't interested.

Brandon's arm dropped from her shoulder to her back and he pulled her in front of him. "Guy's not just drunk, he's blind, because he's not going to find a hotter girl inside than you."

"Ahh, aren't you sweet?" She looked up at Brandon's face. "Thanks for having my back there."

"Always." He grabbed her hand. "Come on, let me drive you home."

Drive her home. Had he changed his mind about wanting to come inside?

Brandon stopped at an old, beautifully restored convertible Bronco. "Wow, this is yours?"

"Yeah, just got it finished a few weeks ago."

"Hang on, you did the work on this?"

He ran his hand down the side of the car. "I did yeah. Took a hell of a lot longer than I'd planned, but she's done."

He opened the door and she touched the butter soft brown leather upholstery, then slid onto the seat. "This is gorgeous, Brandon."

"Thanks. I'm really happy with how it turned out." He walked around to his side and got in behind the wheel. When he fired the Bronco to life, it rumbled and purred. Brandon closed his eyes and nodded his head. She couldn't look away. He seemed to just be enjoying the sound.

Eventually, he opened his eyes and looked over at her and winced. "Sorry."

"Nothing to be sorry for. How'd you learn to restore cars?"

"Umm…" He cleared his throat. "Family I billeted with, uh… he was really into fixing cars."

"That's nice. How long did you billet with them?"

"That family? A couple years, actually."

"Wow, I didn't realize people billeted that long."

"They were friends with my hometown coach, so he hooked me up."

She shifted in her seat to get a better look at his face as he spoke. The way his body tensed when he spoke made it seem like maybe it hadn't been the best experience. "Did you enjoy living with them?"

He flicked a glance at her. "Uh yeah, they were okay. Bill's a mechanic. Okay, no, that doesn't really explain what he is. He's a freaking restoration genius. He wasn't real talkative, but he sure knew his way around a car. He had a shop and didn't believe in anyone getting a free ride, so I learned a lot while I was there."

"So you worked for him as well?"

"Yeah, it worked out pretty good. When I wasn't playing ball, I worked in the shop, just grunt stuff at first but over time I got to get in there and help with little things at first then by the time I left I was able to help with pretty much everything."

"I wouldn't have thought you'd have had time for a job with baseball if you were good enough to be billeted away from home."

Brandon grunted. "It was busy. So left up here?"

She glanced at the road. "Yes," she replied before turning her attention back to Brandon. "Did you grow up in a small town?"

"What?"

"You billeted, so I'm assuming you didn't live someplace with the caliber of ball you needed?"

"Uh…" He rubbed the back of his neck. "My uh, coach didn't feel my town offered me the life I was meant for."

"What do you mean?"

Brandon looked over at her. "I'm guessing I'm not coming inside when we get to your place."

"What? Why would you think that?"

"I don't know. We're doing the whole talking about my childhood thing. That doesn't exactly scream let's get busy."

Annie rolled her eyes. "No, we're doing the whole get to know you better thing, which absolutely screams that you might get an invite inside."

"Might, huh?" He reached across the center console and grabbed her hand. "And what would I have to do to guarantee myself an invite?"

"I don't know, maybe not act like I'm pulling your teeth instead of getting to know you."

Brandon sighed. "How about you get to know me as an adult? Trust me, my life now is much more exciting than anything that happened when I was growing up."

Annie studied him. She wasn't sure that was true. The past shaped who a person was and from what she'd seen of Brandon so far he was a series of contrasts. Everything about his outward appearance and the gruff persona he showed the world seemed to be the exact opposite of the sweet, introspective man inside.

"Turn right on the next street," she said.

Brandon continued to hold her hand as he turned the car onto the next street. His hand was huge. It made hers look so small in comparison.

"Okay, you gonna tell me where you learned to dance like that?" she asked.

He chuckled. "Hate to break it to you, but there's no big secret there. It's just dancing."

She raised an eyebrow. "That was not just dancing."

The left side of his mouth curved up in a cocky grin when he glanced over at her. "What can I say? I was inspired."

"Mmm-hmm."

His thumb flicked back and forth against her hand and she shivered. "So you're just telling me you can dance like that with no training whatsoever?" Annie asked.

Brandon snorted. "Do I seriously look like a guy who did dance class?"

"I don't know. I thought that was a thing athletes did to get limber and more in touch with their body or something."

He scoffed again. "Trust me, I'm very in touch with my body. I don't need any extra training in that department."

"Okay, Mr. Cocky." She rolled her eyes. "My place is just up here on the right. The one with the front porch lights on."

He pulled the Bronco up in front of her house. The moment of truth had arrived. Was this a line she wanted to cross?

She looked over at Brandon. The light from the dash reflected off his face, illuminating him in the darkness. Every time she saw Brandon, she wanted to know more. He intrigued her, unlike anyone else ever had. Of course she was inviting him in. "You want to come in?"

He turned off the ignition. "Is that even a real question?"

Annie licked her lips and let her gaze trail down his muscular body. "Not really. I'm hoping I already know the answer."

"You definitely know the answer."

The heat in his eyes as he looked at her was so hot it practically seared her. Goosebumps danced across her skin.

God, please let him live up to the promise.

Between the way he moved on the dance floor and the way he was looking at her now, her body was on fire. If Brandon wasn't good in bed, it would be a sin. No one should be as sexy as he was and not be able to back it up.

Annie pushed open her car door and stepped out onto the sidewalk in front of her house. She waited for Brandon to round the front of his vehicle before walking up the path.

At her front door, she punched in the code to unlock the door. With every move she made, she could feel Brandon watching her.

Annie kicked off her shoes and Brandon followed suit. She turned to him and let her gaze trail down his muscular body. He stepped closer, then cupped the side of her face softly, a moment before he threaded his hand through her hair and pulled her head back, so she was forced to look up. A shiver ran through her.

Brandon stared down at her. His nostrils flared, but he didn't say a word. Annie licked her lips and his jaw clenched visibly. "You just going to look at me or you gonna take me to bed?" she asked.

"I like looking at you." His fingers tightened in her hair, and she closed her eyes and moaned. *God, she loved having her hair pulled.*

When she opened her eyes, he smirked back at her. Apparently, she'd made it pretty obvious. Instead of feeling embarrassed, she raised her eyebrow in challenge.

His eyes darkened. "Where's your bedroom?" he growled.

"Follow me." She turned, adding a little extra sway to her hips as she walked down the hall toward her bedroom. Annie glanced over her shoulder to make sure he was following and bit back a grin when she saw him glued in place, staring at her ass.

"You coming?" she teased.

He gave his head a little shake like he was clearing away a fog and grunted.

She pulled her shirt up over her head and dropped it on the floor. A low growl sounded behind her a moment before Brandon's long legs ate up the floor and he was directly behind her. She squealed when he suddenly scooped her up and threw her over his shoulder like a fireman before she even had a chance to move.

"You're walking too slow," he said.

She giggled. "You hadn't even moved."

"I'm moving now. Which door?"

She peeked around his side. "End of the hall."

Inside her bedroom, he set her down on the floor at the foot of the bed. His hungry gaze traveled down her chest and across her stomach. She'd always been confident in the way she looked, but the way he looked at her now made her even more so.

Annie ran her hand down his chest, enjoying the way his muscles contracted beneath her fingertips. She grabbed the edge of his shirt and pushed it up, but was too short to get it all the way off. At 5ft8, that wasn't something she'd ever had a problem with before.

Brandon gripped the back of his shirt in one hand and pulled it the rest of the way off his body. The tattoo sleeve on his arm she'd admired previously extended onto his chest. It seemed to be a continuation of the scene on his arm.

She sucked in a breath. Obviously she'd known he was a big, fit guy, but knowing it and seeing it shirtless, and covered in tattoos, were two different things. "Wow."

Brandon's lip twitched. "I was thinking the same thing." His gaze trailed down her body slowly. A shiver ran through her at the intensity of his stare, and she clamped her legs together.

She trailed her finger over his tattoo. "This is gorgeous."

"Thanks. So are you."

"Mmm, not sure we can compare me in my bra to actual art, but thank you."

"I have to disagree." He brushed her hair off her shoulder and trailed his finger down the curve of her neck then across the top of her shoulder. Who knew hands that big could be so gentle?

Everywhere she looked, art covered his muscular body. She couldn't help but admire it. She touched the dragon flying across his shoulder. "This tattoo is like a story."

"Yeah, my mom was an artist."

"This is your mom's art?" She followed the line of his arm to the monster on his forearm.

Brandon nodded, then leaned down and placed a kiss against her bare shoulder. A shiver ran through her.

"Did your mom illustrate books?"

Brandon groaned and stood up. "Doc, you're killing me here."

"Why? What do you mean?"

"You're doing these like sexy touches down my arm and then talking about my mom and it's just ...it's freaking me out." He shuddered. "I'm liking the touch, just can we not talk about my mom right now?"

Annie giggled, then winced. "Sorry, I didn't really think about that. I was just admiring the tattoos."

"Yeah, they turned out great, but I'd really rather focus on other things right now."

He stepped in closer. "Clearly, I'm not doing a good enough job if you are thinking about my tattoos instead of how I'm making you feel. Time to change that."

Oh, my. When was the last time a guy had looked at her like that? Like he was going to devour her and just deciding where to start.

He threaded his hand through her hair, cupping the back of her head. He held her in place.

The controlling move had a slight moan slipping from her lips. His fingers tugged her hair slightly as his mouth crashed down on hers. Hot, wet, hungry. There was nothing sweet about the way he kissed her. His tongue swept into her mouth. Not slowly, like he was testing the waters, but with the confidence of a man who knew exactly what he wanted and was going to take it. And she loved it.

She thought she liked the slow, gradual burn of teasing kisses. She was wrong. This was what she wanted. To be consumed.

She wound her arms around his neck as she sank deeper into the kiss. Brandon grabbed her ass and hoisted her up. Her legs instinctively wrapped around his waist. His hard cock pressed against her and she ground down against him, making them both moan.

Without breaking the kiss, he walked them toward the bed. She expected him to just drop her down, but he didn't. He kneeled and his arm tightened around her back as he hoisted them both further up the mattress.

Brandon released her into the pillow and leaned back on his knees. His eyes darkened as he looked down at her body. She arched her back.

"Jesus, you're perfect."

The reverence in his voice made her feel like it. She smiled. "Glad you approve."

"There was never any doubt."

He pressed a kiss to her belly, then another as he undid the button of her jeans, then slowly dragged them down her legs. He picked up her foot and kissed her ankle bone.

"I can't wait to kiss every inch of your body," he said as he kissed the inside of her knee. He ran his tongue up her inner thigh, stopping at the edge of her panties. She could feel his hot breath through the fabric. Moisture pooled in her core. Teasing her, he exhaled right over her clit, but didn't give her the pressure she wanted. She flexed her hips as he ran his tongue along the seam of her panties.

"You don't want hard and fast the first time?" she asked. "You know, kind of get it out of our systems." She squirmed on the bed. The man was making her crazy. Her entire body was on fire already.

"That might be how it is when I actually fuck you, but right now, I'm taking my time." He pressed a kiss to her hipbone. "I've been thinking about this a lot and I plan to take my time and enjoy it."

He kissed his way up her stomach to the curve of her breast.

What was he doing to her? She was so horny it was ridiculous. She'd never had a man's touch affect her like this before. She just wanted him inside her already.

She threaded her hands through his hair. "Are you sure you don't want to just go hard and fast to start?"

He swirled his tongue around her nipple. "Nope."

"I'll bet I can change your mind," she said, sliding her hand down to cup his hard cock. Oh geez, given his overall size, she'd expected him to be big, but this?

Thank you, Jesus.

Brandon grabbed her hand. "Nope, I'm running this show," he told her.

"Oh, you are. Are you?"

The corner of his mouth curved up slightly as he trailed his palm down her arm before pulling it above her head. Her fingers touched the rail of the headboard. He tapped her hand so she gripped the rail. "Keep your hand there. And if you're a good girl, I won't make you wait too long to come."

Oh my. There was nothing sexier than a man who took charge in the bedroom. "What if I'm a bad girl?" she asked.

Brandon licked his lips, then gave her the filthiest smile she'd ever seen. "I'll keep you on the edge all night."

"That doesn't sound like much of a punishment."

"It will when your whole body is on fire and you want to come so bad you're begging me." He brought her other arm up to the railing of the headboard. "Hold on and be a good girl. Don't let go."

She shivered at the commanding tone of his voice.

Brandon's nostrils flared, his eyes dark with desire. "I've got a body to worship." He sat back on his heels and looked down at her. "Damn, Doc. Everything looks so good I don't know where to start."

Annie arched her back. She had a few ideas. "Want some suggestions?"

Brandon smirked down at her. "I think I got it."

The muscles in Brandon's chest rippled as he shifted his weight above her. She clenched her fingers against the headboard to stop herself from reaching out and touching him the way she wanted to.

Goosebumps danced across her skin as Brandon's breath puffed against her neck. She tilted her head to the side to give him better access. Taking the hint, Brandon placed a kiss against her collarbone, then trailed his tongue up her neck to her ear. When he sucked her earlobe into his mouth, a soft moan escaped her lips.

Brandon shifted his massive body so he was kneeling between her thighs. She bit back a groan when he continued to hover above her instead of lowering himself to give her the pressure she needed.

"Patience, Doc," Brandon murmured as he teasingly kissed his way down her chest. Her nipples beaded tightly, pressing against the fabric of her bra. Grr, why hadn't she taken that off?

He swirled his tongue around her nipple, then sucked it into his mouth. Annie's head dropped back and she closed her eyes. He exhaled against her wet nipple. The cool, damp fabric contrasted with his hot breath, making her nipple bead tighter.

Okay, maybe leaving the bra on hadn't been such a bad idea. Brandon sucked her nipple into his mouth.

As amazing as that felt, she needed more. Shifting her hips, she tried to get some kind of pressure on her clit. She hooked her foot on his back to encourage him to lie against her.

Brandon raised a brow at her knowingly. "So impatient."

He pressed his jean-clad thigh against her core, and she moaned. Yes, that was what she needed.

Teasing her, he gently stroked his fingers over the skin of her lower belly as he swirled his tongue around her nipple. She ground herself against his thigh, rocking her hips back and forth.

He shifted, taking his thigh away, and she groaned. Brandon smirked up at her knowingly. Placing a kiss against her hipbone, he hooked his fingers on the edge of her panties and pushed them down her legs.

Brandon settled his body between her thighs. His wide shoulders forcing her to spread her legs further.

He kissed the inside of her thigh, then slowly dragged his tongue up. Hovering above her pussy, he inhaled and she squirmed in anticipation. The first swipe of his tongue nearly brought her off the mattress. It felt so good. He swirled his tongue around her clit, licking and sucking.

"Oh my god," she groaned.

He added his finger and she bucked up to meet him. "Yes," she hissed, gripping the headboard tightly with both hands to hold on.

Jesus. Fucking. Christ. The man had a magic tongue.

She was so close. Her hips moved in time with Brandon's finger, while his tongue flicked her clit. Brandon sucked her clit into his mouth and Annie's back arched off the bed. Her entire body coiled tight as an orgasm ripped through her.

After several seconds, she finally caught her breath and peeked open her eyes to find Brandon watching her with a grin.

"Wow, so that was...." What was that? Earth shattering? Mind blowing? All the above?

"Intense?" Brandon suggested.

"Definitely." She looked down at Brandon, kneeling between her legs. "I really think you need to fuck me now."

"I can do that." He pushed himself off the bed and shoved his jeans and underwear down his thighs in one smooth move.

Woah. Impressive. Her mouth watered as she stared at his hard cock. "Guess you're a magnum guy, huh?"

Brandon flashed her a little cocky grin then ripped the condom wrapper open with his teeth. He placed the ring on the tip of his cock and rolled it down his thick shaft. Even in Brandon's large hands, the thing looked massive.

A little niggle of doubt slipped through her. She'd never been with a guy that big. "Guess that monster is why you said no to hard and fast." She laughed nervously. He'd rip her in half if she wasn't ready.

"Monster?" He chuckled.

"It's a pretty apt descriptor." She bit her bottom lip. "You sure it'll fit? I've got a pretty decent sized vibrator and you are putting it to shame."

"You've got a vibrator, Doc?"

"Of course I do. I'm a healthy red-blooded woman. Just because I wasn't in a relationship doesn't mean I was going without orgasms."

"No one should go without orgasms," Brandon said.

"Exactly."

"Speaking of, what do you say we get back to giving you another one?" he crawled back on the bed and hovered above her.

"You know how to use that club, do you?"

He winced. "Please don't call it a club."

"You prefer meat stick?" she teased.

Brandon shuddered. "Jesus, no." He looked down at himself, laughed, then looked back at her and shrugged like he didn't know what to say.

Annie giggled. As serious as Brandon often was she hadn't expected him to be the kind of guy who would joke and laugh in bed.

She really liked it.

She really liked him.

She reached down and grabbed his shaft. "Fine, how about you put this cock to use?"

"Gladly."

She placed him at her entrance and shifted to widen her legs around his hips. Brandon eased in and she exhaled. Wow, he was big. He slowly eased in a little further and she lifted her pelvis to change the angle. Mmm, much better.

Brandon rocked forward until he was fully seated. Annie closed her eyes as her body adjusted to his size. After a moment, her arousal grew as her body welcomed the unfamiliar sensation. She shifted her hips, making slow, shallow thrusts.

Initially Brandon let her set the pace, then suddenly he took over and everything changed. The slow seductive glides became much more carnal. Hot. Filling her completely. Nerve endings she hadn't known existed fired to life. "Oh my god," she moaned.

"You like that?" he gritted out.

"Mmm." She more than liked it.

All she could do was hold on as her orgasm built and built. Her breathing hitched as her heart raced to catch up. "Brandon," she grunted. "Oh my god."

Her body bowed tightly. She was pretty sure she looked like something out of the exorcist as the orgasm nearly broke her spine.

All she could do was hold on as Brandon continued to drive into her as he chased his own orgasm. She wrapped her arms around his neck. He thrust several more times, then suddenly stilled above her as he came.

After a moment, he rested his forehead against hers, then placed a kiss on her lips. "Holy shit, Doc."

"No kidding." Emotion clogged her throat. What was she doing? She wasn't the kind of girl who got all emotional after sex. Even mind blowingly amazing sex. Needing to lighten the mood, she gave him a playful little pat. "You sure know how to swing that bat."

"Jesus," Brandon snorted out a laugh and flopped onto the mattress beside her. "I thought we were done with that." Still smiling, he shook his head.

"I'm just saying."

He rolled and planted a kiss on her cheek. "You're crazy, you know that, right?"

Teasing him was so much fun. She giggled and shrugged.

"Do you have a garbage can?" he asked.

"Not in here, no, bathroom." She pointed to the door in the corner of the room.

Brandon stood and quickly went into the bathroom, then returned a minute later and flopped down on the mattress. He held out his arm toward her.

"One sec, I just need to quickly go to the bathroom."

Annie hustled out of the room, took care of business, then hurried back. She crawled onto the bed and Brandon held out his arm again. She smiled as she snuggled up against his muscular chest.

"Good in bed and a cuddler? Be still my beating heart," she joked.

"Eh, don't get used to it. I'm just trying to lure you in."

She trailed her fingers along his body, tracing the muscular lines on his chest. "Lure me into what?"

"Haven't decided yet. But it'll be good." He gave her hip a little squeeze.

"Not sure you can beat that performance." She sighed and burrowed deeper into his body.

"Yeah, that was something else," he agreed.

They both lay silent. She didn't know what the transcendental sex meant, but it meant something. Brandon's heart beat against her cheek and she placed a kiss over it, then dropped her head back in the crook of his arm. Perfect fit.

"I'm gonna have to sneak out soon. I can't leave Leo," Brandon said.

"Mmm, do you need to go now?"

"Nah, you just feel like you're about to fall asleep, and I didn't want you to wonder where I was if I was gone when you woke up."

"If I am, call me tomorrow?" she said.

Brandon placed a kiss on the top of her head. "Absolutely."

She snuggled back in. Feeling safe and secure, her eyes got droopy with sleep.

When she woke, he was gone.

CHAPTER TEN

The following morning, Brandon stood on the back deck with his coffee as he watched Leo running around the yard. He glanced over his shoulder when he heard the sliding glass door open, then turned back to watch his dog as Leo chased after his tail. Not sure how he thought he'd catch it when he could barely see what he was chasing, but it didn't seem to stop the dog.

Carter walked up and set his own coffee on the railing. "So you and the doc?"

"Hmph," Brandon grunted.

"That's all you have to say?"

Brandon glanced at his temporary roommate, then took a sip of his coffee.

Carter huffed out a breath. "B, come on, you gotta have more to say than that."

"Like?"

"I don't know, like sorry Carter, I'm being an asshole this morning because the woman literally fucked my brains out."

Brandon snorted. That wasn't far off the mark. "How about I don't feel the need to discuss my sex life?"

"So you did have sex?"

"And we're done here." He pushed off the railing and jogged down the stairs to the grass. Leo immediately bounded over to him and rubbed against his leg. He gave the dog a scratch on the top of the head.

Carter walked toward them and Leo tensed.

"All good, buddy, it's just Carter." Brandon sat down on the lawn in the hopes it would show Leo it was safe. The dog eyed Carter, then curled up against Brandon's side.

"So you gonna see her again?" Carter asked as he sat down on the lawn beside them.

"Jesus," Brandon muttered.

"What? It's a valid question. I'm just trying to figure out if it's cool I still stay?"

"What the fuck are you talking about?"

"I don't know." Carter shrugged. "I don't want to cramp your style."

"You're fine," Brandon grumbled. Why were they still talking about this? He'd made it pretty clear this wasn't a discussion he wanted to have. Was he seeing the doc again? Fuck, he hoped so, but nothing was set in stone.

"It didn't go well?" Carter pressed.

"What?"

"You blew before you really started, didn't you?"

"What the fuck are you going on about?" The sex had been phenomenal. That was part of the problem. He'd had enough trouble not thinking about Annie before he knew what she felt like underneath him. Now that he knew what she looked like naked. How she sounded when she came. There was no way he was getting her out of his head.

"I'm just trying to figure out why you're in such a pissy mood after getting laid. Normal people are happy after sex. You're the opposite, and I'm just trying to figure out why."

"I'm not grumpy. I just don't feel the need to talk about shit the same way you do."

Brandon rubbed the top of Leo's head. What he needed was some peace and quiet to figure shit out, not talk about his fucking feelings like goddamn therapy. He pushed off the ground. "I'm going to the gym, you coming or you gonna find some knitting circle you can gossip at?"

"Fuck you." Carter chuckled. "It's not gossip when it comes from the source. It'll only be gossip when I tell the guys at the gym that you had shitty sex last night."

"Don't even fucking think about it," Brandon growled.

"So the sex was good? Otherwise, you wouldn't be all protective and shit." Carter's eyes widened. "Holy fuck, you caught feelings, didn't you?"

Brandon sighed. Fuck. Was that the problem? Had he caught feelings for the doc? Who knows? All he knew was he wanted her more than ever. "Are you coming to the gym or not?" he grumbled.

"Yeah, I'm coming." Carter pushed himself off the ground. "Why don't you just call her?"

"I'm not fucking calling her already. I just saw her."

"Yeah, and you're clearly thinking about her, so just call her already. Women love that shit."

Brandon glanced sideways at his friend. "Oh really? And you're so wise about women. When's the last time you were in a relationship?"

Carter's nose scrunched up. "Who said anything about a relationship?"

"Why the fuck else would I call her, dipshit?"

"Sex. Duh." The expression on Carter's face spoke louder than any words.

He definitely thought Brandon was being an idiot. And maybe he was. What was the big deal? Why was he stressing over all this?

They were both adults. Long past the age of playing games.

What the fuck was wrong with him? He'd never given any thought to when he should call a girl. He wanted to hook up, he called. Wanted someone to have dinner with, call. No stress whatsoever. So why the hell was he stressing now over when was too soon to call? This was ridiculous.

Ignoring Carter, he walked back inside and immediately saw his phone sitting on the counter. He grabbed it and shoved it in his pocket as he walked to his bedroom to throw some clothes on to go to the gym. As his shorts hit the floor, he heard his phone thunk against the hardwood. He pulled it out, glanced at the screen. Fuck it. He pulled up a video he'd taken of Leo stumbling as he chased his tail this morning.

There was nothing wrong with sending a dog pic. Everyone loved goofy dogs. Chill, low key, didn't mean anything. Before he could second guess his decision, he hit send.

A moment later, she replied.

Oh my goodness, what a goofball.

He looks great, moving really well.

Shit, okay, maybe he hadn't thought that through very well. Of course she'd see it as Leo's vet and not a cute text from the guy who'd been in her bed the night before.

Yeah, he's doing great. How are you this morning?

I'm good, slept great thanks to you.

He grinned.

Happy to help, I'm available anytime.

Anytime? Really. I'll have to keep that in mind. Never thought I'd have my own personal live orgasm machine at my beck and call.

He sputtered out a laugh. Orgasm machine. He'd been called a lot of things, but that was a first.

I aim to please. But trust me Doc, you ain't seen nothing yet.

The three little dots lit up on the screen like she was replying, then stopped, then started again.

Can't wait.

Oh yeah? You want to do dinner tonight?

Just dinner?

Fuck no. His dick pulsed against his shorts.

To start.

If you're nice, I might let you be dessert.

Mmm. Do you really want me to be nice?
Seems to me you'd prefer me a little bad.

Blood surged to his dick as it came to full attention.

Bad works too.

Thought you might say that.

What time you off?

6

> How much time do you need? Does 7 work?

7 is great.

> Thumbs up emoji

He cringed the second he hit send. Yeah, that was smooth. Nothing like a thumbs up to say you were looking forward to seeing someone.

Gotta go, I can hear my next patient barking in the lobby. Goofy rolling eyes emoji. See you tonight.

He smiled when he saw the emoji. Tossing his phone on the bed, he breathed a sigh of relief. He'd been stressing about calling for nothing.

Last night had been off the charts. It was stupid to think she wouldn't want to get together again. It was great sex; it didn't have to mean anything serious. He hadn't caught the feels, he'd had the best sex of his life. There was a difference. And if things worked out well, he'd be having more of it tonight. He pushed down the little niggle in the back of his head that said it was more than sex. It couldn't be. He wouldn't let it be.

Scanning his closet, he searched for his favorite workout shorts. He grabbed them off the shelf and stepped into them, then yanked a t-shirt off the shelf and threw it on as well. He snatched a pair of socks out of the drawer and walked back out to the bedroom. Leo lay in the middle of his bed.

"What the hell, dude. Off," he ordered. "You know you aren't supposed to be up there unless you're invited." Leo's head dropped and Brandon laughed.

"Jesus," he muttered. If a dog could pout, that would be the face. It was almost enough to make him want to leave him there. Almost. But that was a brand new mattress since Leo'd peed on the old one and there was no way in hell he was letting him mark this one too. "Get off."

The dog hopped onto the bench at the foot of the bed, using it like a step down to get onto the floor.

"You ready to go to the gym?"

Leo's tail wagged.

"Carter, get your ass in gear or I'm leaving without you," he hollered as he walked past the spare bedroom.

His temporary roommate poked his head out of the living room. "I'm right here, all ready to go."

Brandon grunted in reply. He stuffed his wallet in his gym bag and grabbed his keys. "Let's go."

Before he turned on the car, Brandon swiped through his music to find what he was in the mood for.

"Can we listen to like top 100 or something?" Carter asked.

Brandon flicked a glance at the other man. "My car, my playlist. If you want to drive, you can choose."

"I have a rental. I don't want to pay for extra miles just to go to the gym."

"Fuck, if you're gonna be that cheap you can shut up about the music." And just to piss Carter off, he pulled up an old 80s punk list.

When the engine fired to life, Carter groaned. "Seriously?"

"Yep." Brandon turned up the volume, then backed out of the garage.

"You seem like you're in a better mood," Carter said.

"Mmm."

"Good talk," Carter muttered, then with a sigh, he settled into his seat.

Brandon smirked when a couple minutes later he caught Carter's head bashing along to the beat. They rode in silence the rest of the way to the gym.

He parked the car, jumped out, and opened the back door for Leo to hop out. It was amazing how quickly Leo had adapted to only having three legs.

Carter stepped in beside them as they walked across the parking lot. "I wish I healed as quickly as your dog. I still have a little pinch in my shoulder and want regular massage from an injury at the end of the season and he had the shit kicked out of him. Lost an eye and a leg and he's bouncing along beside you like nothing happened."

Brandon pulled open the door to the gym. The loud clanking sound of weights hitting plates made Leo jump. His tail tucked between his legs and he leaned against Brandon.

"Okay, so maybe not like nothing happened," Carter said.

Brandon gave Leo a little scratch on the head. Desensitization time. The first couple times they'd come to the gym, Leo hadn't even wanted to walk in the door. Now after a couple minutes of adjusting to the sounds, he was fine following Brandon into the gym and laying in his spot. Brandon walked over to the spot he'd previously used for the dog and set down Leo's blanket on the floor in the corner, safely away from everyone. He was out of the way, but Brandon could still see him from anywhere he went in the room. Leo took his spot on the blanket while Brandon began warming up near him. Once the dog was relaxed, Brandon would slowly branch out for his workout.

Pete wandered over. "Leo's looking good. Much more chill than the last time I saw you here."

"Yeah it's coming.."

"You left early last night, didn't even get a chance to talk to you."

Carter chuckled. "I don't think talking was on his mind last night."

"Jesus," Brandon muttered.

Pete raised an eyebrow. "Oh, yeah?"

Ignoring his teammates, he executed a couple of walking lunges to warmup. He turned and lunged back to his spot.

"So you hooked up with Leo's vet," Pete said.

Brandon glared at Carter. "Seriously?"

Carter shrugged.

"You gonna see her again?" Pete asked.

"Jesus, you too?" What was with everyone wanting to get in his business? He'd hooked up with girls on the road and Pete had never said a thing. Why suddenly did he care?

"Carter said you're sweet on her. So, are you?" Pete prodded.

"I'm not doing this." He gripped his headphones with both hands and hovered them above his ears. "You need me to spot you, let me know, otherwise I'm here to workout." He dropped the earphones over his ears in an attempt to block out their chatter. With a press of a button on his phone, the music pulsed through, completely drowning them out.

He flicked one last glance at his teammates and scowled at the smirks on both of their faces. "Assholes," he muttered loud enough for them to hear before he walked away.

The last thing he wanted to do was chat with his teammates about Annie. He hadn't even wrapped his own head around things yet. He sure as hell didn't need them adding in their two bits.

Brandon loaded up the barbell. What he needed was to stop thinking about it, and just see what happened between them because if he really thought about it, the last thing he'd do was go out with her again. Annie was sweet and kind and far too good for an asshole like him.

CHAPTER ELEVEN

A nnie leaned in closer to the magnifying mirror as she attempted to make a winged eye with her liner for the third time. Why had she never bothered to learn how to do an everyday makeup look? Caked-on club makeup she could do. A casual everyday look? Nope. The girl on Instagram had made it look so easy, and it wasn't. Not even close.

First, the liner on the second eye was too thick, so she'd tried to make the first match. That had quickly spiraled into cleaning it off and starting again, multiple times.

"Gah," she growled as she tossed the liner down on the bathroom counter. This was ridiculous. She had graduated from an incredibly difficult veterinarian school, surely she could figure out how to do a winged eye properly. Practically every prepubescent teen in America could do it. Why was this so hard?

She grabbed her makeup remover and squirted it onto the pad, then rubbed the liner off her eyes again. Screw it. She was doing her waterline, some eyeshadow, slap on some mascara and call it a day.

Brandon knew what he was signing on for when he asked her out. He'd seen her bloodshot and ragged after a difficult surgery, surely her pitiful attempt at makeup was better than that. So this was a step up from how he normally saw her.

Annie carefully applied her eyeshadow and mascara. She tilted her head to the side to examine her handiwork. Not bad. She gave her hair a quick fluff, then glanced at her watch.

6:22.

Well crap. Brandon wasn't due to pick her up till 7:00. Why had she gotten ready so early? Oh yeah, because the idea of being late for anything made her feel sick. And being nervous about this date, her Type A control freak gene had kicked it into high gear. She could practically hear her dad saying, "You come by it honestly," as he looked lovingly at her mom.

Her phone rang on the bathroom counter beside her. "Speak of the devil," she muttered as she swiped to answer the call. "Hi Mom."

"Hi honey, how are you doing?"

"Good."

"Did I catch you at an okay time? I know it's a Saturday night and you probably have plans. A date maybe?"

Good lord. Annie rolled her eyes. If her mom had her way, Annie would be married with four kids. Her mother's biological grandma clock was ticking loud enough the neighbors could hear it. "Why'd you call, Mom?"

"So no date?" Her mom sighed. "Please tell me you are at least going out with your friends. You'll never meet a guy if you don't put yourself out there."

"Mother." Annie cut her mom off. "I have a date tonight, so can you please stop?"

"Oh." Her mom gasped. "That's so exciting. Who is he? How did you meet?"

"Nope, we aren't doing this. You called for a reason."

"Fine. You can call me tomorrow and tell me all about it. But first, what are you wearing?"

Annie glanced down at her jeans and Converse. No way she was telling her mom she was wearing those. "Mom, I'm an adult. I know how to dress appropriately."

"Annie."

Instantly, it was like she was transported back to college. "Geez Mom, it was one time."

"You wore your pajamas to the store, Annie."

"To be fair, I didn't wear them to bed that night since I'd worn them in public, so can we even call them pajamas at that point?"

"They were Christmas reindeer pajamas, so yes, we can still call them that."

Her mother's droll reply made her laugh. "So what's up?"

"I want to get your dad a dog for his birthday this year."

"I'm sorry, what? A dog? In your house?" Had she walked into the Twilight Zone or something? Her mom didn't do the whole pet thing, never had, and if anyone had asked, Annie would have said she never would.

"Yes, in my house, smartass." Her mom sighed. "Now that your dad has retired, he's driving me crazy. He's bored, and I think a dog will be good company for him while I'm at work."

"I think a dog would be great for Dad. He's always wanted one. I just never thought you did."

"It's not having a dog that was the problem. It was the responsibility of having a pet. It always just seemed like it would be one more thing on my plate."

"And it doesn't feel like that now?"

"No, your dad is retired. He's not traveling, he's home every day. He can walk it and pick up the poop, so I don't have to do it. It'll be your dad's dog."

"Okay, but it's still going to be a dog in your house, tracking in dirt, running around being a dog."

"Yes, and that's where you come in. I figured with your connections you could help me find a good breeder."

"I'll help you find a dog, but if I'm helping, it's going to be a rescue dog."

"What's wrong with getting one from a breeder? I've heard you go on and on about the difference between good breeders and backyard breeders. That's why I'm asking for your help."

"There's nothing wrong with good breeders at all. It's just there are so many dogs in shelters and I'd rather see you give one of them a good home."

"I understand what you're saying, honey, but your dad and I have never had a dog. We don't have the first clue how to handle some of those behavior issues."

Immediately, she pictured Leo. Besides Brandon, she couldn't think of a single person who was willing to take him on. It was hard enough to find homes for healthy dogs, let alone one like him.

"I'm not talking about anything like that. Our local shelter gets all kinds of dogs, from puppies to old dogs, after their owners have passed away and everything in between."

"I was really thinking like a golden retriever puppy or something, honey."

The doorbell rang and her stomach flipped with excitement as she walked toward the front of her place. "My date is here, Mom, so I gotta go."

"Go, go," her mom gushed. "Don't open the door till you look in the mirror first. I know how you always fidget with your hair. You don't want it all over the place when he sees you. And don't forget to let him open the door for you. You don't always have to be so independent."

Annie huffed out an exasperated breath. It wasn't like she never dated. She did know how to behave. "I'll text you some questions to start thinking about with getting a dog, and I'll call you tomorrow night."

"Have fun, dear. Good luck."

"Bye Mom." Annie hung up. Placing her hand on the front doorknob, she paused and exhaled her breath to calm her nerves. The man had seen her naked, for god's sake, so why was she so nervous about a simple dinner?

Annie pulled open the door and sucked in a breath at the sight of Brandon standing on her doorstep with a pretty pink plant in his hands. His gaze traveled down her body and when their eyes met, the look in his eyes raised her body temperature by ten degrees.

It was all she could do not to fan herself to cool down. "Is that for me?" she asked, pointing at the plant in his hands.

He flashed her a crooked grin. "Uh yeah. I know it's supposed to be flowers, but I don't really get that whole thing since they just die, so..." He held out the plant.

The pink and green variegated leaves were really pretty. "Thank you, it's beautiful. I will do my best to keep it alive." She stepped back to welcome him in.

"The lady at the store said it's supposed to be pretty hard to kill."

"She's never met me," Annie muttered.

Brandon chuckled. "You can save an animal's life, but you can't keep a plant alive?"

"Not usually," she admitted. She set the plant on the windowsill, hoping the light would be good for it. "Did the lady at the store happen to say how to care for it?" She chewed her bottom lip. How often was she supposed to water the thing?

"Relax, Doc. It's a plant. You got this."

"Sorry." Embarrassed, she let out a small laugh.

"Nothing to apologize for. I'm not going to be offended in the least if it dies. It lasts as long as it lasts. No pressure."

Was he talking about the plant or them? She wasn't honestly sure.

Brandon stepped closer to her and tucked her hair behind her ear. A shiver ran through her as his thumb caressed the side of her face. "You look incredible by the way."

"Thank you." She licked her lips, enjoying the way he homed in on the movement.

Brandon's nostrils flared slightly before he took a step back. Damn, she'd really been hoping he'd go in for the kiss.

"I thought we could check out Seaport Village, wander around, get some dinner, maybe check out the live music later," Brandon said.

"That sounds perfect. It's such a nice area to walk, but I never think to go there."

"You won't catch me there in the summer. It's so busy. But this time of year it's not bad. The guy who owns the coffeeshop near me is playing tonight so he suggested it. And since he's going to go out of business feeding Leo, I figure I should support him."

Brandon really was a good guy. The more she got to know him the more she realized just how wrong she'd been about him. "Are you bringing Leo tonight?"

"Nah, I have more game than that." He chuckled. "Leo's doing great, but he needs me to be on the ball when we're in public, and that doesn't make for a great date."

"I love that you're aware of that. Most people aren't."

"If that's the kind of guy you normally date, I'm even more offended that you shot me down the first night."

"Sorry, but that's exactly the kind of guy I thought you were." Annie chuckled. "But actually I was meaning most people aren't that in touch with what their dog needs in that kind of situation, so I'm impressed. You've impressed me about a lot of things."

Brandon's mouth curved up slightly and he took a step toward her. "Oh yeah, how else have I impressed you?"

She sucked in a breath at the intense look in his eyes. Holding up her hand, she shook her head. "Uh uh, mister. I know that look. You promised me a date and I want to see how impressive you are out in public. I already know how impressive you are in the bedroom."

"Apparently not impressive enough or you wouldn't care about the date," he muttered.

Annie giggled and patted his chest. "If you play your cards right, I just might let you remind me how impressive you can be in the bedroom as well later."

"I'm counting on it, Doc."

Unable to look away from him, Annie licked her lips and Brandon groaned.

"Jesus," he muttered. "All right, Doc, let's get this show on the road." He held out his hand for her to proceed him to the door.

She could feel him looking at her ass as she walked away. With a small smile on her face, she scooped up her purse from the kitchen counter and headed to the front door. Brandon's Bronco sat at the curb, looking shiny and freshly washed for their evening out.

At the car, he opened her door for her. She could practically hear her mom sigh about him being such a gentleman. "Thank you," she said, smiling at him.

He tipped his head up in acknowledgement before closing her door behind her. Brandon rounded the front of the car and hopped in. He flicked a glance at her seatbelt before firing the car to life.

"Feel free to change the station. I don't know what kind of music you like," Brandon said as he put the car in gear and pulled away from the curb.

"I thought the driver got to pick the music. Isn't that like a universal rule?"

"On a road trip? Absolutely. First date? Nah." His gaze flicked over to her and his eyes twinkled mischievously. "Besides, it's not that far to where we're going, so if your choice sucks, I don't have to listen for very long."

"Oh geez, thanks."

Brandon's big shoulders lifted. "What? You could pick K-Pop or something."

"What's wrong with K-Pop?"

Brandon raised his eyebrow at her. "It's not a long enough drive for me to answer that question."

"Wow," she chuckled. "Who knew you felt that strongly about it? How do you feel about EDM?"

"Jesus," he muttered.

Annie snickered. "Guess that answers that question." She pushed the preset buttons on his stereo. Sports, sports, sports. Suddenly show tunes blasted through the speaker.

She spun in her seat to face him. "You're a closet show tunes guy?"

"The fuck? No, I'm not."

"I don't know, your presets say otherwise."

"This is not in my presets."

"Uh yeah it is."

"No, it definitely is not."

She leaned forward and pushed through the preset buttons. 1,2,3 again. Same results. All sports. She looked at him, then pushed preset 4. Once again, show tunes blasted through the speakers.

"Fucking Daye." Brandon shook his head.

"Who's Daye?"

"A former friend," he growled.

"Former? How would a former friend mess with your stereo?"

"Because he's staying at my house and used my car. You met him the other night. Carter."

Ah, now it became clearer. "And does Carter like show tunes?"

"Not that I know of, but he does like to fuck with me whenever possible. Thus the former friend title."

"Gotcha," Annie couldn't help but bob along when the chorus for Seasons of Love played.

Brandon glanced at her skeptically. "You like this shit?"

"It's from Rent. Of course I like it. Everyone does."

"Not everyone," he mumbled.

Annie leaned forward and hit the next preset button. Disney tunes.

"He's never fucking driving my car again."

With a giggle, she pushed the next button and a hard blues guitar solo pumped through the speakers. She eyed Brandon to see if this was also one of Carter's choices. Brandon's body moved to the music. Interesting that he was a blues man. She never would have guessed that about him.

With the music chosen, Annie sat back in her seat. "So tell me about your friend, Carter."

"Not much to tell. He just got traded to the team. He's in town looking for a place to live, so he's crashing with me till he finds something."

"Have you known him for a long time?"

"Yeah, we came up together in the minors." Brandon looked at the stereo. "I thought he was a good guy."

"Oh, stop it." She gave his arm a little shove. "Clearly he knows how to get a rise out of you."

"Apparently." Brandon turned into the parking lot.

Once the car was parked, she hopped out and rounded the hood to meet Brandon on the sidewalk. It had been years since she'd come here, she'd forgotten how cool it actually was. "Where should we start?" She glanced toward the grouping of stores. "Ooh, an art gallery. Did you want to go in there?"

"Uh, we can, I guess, if you want to."

"Oh, I just assumed you liked art because you said your mom was an artist."

"I like my mom's art, but the rest..." He wrinkled his face. "I don't really get it, honestly." He glanced toward the gallery. "My mom would have loved to have her stuff in a gallery like that though."

"Come on, let's go look." She threaded her arm through his. "It'll be fun to try to figure out what it's supposed to mean."

"Not sure I'm deep enough for that."

Annie chuckled. "Guess we'll find out." She gently pulled Brandon toward the gallery. A large sculpture made of what looked like recycled bottles and plastic filled the front window display.

"That's interesting." She pointed to the piece. Brandon grunted, then pulled the gallery door open and held it for her to walk inside.

In the middle of the room stood a feature wall with a huge abstract painting on it. Annie paused as she tried to make out exactly what the painting was supposed to be.

"Jesus," Brandon muttered, shaking his head. "I do not get art."

"What do you think it is?" she asked.

"Honestly, I have no clue. It just looks like a bunch of splotches." He tilted his head to the side. "But it kind of looks like a vagina."

"A vagina?" Annie sputtered. That wasn't what she'd seen at all. She looked at the painting again. "Holy shit." She laughed. "That's exactly what it looks like. Now I can't unsee it."

"What did you think it was?" Brandon asked.

"Umm, a bug."

Brandon snorted.

She pulled him closer to the piece. "Now we have to go find out what it's called." She looked for a nameplate that told them something about the painting. Nothing. "I'm gonna ask," she whispered to Brandon, then giggled when he rolled his eyes at her.

"Good afternoon." A very put together blonde in a power suit walked toward them.

Annie glanced down at her jeans and converse. Either she was really underdressed or this woman was overdressed. Given the location, she wasn't entirely sure which. "Hi there, I had a question about that piece," Annie said, pointing to the large display.

The woman scanned Annie, then Brandon, clearly finding them lacking if the look on her face was anything to go by. "It's a lovely piece, isn't it? We just got that in today."

"Mmm. I didn't see a tag. I was wondering what the name of the piece was."

"It's called Making an Impression."

Brandon snorted and Annie clamped her lips together to stop from laughing. "That's a perfect name for it."

"Yes, isn't it? There's so much emotion. So much pain."

Brandon snorted again. The gallery employee glared at him.

"Are you interested in buying a piece?"

"How much is it?" Annie asked.

"Fifty-eight hundred dollars."

"Holy shit," Brandon muttered. "Fifty-eight hundred dollars for that?" He pointed at the picture.

"Yes, for that." The woman flicked her hair over her shoulder. "A magnificent piece is an investment. Good art costs money."

"I agree. Good. Art. Should cost money." Brandon punctuated the word good. The implication this was not good art hung in the air.

The gallery employee narrowed her eyes at him. "Perhaps the art shop on the other side of the market is more what you are looking for." The woman looked at Brandon's shoes, then back at his face. "You can paint your own mug over there."

Annie gasped. Wow, that was rude.

Amazingly, Brandon didn't seem offended in the least. He just smirked at the woman. "Yeah, that might be more our speed." He turned to Annie. "You want to go check it out?"

"Absolutely."

Once outside, she turned to him. "Sorry about that. I didn't realize they'd be so snooty. I figured a tourist area would be used to looky-loos and would have some customer service," she said.

"Interesting sales technique, for sure." Brandon glanced back at the gallery. "I lied. That is definitely not a gallery my mom would have wanted to have her stuff shown at."

"Did your mom do showings?"

"No, she never got a chance."

"You said your tattoos were her artwork?"

"Yeah."

She waited for him to elaborate, but he didn't. "Did she sell her art or just do it for fun?"

"She was an illustrator. Children's books mostly." He looked down at his arm and absently twisted it.

"Are those from one of her books?" Annie pressed, hoping he would elaborate a bit more.

"No, these she drew just for me." He looked up, his eyes clouded with memories he didn't seem inclined to share.

"Well, they're really beautiful."

"Yeah." Brandon flexed his hand, then tucked it in his pocket.

With the new position of his arm, it made it difficult to see his tattoo sleeve properly. Annie sighed. Point taken. That conversation was done. "Okay so, do you want to paint mugs? Eat?" She rubbed her hands together. "What are you feeling?"

Brandon's gaze slid down her torso and her traitorous body instantly responded, making her nipples bead. She could feel the intensity of his stare as he homed in on her chest. "Besides that," she said.

"I didn't say anything."

"Your eyes did more than enough talking."

"So did your body, Doc."

She crossed her arms over her chest to hide her nipples. "Yes, well, my words are king."

"Fair enough." He dug his hands into his pockets and rocked back on his heels, and she immediately looked at his crotch.

He shifted his hips as she continued to stare. "I think your body is staging a coup," he said.

Busted.

How embarrassing. She snapped her attention back to his face. "Haha. Quit drawing attention to your junk if you don't want me to look."

"Who said I didn't want you to look?" He stepped closer to her and wrapped his arm around her waist and pulled her toward him. "Not gonna be a time I don't want your eyes on me, Doc."

Her body melted against him. What did it say about her that she kind of wanted to tell him they should forget the date and just go back to his place?

"I gotta stop touching you or I'm gonna be calling an audible here, saying screw dinner, we're going to my place and that's not what I promised."

"What kind of baseball player calls an audible?"

"A horny one." With a sigh, he stepped away from her. "Let's go eat."

Thank goodness he had the strength to put some space between them, because she sure as hell didn't. "Sounds good. I could murder a burger."

"You craving some meat, Doc?" Brandon waggled his eyebrows suggestively.

"Haha, funny man." She swatted his ass. "Let's go."

Brandon reached out and grabbed her hand and threaded their fingers together. He didn't seem like the kind of guy who liked to hold hands, so the gesture was all the more sweet.

They wandered toward a pub type restaurant that was sure to sell burgers. Brandon grabbed the door and held it open for her.

"Thank you."

"No problem."

As they walked up to the hostess stand, an attractive blonde teen looked up and smiled. "For two?"

"Yes, please," Brandon replied.

"Bar side or restaurant?"

Annie looked at Brandon, assuming he'd say bar so he could watch the sports on TV.

"Restaurant." He scanned the room. "Any chance we could grab one of the ones by the window so we can look at the water?"

"Of course. Follow me."

The hostess stopped at a table by the window. Annie looked out at the water. Without all the tourists on the boardwalk, there was an unobstructed view of the water. It was really pretty.

Brandon stepped around the hostess and pulled out Annie's seat.

"Wow, what a gentleman, pulling my seat out."

"Eh, I'm just trying to get lucky," he joked.

"Oh my god. I can't believe you said that." Annie swatted him, her hand bounced off his muscular chest. She looked at the hostess. "Sorry about him."

"Don't be." The teen girl looked at Brandon, then back at her. "You'd be an idiot not to take him up on his offer."

Brandon snickered and held his hands out as if to say what'd I tell ya. "You should listen to the girl, Doc."

"Mmm-hmm," Annie rolled her eyes at him, then smiled at the hostess. "Thanks."

The brazen teen looked over at Brandon, not even trying to hide her blatant appreciation as she scanned his body. "Mmm."

"No," Brandon said. The teen looked up at him and he shook his head. Annie bit back a laugh. He looked like a disappointed father reprimanding his child.

"Sorry." The teen blushed. "Your server will be right with you."

When the girl walked away, Brandon leaned across the table. "I'm sorry that was..." He wrinkled his nose.

Annie smirked. "Interesting?"

"Unsettling."

"Unsettling? Why? I'm sure you get lots of women eyeing you up."

"Women sure. That was a child." He shuddered. "That was just wrong."

She snorted. "She was probably fifteen or sixteen."

"Exactly. She should be looking at high school boys, not grown ass men." He shook his head. "Scratch that. She shouldn't be looking at anyone that way."

"All right, Grandpa." Annie laughed. He was so cute, being all offended over the girl's age. "When I was her age, I probably would have checked you out too."

"Yeah, but when you were her age, it would have been appropriate to check me out. I would have been in high school too."

"That's true. I also would have been way too shy to approach you in high school."

"What? Why?" he asked.

"I was a STEM girl in high school. I didn't exactly hang out with the jock crowd."

"Nothing wrong with being a STEM girl. Brains are hot."

Annie snorted. "Yeah right. I'm sure you were all over the brainy girl, and not the head cheerleader."

"If I'm being honest, I wasn't really all over any girl when I was in high school."

"Yeah right." There was no way that was true. Brandon was gorgeous. Given that he played professional ball, he would have been a high school star in any school. Those guys always had girls falling all over them.

Brandon shrugged. "Between ball and my job I didn't really have time to date much."

"Mmm-hmm, so you were just the sole virgin on your baseball team."

"Come on now, I didn't say I was a virgin. I just said I didn't date."

"Okay, now that I can buy." She leaned back in her chair and looked at him. "I'll bet the girls went crazy for you. The unattainable bad boy who they all wanted to lockdown."

"Something like that." Brandon snorted. "Nah, I didn't go out all that much. I didn't drink or party, so there wasn't a lot of opportunity."

"Why didn't you drink? Did you grow up religious?"

"God no." He laughed. "Nah, my dad was an alcoholic and he didn't make drinking look too appealing."

The server walked up. "Hi there, I'm Steve. I'm gonna be your server tonight. Can I start you two off with anything to drink?"

Annie looked at Brandon. Shoot, what was she supposed to order? She wracked her brain to try to remember if he'd drank anything that night at the bar.

Brandon smirked at her. "I'll have a pint of whatever pale ale you have on tap."

Thank god, he'd put her out of her misery by ordering first. "I'll have the same, please."

"You need another minute with the menus?" Steve asked.

Annie eyed the menus they hadn't even picked up yet. "Yes, please."

"No problem. I'll go grab your drinks."

"So you're a beer girl?" Brandon asked.

"With a burger? Absolutely." She shifted in her seat to get more comfortable. "Thanks for ordering first. When you said drinking wasn't appealing, I wasn't sure where you were at with that."

"I never have more than two, but I don't have a problem with other people drinking." His jaw flexed. "Let me rephrase that, as long as you're a happy drunk I have no problem with you drinking."

"What if I'm a weepy drunk?" she asked. Given how he was with Leo, she couldn't imagine he'd be the kind of person who turned his back on a crying person.

"As long as you aren't a mean drunk, you're good."

"Your dad was a mean drunk?"

"He was, yeah." Brandon picked up the menu. "Have you been here before? What's good?"

Getting the message, Annie picked up her menu. "I've never been, but they call it a burger lounge, so they have to make good burgers, right?"

"Let's hope."

Steve walked up to their table and set their pints down in front of them. "Are you ready to order, or do you need more time?"

"I'm ready," Brandon said and looked at her.

"Me too. Can I get the dirty bourbon with fries?" Annie said.

"Good choice," Steve said. "And for you?" he asked Brandon.

"Can I get the Spenny with fries?"

"You bet. Anything to start?"

Brandon looked at her. Annie shook her head no. "We're good," he replied.

Annie picked up her beer and took a sip of the ice cold ale. "Why don't all places put beer in a frosted mug?"

"No idea, but they should," Brandon replied, then took a sip of his beer.

"So I'm curious what made you choose baseball? A big guy like you, it seems like football would have been the sport of choice."

The corner of Brandon's mouth kicked up slightly. "My mom was not a fan of football. She was convinced my brain would get scrambled. Plus, she loved baseball, so she signed me up as soon as I was old enough to play."

"So you never played football at all?"

"I did a little in high school. My dad wanted me to play. But I knew my mom would have hated it, so I never really got into it."

"It sounds like you and your mom were really close. Losing her must have been really hard."

"Yeah, it sucked. But I had baseball, so that helped a lot." Brandon took another sip of his beer. "What about you? What made you become a vet?"

"Mmm, lots of reasons. Like I said, I was a bit of a science nerd in high school, so obviously I was going to pick a career in that field." Saying she was a nerd was putting it mildly. There was zero chance Brandon would have even looked at her in high school. "I always wanted a pet, but my mom would never let us have one. I blame my brother."

"Why's that?"

"He was a pig." Even now, just thinking about her brother's bedroom made her cringe. "Like next level disgusting. His bedroom was like a toxic waste dump and it spilled out into the rest of the house." She chuckled. "There was many a fight between him and my parents. The more they fought, the grosser he got. I swear he did it on purpose."

Brandon cringed. "What exactly does next level disgusting entail?"

"Let's just say my parents had to ban him from taking any food of any kind into his room?"

Brandon's eyes widened and he looked completely horrified.

"Whatever you're imagining, double that," Annie said.

"Fuck."

"Yep. It was horrifying." She chuckled. "Needless to say, we weren't bringing a pet into anywhere he lived. So I started a dog walking business when I was ten, that morphed into house sitting people's dogs throughout high school."

"People trusted you to house-sit in high school?"

She pointed to her chest. "Science nerd, remember. I wasn't exactly throwing ragers."

"Still, not many people would trust a high school kid to look after their beloved pet, let alone be in their house alone when they were out of town. Even if you weren't throwing ragers, you probably had friends over."

"I think you are overestimating my level of cool in high school," Annie said. Having a party at someone else's house never even crossed her mind. In her social circle, following the rules wasn't optional.

Brandon leaned back, making the muscles in his chest flex as he stretched. The move was so unconscious she wasn't even sure he was aware that he'd done it. But she was. She couldn't take her eyes off him.

"You're so friendly and outgoing I can't imagine you not being really social in school," Brandon said.

"Well, I was pretty focused in high school, not much time for partying and boys. I had big dreams and needed to make sure I got the scholarship to do it."

"Wow, you got an academic scholarship? That's impressive."

"Veterinarian school is expensive. I needed one. My family was comfortable enough for everyday stuff, but there was no way they could afford to send all four of us to school."

Brandon's eyes widened. "You have three siblings? Growing up with that must have been interesting."

"Mmm, that's one word for it. It was loud and chaotic. Probably why I sweet-talked anyone I could into paying me to house-sit when they went away. It got me away from the combat zone of my brother and parents, and allowed me not have to babysit my siblings all the time. The peace and quiet was heavenly, plus it gave me the references I needed to get into one of the best vet schools in the country."

"That surprises me. I just assumed you were really close to your family given all the pictures on your wall and in your office."

"Oh no, I'm very close to my family. So is my brother, now. Once he moved out on his own, he cycled through several roommates before he realized he was the problem and cleaned up his act. Now he's great. I mean he was always great, just gross, so I hated living with him in high school. And my sisters were always fine, just annoying because they were younger. My sister Ella actually lives here in town, so we see each other all the time."

"That's nice?"

The way Brandon said it like a question made her laugh. "It is nice," she confirmed. "What about you? Are you close with your dad now?"

"No."

Annie's chest tightened. That was so sad. Not only had Brandon lost his mom, but he seemed to have lost his dad as well. She couldn't imagine not having a relationship with her parents. Sure, they annoyed her sometimes, but they were her parents. "How come?"

Brandon scrubbed his hand down his face. "The combat zone in my house isn't one I want to forgive." Brandon pursed his lips together and sighed. "To be honest, it's really not something I want to talk about when I'm out on a date with a beautiful woman."

"Fair enough. But just know you can talk to me about anything. No judgement."

"Appreciate it, but I guarantee I won't want to talk about it."

The poor guy. She couldn't even imagine. As much as he pretended it didn't matter, clearly whatever had happened between him and his dad had cut deep. She wished he felt safe enough with her to talk about it. Hopefully, someday, he would. All she could do was let him know she was there if he changed his mind.

Thankfully at that moment, Steve walked up to their table with burgers in hand.

"This looks great." Annie eyed her burger. BBQ sauce oozed out the side and dripped down the edge of the bun. She picked up the juicy burger with both hands. Right off the bat sauce coated her fingers and she hadn't even gotten started. There was no graceful way to eat a burger like this. But if Brandon couldn't handle the way she ate a burger, then he wasn't the right man for her anyway.

"Forgive me for what you are about to witness, but I'm going in and I don't think it's gonna be pretty," Annie said.

Brandon smirked back at her. "Is this gonna be a bloodbath, you need a bib kind of situation?"

Sauce dripped down her hand to her wrist as she held the burger. "I might."

"All right then." Brandon picked up his own burger and tapped it against hers. "Cheers. Let's do this."

He chomped down onto his burger and sauce oozed out the backside of his burger onto the plate below. Brandon winked at her and shook his fingers as he chewed. Instantly her nerves settled. The easy comfort in which he dove into his own food took away any fear she had about being judged.

Annie bit into her own burger. Sauce leaked out the side and she felt it hit the side of her chin. Awesome. Of course her burger went all over her face while his went on his hand.

Brandon grinned at her. "That's a good burger."

God, if her mother could see her now. Annie giggled and wiped her chin with her napkin. She was going to need another napkin before this meal was through. "Yeah, it is."

Half an hour later, Annie looked down at her plate. "You want the last of my fries?"

"Nah, I'm good." He placed a hand on his flat stomach. "You put a decent dent in that. I'm impressed."

"I told you I could destroy a burger." She tossed her napkin down on her plate. There was no way she could eat another bite.

"That you did. I should never have doubted you."

She wiggled her eyebrows and flashed him what she hoped looked like a sassy smile. "No, you shouldn't have."

"Won't happen again."

The heat in his eyes made her suck in a breath. Oh my. Her fingers itched to fan herself. Instead, she looked at her watch to distract herself. "What time does your friend play?"

"They go on at 9:30 pm."

"Perfect. That means we have time to paint mugs."

"Oh goody," Brandon mumbled.

"It'll be fun," she told him.

"That's what the trainer at the gym says too, and he's a liar. It's never fun."

"This will be. I promise," she said as she pushed away from the table.

Brandon stood up and pushed his chair back against the table, then placed his hand against the small of her back. "I'm gonna hold you to that."

CHAPTER TWELVE

A week later, Brandon dropped into the seat at the outdoor cafe and told Leo to sit down beside him. Rayne took her place across from him at the small table. "What are you having?" Brandon asked.

Rayne tugged her bottom lip and stared at the menu board on the side of the coffee truck. "I think I'll have an açai and hibiscus lemonade."

Brandon wrinkled his nose. "That sounds fucking disgusting."

"What about that sounds disgusting?" Rayne asked. "It's literally fruit."

"Yeah, with flowers in it. Why would you drink that shit when you could just have a regular lemonade?"

"Fine, what are you having then?"

"Iced coffee like a normal person." Brandon stood up. "I'll be right back. You mind watching Leo?"

"Of course not."

Brandon stood up and looked down at his dog. "Stay," he commanded. When he was sure the dog would listen, he walked toward the coffee truck. A man was already there ordering. The guy looked a hell of a lot like the owner of the team. The man turned. Yep, it was definitely the owner. Should he say something? Should he not? What the fuck was the protocol to talking to the owner when you saw him on the street? Who the fuck even saw guys like this on the street?

Shit. Eye contact was made, so he did the only thing he could. "Mr. Hoffman." Brandon said.

"Brandon, hi. How are you? What are you doing down here?" Matthias Hoffman asked.

Brandon flicked a finger toward the food truck. "Been doing some dog training and now we're just grabbing some coffee." He pointed toward Rayne and Leo.

Matthias' eyes widened in appreciation, the way most guys did when they saw Rayne for the first time. Just because they were friends didn't mean he wasn't fully aware of how attractive she was.

"I didn't realize you were seeing anyone," Matthias said.

That was weird. Why the hell would the owner of the team know anything about his dating life? But then the owner's eyes drifted back to Rayne and Brandon bit back a smirk. Matthias Hoffman didn't give two shits who he was dating. The man was fishing to find out about Rayne.

"I am yeah, it's pretty new but so far so good," Brandon replied, watching the other man for a reaction.

Matthias' jaw clenched before he replied, "That's good. I imagine it's hard to start dating during the season, so you have to make the most of your downtime."

"True enough."

Matthias' gaze darted back to Rayne again. Taking pity on the guy, Brandon said, "She's gonna meet up with us here in a bit."

Matthias' head snapped toward him. "The woman you're dating is meeting you later? That's not her?" He gestured toward the table.

"No, that's my friend. She's helping me with some dog training."

"She's a dog trainer?"

"No, not really."

"What do you mean, not really?"

Brandon eyed the coffee in the owner's hand. The guy clearly wanted to know more about Rayne, so the least he could do was introduce them. He couldn't imagine Rayne would be attracted to someone who owned as much shit as Matthias Hoffman, but who knows?

"You want to join us?" Brandon asked.

"Oh, I wouldn't want to impose."

"No imposition, we're just hanging out."

Matthias scanned the area, then looked back toward Rayne. "Sure, why not?"

Brandon ordered his drinks and grabbed the order. They made their way back to the table. A low growl slid out of Leo as he slunk further under the table.

"Leo, I got this," Brandon said.

He'd been working on helping Leo learn he was protected when he was around. Brandon sat down and Leo creeped out further, pressing against Brandon's foot. Brandon leaned to stroke the dog's head.

"You're gonna have to come out further than that if you want pets." He held a treat in front of Leo's nose to lure him out a bit so he could pet him easier. Leo slowly made his way out from under the table and rested against Brandon's leg, all the while eyeing the newcomer with suspicion. Brandon looked up at his boss. Shit. He'd just left the guy standing there awkwardly.

Brandon winced. "Sorry."

"No problem."

"Let me introduce you. Mr. Hoffman, this is Rayne. Rayne, this is Mr. Hoffman. He owns the team."

"Please call me Matthias." Brandon's boss held out his hand.

Rayne's eyes widened. "The team? As in the Hawks team?" she asked.

"That's the one," Brandon said.

Rayne wiped her palm nervously on her yoga pants. "Sorry. We've been doing dog stuff." She wiped her hand again, then stuck her hand out to shake his.

Matthias shook her hand, then took a seat in an open chair between them.

Rayne studied Matthias. "You seem young to own a sports team."

"Rayne," Brandon growled. It wasn't like her to say something like that.

"Thank you, I think." Matthias smirked. "For the record, I'm thirty-five, but yes, we are some of the younger owners."

"We?" Rayne pressed.

"My buddies and I bought the team together, although they are pretty hands off for the most part. It didn't turn out to be nearly as exciting as they'd hoped." Matthias shrugged. "More my thing than theirs."

"Nice that you have friends who support you in pursuing your dream," Rayne said.

"It is, yes," Matthias agreed. "What is it you do Rayne besides being a dog whisperer, I'm told?" He glanced down at Leo and winced, then his face softened slightly.

"I have a yoga studio, but I mostly do massage and energy work now."

"Energy work?" Matthias asked skeptically.

"Mmm-hmm." Rayne's body tensed.

Brandon didn't really understand why Rayne's body looked so tense all of a sudden, but he didn't like it.

"Yeah, Rayne is amazing at...I don't know, just reading people, animals and knowing how they're feeling, so she's been a huge help with this guy." Brandon scratched the top of Leo's head.

Matthias glanced down at the dog again. He reached his hand out, then seemed to decide against it and pulled it back. "And what's this guy's name?"

Brandon gave Leo another treat. "This is Leo."

"You said he's a rescue?" Matthias asked.

"He is yeah."

"He looks like he's been through the ringer."

"Yeah, he's been through it that's for sure," Brandon said. "I'm just fostering him right now until we can find him a suitable owner."

"Brandon, you know you need to adopt him. He's your dog," Rayne said.

"And I told you I can't adopt a dog with my schedule, Rayne. It wouldn't be fair to leave him alone."

"And I said I'd help," Rayne said.

Brandon could see Matthias watching them out of the corner of his eye. The man's head bobbed back-and-forth between Rayne and him. It was like the man's head was on a damn swivel.

"What made you foster the dog if you don't want to adopt?" Matthias asked.

"I actually was the one who found him. Someone had left him for dead, so I took him to get fixed up and now I'm just kind of looking after him temporarily," Brandon said.

"You found him?" Matthias asked. "As in, somebody just dumped him on the side of the road?"

"Exactly," Brandon growled.

"What would you need to be able to keep him?" Matthias asked.

Brandon stroked the top of Leo's head. He wanted to keep the dog, but how the hell was he supposed to do that when he was on the road more than he was home? "I don't know. It's not like I can take him with me, so it's not really fair to have him live with somebody else while I'm on the road."

"What if you could take him with you?"

"What do you mean?" Brandon asked.

"If the dog could travel with you on the road, would you keep him or would you still want to give him to somebody else?" Matthias pressed.

Brandon eyed the team owner. Where was he going with this? That wasn't an option, so it wasn't something he ever thought about. Of course, he wanted to keep

Leo. He didn't trust anybody else to look after him properly and he liked having him around.

"Brandon?" Rayne prodded.

"Yeah, I mean if he could travel with me in the plane's cabin, of course I'd keep him, but it's not exactly an option and he'd hate being under the plane."

"What if it was?" Matthias asked.

Brandon studied the team owner. "What do you mean?"

Matthias stood up from the table and crouched down beside Leo. The dog leaned further into Brandon's leg. His body trembled with fear, but he didn't growl, which was enormous progress from where they were a week ago.

"Clearly the dog trusts you. And let's be honest, not many people are going to adopt a dog in his condition. It looks pretty expensive. People want puppies and purebreds, not one-eyed, three-legged dogs."

"I know. Doc said it was gonna be a hard sell to get somebody to adopt him since has a bunch of issues and needs medication for the rest of his life."

"Exactly. So what if you didn't have to give him up? What if you could take him with you when the team traveled?"

"How would that work? It's not like I can just take the dog on the plane with me every time, or to the hotel," Brandon said.

"Why not?" Matthias asked.

"Because you don't take dogs his size in the cabin of the plane."

Matthias looked at Brandon, then down at the dog and back at Brandon. "What if you could take the dog on the plane?"

"I'm sorry?" Brandon asked. What exactly was his boss saying?

"What if I said you could take the dog on the plane and we'd make sure our hotel bookings accepted dogs?" Matthias asked.

Brandon's chest tightened. Was he for real? Was the dude really gonna let him take Leo on the plane? "Would you let Leo go on the plane?"

Matthias chuckled. "Would I have asked you if I wasn't serious about letting him go on the plane? That'd be a dick move, wouldn't it?"

"Yeah, yeah it would." Brandon laughed. "But then I don't really know you, sir."

"Fair enough. I know I have a reputation for being tough, but even I'm not that big of an asshole." Matthias glanced at Rayne and then back at Brandon. "I can be a dick, but I'm not being one now. I'm legitimately asking you. Do you want to bring Leo on the plane? Would that be enough for you to adopt him?"

Would it? Could he keep Leo and look after him? Did he have what it took? Fuck, he didn't know. He barely looked after himself. Could he look after a dog? He looked down at Leo. So far they'd been doing okay.

What was the alternative? Give him up? What if nobody adopted him? Then he'd probably get put down. He wasn't gonna let that happen. "Yeah, I guess if he could travel with me I would keep him."

"Then I guess he travels with you, doesn't he?" Matthias said.

Brandon's chest tightened. Oh shit, did he just adopt a dog?

"Yeah, I guess he does." It was hard to swallow. Brandon looked down at the dog. Emotion clogged his chest.

The fuck was wrong with him? It was a dog. Why was he getting all emotional?

"So, how would this work? What if other people want to bring their dogs now that I can bring Leo?" A piece of him was afraid to believe this was really happening.

"I wasn't making the offer to any other dogs. We charter a plane for most flights, so not a big deal to have a dog on there, assuming he doesn't bite anyone's leg off or anything." Just then, Leo decided to growl at a man that walked past their table. Perfect timing.

"He won't bite anyone's leg off, will he?" Matthias asked.

"I don't think so." Brandon laughed nervously.

"You've got a few months before regular season starts. We'll see how he does at the field during training camp and determine what needs to happen at the field. Work with him, get him some training. You promise me he isn't gonna bite anybody on the plane, then I can promise you I have no problem with him traveling and being the only dog allowed on the flights and in the locker room. Think of him like an honorary mascot," Matthias told him.

"Why would you do that?" Brandon asked.

Matthias glanced at Rayne then shrugged. "Honestly, I have no idea. I just feel like he needs a chance." Matthias stood up and looked at Rayne again.

What the hell is up with that? Why didn't the guy just ask her out if he was that interested?

"Once you know for sure that you're keeping him, talk to my secretary and she'll work out the details for him to be included on all the flight manifests and hotel bookings."

"Thank you, sir. Uh...umm I will," Brandon stammered. Why was the owner being so nice to him?

"No problem, you two have a good day." Matthias looked over at Rayne again. "It was really nice meeting you, Rayne."

"Nice meeting you too," she said.

Brandon stood and offered his hand to shake. "Thank you so much, Mr. Hoffman. I really appreciate it. I promise you won't regret it. Leo will be a perfect gentleman on the flights." He looked down at the dog. "Right, bud?"

As the owner left, Brandon dropped into his seat. His mind raced as he tried to decide if he was up for the challenge.

After several moments, Rayne spoke, "It's amazing that you can adopt Leo now officially."

Brandon looked over at her. He'd almost forgotten she was there. The second his eyes landed on her, it became crystal clear what Hoffman's angle was. Impressing his friend.

"Do you think he meant it?" Brandon asked. He really didn't want to get his hopes up just to have some rich guy change his mind and take it all back.

"Of course he meant it," she said. "He seemed to be legitimately concerned about Leo and what was gonna happen to him. He made a whole point of saying he wasn't that big of a jerk. He's not going to back out. He seems like a great guy, Brandon. I wouldn't worry about it."

"I guess I should thank you for getting Leo plane privileges."

"Me? What did I have to do with it?"

"Because I'm pretty sure Hoffman just wanted to impress you, judging by the sparks flying every time you looked at each other."

"There weren't sparks flying." Rayne rolled her eyes. "Billionaire tycoons don't date woo-woo energy workers."

"You also teach yoga and look like it, babe." Brandon snorted. "I'm pretty sure that's exactly who billionaire tycoons go for. You're all bendy and shit." He waggled his eyebrows at his friend. "I'm surprised he didn't ask for your number."

Rayne rolled her eyes. "You're an idiot. There's a big difference between thinking someone is attractive and wanting to date them."

"I didn't say he wanted to date you, but he clearly wanted to fuck you."

Rayne reached across the table and smacked his arm. "Oh my god, you did not just say that."

Brandon laughed. "Ow, I thought you were a pacifist. What the hell? You're throwing punches now?"

"I didn't punch you. I smacked your arm. There's a difference and you deserved it."

"I deserved it? Rayne, I am shocked. Violence is not the answer," Brandon teased.

Leo had hit him harder flopping down on the couch on top of him for a cuddle. "Seriously, though, he was definitely checking you out."

Rayne waved her hand like she was brushing the idea away. "Anyway, moving on."

She shifted in her seat, reached across the table and squeezed his arm. "Brandon, this means you get to keep Leo."

Rayne's eyes filled with tears. "Oh my god, he has a home." The tears in Rayne's eyes burst free and streamed down her cheeks.

"Yeah, looks like he does." He glanced down at the dog. "Well, buddy, it looks like it's you and me now."

Emotion clogged Brandon's chest. He cleared his throat. What the hell was wrong with him? He felt like he was gonna join Rayne in this weep fest. And he didn't do tears. He didn't remember the last time he'd cried.

No, that wasn't true. He remembered that time vividly. It had been a couple weeks after his mom died and his dad had found him crying in his bed and beat the shit out of him for being a pussy. That was the first time his dad had beaten him and the last time he allowed himself to cry.

Why the hell did he feel like doing it now over keeping a dog? He looked up and his chest tightened for an entirely different reason as he saw Annie walking toward him across the field.

Rayne swiveled in her seat to see what he was looking at. When she turned back to him, she was smirking. "Speaking of fucking," she said.

Pulling his attention off Annie and back to his friend, he tried to process what she'd just said. "What?"

Rayne grinned. "I like her for you. I like seeing you like this."

"Seeing me like what? "

"Happy."

"What are you talking about? I didn't do anything. I just looked up."

"Yep, and your energy completely changed the moment you saw her." Rayne reached across the table and squeezed his arm again. "You deserve to be happy, B, let yourself."

"Hmm," he grunted. How was he supposed to respond to that?

As Annie got closer to the table, he stood up to greet her. Leo did the same, but shifted his body slightly behind Brandon like he was unsure if he wanted to say hello or hide. Annie stood on her tiptoes and pressed a kiss against his lips. Wrapping his arm around her waist, he pulled her against him before she had a chance to pull away. He rested his forehead against her and held her for a moment longer.

"Hey," he said.

"Hey yourself," Annie replied. She leaned back slightly and looked up at him. Her eyes narrowed as she studied his face. "What's going on?"

"What do you mean?"

Annie looked over at Rayne then back at him. "What'd I miss?"

"I'm adopting Leo," Brandon said.

Annie reared back. "You're what?" She searched his face again. "What do you mean you're adopting Leo? What changed?"

"Have a seat." Brandon gestured for her to sit down at the table. "Do you want coffee or something?" he asked.

Annie glanced at the drinks on the table. "Iced coffee would be great."

"Be right back," Brandon said and pressed a quick kiss to the top of her head.

While he waited for his drink, Brandon eyed the two women chatting at the table. Rayne said something that had Annie throwing her head back with laughter.

A smile split across his face as he watched his friend and a woman who he was beginning to care a great deal about. Rayne was right. He was happy and a big part of that was Annie.

Iced coffee in hand, he walked back to the table and set it in front of Annie. He ran his hand over the back of her head and gave the back of her neck a little squeeze before he sat down.

Annie adjusted her body so she was facing him. "All right, you were about to tell me why you decided to adopt Leo."

"Rayne didn't tell you?" He glanced at his friend. That was the difference between Rayne and most of his friends. Had it been Carter, he would've spilled the news without a second thought.

"Not my news to tell," Rayne said.

True, but that didn't normally stop his friends. "We ran into Mr. Hoffman."

When Annie stared back at him blankly, he continued. "The owner of the Hawks."

"Okay, and what does that have to do with you adopting Leo?"

"He said that I could take Leo on the plane."

Annie's forehead wrinkled. "What do you mean, you can take Leo on the plane?"

"We charter a flight for most of our games and he said Leo could come with us on all the away games."

Annie chewed her bottom lip. "I'm not sure that him riding in the cargo area that often is good for him. He's been through a lot. He's not used to that kind of thing. I don't know that's the answer, Brandon." Her face softened. "I'm sorry."

"He wouldn't be riding in the cargo area. He'd be riding in the main area with me. That's not really any different from a service dog, and they travel all the time with their humans."

"How would he travel with you and not in the cargo area? I don't understand."

"That's the beauty of flying with a team. We're the only ones on the plane, so we can do whatever we want. Mr. Hoffman said he'd make sure everything worked fine for Leo to come with me. Stay in hotels that allow dogs and I can bring him to the stadium, assuming he's well trained."

The more he thought about it, the more he loved the idea. He could picture Leo kicking it in the locker room. "He's not a hawk, but I think he'd make a pretty damn good mascot."

Annie eyed the dog. "It'll take a lot of training to get him ready for that kind of lifestyle."

"Good thing I'm not working right now then, because I've got nothing but time."

"Is this really what you want to do? Not that long ago, you didn't even want to foster him."

"Wasn't that long ago for a lot of things. Shit changes. He already lives with me, may as well make it permanent." He nudged her with his shoulder. "Besides, I've got you to help me train him."

"Mmm-hmm," she mumbled. "Why would Mr. Hoffman want to let you do that?"

Brandon glanced at Rayne and smirked. "Because he wants to fuck Rayne."

"And on that note, I'm out. I have a client in an hour." Rayne stood up from the table. She leaned down and hugged Brandon. "I'm really glad you decided to say yes. I think it's the right decision for both you and Leo."

He squeezed her back. "Me too. Thanks for your help today."

"Anytime." Rayne bent down and gave Leo a little pet, then rested her hand on his upper back and one on his chest, and Leo instantly seemed to settle down. "We're gonna get you there, baby. You'll be the best travel companion anyone has ever seen." She leaned forward. "Now give me a kiss so I can take off."

Leo's tongue swiped out and lapped across Rayne's cheek. She giggled, then gave him another little pat before standing up. "Call me when you want to take him out again."

"Will do, thanks Rayne."

"Anytime, you know that." Rayne turned to Annie. "It was great seeing you. Sorry it was so short, but I'll see you at Kia and Jeff's at the end of the month, right?"

Annie's eyes widened and she looked over at him, confusion etched on her face.

"Jesus Rayne, we just got the text like an hour ago, I haven't even had a chance to ask her." He looked at Annie. "But yeah, I'm hoping you'll want to come with me."

"I'd love to," Annie replied.

"Great, I'll see you then," Rayne said before she slipped away.

"Let's talk about how you plan to train Leo to be ready for all this," Annie said.

Brandon grabbed the leg of Annie's chair and pulled her closer to him. "How about we talk about how sexy you look in those shorts? Damn, woman." He leaned in and nuzzled the side of her neck.

CHAPTER THIRTEEN

E ven though she'd been expecting Brandon, Annie still jumped when the doorbell rang. She placed her hand on her stomach. Butterflies danced beneath her fingertips. Why was she so nervous?

She squared her shoulders and opened the front door. The air in her lungs caught when she saw Brandon on her doorstep. "Wow," she whispered.

His mouth tipped up in a crooked grin. "I could say the same thing, Doc." He leaned forward and pressed a kiss against her cheek. "You look beautiful."

"Thanks. You clean up pretty well yourself." She let her gaze trail down his fitted button-down shirt and dress slacks. His clothing looked like it had been custom made for his 6ft5 frame, and it probably had. Thank goodness he'd told her what club they were going to tonight or she would have been underdressed.

"Let me just grab my purse." She turned and picked up her jacket and purse from the entryway table. Brandon held out his hand for her jacket. She passed it to him and he held it open for her. Annie's stomach flipped again. Such a simple little thing to help her with her jacket, but she couldn't remember the last time a date had done that for her. It was nice.

She glanced over her shoulder and smiled. "Thank you."

He nodded, then gestured for her to proceed him to the front door.

"So whose house are we going to dinner at again?" she asked, as Brandon opened her car door for her.

"Kia and Jeff's house, but everyone calls him Smitty."

She waited for him to start up the car before speaking again. "Is everyone on the guest list a teammate?"

"I think so, but I don't honestly know. I've never been to a formal dinner party before with them. It's mostly been BBQs but—" Amusement crept onto Brandon's lips as he smirked. "Kia thought Smitty's 30th should be fancy."

"This is a birthday party?" Annie grimaced. "I didn't bring anything."

"Didn't expect you to. I got something for him." He picked up an envelope sticking out of the cupholder between the seats.

Annie sat back in the car seat and glanced at Brandon. "So how's Leo doing?"

"He's good. You were right about the crate," he said. "He seems to feel more secure when he's in there when I'm gone."

"That's good. Sacrificing one couch to his anxiety is probably enough."

Brandon winced. "I might have left him loose another time after we talked."

Annie raised her eyebrow. "And what did he do?"

"He chewed through the drywall beside the front door and, umm...destroyed the carpet."

Her eyes widened and she covered her mouth. "Oh my god."

"Yeah. Expensive little bugger."

"Why didn't you just put him in the crate like we talked about?"

Brandon shrugged. "I don't know," he grumbled. "I still wasn't convinced."

How many times had she heard that from dog owners? "Now you are?"

"Yeah. He could have killed himself. He was chewing the electrical wire in the wall when I came home. I don't know what would have happened if I'd come home later."

"Oh my gosh, so he, like, really ate your drywall? I was picturing some scratches."

"No, no, he ate it. Like his entire head was in the wall. I'm pretty sure if the electrical hadn't distracted him, he would have busted out of the exterior wall as well, since he was right in there."

"Oh geez, what a little stinker."

"That's one word for him," Brandon muttered. "But after that, I decided maybe your way was worth a shot and he seems to be a lot happier. He goes in there all the time when someone is over. I just figured if I left the door open, he could come and go as he pleased. But apparently, he needs it locked when I'm not home."

"I know you think it feels cruel to put him in there, but it really does help a dog feel safer and more secure to know they are protected."

"Yeah, I can see that now. He's just been through the shit. I don't want him to feel like my place is anything like where he came from."

She reached across the console and squeezed his arm. "From what I've seen, Brandon, there is zero chance of him ever thinking that."

"I hope so."

Brandon turned down a residential street, then turned again, bringing them closer to the water.

"Wow, your friend lives here?"

"Yeah, he's got a nice place, right on the ocean."

She knew ballplayers made good money, but not this kind of money. She'd assumed places like Brandon's were more the norm. Nice, but not don't-touch-anything nice.

Brandon pulled the car up behind a black luxury sedan and put the Bronco in park, then turned to her. "Ready?"

She smoothed her hand down the front of her pants. "Mmm-hmm."

Brandon met her at the front of the car and held out his hand for her to take. His warm palm engulfed hers and the nerves in her stomach instantly settled down. She'd seen Brandon with Leo. If he was half as tuned in to her as he was his dog, she had nothing to worry about.

He rang the front door. A beautiful woman covered in tattoos opened the door. The moment she saw them, she practically beamed and the last of Annie's nerves disappeared.

"Brandon." The woman held out her arms and pulled Brandon into a hug. "I'm so glad you made it."

His huge frame engulfed the other woman in a warm embrace. "You didn't really give me any option, Key."

"True." The woman gave Brandon another squeeze, then stepped back and looked at her. "Hi, you must be Annie. I'm Kia. Nice to meet you."

"You too." Annie glanced around the foyer. When she stepped to the right, she had a clear sightline to the ocean out back. "Your house is beautiful. And that view. Wow."

Kia glanced toward where Annie was looking. A man with striking blue eyes stepped into view and Kia smiled.

"I'm pretty lucky."

Brandon made a fake retching sound beside her. Annie glanced over at him, confused. What was that about?

Kia slapped Brandon on the arm. "Shut up. What can I say? My man is hot."

Brandon fake retched again.

The man in question wandered toward them. "Hey B."

Brandon held out the envelope. "Happy birthday."

"Thanks. You didn't have to get me a gift, but thank you, I appreciate it." The man took the envelope, then turned to Annie and flashed a grin so big it made her take a step back. Uh oh. This guy was far too excited to meet her. She looked at Brandon and he rolled his eyes.

"Ease up, Smitty, she just got here," Brandon mumbled.

"What? I haven't even said anything yet," Smitty replied, then turned to her again. "Hi Annie, I'm Jeff. Nice to meet you."

"Nice to meet you, too. Happy birthday."

"Thanks." He looked at Brandon, then rubbed his hands together. "This is going to be fun."

"Smitty," Brandon growled in warning.

"What? Fairs fair." Smitty dropped his arm around Annie's shoulder.

"So you and Brandon," he said as he guided her toward the back of the house. She was pretty sure she heard Brandon mutter, "Jesus." As they walked away followed by the sound of Kia laughing.

She glanced at the man leading her down the hallway. "Clearly I'm missing something here," she said.

"Nah, not really. I'm just fucking with B since he likes to stick his nose in other people's relationships."

"Brandon does?" She found that hard to believe. He didn't seem like the kind of guy who would care what other people did in their relationships.

"Yep, Mr. Matchmaker over there. Now that he's dating someone, it's our turn to stir the pot."

"Stir the pot? That sounds ominous. Should I be worried?" She wrinkled her nose.

Smitty's eyes widened in surprise. "Oh shit, no sorry, I don't mean we were going to make things uncomfortable for you. This was more about bugging him." He chuckled, then turned to her. He studied her face for a moment before he spoke. "Brandon's a good guy. Don't hurt him."

She blinked at him. Hurt him? Her? If anyone was going to get hurt in this relationship, it would not be Brandon. She looked over at the man in question as he laughed at something Kia said. "I don't think you have to worry about that."

Smitty pinned her with a serious look. "Make sure I don't."

Before she could respond. Brandon walked up. "All right, birthday boy, you done monopolizing my date?"

"For now," Smitty said with a wink. "Besides, I wasn't monopolizing her. I was saving her from the inquisition."

"The what?" Annie sucked in a breath.

"Oh, there's no way you aren't getting grilled by the girls tonight."

She looked at Brandon and at least he had the decency to wince. "Sorry, it's true. There's no way Kia isn't leading the charge on getting to know you." He smirked. "She says it's her job as my big sister."

Wait, what? They were related? Why didn't he tell her that? She didn't know she was meeting his family. She wasn't ready for that. "She's your sister?"

Brandon chuckled. "No, she's not, but since I don't have one, she thinks she should fill the role."

Oh, thank god. She breathed a sigh of relief. Meeting someone's friends was one thing. Meeting their family was something else. "I'm sure I can handle a good grilling from the girls. I've got nothing to hide."

"Don't be too sure about that," Smitty muttered. "You don't know the girls."

"No shit." Brandon laughed again, then winced. "Incoming."

Annie looked over just as four women descended on them. She recognized Brandon's friend Rayne and Kia, of course, but she didn't know who the other two were.

"Annie, I wanted to introduce you to some people," Kia said. "You've already met Rayne."

The welcoming way Rayne smiled at her eased her nerves tremendously. Surely someone as warm as Rayne wouldn't be friends with these women if they were awful.

Kia nodded toward the beautiful, petite blonde. "This is Peyton." Then turned to an equally attractive brunette. "And this is Kendall."

She wasn't one to feel insecure about her looks, but it was kind of hard around these women. They were all incredibly attractive in their own way and not at all what she'd been expecting.

In preparation for tonight, she'd done a deep dive on social media and seen dozens of photos of ballplayers with models and influencers. Women who didn't look like they ever met a carb, let alone eaten one. That had certainly been what most of the women hanging around the players in the club had looked like. But these women looked real. More like women she'd actually be friends with.

"Nice to meet you." She looked around the party at the couples and various single men roaming about. Brandon had said the majority of people would be his teammates, so these must be players' girlfriends, but she had no idea who they belonged with. "Are you both dating players on the team as well?"

"We are," Kendall said. She pointed over to a group standing in the kitchen. "That's mine in the black shirt. Pete, he plays shortstop."

Annie logged the information in her brain.

Peyton pointed in the same direction. "And the guy on Pete's left is Ryan. Best pitcher on the team."

"Ehh." Kendall said.

Peyton scrunched up her nose and stuck out her tongue at Kendall.

"Kendall is Ryan's sister," Kia told her.

Annie's eyes widened. "Oh, okay." That was an interesting dynamic. Wonder how that all happened. She'd have to make sure to ask Brandon.

Smitty slapped Brandon on the shoulder. "Let's get these ladies some drinks."

Brandon looked at the group, then down at her questioningly, like he was asking if it was okay to leave her.

"I'd love a glass of white wine," she told him, hoping he'd take that as permission that it was okay to leave her with the women. As much as she wanted to be with Brandon, she didn't expect him to stay by her side all night at his friend's party.

"You got it. Be right back." He gave her hip a little squeeze.

"Oh my god, I love this," Kia gushed, practically bouncing beside her.

Peyton laughed softly. "You have zero chill, Kia."

"What? I can't help it." She turned to Annie. "I love you two together."

"How do you know that? We just got here."

"I just do. I have a good feeling about you two."

Annie looked across the room and watched Brandon interacting with his teammates. She had a good feeling about them too.

"So Brandon said you're a vet," Kia said.

"I am."

"And I hear you thought he was an asshole when you first met him," Kia pressed.

Annie thought about the night in the bar where she'd met Brandon. He'd seemed like such a cocky player. "That's one way to put it."

Kendall slapped her hands together like a prayer. "Please tell me he hit on you and you shut him down."

"Pretty much," Annie agreed.

Kendall whooped. "Good, these guys need to have to work for it every now and then. Women come too easy to them."

"Says the woman who threw herself at her brother's best friend," Peyton teased.

"Okay, not the same thing at all. I'd known Pete forever and he was oblivious. I had to do something bold. Annie and Brandon were strangers," Kendall said.

"Okay, I'll give you that," Peyton agreed, then turned to Annie. "What made you change your mind? I'm assuming you did change your mind."

Annie looked over at Brandon standing to the side listening to his teammates talking. He wasn't in there loudly demanding attention like some of the guys. He stood there with his arms crossed over his chest, looking a little grumpy. If it wasn't for the slight smirk on his face, she'd think he didn't even care if he was there. Everything about him was just so unapologetically him.

"I absolutely changed my mind. He surprised me. How he presented himself to me in the bar vs how he really is. Night and day." She looked over at Brandon and it was like he could feel her looking because he glanced over. His grumpy perma-scowl shifted into a smile.

Kia squealed. Brandon rolled his eyes and shook his head, making Annie giggle at his response to his friend's enthusiasm about them.

"Let's go join the boys before they start measuring dicks," Kendall said.

"Annie, can I just—" Kia grabbed hold of Annie's arm to hold her back when the others left. "Brandon is ... he's just a really amazing human being..." Kia sighed.

Annie watched the other woman as she struggled to find her words. "I know," she said, hoping to reassure Kia.

"Do you?" Kia studied her. "I know he's built like the freakin' Rock and acts like nothing really gets to him, but..." Kia glanced over at the men, then back to her. "Don't hurt him."

"I won't." Annie looked over at the man in question. Brandon raised his eyebrow at her like he was asking if she needed his help. She waved him off, then focused on her conversation with Kia.

"Look Kia, while Brandon isn't hugely open. I've watched him with Leo. The way he is with that dog—"

How did she explain it? When she looked at the two of them, it was like they were kindred spirits. Two wounded souls who knew firsthand how horribly cruel human beings could be. And while Brandon hadn't told her much about his upbringing, he didn't have to. As much as he tried to hide it, it was written all over him every time he'd come in to be with Leo those first few days.

"I'm not going to hurt him," she told Kia.

"Good." Kia squeezed her arm again. "And don't let him convince you he doesn't believe in love. Because if anyone is a sucker for romance, it's Brandon."

"Oh, really?" Annie glanced over at Brandon. He pushed off the wall and started to walk toward them.

"Oh, yeah."

"What are you two still talking about?" Brandon asked as he joined their conversation.

"I was just about to tell her about all your matchmaking."

"Jesus, not you too," he groaned. "Your boy already tried this shit." He handed Annie a glass of white wine. "Don't believe a word she says."

Kia put her hands on her hips. "Are you calling me a liar?"

Brandon slung his arm around Kia's neck and dragged her toward him.

"Don't you dare noogie me, Brandon Sims," Kia squealed as she tried to squirm out of his grasp.

"Then don't talk shit."

Kia ducked out from under his arms. "Fine, but for the record, it's not shit talking when it's true." Kia fluffed up her hair, then turned to Annie. "I think it's time for shots."

"Shots?" Oh geez, she hadn't expected shots to be involved in the evening.

"Yep, you've always got a built in DD with Brandon. So shots." Kia linked her arm through Annie's and tugged her toward the kitchen.

Annie looked back over her shoulder at Brandon. "Help," she called.

Brandon chuckled. "You're on your own with her, Doc."

"Gee thanks," Annie mumbled. Big help he was.

Kia tugged again and Annie fell into step beside her. "Come on, I promise it'll be fun," Kia said. "Besides, if you overdo it, Brandon can always throw you over his shoulder and carry you home."

"Let's hope it doesn't come to that."

CHAPTER FOURTEEN

B randon pulled the car into the garage and parked. Annie didn't stir from her place in the passenger seat. He glanced over at her. Out like a light.

"Damn, bro, looks like you are out of luck tonight." Carter piped in from the backseat. "Thanks for being DD. Appreciate it."

"No problem."

"You want to play some vids?" Carter asked.

Brandon looked over at Annie sleeping beside him. "Nah, I'm gonna get her to bed, thanks."

"Cool, see you tomorrow." Carter pushed open the back door of the vehicle and shuffled his way into the house.

Brandon nudged Annie's arm. "Doc, we're here."

She curled her body and tucked her hand under her chin. With a chuckle, he pushed open the car door and rounded to her side of the vehicle. He opened her door and gave her another little nudge. "Come on sleeping beauty, time to get inside."

Annie blinked her eyes open and smiled. "Brandon, hey." Her arms wrapped around his neck and she nuzzled her face against him. "Mmm, you always smell so good," she said.

"Thanks. Now come on, let's get you inside."

"Carry me," she said.

"What?" She couldn't be serious. No way the independent doc wanted to be carried.

She wrapped her arms tighter around his neck. "Carry me, my legs are noodles. I can't walk." Annie wiggled her legs and giggled. "See?"

"Good lord," he muttered. He tucked his hand around her back and the other under her legs and scooped her out of the car.

"I love how strong you are." She snuggled in against his chest. "It's really sexy."

"Hmm." He kicked the car door shut and made his way across the garage, then shifted her weight slightly so he could open the door to get them inside.

He paused at the entrance to the living room, where Carter lay sprawled on the couch already. "Lock up, would you?"

"No problem." Carter smirked as he looked at him. "Shame Annie can't hold her liquor better."

"I hold my liquor grr-rate," Annie perked up. "Ooh, do you have frosted flakes?"

"No."

Carter laughed. "Glad I'm not the only one not getting laid tonight."

"Oh, Brandon's getting laid," Annie said with drunken confidence.

"No, he's not," Brandon replied.

"What?" Annie pushed against his chest, and he bobbled to hold on to her when her drunken body didn't support the movement. "We are having sex," she claimed.

"No, we aren't."

"Uh huh, we are."

Carter snorted. "You think you're winning this argument?"

Brandon glanced at his friend. "It's not even up for discussion. Night."

"Good luck," Carter called as Brandon carried Annie down the hallway toward his bedroom.

"What do you mean we aren't having sex?" Annie whined.

"You're drunk. We aren't having sex." He set her down on the edge of the bed then grabbed a shirt out of his drawer and handed it to her. "I gotta take Leo out for a pee."

Annie tossed the t-shirt aside. "I don't need this."

"Alright, drunky." He chuckled. Damn, she was cute when she was drunk. He flicked open the door to Leo's crate and released him. The dog ran out and sat at his feet, practically vibrating as he waited for a pet.

"Hey buddy." Brandon scratched Leo's head. "Let's go pee before bed."

He flicked one more glance at Annie on the bed. She reclined back and smiled seductively at him. Damn, he wished she wasn't drunk. "Be right back."

"I'll be here," she said.

Brandon opened the door to the deck off of his bedroom and wandered down the stairs with the dog. Once the yard was fully fenced, he could just let Leo play outside alone. Leo was going to love it. He wished he hadn't put it off so long, but it had seemed stupid to fence the back when he didn't need to. When he'd thought it was temporary. As soon as he'd made it permanent, he'd called fencing companies, but no one could fit him in until this coming week.

He watched as Leo maneuvered to where he wanted to be. He couldn't believe how well the dog moved on three legs. It didn't faze him at all. Leo ran back and flopped down and exposed his belly for rubs. Leo's excited legs kicked, propelling him further away from Brandon before the dog spun back toward him.

He chuckled as he crouched down to pet the squirming worm at his feet. "You're such a goof." He rubbed Leo's belly. "All right, let's go inside."

Leo hopped up and grabbed the tennis ball at the base of the stairs and dropped it at Brandon's feet.

"Sorry, dude, it's bedtime. We'll play tomorrow."

Leo picked it up and dropped it again on Brandon's feet.

"Nope." He grabbed the ball and set it in the bucket at the base of the stairs. "Let's go inside."

The dog dropped his head and moped toward him. "Jesus, you are dramatic," he muttered.

Leo leaned against his leg and looked up at him, waiting for a pet. He scratched the dog's head and glanced at the open area at the back of the yard. Leo deserved to have free range of the yard when they were home. "Tomorrow is the big day, bud. You get a fence."

God, he was getting soft because he could swear the dog smiled up at him. He gestured for Leo to proceed him up the stairs. "Let's go."

Brandon pushed open the deck door and stopped dead in his tracks. "Jesus."

Annie lay sprawled out naked in the middle of his bed. She rolled on her side and propped her head on her hand. "Took you long enough."

"I thought you'd be asleep."

"Nope. I told you we're having sex."

His gaze lingered on her erect nipples and his dick sprang to life. He willed it to take a backseat so his brain could function. "And I said that wasn't happening because you're drunk."

"I'm not that drunk."

"Yeah, you are. You fell asleep in the car."

"But I'm awake now and all sober." She drunkenly grinned at him. "I rallied."

What the hell was she doing with her face? It looked like she was trying to waggle her eyebrows or something, but every time she moved her eyebrows her mouth scrunched up like it was too hard to coordinate the movement. He couldn't help but laugh. "That's not how it works, Doc."

Annie pushed up on her knees and he bit back a groan. Fuck, why did she have to be so sexy?

"Okay, but we've had sex before, so drunk sex is fine." She crawled toward him, and he stepped further back from the mattress, out of reach.

"I'm sober, you're not. I can't take advantage of that."

"You aren't. I'm offering. Besides, we're dating and drunk couples have sex all the time."

"Yeah, but we haven't had that conversation when you're sober so..."

Annie sat up on her knees and arched her back. She traced her finger around her nipple. "Are you really saying you won't have sex with me tonight, even if I beg?"

"Jesus." He looked up at the ceiling. The woman did not play fair.

"Please," she begged.

He was pretty sure his brain short-circuited as all the blood in his body surged to his cock. "Sorry, Doc."

"Fine." Annie huffed. She lay down on the mattress and spread her legs. "Guess I'll have to take care of myself."

"Wh—what?" he croaked. Please no. She couldn't really mean...

Annie's hand trailed down her stomach, then lower. Brandon couldn't breathe. Holy shit, she was going to masturbate in front of him. She was drunk. The right thing to do would be to leave the room. But he couldn't seem to make his feet move.

Annie's fingers dipped between her legs, and his knees buckled. Holy fuck, he'd never wanted to be a different kind of guy so badly in his life. He looked at Annie spread out on his bed like a gift.

Would it really be so bad to have sex with her? Clearly, she wanted to. But he couldn't. He could practically hear his foster dad's voice saying, "Don't you fucking dare." How many lectures had he had about drugs and alcohol and making good choices and consent?

Nope, no matter how badly he wanted to, he wasn't going to touch Annie when she was drunk.

Fuck, why hadn't he been smart enough to have this conversation before they went out tonight?

Because he hadn't expected her to like his friends enough to get drunk with them. He hadn't expected her to just fit so well.

"You're just gonna watch?" Annie asked, widening her legs.

The woman did not play fair. He couldn't look away. "Apparently," he muttered. He shoved his hand in his pocket to pull the fabric away from his cock. "I should—" He flicked his thumb toward the door.

"Stay," Annie ordered. "You don't have to touch me, but looking can't possibly go against your code, can it?"

"Umm." Did it? He could barely remember his name at this moment. How the hell was he supposed to know if the right thing to do was to leave the room or not? It probably was, but—

"Please, Brandon, you can sit over there." She pointed to the chair in the corner.

"You sure?" he asked.

"Mmm-hmm, I want you to watch." She arched her back and his mouth watered at the sight of her hard nipples standing at attention, begging to be touched.

Unable to take his eyes off her, he stumbled backwards and dropped into the chair in the far corner.

Annie stared at him as she sucked her finger into her mouth. The intense eye contact made it feel like she was sucking him instead. His nostrils flared. Annie's mouth curved up in a sexy grin.

"Don't worry, I'll be quick," she said as her hand trailed down her stomach and disappeared between her legs.

Dammit, from this angle he couldn't quite see. "Spread your legs," he ordered. Shit. He hadn't meant to say that out loud.

Annie's head snapped toward him, and she smirked. "I thought you were just there to watch?" she teased.

So did he, but apparently his dick wanted a front-row seat to the show. "Then I need to be able to watch don't I?" If he was going to hell, he may as well do it with this memory front and center.

Annie shifted on the mattress and spread her legs, giving him a clear view of her perfect pussy. God, he wanted to bury himself inside her. He shifted to get comfortable. His dick practically begged him to take it out, but he didn't.

He watched as Annie flicked her finger against her clit, then rubbed, then flicked again. He homed in on the way she touched herself, the rhythm she liked. She inserted a finger inside herself and moaned.

"Fuck," he growled. Leaning forward in his seat, he rested his elbows on his knees as he watched her fuck herself. He couldn't remember ever seeing anything hotter in his life.

Suddenly, Annie's back arched off the mattress and she screamed out her release. He clamped his jaw tight as he focused on not blowing his own load just from watching her orgasm.

Annie slumped back on the mattress, then lazily turned her head and looked at him. She crooked her fingers. "Come cuddle me."

Brandon stood and walked to the edge of the bed.

Her arm flapped out like a drunken bat, and he stepped back to avoid being hit. "You can't sleep with your jeans on, silly billy," she slurred. It was like the orgasm had zapped out the last remaining soberness in her body.

"I should grab some sweats or something," he muttered.

"Why? I had my orgasm. I'm good. I'm going to sleep." She giggled and swung her arm toward his crotch. "Not sure if you can sleep with a bat in your pants." She snorted. "Bat, get it cuz you're a baseball player."

"Yeah, I get it, Doc." He rolled his eyes, then kicked off his jeans.

"You're hot," Annie mumbled. Curling on her side, she peeked over her shoulder at him. "Spoon, please."

He lay down beside her and pulled her into his arms. Annie wiggled her butt against him and giggled. "Is that a bat in your pants, or are you just happy to see me?" She snorted. "God, I'm so funny."

"Go to sleep, drunky."

Within seconds, she started snoring. She shifted against him, her ass rubbed against his cock, and he was painfully aware of how hard it was. Shit, there was no way he was getting to sleep like this. He eased his arm out from under her head. Annie snuffled and curled deeper into her pillow. She was out.

Easing himself off the mattress, he stood beside the bed. Leo looked up from his own bed in the corner. "Stay," he whispered to the dog.

He silently padded across the bedroom toward the bathroom. Once inside, he closed the door behind him. God, had he ever been this hard in his life? Holy shit. He should be sainted for the restraint he'd shown tonight.

It had taken everything in him not to come when Annie had.

With those memories fresh in his mind and his dick throbbing like this, there was no way he was sleeping without taking care of things. Shoving his boxers down his legs, he fisted his cock in his hand. Images of Annie touching herself instantly flooded his brain. He bit back a groan. Brandon dropped his head and braced one hand on the counter as he worked his cock up and down. He squeezed harder, almost to the point of pain.

"Yes," he hissed. His balls pulled up tight as he orgasmed. On a shuddering exhale, Brandon opened his eyes and grimaced when he saw the strands of cum dripping on the edge of the sink. At least he'd managed to hit the bowl.

After cleaning himself and the sink up, he tucked his semi-hard cock into the waistband of his boxers. Resting his palms on the counter, he looked at himself in the mirror. He'd just had an orgasm, so why did he still feel so on edge? What was his problem? Maybe he just needed to sleep.

He flipped off the bathroom light and opened the door. Leo sat up in the corner. "Go to sleep." After a moment, Leo put his head back down.

Brandon eyed the bed. Annie's naked body lay across the mattress in a drunken sprawl. She couldn't take up more space if she tried. Trying not to wake her, he eased his hip onto the edge of the bed and awkwardly slithered his body into the empty space. He'd barely gotten his head on the pillow when Annie wrapped herself around him. With a sleepy sigh, she rested her head against his chest and all the muscles in his body instantly relaxed. That uneasy feeling he'd had a moment ago disappeared.

Brandon rested his hand against her bare hip, enjoying the way her soft skin felt beneath his fingers. He kissed the top of her head.

Normally the idea of having someone in his bed when he slept freaked him out, made him restless, edgy. But having Annie here like this felt nice. Her drunken snoring felt oddly soothing, kind of like a weird metronome.

His last thought as he drifted off to sleep was that it was probably best not to tell her that.

CHAPTER FIFTEEN

B randon looked up when he heard Annie's feet shuffle down the hall. When she rounded the corner, he sucked in a breath at the sight of her wearing his hoodie and what looked like nothing else. Her bare legs stretched for days. Damn. He'd never seen anything sexier in his life. He hadn't dated much in high school. Hadn't done the whole letterman jacket with his high school girlfriend thing. Hadn't really understood it honestly. But if this is what it felt like, he got why it was such a big tradition.

Annie rounded the table. She picked up his cup of coffee in one hand and dropped onto his lap, then curled herself around him. One arm wrapped around his neck, while the other wrapped around his coffee mug.

"Mmm. Morning," she said and pressed a kiss to his lips.

Before he had a chance to deepen the kiss, she pulled away and took a long, slow sip of his coffee. Her eyes shut and she sighed out a contented moan.

His cock instantly sprang to attention at the sound. Yeah, he knew the moan was about the coffee but tell that to his dick. He had a warm half-naked woman on his lap making sex sounds. What was he supposed to do?

Brandon let his hand slide under the hem of his sweatshirt to cup her ass. He gave the firm cheek a little squeeze.

"Mmm," Annie moaned again.

All right, he could get on board with this kind of morning. He looked at her face, then sighed. Damn, that was another coffee moan. "Hey, that's my coffee."

"I know, but you make it just how I like it."

He squeezed her ass again. "I do a lot of things just how you like." Kissing the side of her neck, he sucked on the pulse point the way he knew she liked.

Annie's head dropped to the side. "Very true. Unfortunately, Dana just called and Jessica called in sick, so they need me to fill in for her today, which means I have surgery in an about an hour."

What he thought was damn, what he said was, "No problem."

He'd been hoping to talk her into spending a lazy day in bed, but he understood she had to work. Unfortunately, with training camp starting up soon, they wouldn't get many more lazy mornings together.

Brandon shifted her slightly on his lap. Speaking of training camp, no time like the present to talk about it. He'd been putting it off because he wasn't 100% sure where she was at with things between them. But may as well rip the bandaid off and find out.

"So, umm...I leave for training camp next weekend."

Annie's body tensed. "Mmm-hmm."

"We haven't really talked about it."

"No, we haven't." Annie pushed against his body like she wanted to stand up. That couldn't be a good sign. "Guess that's it then, huh?" she asked.

He grabbed her hand. "Look at me, Doc."

Emotion burned in her eyes when she glanced over at him.

"Is that what you want?" he asked.

"Me? No, but it is what it is, right?" she said.

"What do you mean, it is what it is?"

Annie shrugged. "I don't know. You're heading into training camp and then the season. You don't date so..."

"What do you mean, I don't date?"

"You don't date. That's what you told me. You don't date during the season." She tried to pull her hand out of his grip, but he held on.

"Normally I don't, but..."

Annie raised her head. He could feel the emotion shimmering beneath the surface as she looked at him. She didn't want this to end anymore than he did. He tugged her hand and she stumbled toward him. He shifted in his seat and pulled her between his thighs. "You make me want to break my own rules," he told her.

"I do?"

"Absolutely." Looking at her while he admitted this was too hard so he dropped his head against her belly. "I'm crazy about you, Doc. I know dating me during the season will be hard. My schedule sucks. I'll have to miss stuff you want to do. Everything has to be on my timeframe. It'll feel like everything is about me and I know it's a lot to ask of you. But I'm asking."

She cupped the side of his face and forced him to look up at her. "What are you asking, Brandon?"

He paused to gather his thoughts. "I don't want this to end."

"Me neither," she whispered.

"Thank fuck," he muttered. He didn't realize until this moment just how worried he'd been about what her response would be.

"Does that mean I get to come to Arizona and be your groupie?"

"I don't know about my groupie, but you're more than welcome to come to Arizona whenever you want."

"Oh, I'm more than welcome to come, huh? That's a ringing endorsement."

He tilted his head up and looked at her. "I'd love it if you came to visit while I was at training camp. And considering how good you look in my sweatshirt, I can guarantee you'll be getting my jersey."

"Ooh, I'll get an official Brandon Sims jersey?" she teased.

He swatted her on the ass, and she squealed. "Not if you keep it up, you won't."

She threaded her arms around his neck. "Please Brandon, can I have an official jersey?" She batted her eyelashes at him. "I'll be good." She licked her lips. "Please."

His dick pulsed beneath his sweats. Fuck, he loved hearing her beg. With a growl, he grabbed her hips and hoisted her onto the kitchen table, then stepped between her thighs. "You're playing with fire, Doc."

She slid her ass foreward so his dick lined up with her body and he bit back a groan. Damn this woman. "Doc," he warned.

"Mmm-hmm." Annie shifted her hips again.

He couldn't help it, he had to. He shifted so his cock ground against her. With just her panties as a barrier, he could feel her heat through his sweats. He shifted his hips and pressed again. Her head dropped back and she closed her eyes.

"How soon do you need to leave?" he asked.

Annie curled her legs around his waist and pulled him in tighter. "How quick can you be?" The corner of her mouth curled as she raised her eyebrow in challenge.

"I can be quick. Let's go."

"Mmm mmm, I want to stay right here." She arched her back, drawing his eyes to her chest.

Unfortunately, with the thick fabric of the sweatshirt, he wasn't able to see her nipples like he wanted to.

The idea of fucking Annie on his kitchen table was something he could more than get on board with. "Lose the clothes while I grab a condom."

"You want me to lie here naked on your kitchen table?" She tilted her head coyly.

Jesus, that sounded hot. "100%."

She glanced around. "Where's Carter?"

"Gym."

Coyly twisting her hair around her finger, she smiled. "That's good."

Annie sat up and pulled his hoodie over her head and dropped it on the chair beside her. "You gonna just stand there and watch me, or are you going to get the condom?"

He tore his gaze off her erect nipples. "Condom, yep, I'm going." After one more look at her sitting on his table in just her panties, he hurried out of the room.

When he returned a minute later, Annie lay naked on his kitchen table. All the blood in his body shot down to his dick. This image was going to be something he pulled out on those long road trips. Holy shit.

"You coming?" she asked as he stood glued to the entrance of the room.

"Not yet, but quick is not going to be a problem."

Annie smiled and dropped her knee to the side, teasing him with a glimpse of her pussy. He groaned.

"Don't be too quick," she teased, bobbing her leg back and forth slowly. Giving him a little peek, then taking it away.

Not taking his eyes off her, he stalked to the table. He shoved down his sweats and kicked them off. He tore the condom wrapper open with his teeth and held it in his hand. Enjoying the way Annie's gaze latched onto his erect cock, he fisted it in his hand and dragged his palm down the shaft once, then twice before placing the condom at the tip and slowly gliding it down in place.

Annie didn't take her eyes off him the entire time. She licked her lips and he clenched his jaw. Fuck, he wished they had more time so he could feel that sweet mouth on him.

With the condom in place, he stepped closer to her. He grabbed her ankles and spread her legs apart. Annie gasped, but the way her nipples instantly became like rocks told him all he needed to know.

Brandon's teeth dug into his bottom lip as he stared down at her pussy. Just because this was going to be quick didn't mean she didn't have to enjoy herself. He looked at Annie. Holding her stare, he brought his hand up to his mouth and flattened his tongue and dragged it up his fingers before he sucked three of the digits into his mouth. Annie's breathing visibly quickened and she made a little whimpering sound.

Without breaking eye contact, he brought his fingers to her body. The moment his hand touched her hot, wet pussy, Annie's eyes closed as she arched her back. Brandon swirled his fingers around her clit and she widened her legs. Leaning down, he flicked his tongue against her nipple. Annie threaded her fingers in his hair as she arched toward him. He swirled her moisture around her clit, then moved his finger down and pushed it inside.

Holy shit. His dick throbbed at how good she felt.

He shoved another finger in and her body greedily sucked him deeper. Brandon groaned and curled his fingers, in that little come here motion he knew she liked.

Annie gripped his hair and she pulled his head back from her nipple. "Stop teasing me and fuck me, Brandon."

He glanced up at her. "Just because we're gonna be quick doesn't mean you shouldn't come."

"Then you better make sure you fuck me properly." She raised her eyebrow in challenge.

With a smirk, he stood up and positioned himself at her entrance. "There's no doubt I'm going to fuck you properly, Doc," he said, then thrust deep.

Annie's head dropped back. "Yes," she hissed.

Brandon grabbed her hips, positioning her where he wanted her as he thrust. Her pussy contracted around his cock. Nothing had ever felt more amazing than sex with Annie.

Her breath hitched as she dug her heels into his ass, matching his thrusts with her own. She shifted her hips slightly and made a little frustrated grunt.

As good as this felt to him, it wasn't working for her. He pulled out. Annie groaned. "Why'd you stop?"

"Because you need to come."

Annie gasped when he grabbed her hips and flipped her onto her stomach. He barely gave himself a chance to appreciate the wonder of her spectacular ass before he buried himself in her pussy again.

"Oh god," Annie groaned when he seated himself fully.

Reaching around, he flicked her clit with his finger as he thrust. He desperately tried to think of something else, anything other than how fucking good she felt as he tried not to come before she did. He was so close.

Shit. Her pussy was so tight in this position. Maybe fucking her this way had been a mistake. He wasn't going to last. He needed her to get there quick.

Bending his knees, he changed the angle, and Annie moaned. That was better. He swirled his finger against her clit, trying to stay focused on what she needed instead of his own orgasm. But that wasn't easy when it was screaming at him to move his ass and come already. If her breathing was anything to go by, she was close.

Knowing his girl liked it deep, he thrust hard. She arched, pressing back against him as she moaned. Brandon pinched her clit between his fingers and she screamed as her pussy clamped down on his cock as she came.

Thank god, now he could come. Her pussy pulsed against his cock with the aftershocks of her orgasm like it was trying to drag his along with it. His balls pulled up tight, and he gripped her hips firmly as he thrust into her again and again. His entire body went rigid as the orgasm ripped through him.

He loosened the grip on her hips. Leaning down, he placed a kiss against her shoulder.

Annie mumbled something incoherent, then turned her head to the side with a sigh. He didn't need to know what she'd said. The satisfied smile on her face said it all.

When she didn't move for several seconds, he gave her a light slap on the ass. "No sleeping. You gotta get to work."

"But I'm boneless. I can't work."

"Come on lazy bones, up you get. No chance I'm letting you be late for work because we had sex."

Annie rolled onto her back. "Why? Can you think of a better reason to be late?"

He smiled down at her. "Me? No. But I'm pretty sure if you're late my chances of having sex before work again just went out the window."

Annie huffed and pushed herself up. "Fine."

She stuck out her leg and wrapped it around his waist to pull him closer to her. He moved in and wrapped his arms around her waist, pulling her tight. Annie's legs tightened around his waist as she threaded her arms around his neck. "For a quicky, that was some serious game, sir,"

Brandon snorted. "Well, you know, I try." He squeezed her hip, making her giggle.

Annie rested her head against his shoulder. "I'm glad we're gonna try to make this work during the season."

He dipped back so he could look her in the eye. "We're not trying, Doc. It's happening."

"Got it."

She ran her hand over the stubble on his cheek, and he leaned into her touch. What was it about her that was so different? Normally, he hated that kind of thing. He wasn't one to hold hands in public, or cuddle after sex, but with Annie he craved her touch, her affection.

Annie exhaled audibly. "I gotta go to work." She scrunched up her nose. "Adulting sucks."

"That it does." He stepped back and held out his hand so she could hop down from the counter height table.

He stepped into his sweatpants while Annie pulled his sweatshirt over her head.

"Just so you know, I'm keeping this sweatshirt while you're on the road," she said when her head popped out through the neck hole.

He swiped out his hand and scooped her panties off the floor. "That's okay, I'm keeping these."

Annie raised her brow. "That's not the same thing at all."

"How do you figure? You keep a piece of my clothing. I keep one of yours."

"Yeah, but this one smells like you, and I can bury my face in it and feel like you're here."

"I think we're saying the same thing, Doc."

"But it's my panties."

"Uh huh." He nodded, enjoying the way her cheeks turned a bright pink as she squirmed.

"That's weird," she said, then shrugged. "Whatever floats your boat, perv."

Brandon barked out a laugh. "Wanting to bury my face in your underwear doesn't make me a perv."

"Whatever you say, hotshot," she called over her shoulder as she walked out of the kitchen. As she walked through the house, the sound of her singing drifted back toward him. He could imagine the little dance moves she was probably doing to go along with the beat.

God, he was crazy about her. For the first time, it felt like there was more to life than baseball. And if he was honest, it was kind of terrifying.

CHAPTER SIXTEEN

This was harder than she'd expected. It was six weeks, so why did it feel like forever? She'd never been the kind of girl who needed a man in her life. She liked her independence, her freedom. So why was she so bummed that Brandon was leaving for six weeks?

She rocked back on her heels as she watched him load up his car. Leo whimpered beside her nervously. Reaching down, she scratched the top of his head. "Don't worry, Leo, you're going with him. He wouldn't leave without you."

Brandon made another trip inside and came out carrying Leo's dog crate in one hand and a bag of all Leo's toys and bowls in the other. Leo barked when he saw it.

"You got more shit than I do," Brandon said to the dog as he walked past.

Leo barked again.

"It's true," Brandon called over his shoulder.

Annie couldn't help but laugh at their interaction. When she first met Brandon, she'd never imagined he would be the kind of guy to have full-on conversations with his dog, but he did, and it was one of the sweetest things she'd ever seen.

The difference in Leo between the day Brandon had carried him in and now was amazing. And that was all because of Brandon. Honestly, if anyone had asked her, she would have said the dog would probably end up getting put down because she'd never seen such a drastic change in a dog, especially not in such a short period of time.

It was remarkable. And a testament to the man Brandon was, whether he agreed or not.

Brandon threw the last load of stuff in his car and walked over to her. "That's the last of it."

"Yep." She pasted on a smile. "Call me when you get there, so I know you're safe."

"Will do." The crinkling at the corner of Brandon's eyes was the only indicator he liked what she said.

He reached out and tucked a stray strand of hair behind her ear. "Don't work too hard when I'm gone."

"I won't."

He raised an eyebrow. "Uh huh, how many times did you sign up to be on call the next couple of weeks?"

"That doesn't count," she replied.

"No?" He smirked. "Explain that to me. How is being on call not working?"

"Well, I might not ever get called so..."

He raised both eyebrows like he was waiting for her to continue. She wrinkled her nose and pushed his chest. "Shut up."

Brandon chuckled. "Love the logic, Doc."

She rested her head against his chest and wrapped her arms around his waist tightly. This sucked.

Brandon rubbed his hand up and down her back soothingly. "You okay?"

Was she? Not really. Gah, she hated being this kind of person. It's not like they saw each other every day anyway. This was going to be fine.

"Of course." She squeezed him tightly. "Text me when you get there."

"Okay, I'll text you tonight."

She tilted her head to look up at him. "No, text me when you get there, so I'm not worried about you."

Brandon's arms tightened around her waist, and he hoisted her up in the air so their faces were level. "Thank you."

"For what?"

He shrugged. "I've never really had anyone give a shit enough to worry about that kind of thing before."

Tears welled in her eyes. Oh, that hurt her heart to hear him say that. "Well, you've got someone now who does, so don't forget to text me when you get there."

He pressed a kiss to her lips. "I won't."

Brandon closed his eyes and rested his forehead against hers. She wrapped her arms tightly around his neck. Even with her feet dangling off the ground, she didn't feel like she needed to wrap her legs around him to hold on. He was strong enough to make her feel completely safe and secure exactly as she was.

"Okay, I better hit the road." He gave her another soft kiss and set her on the ground.

"Drive safe."

Brandon took a couple of steps, then turned back around. "One for the road."

He stalked back toward her and cupped the back of her head as his mouth crashed down on hers. *Oh my.*

His tongue tangled with hers as he deepened the kiss. She grabbed onto his waist, her fingers curling into the fabric of his t-shirt as she let herself be swept up in the passionate kiss. A kiss that was going to have to last her several weeks. It wasn't enough. It would never be enough.

Unfortunately, it had to be.

After what felt like too short a time, Brandon broke the kiss. And rested his head against hers. "I'm not sure if that was a good idea or a bad idea."

"Why would it have been a bad idea?"

"Because now I really want to take you back inside and fuck you again," he groaned.

"You already fucked me three times this morning."

"I know, but now that doesn't feel like enough."

She wrinkled her nose. "I'm afraid it's gonna have to be, big guy. Between last night and this morning, I'm a little raw."

Brandon's eyes widened in horror. "Did I hurt you?"

She placed her hand against his chest soothingly. "Of course not. I'm just not sure I'm up for another round."

His face knit with worry as he looked down at her. "But you're okay?"

"I'm fine. Stop worrying." She patted his chest again. "Leo's gonna go stir crazy if you don't get going soon."

Standing on her tiptoes, she gave him one last quick kiss. "Get going."

"Fine," he grumbled before turning to Leo. "All right, let's get in the car."

Brandon opened the back door for Leo and the dog climbed in. Brandon secured his seatbelt to the harness in the middle seat so the dog could see out front. Then walked around to the driver's side and climbed in.

Annie followed. Once Brandon rolled down the driver's window, she leaned in. "Don't forget to text me as soon as you get there."

"I won't."

"And drive safe."

"I will." He smiled affectionately at her like he found her amusing.

"I'm gonna miss you," she said,

"Yeah." Brandon nodded.

Yes, a big part of her wanted him to admit he was going to miss her as well, but she understood how hard sharing emotions was for him. She didn't need the words when it was written on his face.

She kissed him one last time, then tapped the window frame twice and stepped back on the curb. She stood there watching as he drove away. Six weeks had never felt longer.

Once Brandon's taillights rounded the corner, she sighed. What the hell was she going to do with herself now? She could go home and do laundry. Yeah, that sounded fun. Or she could check in on her parents and see how life with a puppy was going.

As she pulled her car keys out of her pocket, her phone buzzed with a text. Checking the phone, she saw a text from her sister.

> Help me. I'm in wedding planning hell.

Annie grinned down at the phone. As much as she loved Gabby, she couldn't imagine her sister's best friend was an easy bride.

Maid of honor duties not going well?

> That Bridezilla show you made me watch did not prepare me

What's going on?

> Gabby got the invitations today and apparently the paper smells funny

Annie snorted.

Why is she smelling it?

> Who the hell knows?

> Any chance I can steal you away from Brandon today for a drink?

Brandon just left for training camp.

Oh honey. I think you need a drink more than I do.

Probably

Why don't you come over to my place? We can make margaritas and order pizza or something.

Get the blender out. I'm on my way.

On it.

Annie shoved her phone back in her pocket. Thank god for Ella. Hanging out with her sister was so much better than wallowing in self-pity. With a plan of attack, she hopped behind the wheel of her car and headed home.

When she pulled up in front of her place, Ella's car was already parked in the driveway. Annie pulled her car in alongside her and jumped out.

"Wow, you really need that drink," she said as she shut her car door.

"On my god." Ella walked toward her and dramatically flopped against Annie. "Why did I agree to be maid of honor?"

"Because you've been best friends since the third grade." Annie chuckled. "She can't be that bad."

"Oh, honey, you have no idea. She's brutal." Ella shook her head. "I love the girl, but holy shit, she is freaking insane right now."

"Besides not liking the smell of the invitations, what did she do?" Annie asked as she stuck the key in her front door lock.

"Not liking the smell would be fine, but when I said it wasn't that bad, she honest to God grabbed my face and shoved it against the invitation and rubbed my face in it like I was a dog who'd peed on the carpet."

Without thinking, Annie replied, "You shouldn't rub a dog's face in pee."

Ella scowled at her. "Okay, not the point."

"Sorry." Annie winced. "She didn't honestly rub your face on it, did she?"

"Yes, she did. The woman is certifiable right now. I mean... how the hell are we going to make it through the next three months if she is like this already?"

Annie walked into the kitchen with Ella trailing behind her. She pulled out the blender. "Well, at least most things are done already."

Ella's eyes widened and she dropped into the kitchen chair. "Oh my god, what am I gonna do if her dress doesn't fit? I swear to God she will murder a bitch if there is anything wrong with the dress."

Annie snorted. "She's not gonna murder anyone." She pulled out the ice cubes and set them on the island, then grabbed the bottle of tequila and placed it on the island as well. "Besides, with the way she's been dieting, if anything, they will have to take the dress in."

"Oh my god, that's just as bad." Ella dropped her head down on the table with a bang. "Shoot me now."

Annie quickly whipped up the pitcher of margaritas and set one down on the table in front of her sister. "Drink."

Ella raised her head and blinked up at her. "I don't think I can be maid of honor."

Annie grabbed another kitchen chair and pulled it up close to Ella's, then sat down on it. She grabbed her sister's hands. "It's going to be fine."

"You didn't see her today, Annie. She was crazy."

"Talk to her."

Ella rapidly shook her head. "No way."

"Talk to her. I'll bet she's horrified she behaved like that."

"She should be," Ella complained. "I'm surprised I don't have a rash on my face from the chemicals in that paper."

"So it did smell?"

"Yeah, it was gross." Ella picked up her margarita and took a healthy slug. "And I might have angered the beast when I stormed out."

Oh god. Annie cringed. When Ella felt like she'd been wronged, she held nothing back. "What did you do?"

"Umm, I might have made a little Seinfeld reference."

"A little Seinfeld reference?" Annie pressed. "What did you say?"

"First, let me say I'm not proud of it." Ella grimaced.

"What did you say?"

"I told her she was being crazy. Of course she got mad, so I said I was out of there, which pissed her off more." Ella stopped and took a deep breath, then looked down and mumbled something Annie couldn't quite make out.

"What?" Annie asked.

Ella sucked in her lips then blurted, "I might have said have fun licking the envelopes, Susan."

Annie gasped. "Oh my god, you did not say that."

Ella winced. "I did,"

Holy shit, this wasn't good. "Elle, you gotta apologize."

"I know, but she just pissed me off so much. And she owes me an apology too."

Needing to tread lightly, Annie looked at her sister. "I know, but as shitty as it was for her to rub your face in the paper, you took it too far."

"She assaulted me," Ella complained.

"And you implied you wanted her dead."

"That's not what I meant," Ella huffed.

"What did you mean, then?"

Ella dropped her head back and sighed. "I don't know. She was just being ridiculous and it just kind of came out. It's not like I really think she'd die from licking envelopes. But with the way she's behaving I wouldn't have minded if she got a bit of a gut ache."

Annie shook her head. "You need to apologize."

"Fine." Ella picked up her margarita. "At least let me finish my drink first." Ella chugged her margarita and held out the empty glass. "Fill it up, Ann, while I eat some humble pie."

With a chuckle, she took the glass out of Ella's hand and refilled it. She hadn't even taken a sip of her own drink and Ella was already onto her second.

Annie placed the glass in front of her little sister and waited for her to finish sending the text. She picked up her own drink and had a little sip, then wrinkled her nose. It was too early in the day for margaritas. She pushed the glass away from herself.

Ella nervously tapped her fingers on the table and stared at her phone. "She's not answering."

"Did you think she would?" Annie asked.

"Yeah, it's Gabby. She's not really one to back down from a fight."

"You probably hurt her feelings."

"She hurt mine too." Ella slumped in her chair and crossed her arms over her chest.

"I know, honey, but..."

Ella jumped forward and grabbed Annie's hand. "You text her."

"What?"

"Text her and ask her to come over."

"Wh...why...why would I do that?" There was no chance she wanted to get in the middle of this shit show.

"Please, Annie. She's going to ignore me. She won't ignore you," Ella pleaded.

"This is between you two. You guys gotta figure it out." Annie's head was spinning from the one-eighty Ella was throwing at her.

"And we will, but you know how Gabby is. She can hold a grudge. The sooner we get this sorted, the sooner we can move past it."

"Yeah, I don't really want to."

Ella dropped to her knees on the floor. "Please, Annie. When I said the whole Susan thing, I wasn't really thinking about how she'd take it. I was just mad and—"

Tears welled in Ella's eyes. "I feel horrible. I know she's under a lot of stress." Ella sniffed, and a tear slid down her cheek. "Even though I was mad, I shouldn't have said that." Ella wiped her cheek and sniffed again. "Please Annie."

Shit. "Fine," she grumbled. God, she was such a sucker, and Ella knew it. Like her day wasn't already shitty enough with Brandon leaving, now she had to deal with all this drama as well.

"But for the record, if I get her over here, I'm out. That's the only part I'm playing in this. You two are on your own."

"That's fine. That's all I need."

Annie eyed her phone. This was the last thing she wanted to do. "You sure you wouldn't rather just sleep on it?"

"I'm sure. Please, Annie. I'll owe you big time."

"Yeah, you sure as hell will."

She scrolled through her phone until she saw Gabby's name. As much as she wanted to help her sister, she didn't want to lie to do it. What the hell was she supposed to say to get her here without mentioning Ella?

> Today sucks! Brandon just left for training camp. You feel like day drinking?

She eyed what she'd written. It was honest, and she didn't say she would be the one drinking with her. Send.

> God yes.

> Come over. Margaritas will be ready.

> Make mine a double.

"She's on her way." Annie stood up. "I'm going to the gym."

"What? You aren't even going to stay until she gets here?" Ella asked.

"Nope. I told you I have no interest in being a part of this shit show." She walked out of the kitchen and grabbed her gym bag off the hook in the closet.

She turned to Ella who had followed her out of the kitchen. "Keep it civil. Don't wreck anything in my house or it will be you and I who are having words, and you know I'm not nearly as forgiving as you're expecting Gabby to be."

"Got it." Ella nodded. "Thanks Annie."

"Don't make me regret this."

"I won't."

Annie grabbed her car keys off the hook and slung her gym bag over her shoulder. What a nightmare this had turned out to be. One good thing at least it took her mind off Brandon's leaving. And hitting the gym was a lot healthier than what she had planned on doing. She pulled open the front door and stopped on the threshold. "Make this right, Elle."

"I will."

She glanced back inside her house. So much for margarita day. "Oh, and you owe me a bottle of tequila," she told her sister.

"You got it."

Closing the door behind her, she sighed. This had definitely not been how she'd seen today playing out.

CHAPTER SEVENTEEN

B randon heard the bat cracking as he rounded the corner. Damn. He thought he was there early enough he'd be the only one here. He glanced down at Leo. Guess it was time for the first test on how this was going to work.

He spotted a guy he didn't know setting a ball in the tee, line up and swing. Decent form.

"Morning," he said as he stopped at the edge of the cage.

"Oh, uh hey," the guy stammered, then just stood there gaping at him.

"You want me to feed you?" He picked up a ball and gestured toward the tee.

"Really?" the kid asked.

"Yeah." He shrugged.

"But you're Brandon Sims."

"Yep. So?" He gestured to the tee again.

"Yeah, that'd be great," the guy gushed.

"Let me just get my dog set up." Brandon walked to the corner away from where anyone else would be moving around and safely set up a spot for Leo to lie down. He hooked his leash into the fence so he couldn't go after a ball if the urge struck.

"You bring your dog to training camp?"

"I do now." Brandon crouched down and gave Leo a scratch on the head to give him a minute to adjust to his new surroundings. He glanced over at the kid while he continued to pet Leo. "What's your name?"

"My name?"

"Yeah."

"Gabe, uh Gabe Rizzowski."

Brandon nodded in acknowledgment. The guy continued to gape at him.

"Stay," he commanded Leo, then stood up and set the ball on the tee. "Alright Rizz, let's go." He pointed at the tee.

The kid just stood there grinning like an idiot.

"Hit the fucking ball," Brandon grumbled.

"Right, sorry." Rizzowski walked up to the tee and lined up, then stopped and whipped around to face him. "How'd you know my nickname?"

"Seriously? Your last name's Rizzowski, my guy. The nickname seemed pretty obvious."

"Oh yeah, right, I guess." The kid continued to stand and aim his stupid, beaming smile at him.

"This is so cool," Rizzowski gushed. The kid set up at the tee, then looked back over his shoulder at Brandon and grinned again.

"Jesus kid, you gotta tone this shit down or you're gonna be a mess the first time you go up to bat against some of these guys."

Rizzowski hung his head down. "Sorry."

"Shit," Brandon muttered quietly. Now he felt like he'd kicked a fucking puppy. He hefted out a sigh. "Look kid, I get it. Being here for the first time's a big deal. We've all been there. It's umm…" There wasn't even a word to describe it really. Hell, even now there were certain guys he was intimidated to meet, but there was no way he showed that.

"On the field, everyone is just your teammate or your opponent, so get the stars out of your eyes so you can play ball, otherwise you're not going to play well and you won't last."

"Yeah, I know, sorry. It's just guys like you don't really feed the tee for guys like me."

"Like I said, on the field we're teammates, so either hit the damn ball or get out of the way so I can take a turn."

"Right." The kid looked down and Brandon could see his shiny white teeth still beaming.

He shook his head and couldn't help but chuckle. "Hit the ball, Rizzowski."

The kid lined up, then paused and turned around. "Your dog is safe there?"

Brandon looked in the back corner at Leo. "Unless you plan on hitting backwards, he'll be fine. It's a tee, not a batting machine."

"Right."

Brandon sighed. "I appreciate the concern. But he's good, he's not going anywhere. You're good to hit."

The kid lined up and cranked the ball.

"You dropped your hip," Brandon said.

"What?" Rizzowski asked.

"You dropped your hip before you even started your swing."

"I did?"

"Yeah." Brandon dropped another ball on the tee. "Go again."

Twenty minutes later, the kid's swing looked smooth. "Nice job."

"Thanks man, no one's ever said anything about my hip before."

"It was barely noticeable, that's probably why."

"But you noticed it."

"Yeah well, I used to drop my hip." Brandon clapped the kid on the shoulder. "Coach Piper is one of the best hitting coaches in the league. He would have noticed it once he started working with you."

"Yeah, but let's be real. They don't have time to work individually with every guy trying out. They put the time into the position players on the team, so even if they saw it, they wouldn't work with me on it like you. So thanks."

"No problem. You want to feed the tee for me so I can get a couple of swings in before it gets busy?"

"Yeah definitely."

Brandon stretched his neck, then hooked the bat behind his shoulders and did some twists to limber up his spine. He lined up at the tee and swung. His jaw clenched when the ball hit slightly north of the sweet spot.

"Nice hit," Rizzowski said.

"Mmm," Brandon muttered. It felt off. He rolled his shoulders as Rizzowski dropped another ball on the tee. He was just lining up when he heard his name called.

Tipping the bat down, he turned and saw Smitty and Pete. "Morning boys."

"You worried about your spot? You gotta come in early and work with the rooks now?" Pete asked.

"Something like that," Brandon muttered.

Rizzowski rushed forward. "Oh my god, you're Pete Saunders and Jeff Smith."

Brandon rolled his eyes. "Dude, what did we talk about? You've got to chill."

The kid winced. "Sorry."

"Guys, this is Rizz. Obviously, he's new, and still getting used to the novelty of being here."

The guys nodded at the rookie.

"Seriously, why are you here so early?" Pete asked.

"Couldn't sleep, so figured I'd come in and hit a few."

"Ahh, are you nervous about training camp, B?" Smitty teased.

"Fuck you," he chuckled.

"Don't worry, I'll take you under my wing," Smitty joked.

"Gee thanks, asshole."

"Well, you know I promised Kia."

Brandon snorted. "Sure you did."

"Great," Pete muttered as Johnny Knight sauntered toward them.

Johnny nodded at them, then walked to tee and stared at Rizzowski. "Move newb. I want the tee."

Rizzowski scurried back, and Brandon's back went up. "Rizzowski stay." He pointed at the kid, then turned to Johnny. "Knight, go find another tee. This one's in use."

Johnny eyed the kid, then raised a brow at Brandon. "What do you care if I kick some newb off the tee?"

"Knight, it's a new season. How about we try something new this year and don't be an asshole?" Pete piped in.

"How bout you mind your business, Saunders," Johnny replied.

"I can just go," Rizzowski said.

"Nope, I fed the tee for you. You're feeding it for me." Brandon said. "Knight, there are plenty of other cages you can use. I'm in this one."

"I didn't know you were using it. I thought it was just the newb."

"Either way, you knew it was in use," Brandon said. He gave his teammate a look. Johnny liked to pretend he was a tough guy. He'd gotten into a few dustups with guys in the league, but they both knew it wasn't even a contest between the two of them, so he never bothered with Brandon.

"Whatever," Johnny said, then walked away.

"That was so cool," Rizzowski gushed.

"Jesus," Brandon muttered. "Just feed the tee, kid." He picked up his bat and strolled back to the tee.

"Later B," Smitty called.

"Yep," he absently acknowledged his teammates as he lined up at the tee to continue his morning warmup.

Several swings later, he felt like he was getting the feel of things again. It always took a few hits at the start of the season for his body to loosen up and his muscle memory to come back.

He glanced at his watch. Perfect timing. He still had five minutes until he needed to meet the trainer.

"I'm out. It's all yours Rizz."

"Thanks, Brandon. I really appreciate you working with me."

"No problem."

Rizzowski eyed Leo. "Could I say hello to your dog?"

Brandon looked over at Leo. "Yeah sure. Thanks for waiting and letting him get used to you first."

"Yeah, course."

Brandon walked over to the dog, with the kid following close behind. "Leo, this is Rizz, Rizz, this is Leo. He's a rescue and he's been through the ringer, so go slow."

Rizz crouched down and Leo looked at Brandon. "You have any treats?"

"Yeah." Brandon pulled a treat out of his pocket and handed it to him.

The kid held out his hand with the treat and tossed it gently to Leo. The dog eyed it, then looked at Brandon.

Oops. "Break," he said, releasing the dog from his stay position so he could grab the treat if he wanted it. The dog didn't move. "It's okay," Brandon told him reassuringly.

Leo scooped up the treat, then moved closer to Rizzowski to sniff him.

"Nicely done," Brandon told him.

"Thanks. I grew up with dogs." Rizzowski pet Leo's head. "How long have you had him?"

"Just a few months. He's come a long way."

"And now he gets to come to training camp?"

Brandon crouched down and Leo instantly leaned against him lovingly. "Yep, and if all goes well, he'll be coming on the road with us. That's why I gotta go, so we can meet the dog trainer who's gonna help us with all that." Brandon grabbed Leo's leash, then pushed off the ground to stand up. "Come on, buddy, let's go meet the teacher."

"Good luck," Rizzowshi said.

"Thanks." Brandon scooped up his bag and threw it over his shoulder. They wandered past several groups of guys getting ready for the day. Brandon nodded at a few of his teammates milling around, but didn't stop to talk to anyone.

He pulled up short when he saw Matthias Hoffman and the Hawks' publicist, Kirsty McIntyre, standing beside his dog trainer.

Shit. He probably should have expected it since the team owner was the one who'd suggested the trainer, but he'd never seen Mr. Hoffman at training camp before.

"Mr. Hoffman, Kirsty." Brandon nodded at his boss. "Del." He smiled at the dog trainer.

"He looks good," Mr. Hoffman said, nodding at Leo.

"Yeah, we just tried out some batting practice and he did great."

Kirsty's eyes widened. "Batting practice?" she squeaked.

"On a tee. I'm not gonna do anything that would put Leo in any danger."

"Oh, good." She breathed a sigh of relief.

He fought the urge to roll his eyes. He wasn't a complete idiot. He did have basic common sense. "I didn't expect to see you both here," Brandon said.

"My partners and I are looking at acquiring a business here, so I thought I'd tie the two together. I asked Kirsty to be here because I thought it would be great to get some photos of you and Leo at training camp."

"We are going to put those other teams to shame. We don't just have a pet day at our stadium. Every day is Leo day. I mean look at him. We are going to get so much traction out of this," she said.

Brandon's jaw tightened. "He's not a trained monkey you can put in front of a camera," he growled.

He knew he'd signed on for some of this when he'd agreed to it. The team would not let him have Leo travel for nothing. But there was a limit. He wasn't going to do anything that made Leo uncomfortable.

"I wasn't meaning..." Kirsty stammered.

"Kirsty gets excited about the possibilities, but she understands Leo's situation is delicate, so don't worry I have no intentions of making him perform on stage in a dress or anything," Matthias Hoffman said.

The team publicist's eyes lit up. "Do you think you could get him to wear your jersey, though?"

"Jesus," Brandon muttered.

"Pitbulls do often enjoy getting dressed up," Del piped in.

"Seriously?" Brandon glared at the dog trainer. That wasn't helpful.

"I'm just saying they do. It's a funny little quirk about a lot of them. They don't have thick coats, so they like sweaters and stuff." Del shrugged. "Mine loves a good hat as well. And of course when he rides in my sidecar he has to wear goggles."

Kirsty spun toward the trainer. "Your dog rides in your sidecar?"

"Yeah, he loves it. He has a little leather vest that he likes to wear."

"Oh my god, that is so cute." She crooned. "See Brandon, if Del's Pitbull can wear a vest and goggles, surely Leo wouldn't mind a Sims jersey."

"I think that would be a great picture for the website," Mr. Hoffman agreed.

"Ooh, we could get pet jersey's made up and sell them. I bet people would gobble them up," she gushed.

"So we're a yes on the jersey?" Mr. Hoffman said.

Brandon grit his teeth. "Yep." He looked down at Leo sitting at his feet. "Sorry bud, apparently you're getting a jersey."

Leo looked up at him, beaming his big Pitty smile.

"Oh my god, look at that. He's smiling," Kirsty said. She immediately started snapping photos of them with her phone, then swiped to look at the shots. With a smile, she showed her phone to the team owner.

Mr. Hoffman cracked a smile. "The fans are going to eat this up."

Great. Posing for more photos. Fan-freaking-tastic. He closed his eyes and took a breath. If it meant Leo could travel with him, it was worth it. And on that note. They needed to talk about training. "It was nice seeing you, Mr. Hoffman, Kirsty, but Del and I need to discuss today's training before practice."

Kirsty waved. "I'll be around snapping some photos this week, so just ignore me as best you can."

"Right," Brandon muttered.

"I don't think anyone could ignore you, Kirsty," Del said.

"Oh, aren't you sweet?" She clasped Del's arm, then turned to Brandon. "I don't want you to worry. I fully understand that Leo is new to all this, and he needs a lot of training and support. I want this to work as much as you do, so whatever you need from me."

"Thanks."

"So shall we?" Del asked.

"Yep, let's do it." Brandon looked at Leo. "Training time."

Several hours later, Brandon walked off the field and made his way to the back of the dugout. Leo sat at the end of the dugout with Del beside him, safely out of the way of the team. Brandon pushed past his teammates, who were jammed in a little tighter than normal at the front of the dugout to give Leo the room he needed to feel safe.

Thankfully, most of the guys had been super excited about having a dog in the dugout with them and were giving Leo whatever space he needed to be comfortable. Of course a couple of guys, like Knight, had chirped about it, but the rest of the team had shut that shit down fast. It was nice to know the team had his back on this whole thing. He gave Leo a little pat. "He seems like he's settling in," he said to Del.

"Yeah, he's noticeably more comfortable when he knows where you are. But he'll get there."

"I appreciate you doing this, man. I know it's not the norm."

"It's different, but I'm not going to complain. I get to hang out in the dugout during games, and be in the locker room during talks. And I'm getting paid for it. This is outstanding."

"I know it's been a hard day for Leo, so you are more than earning every penny. So thanks."

"Happy to do it, man," Del said.

Needing to focus on the game, Brandon leaned his elbow on the railing of the dugout and watched as Saunders walked up to the plate.

"Looks like you have a bit of a fan club now." Smitty nudged his shoulder.

Brandon followed the direction of Smitty's nod and saw Rizzowski and a couple of guys he didn't recognize all looking in their direction. The kid smiled and nodded when he saw Brandon looking.

"He seems like an okay kid," Brandon said.

"You don't usually spend much time chatting with the new guys."

Brandon raised his eyebrow and looked at his teammate. "Mmm."

He wouldn't be talking to Smitty right now if the guy wasn't forcing the issue.

Smitty chuckled. "I'm just saying it's nice. We could use more mentors on the team, especially now that Gonzo's gone."

"Don't look at me. I'm not filling that roll."

"I don't know. You kind of seem like the perfect person. You're like a whole new guy this season. You've got the dog and the girlfriend. This morning you're shooting the shit with a newbie. I barely recognize you."

Brandon flipped up his middle finger. "You recognize this?"

Smitty chuckled. "Ah yes, I see it now. There's still some of the old B in there."

Brandon shifted and flipped his teammate a double bird, making Smitty snort. The bat cracked against the ball. The sound had them both snapping their attention back to the field. A deep fly ball into right field, caught at the warning track. Damn. It had sounded good.

He pushed off the railing. "I'm on deck," he said.

He made his way past his teammates and grabbed his bat from the holder before taking his spot on deck. He swung the bat a few times to loosen up. Coach had him batting in the six today and with the shitty showing in the first inning, he hadn't even gotten up to the plate.

"Shit," he muttered when Knight swung and missed for strike three. Two down already. Not off to the best start. Brandon walked up to the plate and nodded at the catcher, Jameson.

"You boys are making this too easy on us," Jameson chirped.

Unfortunately, that was the truth. So far they'd been shit on the sticks. But that was about to change.

Brandon brought his bat up into position.

"Did I hear you have your dog in the dugout?" Jameson asked. "You getting soft on us Sims?"

Ignoring the catcher, Brandon dug his feet into the dirt and wiggled his heel to get the right position. He stared down the pitcher in anticipation of the first throw. The pitcher nodded, took his position and threw. The ball soared toward him.

Brandon swung and missed. Fucking curve. "God damn it," he muttered.

Jameson snickered and Brandon sneered at the catcher, then dug his heels in again. The second pitch flew toward him. At the last second, he checked his swing. Outside. Ball one.

All right, that was better. He was getting his feet back. Pitch three. Low. Ball two. The pitcher shook off the call, then shook off another. Brandon heard Jameson curse. Trouble in paradise. The pitcher finally nodded, lined up and threw the sweetest pitch right down the pipe. It was like the thing was sailing toward him in slow motion. It was so pretty. He swung and the ball cracked against his bat. He jogged toward first as he watched his ball fly. It looked like it was going out. At the last second, it bounced off the top of the fence and dropped onto the field.

Damn. Robbed.

He kicked it into gear and pulled up at second. Double instead of a homer. He'd take it.

Carter stepped up to the plate for his first at bat as a Hawk. Brandon took a step off the base as the pitcher lined up. Crack. Line drive between first and second. Brandon took off. When the third base coach told him to stop at third, he knew Carter was safe on first.

Sanchez walked up to bat. "Be ready to go on anything," Coach told him.

Brandon nodded. Two away. First pitch, Sanchez swung and missed. Pitch two. Foul ball. Third pitch strike.

"Shit," Coach muttered.

Brandon walked off the base back to the dugout. Two runners stranded on base. Bottom of the second and still no score for the Hawks. He'd done his part, but it hadn't been enough.

In the dugout, he grabbed his glove and jogged onto the field. Time to get their heads out of their asses and play some ball.

At the top of the fifth, Brandon wandered to the end of the bench and crouched down in front of Leo. "I'm done playing for today," he told Del.

"What? Why?"

"Preseason, we don't play the full game."

"Why?"

"I've already made the team. Coach knows what I can do, no point risking injury. He's got lots of new guys to check out."

"I didn't realize," Del said.

"I thought you were a ball fan."

"I am. I just don't really pay that much attention to spring training."

"Understandable." Brandon patted his shoulder to get Leo to put his paws up. "What do you say we watch some baseball?"

He tucked his hands under Leo's butt and picked up the dog. Leo wrapped his leg around Brandon's shoulder and shifted his body. After a moment, the dog stopped squirming and settled in against him comfortably. Brandon walked to the railing and looked out at the field. Del stood beside him at the railing.

"Given his history, I'm kind of surprised he likes being picked up," Del said.

"He loves it. He's a big suck." Leo hadn't been sure of it at first, but once he'd realized he was safe, the dog couldn't get enough of it. He was like a kid demanding to be carried. Except unlike a toddler, Leo was 70 pounds of pure muscle. Brandon had never met a snugglier dog than Leo. There was no such thing as personal space when it came to this dog.

"You lucked out man, he's a really great dog," Del said.

"Yeah, I know." Brandon rested his head against Leo's. The dog turned and licked his cheek. "Thanks, bud."

The catcher Aiden Patel stepped up to the plate. The pitcher set a perfect fastball right up the pipe. Aiden swung. The sweet sound of the ball hitting the bat perfectly as they connected and sent the ball clear over the right field fence.

"Yeah," Brandon yelled.

Leo startled in his arms. Brandon rubbed Leo's back with one arm to settle him and thumped his other hand on the railing to cheer. Brandon couldn't help but laugh when Leo barked in excitement.

"That's right Leo, way to go Patel," Pete cheered.

"That dog is gonna fit in well," Coach Schneider said.

Brandon rubbed Leo with pets as he held him in his arms. His face hurt from smiling as his teammates cheered for Leo and Leo barked excitedly.

He glanced over and saw not just Kirsty filming the whole thing, but the sports channel crew as well. Looked like Leo would make his TV debut tonight and Brandon didn't even mind that it meant he would be there too.

CHAPTER EIGHTEEN

Annie glanced at the clock. Her stomach jumped with excitement. Only a couple more hours and she'd be in Arizona with Brandon. She put the last of her things away to wrap up before leaving for the weekend.

"Are you excited about seeing Brandon this weekend?" Sarah asked.

"Yeah, I am. It will be nice to see him and watch him play. I've never been to spring training, so it should be fun."

"Do you actually like baseball?"

Since she'd started dating Brandon, she was actually kind of enjoying it. It was fun knowing someone on the team. It completely changed the game for her. "Of course I do. Doesn't everybody?"

"No." Sarah shook her head. "No, they most certainly don't. I can't even. It's like watching paint dry."

Not that she'd admit it, but that's exactly how she'd felt before Brandon. "What? How can you say that?"

Sarah snorted. "Because it's true. But if all the men on the team looked like Brandon, I might consider changing my mind. Especially in those uniforms."

Annie couldn't wait to see Brandon in his uniform in person instead of on the television. She'd stalked him online and seen several pictures and watched some spring training on TV. The man could fill out a uniform. Mmm.

Sarah rested her hip against the counter like she was settling in for a chat. "Flying away to see your boyfriend for the weekend seems so fancy."

"Eh. It's Phoenix. It's not that fancy." Annie laughed.

"Still, you're jet-setting away for a dirty weekend with your boyfriend. I love it."

Annie chuckled. "You make it sound like we're gonna be ordering room service and not leaving the bedroom all weekend. He has training and games every day that I'm there, so it'll mostly be hanging out with Leo and watching baseball."

Sarah wrinkled her nose. "I like what I was picturing way better. Long distance doesn't sound nearly as much fun when you aren't having a dirty weekend to tide you over. Good thing he makes lots of money."

"What does how much he makes have to do with anything?"

Sarah shrugged. "I don't know. You've got a boyfriend who can just fly you in to watch his games."

"Why would you assume Brandon paid for my flight?"

"Because he's rich."

"Nope, I'm a big girl. I can pay my own way. Besides, it's a cheap flight and I'm just shoving everything into a backpack, so I don't even need to pay for carry-on."

"Annie, you are dating a professional athlete and you're just throwing clothes in a backpack. What if he wants to take you out someplace nice? If I was dating him, I'd make him pay for me and my suitcase so he could take me someplace fancy. You're going to visit him. The least he can do is take you someplace nice. Isn't that the whole point of dating a rich ballplayer?"

Annie stared at her employee. Was that really how people thought? "I think the point of dating someone like Brandon is that he's a good guy and we have lots in common. Him being rich doesn't really come into play."

"Oh, of course not. I wasn't meaning that you only liked him because of his money. I was just meaning. Umm. That it's a nice perk. And he wants to see you. It seems like he should pay for your flight. That's all."

"Right." Not wanting to continue this conversation. She picked up a chart and scanned the records to see what needed to be done with the dog over the weekend. "I don't want Brutus going home until he's managed to keep some food down. Umm, he should be able to handle something to eat in about an hour. If he keeps it down, then you can call his owners to pick him up. If not, talk to Jess and see what she thinks."

"Will do." Sarah shifted her weight, then shifted again uncomfortably. "I didn't mean to offend you or anything."

"It's fine." It wasn't really but talking about it wouldn't change anything. Annie was a feminist through and through, but she'd realized a long time ago not everyone shared her opinion. She just hadn't realized Sarah and her were so different. It boggled her mind that in this day and age, people still thought about relationships like that. She'd worked really hard to put herself through vet school, to become a partner in this practice and with one throw away comment she'd been reduced down to a rich man's arm candy. Hell no.

Annie picked up her bag. "I'll see you Tuesday."

"Have fun."

"I plan to," she called back over her shoulder.

Forty minutes later, Annie parked her car in the overnight parking lot and wandered to the shuttle station. She pulled out her phone while she waited and fired Brandon a text.

Just got to the airport.

A moment later, her phone buzzed. Her eyes widened when she saw a reply from Brandon. She hadn't expected him to even see her message till she was already at his game.

Good. I left your name at the ticket window. Sorry I can't be there to pick you up.

No problem. What are you doing texting? I thought you had practice.

Lunch

Get all fueled up for the afternoon.

Gonna need it for what I have planned.

Oh yeah?

Absolutely. Is it bad that I can't stop thinking about the absolutely filthy things I want to do to you?

Filthy?

It might actually be illegal in some states, possibly this one. Who knows?

Illegal

If it's not, it should be....

She gulped. Wow!

Before she had a chance to reply, the shuttle pulled up. She nodded to the driver as she climbed aboard and dropped into her seat. She immediately saw several missed texts from Brandon.

Doc?

Hello? You still there?

Shit, sorry.

Too far?

Haha, sorry the shuttle just arrived so I had to get on

Thank god. I thought you freaked out.

Definitely not, although now I am very intrigued. Just how illegal are we talking?

How illegal are you willing to do?

Don't answer a question with a question.

I like it. You're doing that impatient thing you do when you're horny.

I'm not horny.

You sure about that?

No, she was definitely not sure. She shifted in her seat as she imagined all the possible things he could be thinking about doing with her when she arrived.

> Seeing how long it's taking you to reply I'm gonna take that as a no. Don't worry, Doc. I'll take care of you when I see you.

You better.

> I got you, babe.

> Shit, sorry, Doc, I gotta go. I'll see you at the game.

Good luck.

She placed her phone in her purse just as the shuttle pulled up in front of the departure doors. Annie grabbed her backpack and made her way off the shuttle.

Inside the terminal, she looked around, taking note of the long line of people at the airline counter. Thank god for the online check-in, she didn't have to deal with all that.

Making her way toward security, her phone buzzed. She pulled it from her purse. An alert from the airline that her flight had been delayed for an hour. Fantastic.

Looks like my flight is delayed for an hour.

Not expecting a reply, she shoved her phone back in her pocket so she could easily get to it again.

After clearing security, she wandered to her gate, found a seat, and pulled out her book to wait. When her phone buzzed again forty minutes later, she glanced up at the boarding screen. All it said was delayed. She pulled out her phone and checked the notification. Another hour delay. Fantastic. At this rate, instead of arriving just after the game started, she'd be lucky to see any of it at all.

The speaker crackled on. "This is for Flight 3454 to Phoenix. We are now ready for boarding. Now boarding Zone 1."

Finally. Only two and a half hours late. Annie flicked over her wrist to look at her watch. Darn it, they hadn't had the Daylight Savings change yet, so she was going to lose an hour, and then it was about an hour from the airport to the sports complex. She quickly did some mental math. She would be lucky to get there by 6:00pm. The game had already started, which meant it would probably already be done.

The PA clicked on again. "Now loading Zone 2."

Ugh, why had she been so cheap? She couldn't even load till Zone 4. She tapped her foot impatiently. Why was this taking so long? After a moment, she paused, closed her eyes, and took a deep breath.

Relax.

Even if she'd already loaded the plane, they still had to wait for everyone to board, so it's not like they would have been leaving any quicker if she'd paid for first class. She would have just been sitting on the plane longer.

She took another deep breath to relax. It was fine. She was still going to see Brandon tonight. She'd just have to wait till tomorrow to see him play. Not a big deal.

Suddenly, someone bashed into her, and she stumbled to the side. "Why don't you watch where you're going," the man who'd bumped her snarled.

She'd been standing still. How was she the problem?

Annie clenched her jaw to stop from snapping back. Ah, the joys of travel. It did not always bring out the best in people.

"Flight 3454 to Phoenix, now boarding all zones," the announcer said.

Annie made her way to the lineup for her flight and onto the plane. Once seated, she pulled her phone out of her pocket.

> Flight is 2.5 hours late so just leaving now. I'll text you when we land. Should be around 5.

With the text sent, she flicked it into airplane mode and looked out the window of the plane. When the seat beside her shifted, she glanced over at the little boy who climbed into the middle seat. She smiled when she saw his Hawks jersey.

"Hi," the little boy said.

"Hi." She smiled at the boy and his dad.

"I'm Mason," the boy said.

"Sorry," the dad said to her, then touched his son's arm. "Mace, how about we just leave the nice lady alone?"

Mason turned to her. "Sorry I bugged you."

"You're not bugging me at all. I'm Annie."

"Hi Annie," Mason grinned at her.

"So you're a Hawks fan?" she asked.

"Yep. We're gonna go watch them play."

"That's cool. Me too."

Mason's eyes bugged wide. "You like baseball?"

"I do."

"But you're a girl."

"I am," she agreed.

"But girls don't like baseball," Mason declared, then turned to his dad. "Right Dad?"

"Uh, some girls do." The dad winced, then said, "Sorry," again.

"No problem." She shifted in her seat so she could face Mason. "So, who's your favorite player?"

"When I was little it was Ramon Gonzalez."

She couldn't help but chuckle at his response. The kid couldn't be more than about seven, so little was a relative term. "When you were little, huh?"

"Yep, but he got traded to New York." Mason scrunched up his face. "We hate New York. They suck."

"Mason." The look of shock on his dad's face made her laugh. Out of the mouths of babes. She dipped her head down closer to Mason. "I agree they're the worst. San Diego is way better."

"Yep." Mason kicked his shoe off.

"Mason, leave your shoes on. I'm sure Annie doesn't want your stinky feet next to her."

He brought his foot up to his nose and inhaled deeply. "They don't stink," he declared.

She bit her lip to keep from laughing. God, kids were wild.

For the next hour, Mason chatted her ear off. Before she knew it, they were there. As they waited for the captain to turn off the seatbelt sign, Mason bounced in his seat. "Do you think the Hawks won today, Dad?" he asked.

"I don't know. We'll check the score when they say we can turn our phones on," his dad replied. "Thanks for keeping Mason entertained, Annie."

"My pleasure. It made the flight feel a lot faster."

"Do you have kids?" Mason's dad asked.

"Nope, not yet."

"Well, you're great with them. I would have thought you had your own with how patient you were with this guy's million and one questions." He ruffled Mason's hair.

"Thanks." She smiled, then looked down at Mason. "Hope you have fun at the ballgame tomorrow. Make sure you look for me."

The captain began speaking overhead. "Welcome to Phoenix. It is currently 5:03 local time. Sunny and 74 degrees. You can now turn your devices back on, but please remain seated until you see the fasten seatbelt sign turn off."

"Check the score, Dad," Mason pleaded.

"7-4 for the Hawks, bottom of the Seventh."

Shoot. She was still an hour from where she needed to go. Annie pulled out her phone.

Plane just landed. Saw you are already in the 7th, so I'll just take a cab to your place and meet you there. Text me when you get

this, so I know you aren't waiting for me at
the stadium.

Slowly making her way through the arrival terminal, she scanned for the sign announcing taxis. Annie made her way to the line of cabs, hopped in one and gave the driver Brandon's address.

They'd been driving for about forty-five minutes when her phone buzzed.

> Just finished the game. I'll get there as soon as I can. If you get there first, there's a pool around the back and patio furniture set up, so make yourself comfortable.

See you soon.

Ten minutes later, the cab pulled up in front of a large modern house. She eyed the address. Good lord, the place was huge. Why would Brandon need something this big for just him and Carter?

Standing on the sidewalk, she pulled out her phone.

Just got here.

> Be there in 20

She shoved her phone in her back pocket and flicked open the latch on the gate. She wandered down the decorative paving stone path and around the side of the house.

Wow, the backyard was even nicer than the front. This place was insane. Annie set her bag down and made herself comfortable on the chaise lounge. Dropping her head back against the pillow, she closed her eyes. Something about flying always made her so tired. She didn't know how Brandon and them did it. She'd flown for an hour and felt like she needed a nap. How did they do this and then play?

"Doc?"

She blinked her eyes open and saw Brandon standing over her, smiling down.

"Hey." She held out her hand. When he took it, she tugged him toward her. His enormous frame took up all the vacant space on the lounger.

Brandon leaned in and she wrapped her arms around his neck. The moment his lips touched hers, she sank into him. It had only been three weeks, but she'd missed him like crazy.

When the kiss broke, she didn't want to let go. Brandon shifted his body so he was leaning back on the lounger with her, allowing her to cuddle against his side.

"I missed you," she murmured.

"I'm glad you're here." Brandon kissed the top of her head. "Sorry, your flight got all messed up."

"All good, it happens. Sorry I missed your game."

"Eh, you'll see it tomorrow."

She scooched in a little closer to him and looked at the surrounding yard. "Pretty swanky digs for a rental."

"No shit." He chuckled. "It's a friend of the owners."

"And he just rents it out to the team?"

"Yeah apparently."

"This place is huge. Why don't more of you stay here?"

"Oh, no, we just rent that." Brandon pointed to the pool house.

"That makes more sense." She sat up. "Where's Carter?"

"You were conked out so he went inside to give me a chance to wake you up and say hello." Brandon placed his finger under her chin and tipped her face up at the same time he dipped down. "So hello."

"Mmm, hi." She threaded her hands through his hair and brought his face down the last few inches so their lips could touch. The kiss started soft and slow, then built. As their tongues tangled, Annie shifted to get closer. She brought her leg over on top of his.

As soon as she did, Brandon gripped her hip and pulled her on top of him, so she was straddling his lap. She sank down, allowing his hard cock to press against her clit. She shifted her weight, dragging her body against him. His hands dug into her hips as he deepened the kiss.

"All right you two. This is communal space. Enough of that shit," Carter called.

"Fuck off," Brandon growled.

With a giggle, Annie shifted her body and turned toward the pool house. "Hi Carter."

"How was the flight?" Carter asked.

She tried to move off Brandon's lap so she could properly face Carter to talk. His fingers gripped her hips.

"Stay," he ordered and shifted his hips so his hard cock pressed against her core.

A little pulse of arousal shot through her at the commanding tone of his voice. Brandon smirked at her. She narrowed her eyes. He knew exactly what that tone did to her.

Fine, she'd stay, but that didn't mean she wouldn't torture him just a little in return. Adjusting her body so she could see Carter better, she pressed her hips firmly against him, making sure to drag her body along his length as she shifted.

"Doc," he growled.

She batted her eyelashes at him innocently, then turned her attention back to Carter. "It was good. I sat beside a little Hawks fan."

"Oh, yeah?" Carter leaned against the door frame. "Who was his favorite player?"

"It was Gonzalez, but he's undecided at the moment."

"Hope you told him he should stick with third base," Carter said.

"Sorry, I told him Sims was by far the best player."

Brandon squeezed her hip as if to say thanks.

Carter snorted. "Come on Annie, no one's favorite player is right field."

"Fuck you." Brandon raised his hand and flipped up his middle finger.

Carter snickered. "Don't be jealous, B, you know in-field gets all the love."

"We'll see when my batting average leaves yours in the dirt," Brandon said.

Leo stirred from his place at the edge of the pool deck, and Annie noticed him for the first time. "Oh my gosh, Leo."

"Break," Brandon said, releasing the dog.

Leo wandered over to them. Brandon dropped his hand down to the edge of the chaise and Leo's body wriggled to get close enough to touch his person. Annie reached down and gave him a little pat. The dog seemed virtually unaware of her hand. He was much more focused on Brandon.

"How's he been doing?"

"Really good." Brandon's smile split across his face. "It's fucking awesome, actually. I can't wait for you to see him at the field tomorrow."

"I can't wait."

"I talked to Del about doing some training and thought him and Leo could sit in the stands with you."

"That sounds great."

"Del said he's ready for that next stage of training and I think having you there will help him feel safer."

"Of course."

"Cool, thanks."

She turned to face him. "Have I ever told you how hot it is that you are so sweet about Leo?"

"I don't think so." Brandon shifted his hips, and she bit her lip as his cock thickened beneath her. "Why don't you tell me how hot it makes you?"

"I didn't say it made me hot. I said it was hot," she teased.

Brandon flexed his hips again slightly and she sucked in a breath. "I'm not sure I hear a difference, Doc,"

"Umm, guys?" Carter said.

Brandon licked his lips. Between the heat in his eyes and the way his dick pulsed against her core, every nerve ending in her body fired to life. Her breath hitched. God, she wished they were alone.

"Guys seriously?" Carter complained. "Look away Leo."

Suddenly, Brandon gripped her hips and stood up. Instinctively, she wrapped her legs around his waist to hold on.

"Watch Leo," he said as they walked past Carter.

"Leo, come on buddy, you're too young to watch this," Carter said. "Stay with me."

Annie buried her face in his neck and giggled. She should probably be embarrassed about Carter knowing they were going to have sex, but she wasn't. Not in the least.

All she could think was finally!

CHAPTER NINETEEN

T he following afternoon, Brandon walked up to the plate, rolled his shoulders. It might only be spring training but they needed to come out of the gates swinging, put the fear of god in the other teams early.

"Gonna be a big come down when you guys don't even make playoffs this year," Piatelli said from his crouched position behind the plate.

Brandon looked down at the catcher. "Don't you worry about that. We'll be trouncing past you all the way to the World Series."

"You think you can do that without Gonzo?"

"Yep." It might be a little harder, but Carter was a solid third baseman. And there was more to a team than one player, no matter how good that one player was.

Taking his stance, he lined up at the plate. Manuela positioned himself on the mound. Everything else fell away as Brandon watched the pitcher. The ball rushed toward him. In the split second he had to decide, he checked his swing.

Ball one.

The second pitch soared toward him.

Swing and miss.

Fucking breaking ball.

He adjusted his feet in the dirt and dug in a little deeper. Piatelli shifted his weight behind him, moving into a slightly different position. Narrowing his vision, Brandon focused on Manuela. The ball flew toward him. He swung, the bat cracked against the ball and he took off toward first base. The ball landed safely in the gap, giving him plenty of time to get on base.

He peeled off his elbow and leg guards and handed them to George Lammont, the first base coach, while Pete walked up to the plate.

He glanced toward the stands where Annie was sitting.

"Focus, Sims," Coach snapped. "We got two outs, so be ready to run."

"Yep." He pulled his attention back to the game as Pete lined up at the plate.

First pitch right down the pipe, followed by that gorgeous sound of the sweet spot hitting the ball.

He didn't wait to see where the ball went. He took off. As he rounded second, the roar of the crowd told him the ball had cleared the fence. He slowed to a jog as he continued his way around the bases to home plate. Once he crossed the plate, he turned and waited to congratulate Pete as he crossed home. They high-fived, then made their way back to the dugout. Smitty held open the home run jacket and Pete slid into it.

"Way to keep the inning alive, boys," Ryan said as he slapped Brandon, then Pete on the shoulders.

Unfortunately, Sanchez struck out ending the inning. They were up 4-2 at the top of the 5th.

Brandon grabbed his glove off the bench and made his way onto the field. This would probably be his last inning this game, as Coach tended to bench his starters so he could see what the prospects could do.

The pitcher took to the mound. Maarx, a kid from the farm team that he hadn't gotten to know yet. Probably wouldn't bother until he knew if he was going to make the cut or not.

Davidson walked up to the plate. Shit. The kid wasn't catching a break with his first shot at pitching in the majors. Davidson had lit them up all last year every time he stepped to the plate. Hopefully, this season was different.

First pitch, just a bit outside.

Maarx, lined up for the second pitch and threw. Davidson swung. The ball soared toward right field. Fuck, it was deep. Brandon raced back toward the warning track. Dammit, this ball looked like it was going over. At the fence, Brandon jumped and kicked his foot off the wall and snatched the ball just as it went over the fence. He landed on the dirt with his stolen home run in his hand. The crowd roared in approval.

Fuck that Davidson, this was a new season.

Brandon tossed the ball back toward the infield. One away.

Followed by two more quick outs.

He walked back to the dugout, Coach Schneider nodded to him as he walked past. "Good job, Sims. You can sit."

Brandon nodded to his coach in understanding, then dumped his glove on the bench.

Coach Schneider bellowed, "Ramirez, you're going in for Sims, Gustafson in for Saunders."

Taking advantage of not having to worry about where he was in the lineup, he wandered over to Carter, who stood leaning against the fence.

"Nice snag," Carter said as he glanced over at him, then looked away to spit his sunflower seed shells over the fence.

"You got any more of those?"

Carter raised his eyebrow. "Yeah, in my bag."

Brandon scooped up the spitz bag, wrinkled his nose at the dill pickle label, then shrugged and poured a handful into his palm. He tossed some into his mouth. Yep, that's about what he expected it to taste like. "Why the fuck do you have dill pickle?"

"Because it slaps," Carter said, tossing another handful into his mouth.

Brandon rested his elbows on the rail as he looked out at the field. "How you feeling?"

"Good. Saunders is a beast. It's nice having him beside me. He covers a lot of ground."

Brandon nodded in understanding. That's how he felt playing beside Smitty. He knew the guy would do his job. "Yeah, he's good. You guys seem like you're gelling well."

"So far, yep." Carter glanced toward the stands. "I'll, umm...make myself scarce after the game."

"Why?"

Carter wrinkled his brow. "Dude, I love you and all, but hearing you two fuck like rabbits is not really my thing. If I keep hearing her scream your name, I might start wanting to fuck you."

"Fuck off." Brandon shoved his shoulder into Carter and the other man stumbled.

Carter chuckled. "I'm serious. From the sounds of shit in there, I should be sitting outside the door taking notes or something."

"Maybe stop being a perv and listening to us."

"Kind of hard not to hear when you shake the whole fucking house at 2:00 in the morning, then decide to do another marathon wakeup round at 6:00. How the fuck are you not tired?"

"Healthy living," Brandon said.

Johnny Knight leaned over from his place on the other side of Carter. "Who knew eating pussy was the breakfast of champions?" Knight mocked.

"Who knew being a pussy meant you played like you?" Carter replied.

"Don't strike out," Carter called after Johnny when he walked away to pick up his batting gear.

"Fuck you, new guy," Johnny snarled.

Brandon smirked at Carter. "Still making friends wherever you go I see."

"Eh, every team's got a couple of dicks. Doesn't take long to figure out who they are."

"Unfortunately."

"I'm on deck," Carter pushed off the railing.

"Crank it."

Carter winked. "It'll be like watching batting practice, baby."

"Yeah, right," Brandon snickered. "Except you sucked ass at practice this morning."

"Settle down." Carter held up his hand. "I got that shit out of my system. It's smooth sailing from here on out."

"We'll see." Everyone had their own batting routine. For some reason Carter's had always been trash talking his teammates. It had never made much sense to Brandon, but it always seemed to work for Carter.

As Carter sauntered away, Pete stepped up beside Brandon and leaned on the railing. "How's he feel like it's going?" Pete asked as they watched Carter on deck.

"Good, he's liking playing with you."

"Awesome. It's always an adjustment on a new team."

"Yeah, for both of you," Brandon said.

Pete made a snorting sound. "No shit," he muttered. Then they stood in silence, neither of them saying a word through the next two batters. As Carter ran to first on a walk. Pete nodded his head. "He's a good fit."

"Yep."

"You and Carter want to come by for a BBQ later?"

"Thanks, but I'm going to pass since Annie is in town."

"Bring her," Pete said.

"Thanks but no, she's only here for a couple days, but if you want to take Carter off my hands for the night, I'd appreciate it." Having Carter go for a BBQ guaranteed they'd have the place to themselves for a couple of hours at least.

Pete smirked. "Understood. We'll take the new guy off your hands for the night."

"Cool."

"So things with Annie are going good?" Pete asked.

"Yep." Brandon watched as Hernandez walked up to the plate.

"That's all you're going to give me?"

"Yep."

Pete shifted his body. "You must be kind of serious if she came down to visit."

Annoyed, Brandon glanced at his teammate. Did the guy really think they'd just share their feelings standing here on the sidelines? "We're not doing this." He flicked a finger between them.

Pete snorted. "So you get to play matchmaker with Smitty and Gonz, but we don't get to know anything about you?"

"Yep."

"Well, that hardly seems fair. Smitty," Pete called as Jeff Smith walked back into the dugout after striking out.

"What's up?" Smitty asked.

"Annie came to visit."

Smitty's eyebrows raised and he waggled them. "Oh, really?"

"Jesus," Brandon muttered.

"So you must really like her?" Smitty pressed.

"Pay attention to the game."

Smitty waved his hand. "I just shit the bed at the plate, give me something to work with here."

"How bout you work on baseball? Clearly you need it," Brandon said,

"Nah, I'd rather hear about Annie. You know Kia is going to ask me."

Brandon rolled his eyes. "Tell her to mind her business."

Smitty snorted. "That'll go over well. Just nut up and give me something I can tell her."

Glancing over to where Annie was sitting in the stands with Leo safely tucked by her side, Brandon smiled as he watched her. She'd said she didn't really like baseball, so he'd been expecting her to look bored. But she was anything but. She raptly watched the batter. She was really into the game.

It shocked him how much he liked having her there. He'd never really had someone in the stands for him that he cared about. His mom had already died before he really got into baseball and his dad sure as hell hadn't shown up to watch. He shuddered, but that was probably a good thing. Sure he'd had girls he'd been casually dating watch him, but this felt different. Annie was different.

"Cool. I'm gonna tell you that you're completely gone," Smitty said.

Brandon pulled his attention off Annie and back to his teammate. "Huh?"

Smitty slapped him on the shoulder. "All good, man. We've both been there."

"Been where? I'm not gone. I'm—" What was he? "I'm—" Jesus. He had no clue.

Smitty chuckled beside him, and Brandon dropped his shoulder into his teammate's side, making Smitty stumble sideways.

"Just shut up and watch the fucking game," Brandon snarled and forced himself to do the same, despite how badly he wanted to turn and look at Annie again.

CHAPTER TWENTY

A nnie felt Brandon kick the sheet a moment before he flipped her off him and launched her across the bed. Her eyes flew open and she saw Brandon sitting up in bed beside her, gasping for air.

"Brandon," she said carefully.

His wide-crazed eyes shifted toward her and he rubbed both hands down his face and let out a shuddering breath. "Fuck, are you okay?" he asked.

"I'm fine. Are you?"

He scrubbed his hands over his face again. "Yeah, yeah, shit. I'm so sorry, Doc. I was asleep and just..."

His body vibrated. The end table sat at an awkward angle beside the bed. It being there was probably the only reason Brandon was still in bed since he'd crashed into it when he jumped up.

She eased closer to him and placed her hand on his arm. "It's okay, we're both fine," she soothed.

He blew out a loud breath. "You're sure I didn't hurt you?"

"I'm fine. It's a bed, it was a soft landing."

Brandon pushed off from the bed and stood up. He shoved his legs into his sweatpants and pulled them up, then turned to face her. "You want breakfast?"

"Brandon, sit down, talk to me. What happened?"

"Nothing," he muttered. "You want eggs?"

She reached out her hand and grabbed his arm. "Brandon, talk to me. You're clearly rattled."

"Yeah, I fucking launched you across the bed. Of course I'm rattled. Fuck."

"You didn't launch me across the bed. You were dreaming and your body obviously needed space."

He stopped pacing around the room and stared at her.

She grabbed his other hand and tugged him toward the bed. "Brandon, I'm fine. I promise. You didn't hurt me at all. It was a jarring way to wake up, but that's all. I'm totally fine." She tugged harder and he dropped onto the mattress beside her.

"Did you have a bad dream?"

"No, not really. I don't think so. I don't..." He looked over at her and ran his hand down her head and cupped the side of her cheek. "You're sure you're okay?"

"I'm fine. I promise." She moved her head and kissed his palm. "It's okay."

"No, it's not. I could have seriously hurt you."

"But you didn't."

Brandon pinched his bottom lip between his fingers and shook his head. "I've done everything I can to not be like him," he whispered.

"Be like who?"

"What?" He blinked at her.

"You've done everything you can not to be like who?"

He shook his head. "Forget it."

When he tried to stand up, she grabbed his arm. "No, Brandon, clearly we need to talk about this. You don't want to be like who?"

"My dad, okay."

Treading carefully, she reiterated what he said, "Your dad?"

"Yeah, fuck," he growled, then shifted so he was facing her. "I need you to know I would never hurt you on purpose."

"I know that, Brandon. You're one of the sweetest guys I know."

"But I've got him in me, don't I, so it's there." He looked up at the ceiling and sighed. "Fuck."

Got him in him. What did that mean? What kind of guy was his dad? "You had said your dad was a drunk, but was it more than that? Is your dad not a nice guy?"

Brandon snorted. "Not even close." He looked down at his arm and absently ran his hand over the inside of it.

Annie looked more closely at the tattoo sleeve covering Brandon's arm. Was his dad the monster? "Is that what your tattoo is about?"

"Nah, no." He shook his head. "No, this is a couple of drawings of my mom's that Kia blended into a sleeve."

"You keep rubbing your arm, so I wasn't sure."

He turned his wrist and looked at the inside of his biceps. "Yeah."

Annie waited, but he didn't elaborate, so she pressed on. "What does your dad do?"

He flicked a glance at her. "Besides drink?"

Oh boy. "Yeah."

"Last I heard he was still running his landscaping business."

"Last you heard? You don't talk at all?"

"Nope, haven't spoken to him since I was fifteen."

Annie's chest tightened. Fifteen, she couldn't even imagine. At fifteen, he'd had no family. "How come?"

He pushed off the mattress and paced around the room. "You really want to do this?"

"Yeah, Brandon, I do. I think we need to. It's part of who you are. If we're going to make a go of things, I think we need to be able to talk about this kind of stuff."

He leaned his butt against the dresser and faced her.

"How come you stopped seeing your dad when you were fifteen?" she pressed.

"Because I beat the shit out of him and he had me arrested."

Annie reared back. "You what?" How was that possible? The man she knew was kind and gentle. How could he have assaulted his dad?

"Still think I'm a good guy, Doc?" Brandon crossed his arms over his chest. The muscles in his body all coiled tightly as he waited for her to respond.

"Yes, I know you are. If you assaulted him, you must have had a reason."

"You sure about that?"

Annie studied him. It was like he expected her to reject him with this admission. She pushed off the bed and went toward him. She stopped in front of him, close enough to touch.

"Yes." She grabbed his arm and gave it a little pull. When he finally released his hold on himself, she took his hand and looked down at it. His hands were huge, making hers look tiny in comparison. She placed a kiss against his palm and he shuddered.

He wrapped his arm around her and pulled her against his chest. "Thanks, Doc." He kissed the top of her head.

"What happened?" she asked.

"My dad wasn't a nice drunk and one day I got sick of it."

It didn't even sound like Brandon when he spoke. There was no emotion in the words, but she knew he had to be feeling them. How could he not? Annie placed a kiss against his chest.

"So you fought back?"

"Yep, but didn't really stop like I should have and I broke his arm—payback for when he did mine, I guess."

Tears welled in her eyes, and she wrapped her arms tighter around his waist. "Your dad broke your arm."

"Yeah, among other things."

She looked up at him as the tears spilled down her face. Brandon wiped the tears off her cheeks. "No need to cry about it, Doc. It was a long time ago."

"Brandon, I'm so sorry."

"Eh, it's fine. I got bigger and stronger and made sure he knew it."

"But you lost your home as a result."

"Best thing that ever happened to me. Coach took me in for the rest of the season, then the next year he set me up with a billet family to play ball and the rest is history."

"So you just billeted after that and never saw him again?"

"Nope, never wanted to." He dropped his arm from around her. "We done with this?"

She stepped back and looked up at him. "For now, I guess."

His body tensed. "What do you mean for now?"

"I don't know. It seems like there's a lot you aren't saying."

"Of course there's a lot I'm not saying. It's not exactly a bedtime story."

"Good thing it's almost breakfast time then."

He sighed. "Fine, let's just get this over with. What else do you want to know?"

"Brandon, hang on, I'm not trying to push you into anything you don't want to do."

"But you are." He stepped away from her. "I don't like talking about this shit with anyone, especially you."

Pain lanced in her chest. "What do you mean, especially me?"

He growled and rolled his eyes. "Don't be that way. That's not what I meant and you know it."

"No, Brandon, I don't know it. How did you mean it?"

"I don't want you to see me like that. "

"Like what?"

"Weak." He dropped onto the mattress. "Poor little, Brandon, his dad used to burn him with cigarettes and he was too much of a pussy to stop him." He sniffed. "Till I did, and I became exactly like the fucking monster I hated." He looked up at the ceiling and blinked rapidly.

Her heart broke for him. Rushing over, she dropped to her knees in front of him. "You're not a monster, Brandon, and you're anything but weak."

He flipped over his arm and looked down at the inside of her elbow. "The scars say otherwise."

Scars. "Oh my god." She touched the large scar on the side of his ribs. "So, this wasn't from boiling water?"

"No, it was." He looked down at his side. "Just my dad spilled it, not me."

"Spilled it?"

"Spilled, dumped, same thing."

Oh my god, that poor boy. Tears poured down her face. "No, Brandon, it's not."

He absently fingered the inside of his elbow. She'd never noticed the scars on his arm before. The tattoo covered them, blended them into the story so beautifully they weren't even noticeable. She touched one of the scars. "Kia tied them into the story."

"Yeah, she's kind of pushy like that." He smiled. "Makes sense to use 'em since they're part of the story as well. Light and dark, good and bad and all that. The two parts that made me."

"This is from a cigarette?"

"Yep."

She pressed a kiss to the scar at the inside of his elbow. "This one was deep."

"Yeah, he liked to hit the same spot."

"Brandon," she cried.

"Doc, it's all good. It was a long time ago."

"It's not all good, Brandon. How could he have done this to you? Why did no one protect you?" She sobbed.

"Hey, hey," he cooed. Suddenly, he scooped her up and pulled her onto his lap. "I'm fine."

Tears streamed down her face as she thought of the little boy. His mother dead. Nowhere to turn. Annie sobbed. She was supposed to be comforting him and yet here he was rubbing soothing circles on her back.

"I'm so sorry, Brandon."

"This is why I didn't want to tell you."

She pulled back so she could look at him. "Why? Because I hurt for the little boy you were?"

"I wasn't that little," he muttered.

"Brandon, you were a child. He was your dad. He should have protected you, not hurt you."

"I don't like to talk about all this shit. It was a long time ago. Besides, if my dad hadn't been a such a dick, then who knows maybe I wouldn't be playing ball now. Needing a place to go was what got me billeted and away from my old man."

"They wouldn't have billeted you if you weren't good, Brandon."

"True, but who knows? I don't talk about it. I don't think about it."

"Talking helps, Brandon."

He shrugged. "I talked about it enough when it happened, not much point in talking about it now." He tucked her hair behind her ear. "Look at how upset you are about it. How is this helpful to know this shit about me?"

"Oh my gosh, B, how is it not helpful for me to know this?"

"Why would it be?"

Men could be so obtuse sometimes. "It explains Leo."

"What do you mean?"

"Why you had to save him?"

"It was the right thing to do," he mumbled.

"Sure, but not everyone would have gone to the lengths you did for an abused dog." As she looked at his gorgeous face, she couldn't help but see him in a new light. "You haven't talked to Rayne about this have you?"

"No, why would I? Kia's the only one I've told recently, and that's only because we were talking about my tattoo."

She smiled to herself. No, of course he wouldn't have told Rayne. But her energy and the healing she was able to do with no words explained why they were so close and why he was so adamant Rayne spend time with Leo.

She'd been right. They were the same, Brandon and Leo. Fighters. "No reason." Annie cupped his cheeks and pressed a kiss against his lips. "Thank you for telling me all this."

"You didn't really give me much choice, Doc."

"I know."

He pursed his lips, then sighed. When his eyes met hers, he looked resigned, like this was the beginning of the end. That couldn't be further from the truth.

"Trust me, this is a good thing," she said.

Brandon snorted. "Yeah right."

"I'm not going to lie and say it doesn't change anything. Because it does." Annie pressed another gentle kiss to his mouth. "For the better. I see you, Brandon. And I really like what I see."

"Oh, yeah?" He grabbed her around the waist and hoisted her up so she was forced to straddle him.

His dick twitched against her. How the hell could he be hard after that conversation? "Really?" She smirked.

"Definitely." He cupped the back of her head and just as his lips touched hers, Leo barked.

"Leo," Brandon groaned. "Not now, buddy."

Leo barked again, this time more urgently. Annie giggled. "I think he needs to go out."

"Yeah probably." He pressed his forehead against hers. "To be continued."

"Count on it." She pushed herself off his lap.

Brandon stood and adjusted himself, then walked over to the closet when he kept Leo's crate. When he opened the door, Leo's entire body wiggled as he walked out and greeted Brandon. "You know, if you wouldn't pee on the floor and eat shit, I'd let you sleep in the bedroom."

Leo bumped against Brandon's leg as he wiggled for pets. Then peed on the floor.

"Dude," Brandon said. He grabbed the disinfectant spray bottle off the shelf and the paper towel and wiped up Leo's excited pee. Crouching down, he leaned over and gave the dog a pat. "You know, dude, I wouldn't have to keep cleaner in the closet if you'd stop doing the wiggle spray."

The dog pawed Brandon. With a laugh, he sat down on the floor and Leo crawled onto his lap for a cuddle.

Annie grinned as she watched them. If someone had told her the big player who hit on her in a bar would be the type of guy to casually clean up pee or cuddle a dog on the closet floor, she would have thought they were crazy. But it worked. The pair fit like puzzle pieces. Each one afraid to be loved, yet both desperately needed it. How Brandon could ever think he was like his father was beyond her.

Brandon kissed the top of Leo's head. "All right, buddy, let's go do a proper pee outside so we can save my floor." He pushed up off the ground and pulled up short when he caught her staring. "What?"

"Nothing."

"Why you looking at me like that?"

She walked over to him. Even standing on her tiptoes, she was nowhere close to his face, so she reached up and pulled his head down. "You're a good man, Brandon."

Leo wedged himself between them, making her laugh. She reached down. "You're a good boy too, Leo."

The dog shifted his weight, hip-checking her slightly as he rubbed against Brandon's leg, making her laugh again. She ran her hand along the dog's head. "No need to be jealous. There's plenty of him to go around for us to share."

"And that's another reason he's in his crate when you sleep over. No chance in hell I'm having him jump on the bed mid-way. It's bad enough I could feel him watching me from the closet."

Annie giggled. "He can't see us from the closet."

"He knew what was going on."

She shoved Brandon's side. "Go take him for a pee, you weirdo."

"Meet you in the kitchen?"

"Yep." Annie watched the pair leave the room, then leaned against the wall. She was in trouble. How was she supposed to not fall in love with him now? She looked up at the ceiling. "Please don't let him break my heart," she whispered.

CHAPTER TWENTY-ONE

I t was nice being back in his own house. As much as he enjoyed training camp, there was nothing like sleeping in his own bed. Even if it was just for a couple of nights before they hit the road. Brandon filled up the dog food bowl and waited for Leo to sit before setting it on the ground.

"Break," he said and Leo sprang up and dove into his bowl like he hadn't seen food in weeks.

Annie walked into the room, and Leo growled, guarding his bowl. "Uh uh," Brandon ordered.

He poured a cup of coffee for Annie and doctored it the way she liked before handing it to her.

"Thank you." She brought the cup to her nose and inhaled before taking a sip.

"What should I be doing to get him to stop resource guarding like that?" he asked.

Annie rested her hip on the counter beside him as they both watched the dog. "Honestly B, he's doing amazing. I never dreamed you'd be able to get him any-where close to where he already is. The rest is just going to take time. He was half-starved when you brought him in. It's normal for him to be protective of his food."

"But that's not something he has to worry about now."

She cupped his arm. "No, but he doesn't fully trust it yet. Give him time."

He bit into his apple and broke off a piece and walked closer to Leo. The dog raised his head but didn't make a sound. Brandon tossed the piece of apple into the bowl and Leo scarfed it down. When his bowl was empty, Leo walked over and sat down at Brandon's feet.

"You've got yourself quite the shadow there," Annie said.

He looked down at the dog that had practically made himself a part of his leg.

"No shit." He'd never had a dog before, so didn't have a clue if it was normal or not. "He needs to work on the whole bathroom etiquette thing. You're not supposed to maintain eye contact when someone is using the can."

Annie snickered. "Just because he's watching you doesn't mean you have to watch back."

"He's giving me the stink eye when I'm holding my junk. I'm not looking away. I just don't get why he wants to sit so close to me when I'm going. It's a big fucking room. He could sit on the other side."

"That's not how it works when you have a velcro dog."

"Apparently." He chucked a piece of apple up in the air and Leo caught it. He rubbed the top of Leo's head. "Nice job, bud."

When they'd first started playing toss, Leo couldn't catch anything. He wasn't sure if it was the one eye, the missing limb or just lack of practice all together but more things hit his forehead than went in his mouth. Now he was about 50/50 more if what was being tossed was food rather than a ball.

Brandon leaned back on the counter beside Annie. "So you looking forward to your girls' night thing tonight?"

"It should be fun. I haven't seen some of the girls in a while, so it'll be good."

"What's on the agenda?"

"We're doing a spa day, then dinner and drinks."

"That's it?"

"No, there's this umm...dance show that Gabby is itching to see."

Brandon smirked. "You're going to the rippers?"

Annie scrunched up her nose. "They're male dancers."

"Who take their clothes off. You can call it what you want, but they're rippers."

"Okay, yes, we are going to the strippers."

"Call me when you're done and I'll pick you up."

"Don't be silly. You have a game tonight. You're not going to pick me up from the strip club."

He grabbed her hand and pulled her in front of him and rested his hands on her hips. "Babe, if you're getting drunk with the girls and going to the rippers, I'm picking you up."

"I can catch an Uber home."

"Nuh uh, I've heard all about how you ladies get with the whole Magic Mike thing. I'm not missing out on your coming home all horny."

Annie snorted. "I'm not coming home all horny. Have you seen those shows? I'll be hiding in the back, nursing my drink."

"Uh-huh, that's what they all say before they're shoving dollar bills down his g-string with their teeth."

"Eww, I'm not putting money in my teeth. That's gross. Do you have any idea how dirty money is?"

Brandon threw his head back and laughed. "But you will be shoving money into his pants?"

Annie trailed her fingers up his chest. "Do I hear some jealousy there?"

"No," he scoffed. "I don't do jealousy."

"Right, I forgot," she teased.

"Seriously, when you're ready to come home for the night, call me and I'll pick you up."

"That's silly. There's no reason for you to miss out on sleep just to see me drunk and falling into bed."

He pulled her close. "Humor me. I don't like the idea of you getting in some Uber alone when you're drunk. Call me. I'll pick you up, tuck you in, and make sure you're home safe."

"I don't want to ruin your sleep when you play again tomorrow."

"Babe, I'm not going to be sleeping till I know you're home safe anyway, so I may as well pick you up."

"Are you sure?" Annie stood on her tiptoes and cupped his face with her hands.

Why was she looking at him like that? It was a ride. He wasn't buying her a car, he was picking her up.

"Yep." He gave her a kiss. "I'm still hoping you're going to be all horny from the strippers, and I'm more than happy to let you use me to work it off."

"Oh really, you'd just let me use you however I see fit?"

"Honey, you can use me however you want. Bounce, grind. My body is yours to use however you need to get yourself off."

She wrapped her arms around his neck. "What if I decide I need to sit on your face?"

Brandon growled. Grabbing her hips, he hoisted her onto the kitchen counter. "You could fucking smother me with your pussy and I'd be okay with it." He pushed her legs apart and stepped between her thighs.

"Well, I wouldn't want to smother you," she teased.

He gripped her hips and pulled her tightly against his cock. Leaning down, he ran his nose up her neck.

"What happened to no sex when I'm drunk?" Annie teased.

"I feel like this conversation counts as consent unless you change your mind later."

"Oh, it definitely counts as consent." She pushed her hips against him. "You can just assume you always have consent unless you hear otherwise."

"I always have consent, huh." He ground his pelvis against her, enjoying the way her eyes darkened with arousal.

Leo pawed him in the leg, pulling his attention from Annie. He glanced down at the dog. "What?" he asked.

The dog pawed him again, then ran to the front door and barked. Brandon dropped his head back. "You've got to be kidding me," he groaned.

"To be continued." Annie patted his face. "The joys of being a daddy."

Leo was a dog, not a kid. Thank god, because he was not dad material. Not now, not ever. "He's a dog. I'm not his dad," he growled.

"Right. Sorry." Annie giggled.

Brandon scooped the leash off the counter. Pausing at the front door, he attached Leo's leash. "All right, cockblock. Let's go."

Leo looked up, his pink tongue hung out the side of his mouth as he bounced excitedly beside him. Brandon rubbed his hand along the top of the dog's head affectionately. There was no way he could stay annoyed at that face.

When they returned from their walk around the block, Annie stood in the kitchen fully dressed, looking like she was ready to leave. He unclipped Leo's leash and tossed it on the counter. Wrapping his arms around her waist, he pulled her against him. "Have fun tonight."

She smoothed her hands over his back. "I will. Good luck at your game."

"Thanks." He brushed her hair back from her face and tucked a stray piece behind her ear. "Make sure you call me when you're ready to come home and I'll come get you."

"Brandon, it really is unnecessary. What if I'm going to cab it with some of the girls?"

"Then I guess I'm driving them home, too."

"You'd do that?"

He rolled his eyes. What part of this was she not understanding? He was picking her up tonight. It didn't matter what that looked like, it was happening. "Mmm," he grumbled.

She stood on her tiptoes and pressed her lips against his. "You really are the sweetest."

He snorted. He'd been called a lot of things in his life. Sweet wasn't usually one of them. "Like I said, if you're gonna be drunk and horny, then I'm gonna be there."

"All right, tough guy. I'll let you pretend." She kissed him again. "Thanks, B, it means a lot to me to know you care enough to pick me up."

Why did she keep looking at him like that? He rubbed the back of his neck and looked away from her. "Yep," he mumbled.

As the door shut behind Annie, he glanced over at Leo. "Okay, dude, I gotta get ready to head to the field."

An hour later, he wandered into the locker room and dropped his bag on the bench.

About half the team was already there in the various stages of their pregame routine. He nodded at Smitty a couple of lockers down.

Brandon turned up the music on his headphones, closed his eyes and rolled his neck, then dropped his elbows onto his knees as he began his own routine.

His head snapped up when someone pulled his earphone away from his head. "What the fuck?" he growled at Carter.

"My bad." Carter held his hands up in surrender. "I said your name a couple of times, but you didn't hear me."

Brandon raised his eyebrow at his teammate. "Maybe I was ignoring you."

"Whatever." Carter dropped onto the bench beside him. "My parents showed up at my door this morning."

"They just showed up?"

"Yeah, they're doing this RV trip along the coastline, taking a few months and doing Vancouver to Mexico and apparently made good time and here they are."

"When were you supposed to see them?"

"I wasn't. They thought the timing wouldn't work with our schedule."

"Anyway, they want to grab a bite after the game and asked if you wanted to come."

God, that sounded awful. "For dinner with your parents?"

"Yeah, come on, they're happy we're playing together again."

"Yeah right, cuz they loved me so much."

Carter shrugged. "They didn't dislike you. My mom is just nosey and didn't like that you wouldn't give her anything to work with."

Nosey was an understatement. The woman should have a been a military interrogator. "Don't think she's going to like me any more now, since I still am not telling her jack."

Carter waved his hand. "It'll be fine. They already know about Annie, so you can just talk about that."

"Why the fuck would you tell them about Annie?"

"I said you might not be able to make it because of her."

Jumping on the out, he said, "I can't make it."

Carter smirked. "Do you have plans with Annie?"

"No, I just don't want to fucking have dinner with your parents."

"Come on, man. It's going to be all awkward and un-comfortable. Help me out."

"Oh geez, that sounds great. Sign me up." Brandon scrunched up his face in discomfort. "Fuck no."

"I'd do it for you," Carter pleaded.

"I wouldn't ask."

"That's not really fair. You don't talk to your dad, so it's different."

Even if he did have to talk to his dad, there was no chance he'd subject anyone else to him. "They're your parents. Nut up and have dinner with them. What's the big deal?"

"Nothing." Carter rubbed the back of his neck. "I'm not married, I don't have prospects, I'm not getting any younger. You know the drill."

"Not really, no." Brandon pulled his shoes out of the bottom of his locker. "How is me being there going to help at all?"

"It probably won't, but at least I'd have a DD if I decide to have a couple."

The coaches walked into the change room. "All right, listen up. Big game today." Coach Schneider looked around the locker room. "Seattle is going to be gunning for us after the thrashing we gave them last night. Saunders, get with Daye. I want that infield locked down. Nothing gets through that side."

"You got it," Pete said.

"We need to be on the sticks." Coach looked around the room and paused at Lourdes. "Don't swing at shit pitches."

"Yeah, it's baseball not golf, Hernandez," Knight mocked.

Lou pretended to scratch his face with his middle finger.

Chase snickered, then said, "How many times did you get on base again last night, Johnny?" Chase scratched his chin like he was deep in thought. "Oh yeah, zero."

"Fuck you," Johnny growled.

"All right, all right, focus," Coach said. "Infield, you know Batiste likes to bunt so balls of the feet when he's up." Coach scanned the room and stopped at Brandon. "Sims, during batting practice, Matthews was cutting right, so be ready."

Brandon nodded. No way Matthews was getting one by him.

"Let's have some fun and win us a ballgame," Coach said. "Let's go. Everybody in."

They all crowded into the middle of the floor, and Lou led them in a cheer. With one final Hawks roar, they broke.

Carter dropped in beside him as they walked toward the tunnel. "So tonight? Yeah?" Carter asked.

"Fine, but you're buying."

"God, you're cheap," Carter grumbled.

"I'm not cheap when it comes to things I want. I don't want to do this, so if you want me to come, you're buying."

"Fine."

"Just so you know, I told Annie I'd pick her up when she was done with girls' night, so when she calls I'm out even if your mom is still eating."

"You can't leave in the middle of dinner. That's rude."

At the entrance to the field, Brandon spun back toward his friend and held out his arms. "Take it or leave it. When Annie calls I'm leaving."

"You're whipped," Carter grumbled.

"Yep."

Carter snorted. "Pathetic."

Brandon raised his eyebrow. "You need me to go to dinner to protect you from your mommy and you're calling me pathetic?"

"Touche," Carter dipped his head and nodded. "Yeah, I definitely need you to run interference, so I'll take what I can get."

"For the record, I'm ordering a big ol'steak," Brandon said, then jogged off to the outfield.

"How big are we talking?" Carter called after him.

Brandon glanced toward the stands. Damn, if there weren't so many people with cell phones constantly filming, he probably would have grabbed his junk, but he didn't really need that posted online. Instead he just yelled, "Hope you have a black credit card."

"You're an asshole," Carter called.

He wasn't wrong.

Didn't mean he wasn't going to eat his weight in steak. At least if he was chewing, he couldn't be answering questions. God, tonight sounded painful.

Well, not all of it. The idea of seeing Annie horny from the strippers was actually pretty fucking outstanding. He couldn't wait.

But first they had a game to win.

CHAPTER TWENTY-TWO

The moment Annie walked into the restaurant, she heard her group before she even saw them. Oh boy. It was going to be one of those nights. "Buckle up," she mumbled under her breath.

"Annie," the bride-to-be yelled her name from across the room.

Waving in acknowledgment, she wove her way past tables until she met her group. She smiled at Gabby and wrapped her arms around her sister's best friend. "Looking good, Gab's. I can't believe you're getting married."

She pulled back and looked at the bride-to-be in her veil and fitted white dress. If you could call it a dress. It looked more like lingerie than clothing, but if anyone could pull off a dress like that, it was Gabby.

"I know," Gabby squealed. "It's my last night of freedom, so we are going hard tonight."

"You don't get married for almost a month."

"After tonight I'm going to be so busy with the final arrangements, I won't have time for a proper girls' night."

Their friend Sydney threw her arm around Gabby's shoulder. "What she means is this is her last chance to get pulled up on stage at the strippers."

Annie's eyes widened. That sounded awful. "Do you want to be pulled up on stage?"

"Umm, yeah, of course I do," Gabby agreed.

"All right then. I'm gonna need a drink." Looking for her sister, she scanned the group of women. Finally, she spotted Ella at the other end of the table. Annie made her way toward her.

Ella stood and wrapped her arms around her. "Finally!"

"Sorry, you know me." She wrinkled her nose. "Little Miss Sensitive." She'd had to skip drinks and run home to shower off the conflicting scents. She didn't know which one was the problem, or the combination of them all but something had been making her allergies flare up. If the itch was anything to go by, it had only been a matter of time before things got ugly. The last thing she needed was some rash to take over her body.

"Definitely. I don't know why they used so many different scents. Each treatment made me smell like something else. Why not just pick one?"

Ella threw her head back and laughed. "Oh my god, you sound like Mom."

Annie shoved her sister. "Take that back."

"It's just wasteful to use so many products on one person," Ella mocked.

Annie swiped at her again. "Shut up, I don't sound like that." She chuckled. "Oh my god, do I?"

Ella snorted, then wrapped her arm around Annie's shoulder. "No. I'm just bugging you."

Gabby squealed at the other end of the table, drawing their attention to the bride-to-be. "What are you doing down here? As maid of honor, isn't it your job to be attached to the bride?"

"Nah, Gabby has enough people to hold court with. My job is to make sure everyone has fun. Nobody is checking off lame on the comment cards on my watch. Any chance you could have dinner down at this end with Gabby's cousin?" Ella pointed at the only woman Annie didn't know at the table. "She's just here for dinner and already grumbling, and you have a way of always making everyone feel so comfortable."

"No problem. What do I need to know?"

"Her name is Diane. She has two kids and from what Gabby said she's super religious and so..." Ella dragged off the implication.

"She's religious and came out to a bachelorette party?"

"Thus why she's skipping the Savage part."

Probably a good thing Diane was skipping the stripper portion of the evening. Annie expelled a deep breath. "I'm on it. I'll make sure she has a good time."

"Thank you. I owe you one. She's umm...she can be difficult."

Fantastic. She gave her sister's arm a little squeeze. "I got this. Go have fun."

Annie walked to the far end of the table and gestured to the vacant seat. "You mind if I sit down?"

"You drew the short straw on babysitting?" Diane asked.

"What? No, of course not. My sister Ella just said you were Gabby's cousin. I didn't realize she had any family coming."

"You're Ella's sister?" Diane studied her.

Annie couldn't tell from the way the woman was looking at her whether being Ella's sister was a good or bad thing. "I am."

"She's nice," Diane replied. "Not sure why she's friends with my cousin."

Okay, so it was going to be like that, was it? Annie smiled. "They've been friends forever. Once you go through braces and training bras together, the bond is set."

A small smile cracked on Diane's face. "I suppose that's true. Once someone helps you figure out how to put in a tampon, there are no secrets."

"That's for sure. My house saw some things it can't unsee." Annie chuckled.

"So you've been friends with Gabby a long time too, then?"

"Umm, I wouldn't say we were friends back then. I'm four years older than them, so we didn't have much in common when I lived at home. I'm more the honorary big sister of the group."

"That explains why you got stuck down at this end of the table," Diane said.

Annie flagged down the server. "Hi there, can I grab a drink?"

"Of course, for your group, we have three drink specials. We've got a blushing bride, a pretty in pink and a Malibu Barbie."

Okay, she didn't have a clue what any of those were. "What's the most popular?"

"The blushing bride." The server pointed at the woman beside her, drinking what looked kind of like a mimosa.

"Does that have champagne in it?"

"It does, yes."

Annie shuddered. "Pass. Any chance any of these have gin in them?"

"The pretty in pink does."

"Perfect, let's go with that one." Annie turned to Diane. "Do you want anything?"

Diane chewed the inside of her cheek and looked around. Finally, she shrugged. "What the heck. I'll have one of those blushing brides."

"All right, Diane," Annie said.

Diane giggled. "When in Rome, right?"

A couple minutes later, the server returned with their drinks. Annie held up her pink concoction to Diane to toast. The other woman clinked her glass against Annie's. "To the bride," Annie said.

"To the bride," Diane replied.

She glanced down the table toward the bride, and Ella caught her eye. "Oh my god," Ella mouthed, then made a drinking gesture. Her sister put her hand on her chest and mouthed. "Thank you."

Annie nodded and toasted her drink in that direction before taking a sip. Not bad.

Several hours later, she looked around Savage. When did she get so old? It didn't seem that long ago that a girls' night would last till the sun came up. But now? She just kind of wanted to go home. The one drink she'd tried to have at dinner didn't go down very well. It had tasted funny, probably because her nose was all out of whack from the spa. So now she was nursing a glass of water, surrounded by drunk people, while they fawned all over half-naked men.

Had there ever been a time when she'd have found the skeezy strippers hitting on them hot? God, she hoped not. But her girlfriends were sure eating it up. Especially the bride-to-be. It was kind of gross. The motherly big sister in her was rearing her ugly head, so if they were going to have a hope in hell of remaining friends after tonight, she needed to leave.

Pushing her way through the crowd, she elbowed the stripper out of the way so she could talk to the bride-to-be. "Gabby, I'm going to take off."

Gabby shoved her veil back from her face. "What? No, you can't leave. The guys have another set still."

The stripper, she thought his name was Ty, but she could be wrong, wrapped his arm around her shoulder. "Yeah, you can't leave yet. I was planning on bringing you up on stage with me."

She shuddered. Hell no. "No thanks, I'm good."

"Come on, beautiful, relax a little, have some fun."

"I'm sorry, but getting dry humped on stage in front of all my friends isn't really my idea of fun."

He leaned in close, his breath brushed against her neck as he spoke. "Trust me, you won't be dry."

She reared back and glared at him. "Eww. Does that really work?"

"Every time."

She shook her head. "Clearly not every time."

"We'll see when you're up on stage."

Oh hell no. Did this guy really think he'd bring her up on stage and she'd suddenly just melt beneath him? Not a chance in hell. "If you pull me up on stage, the only wet thing up there is going to be your bloody nose."

"No need to get aggressive, babe. I thought you were just playing hard to get."

"I'm not playing. I am hard to get and I am not interested."

"I am," Gabby called.

"I know you are, sugar." The stripper smiled at Gabby.

Annie blew out a breath and looked at her watch. 11:30. Was that too early? The lights flickered and the music turned off.

"Looks like we're up, ladies," Ty said, then turned to her. "Message received, gorgeous." He flicked her hair off her shoulder and winked.

What the hell did that mean?

"Ooh, I hope he brings me up on stage with him. He's so hot," Gabby said.

"Gabs, don't do anything you're gonna regret okay?"

Gabby giggled. "It's my bachelorette. I'm allowed to dance with strippers. It's a rule."

"Really? And is Dex allowed to dance with strippers too?"

Gabby's eyes hardened. "Why are you trying to ruin my night?"

What the hell? She wasn't trying to ruin anything. In fact it was the exact opposite. Watching her friends tonight was like some awful girls gone wild video. Not exactly the makings of a happy marriage. "I'm not."

"Yes, you are. Dex told me to have fun. That's what I'm doing." Gabby stumbled toward her and threw her arms around Annie's neck. "Just let me have fun."

"Okay. Sorry. Grind away on the sweaty stripper."

"Oh I will. I can't believe you're passing up that sexy man. Mmm, he's so yummy."

"I'm pretty happy with what I've got going on."

"Right, your sexy ballplayer. When do we get to meet him?"

"I don't know." Introducing him to her friends was one thing. Introducing him to her sister's was something else. Gabby had zero filter.

The music changed, and the women around them screamed. Four men stepped out on stage and began to move. Her friends were practically salivating as they watched.

As the song changed, Ty was the only man left on stage. He walked down and pointed at her and wiggled his finger to indicate she come forward.

Not a chance.

Did the guy seriously think she'd been playing?

Suddenly, one of their friends pushed Gabby forward. The bride-to-be practically ran to the stage.

Ty continued to look at her, then with a smirk he grabbed Gabby's hand and led her over to the chair in the middle of the stage.

Her girlfriends hooted around her as the only thing keeping the stripper and Gabby from having sex on stage was his jeans. Gabby's skirt had hiked up around her hips. Annie looked around their group. Several cell phones were aimed at the stage videotaping the show.

This whole thing was a bad idea.

Pulling her phone out of her purse, she opened her text thread with Brandon.

I'm watching this stripper dry hump Gabby on the stage

Jesus what the hell kind of stripper are you seeing?

It's got me thinking about how hot it would be if it was you

What stripping? Yeah not gonna happen.

What if I asked really nicely?

Don't think it's possible to be that nice

What if I begged?

No response

What if I got down on my knees and asked really nicely?

Keep talking

You want me down on my knees?

How many drinks have you had?

I've only had one all day. Besides even if I was drunk I've already given you permission to fuck me tonight.

You're killing me Doc.

I'm getting all hot just thinking about it.

Yeah strippers will do that to you.

It's not the stripper that's doing it. It's imagining you stripping.

Say the word and I will pick you up anytime.

She watched as Ty flipped Gabby onto her stomach while grinding against her. Suddenly he hooked his leg and they flipped over. Wow. Impressive. Kind of gross with a stripper, but if Brandon did something like that with her. Oh hell yeah.

Come get me.

Now?

Yes, please.

Sure, where are you?

Savage Male Revue.

Jesus

As soon as she read his response, she laughed. She could picture his face perfectly. The slightly grumpy look as he rolled his eyes.

Thank you.

Yep. I'll text you when I'm outside.

I'm not coming in.

Annie giggled again.

Party pooper

Three little dots formed and she waited for him to reply. It stopped and started again.

Leaving now

Nerves danced in her belly at the idea of seeing Brandon. It was funny, her friends were all going nuts for the guys on stage and it was doing nothing for her. But knowing Brandon was on his way instantly had a little zing floating through her.

She looked up on stage as Ty flipped Gabby onto her stomach and pulled her hair. Gabby looked like she'd died and gone to heaven.

Annie stood up and wove her way over to her sister. She crouched down beside Ella's chair. "Hey, I'm taking off."

Ella spun in her seat. "What? Why?"

"I just texted Brandon. He's on his way."

"Okay, if I had a big sexy guy like that waiting for me, I wouldn't want to be here either." Ella leaned in and wrapped her arms around her in a drunken hug. "I love you, Annie. You're the best sister ever."

Annie squeezed her sister. "I love you too, sweetie."

"Get it, Gabby," someone yelled.

Annie looked toward the stage. "Holy shit, did she just stick her hand down his pants?"

Ella laughed. "Looks like it."

Annie shook her head. "Wow. Okay, and you're fine with that?" she asked her sister.

Ella shrugged. "She's a big girl. She makes her own choices."

"But—" Annie started to speak, but Ella held up her hand.

"She's a big girl. I think we've both learned if I want to stay friends with Gabs I have to take the bad with the good and keep my mouth shut."

"I guess."

Annie's phone vibrated in her pocket.

"Is that Brandon?" Ella asked, then made kissy noises.

"You're a goofball."

Ella threw her arms around Annie's neck again. "I know, but you love me."

"I do." She kissed her sister's cheek. "I'm assuming you don't want a ride home?"

"Nope."

"Okay. Be safe." She pinned her sister with a stern look.

"I will."

"Text me when you get home."

"I'm not texting you when you're having sex with your boyfriend," Ella said.

"I won't answer it when I'm having sex." Annie laughed. "But I want to know when you're home. So text me."

"Okay, Mom."

"Thank you." Annie gave her sister another squeeze, then stood up. "Love you."

"Love you, too," Ella said. "Now go have hot sex."

She wiggled her eyebrows at her sister. "I plan to."

"Yes," Ella threw her arms up to cheer.

With a laugh, Annie turned and walked toward the exit.

CHAPTER TWENTY-THREE

B randon pulled up in front of Savage and threw it in park. He picked up his phone from the cup holder and pulled up his texts.

> Here

> You sure you don't want to come in? Lol

> Not a fucking chance

> hehe I'll be right out

A couple of minutes later, Annie walked out of the bar. She paused on the sidewalk and scanned the area.

The moment she spotted his car a smile spilt across her beautiful face. His chest tightened. He couldn't remember the last time someone had been truly excited to see him. Not Brandon Sims, professional ballplayer, but just him, plain old regular Brandon.

Annie opened the car door and hopped inside. Her butt had barely hit the seat before she leaned over and kissed him.

He'd expected a peck and what he got was so much more than that. Annie's tongue pressed into his mouth and she made a soft mewing sound that instantly made his dick hard. He cupped the back of her head and deepened the kiss, loving the way her body melted toward him.

"Damn," he murmured when he broke the kiss. "That's a hell of a hello."

"Mmm." She smiled, her eyes bright with excitement.

"How was your night?"

Annie dropped back in her seat, her head resting against the headrest as she turned to look at him. "It was good. Gabby was enjoying her last girls' night as a single lady."

He glanced at the male revue club. He could just imagine what that meant. "She get a lap dance?"

"Mmm, she got something alright."

He put the car in gear and pulled away from the sidewalk. "What's that mean?"

Annie shifted in her seat so she was facing him. "I think I'm too old to go to see the strippers."

Brandon snorted. "Why's that?"

"I don't know, it seemed kind of skeezy."

"Skeezy?"

"Yeah, I felt dirty. Don't get me wrong. I'm not a prude or anything. I just think some guy dry humping you on stage in front of a bunch of people is a bit much."

"Fair enough." He glanced over at her. "So I guess you didn't get up on stage."

"God no." She shuddered.

Brandon breathed a sigh of relief. He wasn't a jealous guy by nature, but the idea of some random guy grinding on Annie made him see red.

"I don't want some guy I don't know licking me, pulling my hair and pouring water all over me."

"Jesus, they do that?" They sure as hell didn't do that at the strip clubs he'd gone to.

"Yep, the guy put Gabby in a chair and then picked her up, chair and all and put her on the ground, then he did like this weird back up thing where he flipped her over and pulled her hair." She sighed. "Gabby seemed to be enjoying herself. But I'm not one to be dry humped on stage."

He tried to picture what she was talking about. The guy picked up her chair, then somehow flipped her over. Where did the chair go? "I have no fucking idea what you're talking about."

"I'll show you a video."

He glanced over at her. "You videotaped it?" That surprised him. Annie didn't seem like the kind of person who would videotape her friend at the strippers.

"God no, the guy has an Instagram page and shows that move a lot. He's the reason they picked this place tonight for the bachelorette party, so hopefully he'd do it to Gabby."

"Oh, all right. How does Gabby's future husband feel about this?"

Annie shrugged. "No idea, but I can't imagine he'd love it."

"Probably not."

"How would you feel about me being up there?"

He sat silent for several seconds before he finally admitted. "Wouldn't love it."

"Good." She trailed her hand down his arm. "I had no interest in being up there with him. But I think it would be pretty hot if you did that to me."

"Not a stripper, babe." He chuckled.

"No, but I've seen you dance and the way you move is so much sexier than what that guy was doing."

Brandon snorted.

"I'm serious. You're really strong." She shifted in her seat again. "I think it'd be really hot to have you pick me up like that and flip me over."

"Ri-ght." He raised a brow at her, then back to the road. "You're all drunk and hot and bothered by the stripper."

"First, I'm not drunk. Second, I'm hot and bothered by the thought of you doing to me what the stripper was doing. It had nothing to do with him, and everything to do with the idea of it being you."

He pulled the car into Annie's driveway.

"You're coming in right?" she asked.

He turned off the car and undid his seatbelt. "Well, yeah, I've got to see this magic stripper dance you're fantasizing about."

She smacked his arm. "Shut up."

Brandon rounded the front of the vehicle and held out his hand for Annie. She laced her fingers through his as they walked to her front door. As Annie unlocked her door, he placed his hand on her hip and kissed the top of her shoulder.

"How much did you drink tonight?"

She glanced over her shoulder. "Why? You still worried about taking advantage of me?"

"Little bit, yeah."

She turned and cupped his cheek. "That's very sweet, but I only had one drink the entire night. Definitely not drunk."

"Good." He placed his hands on her hips and backed her toward the door.

Annie placed her palm on his chest. "Uh uh. I'm still hoping you'll do this Magic Mike thing for me."

"Jesus," he groaned.

He reached around her and finished opening the door. Annie kicked off her high heels and padded barefoot into the living room. With a sigh, he followed her. If someone had told him six months ago that he'd even be thinking about trying some stripper move with a woman, he'd have laughed his ass off.

Now here he was seriously considering it. If Annie had been that turned on just thinking about, he could only imagine how hot she'd get with the real thing. Assuming he didn't humiliate himself.

He was an athlete. How hard could it be?

"All right, show me this video."

"Really?" she squealed and snagged her phone from her purse. She pulled up Instagram, then did a couple of swipes on her phone. Annie held out her phone so they could both see the video.

The guy buried his face in the woman's crotch, then as he stood he dragged his face up her body. His hands followed the same path, starting with her pussy and up over her breasts. Then he started grinding on her and shoved her hand down his pants.

"Holy fuck, I can't believe you do that at strip shows. That is so much different from when I go."

He definitely could see why Annie wouldn't be into that happening at the strip show. She played another video. This one the guy had the woman on the floor and backed into her, then flipped her over, pulled her hair, then flipped her back and started grinding on her.

Kind of wild that people wanted to do that at the strip club, but he absolutely could see how it might be fun for the two of them.

"All right, one more time so I can see that flip again." He pushed the rewatch button.

He scrubbed his hand over his face. The video looked easy enough. Fuck, he hoped he didn't mess it up. Executed properly, it would be hot. Wrong and there went his chances of getting laid.

He glanced around the living room. "We doing the whole chair thing?"

Annie's eyes widened as her mouth dropped open. "You're really going to do this?"

"Apparently I am."

"Eek," she squealed. Standing on her tiptoes, she gave him a quick kiss. "Thank you."

"Uh-huh. Don't expect much. That guy probably practiced that move for days before he actually did it at a show."

"Oh my god, this is going to be so good," she squealed again, then ran out of the room.

What the hell?

A moment later, she returned with a kitchen chair and plopped it down in the middle of the living room. She sat down, then promptly jumped up and began shoving the coffee table out of the way.

Jesus, they needed to clear the room? Just how elaborate did she think this was going to get?

Annie dropped into the chair and grinned at him. Her entire body vibrated with excitement.

Amused, he shook his head as he looked at her. "You got a song picked out?"

Her head bobbed enthusiastically. "I do."

A moment later, music started playing through the bluetooth speaker. He chuckled. "Mercy? Really."

"Mmm-hmm." She wiggled her hips in the chair. "You need to lose the shirt so I can get the full effect."

He smirked and reached behind his head and pulled his shirt off and tossed it onto the sofa. Annie sucked in a breath. Without breaking eye contact, he undid the top button of his jeans and slowly unzipped them.

Annie shifted her body, her legs dropped open slightly. He pushed his hand through his hair, took a breath, and moved to the music.

"Wow," she sighed.

He straddled her chair and did a body roll that made Annie gasp. He winked, then took her hand and dragged it down his body and into his pants. As much as he wanted to let it stay there, he pulled back before she got a chance to do much more than graze her fingers over his cock.

He dropped to his knees and spread her legs wide. Gripping her hips, he pulled her to the edge of the chair and pressed his mouth against her panties. He exhaled against her clit, and she shivered.

He hooked his finger in her panties, and she put her hand on top of his. "Uh uh, the stripper doesn't get to take the girl's panties off," she said.

"He also doesn't get to fuck her as soon as he's done dancing either, but I certainly plan to."

"Well, I'm sure we can bend the rules if you turn me on enough."

"Oh, is that right? You telling me your pussy isn't wet right now?" He dragged his nose over her damp panties and inhaled. "Because I'm going to call you a liar."

"No," her voice quivered. "I'm not saying that."

"Okay, baby, you want the whole fantasy thing. I get it." He crouched and grabbed the back of the chair and hoisted both her and the chair up in the air. In one quick move, he pulled her legs over his shoulders so her pussy was in his face and dropped the chair with a bang.

Annie gasped. "Oh my god that was hot."

He grinned and nipped her inner thigh.

Holding her hips, he let her body drop so she was upside down, Her legs tightened around his back, pulling her pussy closer to his face. He ran his tongue along her seam through her panties.

"May—maybe I should have let you take those off."

"Too late now, darlin," he said as he pressed his tongue into her pussy through the material.

"Oh my god," she moaned.

He arched his back and bucked his hips at the same time he grabbed her waist and pulled her upright again. Moving to the beat, he spun and lay her down on the ground. He dragged his mouth down her chest, over her stomach, and paused at her pussy. He could feel how hot and wet she was through her panties. And he fucking loved it.

He stood with his back to her. Glancing over his shoulder, he winked, then jumped down, hooked his legs with hers and flipped her onto her stomach. He grabbed her hair and pulled her head back so he could plant a searing kiss on her.

She tried to move her arms, and he flipped her back over. Annie's lust filled eyes watched him. Kneeling over her chest, he grinned and pushed his hair back from his face. He licked his fingers, then reached behind him and dipped his finger beneath the elastic leg of her panties and rubbed his finger around her clit before he buried it in her pussy. Annie's head dropped back and her eyes closed as she moaned.

"Don't think you need these anymore." He peeled her panties down her legs and tossed them away.

Standing, he moved so he was at her head and looked down at her panting face. He dragged his hand down his body, slid his hand into his pants, and palmed his dick. He was so fucking hard. He'd expected the dance to turn her on, but he hadn't expected it to turn him on just as much.

He jumped into a plank, with his head at her pussy and his dick at her mouth. He gyrated against her. Annie's entire body trembled. He slithered down her body, then hooked his legs with hers and flipped her again. She gasped and arched her back.

Her hand snaked around his neck and she held on. "B, you need to fuck me," she begged.

"You want me to stop dancing?"

"I want you to stop teasing me and fuck me."

"Gladly," he growled.

He flipped her onto her back. Kissed his way down her stomach, then crouched down and hooked her legs over his shoulder and picked her up.

"B, stop, I said I needed you to fuck me. I can't take any more."

"Oh, I'm going to fuck you. Don't you worry." He definitely could understand why a guy would get off on this.

Brandon carried her over to the wall and pressed her back against it. He boosted her hips up slightly and buried his face in her pussy.

"Oh my god," Annie moaned, bucking her hips toward his face.

Her hand slapped against the wall. He could feel her searching for something to hold on to as he fucked her with his tongue. Finally, she grabbed the edge of the bookcase and the angle of her body shifted.

He moved his face back and looked up at her. "You good?" he asked.

"Don't you dare stop," she ordered and pushed her hand against the back of his head.

Brandon chuckled. He nipped her clit and Annie bucked against his face. He nibbled and sucked the tight little bud. Loving the way her nails dug into his scalp as she moved against him.

He cupped her ass with both of his hands and pulled her hips off the wall. Brandon thrust his tongue into her pussy, fucking her with his tongue. Annie's breath hitched, letting him know she was close. He slurped her clit into his mouth and sucked hard. Loving the way she exploded against his mouth. Annie's legs clamped down on his ears as she bucked against him. He continued to suck her clit until she went boneless above him.

With her legs still wrapped over his shoulder, he held her in place against the wall to give her a minute to catch her bearings.

"Oh my god, Brandon," she said, then chuckled. "Holy shit."

"We're not done yet, Doc," he said. Holding onto her, he backed up to the sofa and sat down, then muscled her off his shoulder onto his lap. "I want you to ride me," he told her.

Annie nodded her head. She licked her lips, then looked around. "One sec, let me grab a condom."

"There's one in my back pocket. Let me lose the jeans and I'll grab it."

"Uh uh, the jeans are staying on. In my stripper fantasy you aren't naked."

Brandon draped his arms along the back of the sofa. "It's your fantasy, Doc. Use me however you want."

She stood up, and a moment later she was back with a condom. Standing at the edge of the sofa, she licked her lips as she looked down at him. The look of pure lust on her face made his dick harder than ever. It flexed against the rough denim fabric.

"Just pull your jeans down your hips a little like you need to be able to pull them up if someone catches us."

Brandon smirked at her. "Damn. Okay." He hooked his hand in the waistband and slid his jeans down just far enough for him to pull out his cock.

Annie bit her lip as she stared at his cock. He wrapped his hand around his dick and slid his palm down the length. "This what you had in mind?" he asked.

She nodded, then held the condom out to him.

"You aren't putting it on for me?" he asked.

"Mmm mmm. I want to watch you do it."

Holding eye contact with her, he ripped the wrapper open with his teeth, then rolled the condom in place.

He held out his hand for her. "Ride me, Annie."

She placed her thigh on the edge of the couch, then set the other one on the other side of him so she was straddling his waist. Annie reached between them and gripped his cock in her hand. He clenched his jaw and bit back a groan.

With a teasing smile, Annie placed him at her entrance, then slowly lowered herself down. Her hot pussy clamped down on his cock. "Jesus, you feel good," he told her.

"So do you." She shifted her pelvis, then pulled almost all the way off him before firmly seating herself again.

"Fuck," he said through gritted teeth. "Your turn to tease me now?"

Annie swiveled her hips. "Maybe."

Brandon grabbed the back of her head and threaded his fingers through her long, dark hair, wrapping it around his hand. Annie gasped, her eyes closed, her head dropping back as he pulled her hair slightly.

He gripped her hip with his other hand, holding her where he wanted as he drove into her. Annie rocked up and down on his cock as he thrust up to meet her. He shifted lower on the couch so he could drive deeper. Annie's eyes darkened with the new position. Her breath hitched, and she rode him harder.

"Yes, right there, Brandon, right there," she gasped.

He tightened his grip on her hair as Annie's pussy clenched around him. His balls pulled up tight. "I'm close, Doc."

"Me too." Annie swiveled her pelvis and ground her clit down on his pubic bone.

"Yes," she hissed as she came. Her pussy pulsed against his cock, clamping down on him like a vise.

He thrust one last time. The orgasm that ripped through him took his breath as every muscle in his body went rigid.

Annie's head rested on his shoulder, the rest of her body limp against his. Both of them completely spent.

Holy shit. He could die right now and be completely fine with that. "That was incredible."

Once he'd caught his breath, he rubbed his hand gently up and down her back. "I can't stay too late. I have to get home to Leo," he said.

She pressed a kiss against his shoulder. "I kind of want you to leave now," she told him.

He shifted his weight so he could see her. "What do you mean you want me to leave now?"

Annie sucked in her lips and gave a cute little shrug. "It kind of gives more dirty fantasy vibe if you just kind of use me and leave."

"Yeah?" He raised an eyebrow at her, and she nodded. "You keep surprising me, Doc."

"Is that a good thing?"

"It's definitely not a bad thing." He cupped the back of her neck and kissed her. Purposely tangling his tongue with hers, hoping she could still taste herself on his lips. If they were doing the dirty fantasy thing, then they were doing it all the way.

When he pulled away, they were both breathing hard.

"That was fun," Annie said.

Brandon smirked at the way she remained in character. "Yeah, it was."

He gave her hip a little tap. "Up you get, darlin'. As fun as this was, I've got a few things I need to do before I can call it a night."

Annie bit back a smile. The crinkle at the corner of her eyes betrayed her amusement. "Right, of course," she said. "So any chance I can see you again?" she batted her eyelashes at him coyly.

"I'm heading out of town tomorrow night after the game. It's a five game road series, so I'll call you."

Annie picked up his t-shirt off the floor and pulled it over her head. He eyed her. "What are you doing? That's mine."

"I like it, so I'm going to keep it," she said.

He let his gaze trail down her long legs beneath the hem of his shirt. Fuck, he loved seeing her in his clothes. He gripped the front of his t-shirt and pulled her against him. "You're getting quite a collection of my clothes."

"I know. I like it."

"I do too." He pressed a kiss against her lips, then gave her ass a little swat. "Be good while I'm away. I'll call you from the road."

"Good luck at the games."

He grabbed his sweatshirt off the floor and pulled it over his head. Once he was fully dressed, he turned to her. "Night, Doc."

"Night, Brandon. Thanks for doing all this." She smiled shyly at him.

"Anytime, Doc," he said before walking to the front door.

At the door, he paused. "Lock this behind me," he said. "I'll call you from the road." He took one last look at her before he opened the door and stepped outside.

As hot as the fantasy was, a little part of him was disappointed he wasn't spending the night.

CHAPTER TWENTY-FOUR

The team walked off the field with their heads down. They'd played like complete shit.

And where the fuck was Carter?

Brandon rubbed his sternum as fear for his best friend made it hard to swallow. During the game, he'd knocked it down. Done what he needed to stay focused. But now that the game was over the fear crashed into him, gripping him tight. Where was he?

Something had to be wrong. There was no way Carter just wouldn't have shown up for the game. Fuck. What if something serious happened? He needed to find him and make sure he was okay.

They'd barely made it into the locker room when Coach Schneider called them all to attention.

"Tough loss tonight, I'm about to make it even worse. I know we were all worried about Carter and why he wasn't at the game. We got word that he's been in a car accident. He's in surgery. Unfortunately, I don't know anything more than that." Coach made eye contact with him. "They took him to UC Hospital. That's all I know at the moment. Dr. Dave is on his way there and will update us once he knows more."

Brandon dropped onto the bench. Pete clasped his shoulder. "You okay?"

He scrubbed a hand over his face. "Umm, yeah."

"You're heading to the hospital?" Pete asked.

"Yeah." He pulled his bag out of his locker. He could shower when he got home later. "How do they not know more? He missed the entire fucking game. Obviously, he got hurt before then." He ripped his jersey over his head. "Surgery could mean anything."

"I don't know, man. But I'm sure coach would tell us if he knew more." Pete eyed him. "You gonna be okay to drive?"

"What?" Brandon's head snapped up. "Yeah, I'm fine." He grabbed one of the towels off the shelf and quickly wiped any dust off himself, then threw his clothes on. He glanced over at Pete and Smitty. "I'll see you there."

Brandon stood in the waiting room, surrounded by his teammates as they waited impatiently for the doctor to come out and talk to them. Fuck, he hated hospitals. The noise, the smell. Everything. Typically he avoided it at all costs. Way too many memories from when his mom was sick.

His phone buzzed in his pocket. Unknown name and an area code he didn't recognize. Decline.

A moment later, his phone buzzed with a text message.

Is this Brandon Sims' number?

What that hell? Sorry buddy, but no chance he was answering that. The last thing he needed was some weirdo knowing they'd tracked down his number.

This is Sonya Daye. Carter's mom.

Holy shit.

Sonya, yes this is Brandon.

His phone instantly rang. The same number appeared on the screen.

He swiped to answer the call.

"Oh thank god, Brandon. How's Carter? Have you been able to see him?"

"Not yet. We're still waiting for more of an update."

Sonya started crying. "They had to—to take—" she sobbed. "His leg, Brandon. He lost his leg," she wailed.

He dropped onto the seat with a thud. "What?"

"They had to take his leg." Sonya sniffled. "They couldn't save it."

"How do you—how do you know? I mean, we haven't seen the doctor. Maybe they could." Carter couldn't have lost his leg. They would have told them that, wouldn't they? They wouldn't just leave them all out here wondering when they were in there taking his fucking leg. She had to be wrong.

"No, we spoke to the doctor." She began to cry again. A moment later, a male voice came on the line.

"Brandon, it's Paul Daye. Sorry, my wife is under-standably upset. We are just heading to the airport to catch a flight. We'll be there as soon as we can. I told Dr. Avery that you were our contact point until we arrived."

"Me?"

"Yes, we know you. Carter trusts you. So we've asked that they treat you as the family contact until we arrive."

"What about the team? Shouldn't it be Coach or something?"

"Carter lost his leg. The team won't give a damn about him now," Paul growled.

"That's not true." Was it?

Paul made what sounded like a scoffing sound. "We'll see." Silence hung in the air.

Finally Paul spoke. "It'll be politics with the team, Brandon. You're his friend. We need you to do this for us. We are at the airport just waiting for our flight. We won't be available when we are in the air. But keep me posted. I'll make sure my phone is on whenever possible."

The doors opened and everyone stopped talking. "The doctor just came out," Brandon said into the phone.

"Call me back once you've talked to him," Paul ordered.

"Will do," he said, then flicked his phone off.

"Which one of you is Brandon?" the doctor asked.

Brandon raised his hand and stood up, and the coaching staff all followed suit. They met in the middle of the room.

"Brandon." The doctor squared his shoulders. "I'm Dr. Avery. Chief of Orthopedics."

"Hi," Brandon said, then pointed at the man beside him. "This is Cal Schneider. He's the team manager."

Dr. Avery nodded in acknowledgement.

"How is he?" Brandon asked.

"He's in recovery." The doctor paused. "He's heavily sedated, so it might be a couple of hours before he wakes up."

"His mom said you had to take his leg," Brandon said.

Coach gasped beside him. "What?"

He could practically feel the air in the room stand still as a collective gasp echoed around him. Brandon flicked a glance at his teammates and coaches, then back at the doctor. "Is that true?"

"Unfortunately, yes, we had to amputate his leg below the knee."

"Jesus," Brandon muttered.

"You couldn't save the leg? Did he agree to that? Was he even conscious?" Coach snarled. "He's a professional athlete for god sakes. You should have done whatever it took to save it."

"We do our best to save all of our patients regardless of who they are." The doctor pinned the coach with a stare. "Unfortunately in this case, there was no decision to make. The accident made it for us."

Jesus that sounded horrible. Poor Carter. He couldn't even imagine what his friend had gone through. "He's alive, that's all that matters." Brandon dragged his hand down his mouth.

"You're right," Coach replied. "Sorry."

"When can we see him?" Brandon asked.

"Like I said, it could be some time before he wakes up." He looked around the waiting room. "And even then he'll need to rest, so no more than two visitors at a time once we get him to his room. While he's on this floor, it's family only, which his parents said means you."

"Yeah," Brandon mumbled. "Other than his leg he's going to be okay?"

"It was an incredibly difficult surgery. By the time the paramedics got him here, he was in shock and had lost a lot of blood. But he's young and healthy, so he should make a full recovery."

"Thanks Doctor." Brandon held out his hand for the doctor to shake.

The moment the doctor left the team swarmed around him. Brandon's ears buzzed as he tried to process what the doctor had said. What were the odds he'd have to deal with two amputations in a six-month period? Somehow he didn't think Carter's recovery would be quite as smooth as Leo's.

Brandon's ears slowly came back online as the buzzing lowered.

"They should have let him die," Johnny said.

"What the fuck did you just say?" Brandon roared at his teammate.

"If it was me, I wouldn't want to live without my leg. His life is over."

Brandon grabbed his teammate by the scruff of his shirt and yanked him hard toward him. "If you fucking spew that kind of shit anywhere near Carter I will fucking end you." He tightened his grip. "You hear me?"

Johnny nodded his head. Brandon couldn't make his fingers ease their hold on his teammate's shirt.

A hand gripped his shoulder. "Ease up, B," Pete's voice cut through the roaring in his head. But he couldn't unclench from Johnny's shirt. He was afraid if he let go he'd plow his fist into the asshole's face.

Pete's hand dug into his shoulder tightly. "Brandon, let go," Pete ordered.

Brandon pulled Johnny in closer and a sick piece of him enjoyed the flash of fear in his teammate's eyes. "If you plan on sticking around here, you better change your fucking tune real quick, because I hear anything like that again, Saunders won't be able to save you. You hear me?"

Johnny's head bobbed up and down in rapid agreement.

"Good." Brandon gave him a little shove as he released him.

Johnny stumbled back and quickly moved to the back of the group, as far away from him as possible.

"Sims, I know you're upset. We all are, but you can't be taking it out on your teammates," Coach Schneider said.

Brandon raised an eyebrow. Was he kidding right now?

"This is a shitty situation and Carter is going to need all of us when he wakes up." Coach clapped his hand on Brandon's back, then turned to the rest of the group.

"Carter isn't going to be able to have visitors until tomorrow, so there's not much more any of you can do here tonight. Why don't you all head home to your loved ones." Coach glanced at Brandon, then back at the group. "I'm sure the family appreciates you all being here. Sims is the family contact until they get here. So if there are any updates we'll keep you posted."

One by one his teammates came up and told him they were sorry. He didn't have a clue how he was supposed to reply to that. All he could do was nod.

Finally it was just a couple of the coaching staff and Pete, Smitty and Ryan left. "You gonna be okay?" Pete asked.

"Yeah."

"You staying until Carter wakes up?" Ryan asked.

Brandon nodded. There was no way he was going home before he saw Carter with his own eyes. The doctor had said he was going to be okay, but he needed to see that for himself. The buzzing in his ears came back and he rolled his shoulders to try to relax. Fuck hospitals.

"You want me to stick around with you?" Pete asked.

"Nah, it's fine." He was a big boy. If he could handle the hospital when he was a kid, there was no way he was pussing out as an adult. "I gotta call his parents and fill them in anyway."

"Did you call Annie yet?" Smitty asked.

"I sent her a text when I got here and said I'd call when I knew anything. I'll call her after I call his parents back." What he wanted was to be alone. He was hanging on by a thread and he really didn't need an audience for the show.

He pasted on what he hoped was a reassuring smile. "Appreciate you hanging back, but I'm good. Go home. Be with your families."

"Why don't I hang until you talk to her, make sure she can come so you aren't alone," Pete suggested.

"I appreciate it, but I'm good, man."

"Make sure you call Annie," Smitty said. "Trust me, it'll be easier with her beside you."

And like she had been conjured, suddenly there she was, coming down the hall toward them.

His chest tightened. "Wha—what are you doing here?" he asked as she hurried toward them.

"I came as soon as I could." She jogged the last couple of steps, then threw her arms around his waist, wrapping him tightly in her embrace.

Emotion clogged his throat.

She came.

Closing his eyes, he rested his forehead on the top of her head.

"Oh Brandon, I'm so sorry," she whispered.

He tightened his arms around her. Until she'd arrived, he hadn't realized how much he wanted her there. He was used to doing things alone. Preferred it usually. But Smitty was right. It was better with her here. Having Annie in his arms took the buzzing away. He didn't feel like he needed to run. "I'm glad you're here."

"Me too." She squeezed him, then stepped back. "How's Carter?"

Tears burned behind his eyes, and he shrugged. His best friend had lost his leg. He'd never play ball again.

Annie grabbed his hand. "Talk to me."

"We're gonna take off. Call us when you know more," Pete said.

Brandon nodded. He watched as his teammates walked away. The coaching staff sat huddled on the chairs in the far corner of the room, probably discussing what they were going to do next.

"I gotta call Carter's parents back, quickly."

"Of course."

He dialed Sonya's number. It rang several times, then went to voicemail. "Hi Sonya, Carter is out of surgery. The doctor said he's doing well. He's still resting. They're going to take me in to see him shortly. I'll stay with him until you arrive. Have a safe flight."

With a sigh, he stuck his phone back in his pocket and looked at Annie. She smiled sadly. "So surgery?" she asked.

"Yeah." He dropped his head back and growled. "Fuck."

Annie stood silently beside him, not saying a thing, not pressing him to talk like most people would. He pressed a kiss against the top of her head. "You want to sit?" he asked.

"Sure."

Brandon dropped into the chair, and Annie took the one beside him. Still she waited. He didn't know how she knew he needed time to process, but she did. He scrubbed his hand over his face and dragged it down his jaw, then sighed. "They had to amputate his leg."

Annie gasped. "Oh my god." She covered her mouth with her hand. "But he's okay?"

"I think so. The doctor said he lost a lot of blood and I got the feeling the surgery took a while, but the doctor said he'd be okay."

"That's good." Annie shifted and placed her hand on his knee. "And how are you?"

He shrugged again. "I don't know. This sucks."

A cleaning person walked past with their trolley and suddenly he was nine years old again watching his mom cry in pain, while apologizing for puking on the floor.

"Brandon?"

Coming out of the memory, he blinked over at Annie.

"Where'd you go?" she asked.

"Nowhere, sorry."

"Brandon, talk to me." She slid closer so their knees were touching.

"Sorry, just thinking about my mom."

"What were you thinking about?"

"It's stupid really. I was just remembering this time my mom was sick and puked on the floor and housekeeping was kind of annoyed that I didn't think to give her a bucket to use." He gave a little laugh. "I didn't even know they had them."

"That must have been really hard to see your mom like that."

"Yeah, it sucked." He dropped his shoulders. The housekeeping cart squeaked down the hall and he winced.

"Stand up," Annie said.

"What?" He looked around the empty waiting room.

"Stand up."

"Why?"

"Just do it, please." Annie hopped up and held out her hand.

With a huff, he pushed to his feet. "Now what?"

"Shake."

"Huh?"

"Shake." Annie started shaking her arms and wiggling her head and body. "Shake," she ordered.

Brandon rolled his eyes, then shook his arms.

"No, really shake," Annie said as she started shaking her arms around and bouncing on her feet.

Good lord. He shook more vigorously.

"Jump," Annie said.

Feeling like an idiot, he hopped and shook beside her. Oh Jesus. Emotion clogged his throat. Where the fuck did that come from? "Umm?" He looked at Annie for help.

"Keep shaking."

He stopped jumping and kicked his foot out, then the other, then rolled his neck and his chest eased. The emotion slid away. After a few more seconds, he stopped moving. He looked at Annie. "What the hell was that?"

"You feel better?" she asked.

He rolled his shoulders. "Yeah actually." Surprisingly, he felt significantly calmer than he had before.

"Good."

"How'd you know?" Who the hell would have thought shaking would help calm him down?

"I learned it at a conference. Animals shake after a fight-or-flight response. People don't, but they should."

"I wasn't planning on going anywhere."

"I know, but your body was starting to think about it. We just shook to move it through."

"Thanks, Doc. That's something I would have expected from Rayne. I didn't realize you knew that kind of stuff too."

"Wow, high praise," Annie teased. "I wouldn't put me in the same category as Rayne, but I'm glad it helped."

He took her hand and brought it to his mouth and placed a kiss against her palm. "Thank you."

"Anytime."

Dr. Avery walked toward them, and Brandon stood up. "How's Carter?"

The doctor looked at Annie.

"This is my girlfriend, Annie Wright. This is Carter's surgeon." Girlfriend. It was kind of ridiculous to call a grown woman his girlfriend, but he didn't really know what else to say. Partner was so—whatever. It didn't matter.

"Nice to meet you." Annie smiled at the doctor.

"Nice to meet you as well." The doctor nodded at her. "Carter woke up briefly, but he's back asleep now. I expect him to be that way for several hours given the medication we have him on. You can go in and see him now."

"Great thanks. Just give me a sec," he told the doctor.

"Of course."

Brandon turned to Annie. "I'm gonna sit with Carter till his parents' get here."

"You want me to stay?" she asked.

"No, no, it's gonna be a bit still since they were flying in from Vancouver."

"Are you sure? I don't mind waiting."

He wrapped his arms around her waist and pulled her into a hug. "No, you go home and get some rest." He kissed the top of her head. What would he have done without her? "Thanks, Doc. I really appreciate you coming."

"Nowhere else I'd rather be," she said.

He couldn't help himself he leaned down and pressed a kiss to her lips. "Thanks."

"Call me later," she said and then turned to leave.

Strangely, he didn't want her to leave. "Doc, hold up," he called.

Annie turned and looked at him expectantly.

He pulled his keys from his pocket and pulled his house key off. "You want to stay at my house?"

"Oh sure, you need me to check on Leo?"

Oh shit. He'd forgotten all about Leo. Fuck. "Yeah, that too, but I just kind of wanted you to be there when I got home."

Annie smiled back at him and his chest tightened. "You got it."

"Leo's in my truck in the parking lot. Can you grab him too?" Hopefully, he hadn't destroyed too much in the truck. Thank god, he'd decided to drive his crappy beater today.

"Of course."

He handed her the separate house key. "House." He held out the truck keys. "I drove the truck today."

"I know I saw it when I parked." Annie slipped the keys in her pocket, then stood on tiptoes and pulled his face down to hers. She gave him a kiss. "I'll leave the keys at the nurses' station."

"You can just text me and I'll come find you," he said.

"It's fine. I'll just leave them with the nurse so you can be with Carter." She kissed him again. "Give Carter my best."

"Will do." He stood and watched her leave.

The doctor cleared his throat. "Ready?"

Was he?

No, not really. What the hell was he going to say to Carter? Brandon took a deep breath. "Lead the way."

CHAPTER TWENTY-FIVE

Hovering on the edge of sleep, she didn't want to open her eyes. Brandon's warm body curled against hers. His morning erection poked against her butt. Mmm, she loved waking up with him. With his schedule, it didn't happen nearly enough. His hand wrapped around her waist, and she wiggled back tightly against him.

"Unless you want to be fucked right now you better stop that, Doc," Brandon's sleep roughened voice sent a shiver through her, making her nipples tighten. She wiggled again.

He chuckled. "There's my girl."

Annie shook her hips again, loving the way his cock hardened even more against her ass.

Brandon's fingers slid up her stomach and he cupped her breast. Annie shifted to turn toward him.

Suddenly, a wave of nausea ripped through her. She shoved against him and he instantly released her.

Launching herself off the bed, she raced to the bathroom, slamming the door behind her.

She dimly registered Brandon's worried voice through the door, asking if she was okay as she threw up.

Annie rested her head in her hand as she caught her breath and groaned. Throwing up was the worst. Everything about it was disgusting, including hugging the bowl afterwards. Gross. Taking a deep breath, she tested how she felt. Not bad. She sat back on her heels and waited to see if another round was going to hit. Nope, seemed fine.

She pushed herself off the floor and walked to the sink to brush her teeth. Looking in the mirror, she sighed. Guess she wasn't putting this conversation off any longer. With everything that happened the day before with Carter, she hadn't been sure if now was the time to tell him, but apparently her body was deciding for her.

After several calming breaths, she pulled open the door prepared for her entire world to change.

She stepped into the bedroom and Brandon jumped up from his seated position on the end of the bed and rushed toward her.

"You okay." He brushed her hair back from her face and stroked her cheek affectionately.

"Yeah." She dropped her head against his chest. Damn it, this wasn't how she wanted to have this discussion.

Brandon's hands gently rubbed up and down her back as he held her. "Why don't you get back in bed?" he said as he stepped back from her. She instantly missed the safe protection of his arms.

Annie's stomach rolled, whether from nausea or nerves she wasn't sure. She looked around for her purse and saw it sitting on the floor by the dresser. She picked it up and took the sleeve of saltines out from the depths. She pulled one out and nibbled the corner.

"Uh, why do you have saltines in your purse?" Brandon asked.

With a sigh, Annie looked at him. "Maybe you should sit down."

Brandon's back stiffened. "Why?"

She gestured to the bed again. "Sit please."

He rubbed the back of his neck nervously and rocked back on his heels. "I'm not sure I want to."

"Fine." Feeling a little lightheaded, she walked over to the bed and rested the pillow against the headboard, then sat down with her back against it. Needing a little more time, she nibbled on another cracker.

"What's going on, Doc?"

"Umm, so—" She tucked her hair behind her ear nervously. "Turns out I'm pregnant. Surprise." She laughed nervously.

Brandon stumbled backwards and rested his hand on the dresser. "You're what?"

"I'm pregnant."

"No, no, you can't be. We always use protection." He shook his head, then paced around the room. "Nope, no, no, no. How long have you known?" he asked.

She swallowed past the lump in her throat. "Umm, I started to suspect it a couple of weeks ago, but I've known for sure for about a week."

Brandon's eyes narrowed as he pinned her with a stare. "You've known for a week and you're just telling me now? The day after my best friend almost died."

Uncomfortable with the admission, she looked down at her lap. "Obviously the timing isn't great," she admitted, but honestly, was there ever a good time to say 'surprise unexpected baby alert'?

"The timing isn't great, you think?" He shook his head. "I gotta take Leo for a pee."

"You're taking the dog out now?"

His chest rose and fell as his body vibrated with barely contained energy that she could feel from across the room. "Jesus, Annie, you've had two weeks to think about this. Give me a minute to catch up. Please."

He walked to Leo's crate and crouched down to open the door. The dog walked out, but instead of moving, Brandon put his back against the wall and slowly slumped down to the floor. Rubbing his chest, his mouth opened and closed like a fish as she helplessly watched.

"Brandon? Are you okay?" What was happening here? While she hadn't expected him to be thrilled about this, she hadn't really expected him to look like he was going to have a panic attack either.

She got off the bed and stepped toward him. He looked at her with wild eyes. She stepped closer and he held up his hand like he didn't want her to come near him.

Oh, that hurt. She stepped back to give him space.

He pulled the collar of his shirt away from his neck and looked up at the ceiling like he was struggling to breathe. He pulled his collar further away.

Leo nudged his arm. Almost unconsciously, Brandon shifted to give the dog room as he continued to breathe rapidly.

What was she supposed to do?

After a couple of minutes, Brandon wrapped his arms around the dog and pulled him against his chest. Leo curled his head into the crook of Brandon's neck.

Okay, that really hurt too. Why was he pushing her away and cuddling the dog when she was right there? She'd never been more jealous of a dog in her life.

Not knowing what to do, she sat back against the headboard and brought a pillow to her chest.

Finally he looked at her, his eyes shining with unshed tears. The pain on his face made her stomach knot. She braced herself for what he was about to say. "I'm sorry, Annie, I can't."

"What do you mean you can't?" She gripped her knees tighter.

Brandon let out a shuddering breath. "I just...I can't...I can't be a dad."

"It's a little late for that, Brandon. I'm pregnant."

"I know." He dragged his hand over his mouth. "I'm sorry. I just I can't be a part of that."

Her spine stiffened. Was he kidding right now? "Not really an option, Brandon."

"But it is," he said.

Fear and anger battled in her gut. He was not doing this. There was no way. He was freaking out that was all. She took a deep breath. "Look I understand this is a lot to process. Why don't you go have a shower and give yourself some time to clear your thoughts? Like you said I've had a couple weeks to process this and you haven't."

"It's not—"

"Go have a shower." She cut him off before he could finish speaking. "I think we both need a minute."

Brandon pushed away from the wall and walked into the bathroom without saying anything else. The bathroom door closed behind him and she pulled her knees up to her chest and wrapped her arms around her legs. Emotion clogged her throat.

He better come out of that bathroom in a different mindset or she was going to lose her shit. It's not like she got pregnant on her own. They'd both been there. She tapped her foot anxiously on the mattress.

This was not happening. She hadn't met the man of her dreams only for him to be the kind of guy who walked away from his own kid. There was no way. Tears burned in her eyes.

After what felt like an eternity, he emerged from the bathroom. One look at his body language and she kind of wished he'd go back inside to give her time to prepare. He looked so defeated. Damn it. "Not feeling any better?" she asked.

"I don't want to be a dad, Annie."

"Well that's too bad because you're going to be one."

"Obviously I'll give you money and sign whatever you need me to sign." The coward couldn't even look her in the eyes when he said it.

She stormed over to him and planted her feet in front of him. "You'll sign whatever I need? Are you fucking kidding me?"

"Keep your voice down," Brandon said.

"Why? You don't want the world knowing you're acting like a piece of shit?"

"How am I a piece of shit? Because I want to take care of you and my kid?"

"Take care of? Are you kidding me, Brandon? You want nothing to do with us."

"I'm not cut out to be a parent. Jesus Annie, look at what I came from. I can't do that to a kid. I won't."

"Don't give me that shit, Brandon."

"I can't be a dad."

She shook her head. "That's too bad because my kid sure as hell deserves one. But you're right, it deserves one that would slay a dragon for them, not a coward. I thought the guy who rescued an abused dog would rise to the occasion."

"A kid isn't a dog."

"No, it sure isn't." Her chest constricted. "It's sad you can't see what's inside you."

Brandon made a scoffing sound. "I know all too well what's inside me."

She grabbed his arm and poked his tattoo sleeve. "You also have the woman who drew this inside you. The woman who, on her deathbed, drew pictures and created stories to help her son get through her illness. The mother who put her own pain aside to care for her son. Are you seriously saying his shitty genes are more powerful than hers?"

"I'm not saying they are more powerful, but they are fucking there. He's in me." He thumped his hand against his chest. "Don't you get that? I have that sickness inside me. I can't do that to a kid."

"Grow up Brandon. We are all damaged. We all have scars. You can either let it define you or you can do the work to change your story." She poked his tattoo again.

"I never met your mom, but I'm pretty sure I know which one she'd choose."

"Easy to say from your ivory tower, Annie. With your two parents and your picket fence."

"No one's life was perfect, Brandon, and each generation has the opportunity to do better."

"Yeah, well, sometimes better still isn't good enough," he muttered. "And I'm not willing to take that chance. I'll make sure you have more than enough money for everything."

"I don't want your fucking money," she screamed. "I want you to be a fucking man."

"That's what I'm trying to do."

"Bull shit. A man would do whatever it took to be there for his family. Not run away and hide."

"I'm not hiding," he said stubbornly.

The man was infuriating. Why couldn't he see who he could be? She couldn't do it for him, and it was pointless to keep doing what they were doing. She scooped up her purse from the floor. "You're being a coward, Brandon, and you need help."

"I don't need help."

"Yeah, you do," she scoffed. "And if you won't do it for me, for your child, then at least do it for yourself because this..." She waved her arm to encompass the room. "Is bullshit. This isn't normal, Brandon. That panic attack should tell you something."

"Yeah, that my best friend just lost his fucking leg yesterday and today you drop a bomb on me with this kid thing."

"This kid thing?" she sneered.

"Yeah, you blindsided me and maybe I wasn't as articulate as I could be."

"As articulate as you could be? Really? So you're saying with a little more time you'd be all over having a child?"

"No." He sighed. "Look Annie, I wish I could be who you want me to be."

Tears burned behind her eyes, but she refused to let them fall. "But you are, Brandon, that's the thing. You just don't see it."

"You're right. I don't. Because I can't do that to a kid. I wouldn't inflict what I had on my worst enemy, let alone someone I loved."

"So don't." She stepped toward him and he stepped back.

"I wish it was that easy."

"It is if you want it to be."

"No, it isn't." Brandon sighed.

"Well then, I guess there's nothing else to say, is there?" She walked toward the door. At the threshold, she stopped and looked at him. "You're not the man I thought you were."

"I'm trying to do the right thing here," he said.

Tears spilled down her cheeks. "Sadly, I think you really believe that."

Turning on her heel, she left and didn't allow herself to look back.

She forced herself to keep moving until she got into her car. Everything in her wanted to curl up in a ball and sob but she forced herself to put the key in the ignition and drive away.

She made it a block before she had to pull over. Annie dropped her head against the steering wheel and let the tears fall.

How had everything turned to shit?

CHAPTER TWENTY-SIX

The elevator doors opened and Brandon stepped out onto the VIP hospital floor. He glanced around. Holy shit. This didn't even feel like the same hospital. He paused outside Carter's room and took a deep breath as he prepared to see his friend. He rapped his knuckle on the doorframe. "Knock knock, I come bearing food," he said as he peeked his head in the door.

Carter lay propped up on the bed. Between the scruff on his face and the bags under his eyes, the guy looked rough. The corner of Carter's mouth turned up slightly in a half smile. "Hey man."

Brandon held up the takeout bag. "Philly Cheesesteak. Figured you could use some decent food."

"Thanks," Carter murmured but made no move to take the food from Brandon's hand.

Brandon opened the bag and set the sandwich and drink on the wheelie table and slid it closer to Carter in the hopes that he would eat.

He grabbed the back of the chair and pulled it across the floor closer to the bed, and dropped into it. "How you feeling?"

Carter raised an eyebrow at him, and Brandon winced. "Right, stupid question. I just meant are you in pain, or..." Unsure how to finish the sentence, he just sort of trailed off.

Carter made a scoffing sound.

Brandon shifted uncomfortably in his chair. "Your parents come today?"

"Yeah."

"Have the doctor's given you any idea how long you'll be in here?"

"Bout a week, give or take. They want to start me on some PT and coordinate with the team or something."

"With the team?"

"Yeah, Mr. Hoffman was here this morning to get consent for him to talk to my doctor's so he can try to coordinate therapy." Carter shrugged.

"The team owner came to get consent? I would have thought he would have sent someone."

"I don't know." Carter scrubbed his hand over his face. "We'll see. When he showed up this morning, I assumed it was to tell me they were releasing me."

"Jesus," Brandon muttered.

"What? I'm never going to play ball again. Figured they'd be here to just cut me loose."

"You just had major surgery a couple of days ago."

"Yeah, major surgery that ended my career." Carter shrugged. "I'm just being realistic. Figured the team would just cut their losses."

"And that's not what they are doing?" Brandon asked.

"I'm sure that's coming, but for now Mr. Hoffman wants the team doc and physio to work with the hospital." Carter scoffed. "Not like they have a lot of experience working with amputees."

Carter dropped his head back against his pillow and grunted. "Fuck." When he looked back, Carter's bloodshot eyes glazed with unshed tears.

Brandon had to look away unable to handle the pain he saw on his friend's face. He couldn't imagine what Carter was going through. "I'm glad the team is stepping up to make sure you get treatment."

He stood up and walked to the window, and looked out at the landscape. "Jesus, what the hell is with this hospital room? It's like a hotel."

"No shit. The perks of the US medical system and platinum insurance apparently. We sure as hell don't have anything like this in Canada."

"I didn't know we had it here either." Brandon eyed the big flatscreen tv that took up half the wall. Who the hell needed a TV like that in the hospital?

Brandon walked over to the window and looked out at the San Diego skyline. His gaze landed on a play park and his shoulder slumped forward. What the fuck was he gonna do with his life? He couldn't be a dad.

"What's up?" Carter asked.

Brandon glanced over his shoulder at his friend in the hospital bed. He really couldn't be that big of an asshole and unburden himself on the guy when he was laid up in the hospital. Brandon stuck his hands in his jeans pocket and rested his hip against the windowsill. "So how long are your parent's able to stay?"

"You seriously not gonna tell me what the fuck is going on?" Carter pressed.

Brandon turned and looked out the window again. "You have enough on your plate without me talking about my shit."

"Maybe talking about your shit would make me stop thinking about mine, so what's going on?"

Brandon scrubbed his hand across his face, the noise from the whiskers of his scruff reminded him he needed to shave. "Nothing really. Just got some shit to figure out."

"Don't we all? How's Annie?" Carter asked. "My Mom said she came by while I was asleep."

"Annie came by?" Brandon choked up. That was so like her. Even with everything so fucked up between them she still came by to see his best friend.

"Yeah, weird she came by herself. I would have thought she'd come with you."

Brandon cleared his throat. "We broke up."

"What? What do you mean you broke up? You're crazy about her."

"Yeah, I am. Just a lot of shit going on. "

"Like what?"

"You really wanna do this right now, man? You got enough on your plate."

"Just tell me what's going on. How the fuck did you screw things up with Annie?" Carter asked.

"How do you know I screwed it up?" Brandon grumbled.

Carter snorted. "Because it's you, dude."

He couldn't argue with that. Brandon turned and faced the window again and looked outside. He didn't have the first fucking clue what he was gonna do, but maybe talking with Carter would help. God knows trying to figure it out himself hadn't done shit. "She's pregnant."

"Pregnant? Holy shit."

Needing to move, Brandon turned and wandered around the room, hoping the movement would expend some energy. "She told me yesterday before the game."

"Hang on, you said you broke up. Is the kid not yours?" Carter asked.

Brandon reared his head back. "What? Of course it is. Why would you even ask that?"

"I don't know because you said you broke up and she's pregnant, so I just figured."

"No, the kid is mine, umm, I just... I can't... I can't fucking be a dad."

"Pardon?" Carter pushed himself up in the bed. "What the fuck do you mean you can't be a dad? Sounds to me like you're gonna be one."

Brandon turned back toward the window. That was the problem. Things were always so good with Annie. He honestly thought she was the one, but now? He couldn't fucking do that to her, to a kid. They deserved so much better than an asshole like him. Something pelted him in the back of the head and he whipped around. A plastic cup lay on the floor beside him, obviously the culprit.

"Did you seriously just fucking hit me in the head with a cup?" Brandon asked, glaring at his friend.

"Are you seriously fucking telling me you broke up with Annie because she's pregnant?"

"I knew you wouldn't understand," Brandon said

"You're right, so explain it to me," Carter growled.

"Why the fuck are you mad?" Brandon snarled. Where the hell did he get off being pissed off about this? It didn't even affect him.

"What the actual fuck, Bran? Please tell me you're not that guy."

"What guy is that?" he asked, knowing perfectly well what Carter was talking about.

"You're seriously gonna be that fucking professional athlete. The kind we hated. You're really the guy who just knocks a woman up, then pays her a bunch of money and fucks off?" Carter shook his head. "Jesus, I never thought you would be one of those fucking guys, of all people."

"Fuck you. It's not like that."

"No? What is it like then, asshole?" Carter asked. "Because from where I'm sitting, that's exactly what it sounds like."

"I'm not dad material." Brandon's throat constricted as he even thought about it. "We talked and agreed she's better off raising this kid on her own."

A box of tissues flew across the room toward him. Brandon threw up his arm, just in time to stop it from hitting him in the face. "What the fuck, dude? Why do you keep throwing shit at me?"

"Better off on her own, without you. What the fuck are you talking about?" Carter asked.

"I can't be a dad. I don't wanna be a dad. I...I..." Brandon looked up at the ceiling. How was he supposed to explain this? "This wasn't part of our agreement. Annie and I've only been dating a few months and we hadn't even gotten to the part of talking about kids or

I would've told her that I was never gonna be a dad. It's just not something I ever wanted to do or be."

"Too fucking bad. Annie's pregnant. Sounds to me like you're gonna be a dad whether you wanna be one or not. No, scratch that. Make that a sperm donor. Question is, are you man enough to be a dad?"

Brandon glared at his friend. "This has nothing to do with being a man."

Carter snorted a sound of disbelief. "I can't fucking believe you. When the fuck did you become this selfish prick?"

"How am I being selfish? Because I don't wanna be a dad? Because I don't wanna saddle some kid with me for the rest of his life? I'm being the exact opposite of selfish here. I'm saving this kid from having me as their dad."

"Sure," Carter scoffed. "Keep telling yourself that. Sounds to me like you're saving yourself and not giving a fucking thought to any kid." Carter shifted his bed and winced in visible pain. "You're right, you shouldn't have fucking told me."

"What?"

"Maybe you should go before I say something I shouldn't. I'm not really in the mood for this," Carter muttered.

"You're not in the mood? You pushed me to talk and now you're mad that I did?"

"Jesus, no, I'm not mad that you talked. I'm mad that you're this big of a fucking asshole. I can't believe I'm friends with somebody like you."

"You can't believe you're friends with me?" Brandon asked incredulously. How could he say that?

"Not really, no. The guy I thought you were and the guy you actually are? Two very different things, my friend."

"How do you figure?"

"You really want to do this?" Carter asked.

Brandon held out his arms openly. "Let's hear it."

"Fine." Carter winced as he shifted his weight. "First time I met you I thought, fuck this guy is a beast. Huge. Fearless. Kind of scary at first, but like a good guy, you know. The kind of guy who'd give you the shirt off his back. Now? You're not fearless, you're a pussy and worse than that a selfish one. That's not at all who I thought I was friends with."

"Hey," Brandon snapped.

"No, you asked and I'm going to finish." Carter pointed his finger at him, punctuating his anger. "I'm sitting here in this fucking hospital bed. My life is complete and utter shit. I'm never going to play ball again. Fuck, I need someone's help to go to the goddamn bathroom because I can't fucking walk on my own. My life is over and you're over here feeling sorry for yourself because you have an amazing woman who loves you and she's pregnant with your fucking kid. She wants a life with you. A family with you and you're too fucking big of a pussy to take it. No, you're a fucking asshole who wants her to do this alone."

Brandon could see the tears burning behind his friend's eyes when he looked at him.

Carter sniffed. "I would fucking kill to be in the position you're in. But I'm here." Carter slapped the mattress. "Look at my fucking life and you're coming in here complaining that you have a woman who loves you and wants to start a family with you. And you're throwing away this fucking gift. Fuck you, man, fuck you. Get outta here." The tears that had been shimmering in Carter's eyes broke free and slid down his cheek, and he angrily wiped it away.

"Carter," Brandon didn't know what to say.

"Go," Carter snarled.

Brandon didn't move.

"Get out." Carter screamed.

The last thing he wanted to do was leave his friend like this, but what was he supposed to do? He couldn't even come back later that day since he had to be on a plane in a couple hours. "I'll text you from the road."

Instead of answering, Carter picked up his head-phones and slid them over his ears.

With a sigh, Brandon left the room. That had gone well. Not only had he fucked up his life with Annie, now he'd fucked up his relationship with his best friend as well.

He felt like an asshole. What had he been thinking, complaining about things to Carter? The guy's life was in bigger turmoil than his. He couldn't even imagine what Carter was going through. The idea of never playing ball again made him feel sick. His stomach twisted the same way it did when he thought about Annie and this baby.

Carter was right. He was an asshole. He just didn't know how not to be. Jesus, he really was like his old man. And that's exactly why Annie and the baby were better off without him.

CHAPTER TWENTY-SEVEN

How did she end up here? This was not how her life was supposed to turn out.

Damn it. How could she have been so stupid? She knew better than to fall in love with a professional athlete. She thought she knew better than to get pregnant too, but there she was.

Annie pulled the blanket up under her chin and snuggled deeper into the couch. The half-empty box of tissues that had been on her lap fell to the floor. She eyed them and debated leaving them where they were even as fresh tears slid down her cheeks. With a huff, she leaned over and picked them up. Yanking a tissue out of the offending box, she blew her nose.

God, these pregnancy hormones were wreaking havoc on her already. She could only imagine what a mess she'd be in nine months. How was she supposed to do this alone? This wasn't how this was supposed to be. This wasn't how Brandon was supposed to be.

She'd known it was a risk to get involved with Brandon, but she'd fallen for him anyway. Fallen for his stupid crooked smile and the slightly grumpy disposition that he used to mask how kind and caring he really was.

How could she have been so wrong about him? She never dreamed someone who would adopt an abused dog would run from his own child. Sure, he had insecurities, but who didn't? But she'd thought he was more like her. Someone who ran toward the fire not away from it. Clearly, she'd been wrong.

And now here she was, pregnant and alone.

The doorbell rang. Annie groaned and burrowed deeper into the couch. Nope. There was no way she was answering it.

The doorbell rang again. Followed by pounding on the door. "You may as well answer because I'm not going to go away. I know you're home, Annie," her sister's voice pierced through the door.

Bang. Bang.

Then silence. A moment later, her cell phone rang. Quickly followed by an incoming text.

Ella: I can keep this up all day.

Ella: You know I will.

"Ahh," Annie growled as she shoved the blanket off her lap. She stormed to the front door and threw it open.

Ella stood on the stoop with a pizza in one hand and a shopping bag in the other. She held each hand up in the air. "I brought reinforcements."

Annie could just make out the ice cream carton and what looked like a can of whipped cream poking out the top of the bag. She stepped back to allow the door to open wider.

Ella looked Annie up and down and shook her head. "Damn."

She reached into the shopping bag, pulled out the cannister and shoved the whipped cream at Annie. "You look like you need that."

Annie popped off the cap. Opening her mouth, she tipped her head back and squirted a gigantic mouthful of whipped cream into her face. "Thanks," she muttered as the excess cold sugary fluff fell out the side of her mouth.

Ella nodded. "I got you, girl." She wrapped her arms around Annie's shoulder and led her back to the living room.

Annie should be embarrassed about the crumpled tissues littering the floor, but she just didn't care. Maybe if it had been anyone but her little sister, she would have been, but they'd been through enough breakups together that it didn't matter.

Ella led them back to Annie's makeshift nest on the couch. Annie dropped back into her spot and her sister sat down beside her. "Guess I don't have to ask how you're doing."

Annie squirted another mouthful of whipped cream into her mouth. "Nope."

"He hasn't called."

Instead of answering, Annie squirted again.

"Asshole," Ella muttered. "I really thought he was one of the good guys."

"He is." Tears welled in Annie's eyes. "That's what makes this so hard."

"If he was one of the good guys, he'd be here."

"That's not really fair. He didn't sign up for this," Annie argued.

"Neither did you," Ella said. "And you're not running."

"That's different."

"No, it's not," Ella argued. "Is this shit scary?" She shook her head. "I can only imagine. But you don't run. You figure it out. Together."

Tears burned in Annie's eyes. That's what she'd hoped would happen, but it didn't. "Apparently not." Her voice cracked as she spoke. "What am I going to do?" she whispered.

Ella leaned over and pulled Annie into a hug. "You become an amazing mom and give this kid an amazing life. Because whether they have a dad or not, this baby has you and they are going to be the luckiest kid on earth."

"Thanks." Annie squeezed her little sister's hand.

"Plus, you've got me and Mom and Dad and Bryce and Leah. With the Wrights at their side, this kid doesn't stand a chance of growing up anything but awesome."

She looked at her sister. Annie had always been the one looking after her. She'd never needed Ella to be there for her, and now she was. Just like she needed her to be. "Very true."

Ella picked up the pizza box off the coffee table, opened the lid and held the box out to Annie. "Eat. We gotta make sure this baby learns the value of a good pizza in a crisis."

Annie pulled a piece out of the box. Tears burned in her eyes when she looked at her sister. "I'm on it," she said and stuffed a bite in her mouth. That amazing combination of cheese and sauce and grease hit her tongue. Instantly, she felt slightly better. Magic.

"Better?" Ella asked.

It was going to take more than a box of pizza to get things better, but having Ella there helped a lot. "Getting there."

"I'll take that." Ella squeezed Annie's leg. "Now my little closet control freak, let's see the list."

"What list?" Annie feigned innocence.

She worked hard to give off the illusion of being carefree and fun, but deep down she was a planner. Responsible. And yes, a list maker.

Ella chuckled. "Don't give me that. I know you've got one. Hell. you probably have several. Bet you've got a notebook beside your bed."

Annie wrinkled her nose at her little sister. "Ha, wrong."

Ella raised her eyebrow.

"Fine, it's on the kitchen island. I was writing something down in it this morning," Annie muttered.

"Knew it."

She prided herself on being prepared and planning. But this wasn't something she'd planned for. Not yet anyway.

"What am I gonna do, Elle?" she asked. "How do I help him?"

"Help who? Brandon? Screw him," Ella growled,

"It breaks my heart that he doesn't realize how good of a person he is."

"Well, it breaks my heart you're defending this asshole." Ella tossed her napkin down on the paper plate and set it on the coffee table.

"I could have handled things better with him. Apparently the being kind of a dick when you're hurt thing runs in the family."

"Oh hell no," Ella growled. "We aren't doing this shit."

Annie blinked at her sister. "What?"

"Nope, there is no way. How many lectures have you given me over the years about boundaries and owning what is mine and only that?" Ella shook her head. "So no. I'm not letting you blame yourself for Brandon's decisions. He's a grown ass man. He's the only one responsible for his choices. Isn't that what you always say to me?"

"Yeah," she grumbled.

"So take your own advice." Ella curled her feet up underneath her on the sofa. "Did you say some things you wish you didn't? Maybe. Did he need to hear them?"

Annie nodded. "Yeah, but I could have said it nicer."

"Boo hoo, he's a big boy. He can handle it."

Annie let out a little laugh and placed her hand on her chest. "Oh, you were listening all those times I lectured you."

"Yep, so take your own advice. It's not your job to fix Brandon. That's his job. He's the only one who can do it."

"I know. It just sucks." She picked up the whipped cream cannister from the coffee table and squirted a big dollop in her mouth.

"Yep." Ella shoved her foot into Annie's leg. "Now quit bogarting the whipped cream."

"I thought you bought this for me," Annie grumbled.

"In what world would I buy whipped cream and not expect to eat some?"

"When you're being a good sister and taking care of me." Annie squirted another mouthful of whipped cream in her face.

Ella's hand whipped out and snatched the whipped cream from her. "Now I'm saving you from yourself. When Brandon comes crawling back, you want to look your best not be all bloated from excessive lactose consumption."

"Then you shouldn't have brought cheese and whipped cream," Annie said.

"Those are the top two FDA approved foods for heartbreak I'll have you know," Ella countered.

"Yeah, I'm sure they are." Annie sighed, then looked at her sister. "Do you really think he'll come crawling back?"

"If he's the guy you still seem convinced to believe he is, then he'll get his head out of his ass and figure his shit out."

"I hope he figures it out soon."

"You and me both." Ella sat up, then slid her way into the spot between Annie and the back of the couch so she was snuggled up against her like she'd always done when they were kids. "Until then you've got me, babe."

Tears welled in her eyes again as Annie wrapped her arms around her sister. "Thanks," she whispered. What would she do without her family?

Brandon didn't have that. He didn't know what it was like to know someone always have his back. As much as she hated it, she couldn't really blame him for being scared.

But Ella was right, she couldn't do the work for him. He had to get there on his own. She just hoped he figured things out before it was too late.

"Anytime."

CHAPTER TWENTY-EIGHT

D ejected, Brandon hung his head and looked back through the tunnel at the field. That was quite possibly the worst game of his entire career. He couldn't get his head in the game. He kept seeing Annie's face. How disappointed she was with him. He could just imagine what his mom would say about him walking away, abandoning his own kid. What kind of person did that?

But it just freaked him out. All he kept thinking was how no kid deserved to have a dad like he'd had. Didn't they always say you learned how to be a parent from your own? Look at his role model. No, he wasn't doing that to a kid. He couldn't.

But he couldn't imagine his life without Annie.

Wandering into the locker room, Brandon chucked his glove in the top of his locker and dropped onto the bench. He ignored the guys around him. He pulled off his gear and headed for the shower.

When he walked out a few minutes later. Pete sat on the bench, waiting for him. No doubt to lecture him about how he was letting down the team. Give him a break. That was the last thing he needed to hear. He knew that already. He didn't need someone to tell him. Ignoring his teammate, Brandon pulled his clothes out of his bag.

"You just gonna ignore me?" Pete asked.

"That was the plan." Brandon eyed his teammate. "You just gonna be a perv and sit there and watch while I get changed?"

"Don't flatter yourself," Pete scoffed. "But I am going to sit here until you fucking tell me what got up your ass at the game today."

"You seriously have to ask?" Brandon dropped his towel and stepped into his underwear.

"No, not a chance. You're not blaming that shit on Carter," Pete said.

"Blaming it on, Carter, are you fucking kidding me?" Brandon turned and glared at his teammate. "If anyone should understand what it feels like not to have Carter on the field, it's you."

"No, I'm fully aware it sucks, but that's not the reason you played like shit. We both know it. What the hell is going on?"

Brandon ignored his teammate and continued to get dressed. Pete nudged him with his foot. "You need to talk to somebody, man, or go hit something, but either way you need to get your shit together because we need you to be on the field. You sure as fuck weren't there today."

"I have one fucking bad game and you're gonna be like this?"

"It wasn't a bad fucking game. You weren't even there," Pete said.

"I was fucking there," Brandon snarled. "I dropped one goddamn ball."

"Fucked up a couple of throws. And don't even get me started talking about your hitting," Pete said.

"Nice fucking pep talk," Brandon muttered.

The equipment manager walked up and looked at the two of them and cleared his throat. "Brandon, Coach Schneider wants to see you in his office."

Great, just what he needed. "Thanks, man. I'll be right there."

"Figure your shit out before you get in there," Pete told him.

Brandon glanced around the locker room at his teammates, then back at Pete. "How the hell are you the best we've got for this kind of conversation?"

"Look, man, I know shit with Carter was hard. I get it. We all do, but you can't let it get in your head and wreck the game. That doesn't do anybody any good and it shits all over what Carter's going through. He'd give anything to be on this field and you know it. When you get the chance, you play. You play like he'd fucking want you to play." Pete stood up. "Since we both know there's something else going on with you. I'm here if you wanna talk." Pete slapped him on the shoulder. "Good luck in there."

"Thanks," Brandon muttered.

After making a quick stop to grab Leo from the trainer, Brandon walked toward the coach's room, paused outside the door, took a deep breath, and knocked.

"Yeah," came the response from inside.

He peeked his head inside the room. "Hey Coach, you said you wanted to talk to me."

Coach set the pen down on the desk. "Come in. Close the door behind you."

Brandon shut the door and took another deep breath. Shit. He sat in the chair across from his coach, told Leo to sit on the floor beside him, and waited.

Coach stared at him for several seconds before finally taking a deep breath. "That was a tough game out there, son. Worst one I've ever seen you play."

"Yes, sir."

"You wanna tell me what's going on? I know you and Carter are pretty close."

"Yeah."

"That what today was about?" Coach asked.

Was it? Maybe partly. Definitely not entirely. But he wasn't exactly gonna tell his coach that he didn't have his head screwed on straight because he'd knocked up his girlfriend. No, not knocked up his girlfriend. Gotten the woman he loved pregnant and he was freaking the fuck out.

"Sort of. I mean, of course being out on the field without him it's gonna make me think about what happened and how shitty his situation is," Brandon replied.

"From what I understand, you're usually pretty good at compartmentalizing shit," Coach said.

What was that supposed to mean? Brandon narrowed his eyes and looked at his coach. "Excuse me?"

Coach leaned back in his chair and crossed his arms over his barrel chest. "I'm gonna be real with you, Brandon. I didn't like what I saw out there today. I see a lot of guys get a case of the wobbles and it can be hard to come back from. You get in your head and you start questioning everything, so I'm gonna be keeping an eye on you to make sure this is a one and done kinda deal."

"Yes, sir," Brandon replied.

"Is there something else I should know about?"

Yes, but there was no way he was having this discussion with his coach. "Umm...no, sir."

"Look I'm going to be straight with you, Brandon. I like you. I think you're a good guy, but I'd be lying if I said I wasn't aware you're battling some demons. It's part of what makes you such a great player. But if those demons are knocking on your door and making your game go to shit, then I'm going to step in and make you deal with them."

Brandon didn't respond. How could he? He didn't know what his coach knew about his past, and he sure wasn't going to volunteer the information.

"Part of our scouting report includes your history, high school, minor leagues. Everything we can dig up. I like to know what I'm signing on for when I get a player." Coach smiled sadly at him. "I don't have all the details and I don't need them, but I know you had it pretty rough growing up."

Jesus, he didn't know anyone here had a clue about his past. He could just imagine what those reports would have said. Hell, there were more than enough people from his past who were only too happy to talk about the poor little Sims kid. Shame filled him at the idea of someone he looked up to like Coach Schneider knowing that about him.

"Honestly, that grit and fight is one of the reasons I pushed for you to come here," Coach said.

At the moment, he didn't feel like he had much fight left in him. Everything had fallen to shit.

Coach leaned forward and steepled his hands on the desk. "We are not at the point where I'm going to push this, but you may want to talk to the team psychologist."

"Are you kidding me? It was one bad game." This was ridiculous. Gritting his teeth to stop himself from saying something else, he tried to breathe. Leo shifted his bodyweight against Brandon's leg. He reached down and gave the dog a little rub. At least the dog had his back.

"Don't get defensive. I'm worried about you, and I know how quickly things can spiral to shit, and I don't want it to get to that point." Coach sighed. "Judging by your reaction to me suggesting you use the team psychologist, you've never talked to anyone."

"I'm not much of a talker," he grumbled.

"Hadn't noticed." Coach chuckled. "Seriously though, what happened to Carter is a lot to deal with. You two are close. He's going to need you. And the team needs you to have your head in the game, so I'm strongly suggesting you talk to the team psychologist."

Annoyed, Brandon smacked his teeth. "Strongly suggesting."

"At this point, it's a suggestion. Don't make me make it a requirement." Coach pinned him with a stare. "I'm saying this because I care, Brandon. Talk to someone."

"Right. We done here?" he asked.

Coach let out a loud sigh. "For now."

Brandon pushed himself off the chair. "Let's go, Leo. Break." The dog stood up and looked at him for direction.

They had just taken a step toward the door when the coach called him back. He turned and Coach held out his hand with a card in it. "The psychologist's number. They'll fit you in anytime. Can even do it via zoom while we are on the road," Coach said.

Brandon snatched the card from the coach's hand. "Fantastic."

Turning on his heel, he walked out of the office and didn't stop till he got to his vehicle. He drove home on autopilot.

By the time he got home, he was practically vibrating. Who the hell did Coach think he was, acting like he gave a shit about him? One bad fucking game and suddenly he needed psychological help.

He dropped onto the sofa and put his feet up on the coffee table. Leo whimpered, drawing his attention to the dog at his feet.

"Okay, come on up." He patted the seat beside him. Instead of laying down like normal, Leo sat up straight and stared at him. If he didn't know better, he'd say Leo looked worried. He gave the dog a reassuring pat. "Lie down, bud. Everything is fine."

The dog lay down and plopped his head on Brandon's lap. Brandon rubbed the dog's head, then stroked his soft ear between his fingers. "Okay, maybe everything isn't good. Clearly, I'm not holding it together as well as I thought. But a fucking shrink? Really?"

Leo pawed his arm and cocked his head to look up at him. Brandon could practically hear the dog say 'yeah, really'.

Jesus, when even the dog thought he needed help, maybe he really did. Annie sure as hell thought he needed to talk to someone. And he'd royally fucked things up with Carter, so it wasn't like he could talk to him.

Absently playing with Leo's ear, his mind drifted to Annie. His chest tightened. Fuck, he didn't want things to be over between them, but the idea of being a father absolutely terrified him. Some people just weren't meant to have kids.

Leo pawed his arm and he realized he'd stopped petting him. He glanced at the dog and some of the tension in his chest eased. He picked up Leo's face and leaned down and kissed the dog between the eyes. Leo gave him that goofy, Pitty smile of his and Brandon couldn't help but smile back. "I love you, buddy."

The dog raised his eyebrows and looked back at him. Brandon sat up straight. He loved the dog, like really loved him, would kill to protect him kind of love.

His dad wasn't like that. He clearly remembered his dad hitting a dog with his car and being annoyed it left blood in the grill.

When it came to dogs, at least, they were completely different. And he knew he'd never purposefully hit a kid. Not planned and malicious like his dad did to him, but that anger was inside him. He'd assaulted his dad, he'd gone after Johnny the other day. That instinct to attack, to use violence when he was stressed it was like a burning knot in the pit of his stomach. What if he snapped on his kid? That was who he was. It was in him and he'd rather die than do that to a kid. It just seemed safer for everyone not to put himself in that situation.

Leo scratched against the couch. His claws made a noise as they dragged against the fabric. "Hey, none of that. You already destroyed one couch."

The dog glanced at him, then scratched again. "I'm serious, dude. You'll get off the couch if you're gonna do that."

When he'd come home and seen the destroyed couch, he'd been mad, but there wasn't a single part of him that thought about hitting the dog. Sure, he'd been annoyed, but more at himself for letting it happen. The dog was a dog. He didn't know better. They both knew better now and would do better.

Brandon ran his hand over the fabric of his new sofa. Could he possibly be like that with a kid as well? His dad sure as hell couldn't. But then his dad would have killed the dog and that hadn't even crossed his mind.

Brandon gave Leo a firm pat. "Thanks, Leo. Who needs a shrink when I've got you?"

Leo let out an exasperated sigh.

"Are you saying I do need a shrink?" Brandon chuckled.

Leo burrowed his head deeper into Brandon's lap. "All right, point taken."

If he wanted to have a hope in hell of being with Annie, he needed to at least try to figure this out. He pulled the business card out of his pocket and looked at the number. He didn't have a clue if he could be the kind of man his kid deserved, that Annie deserved, but he sure as hell wanted to try.

Before he changed his mind, he picked up his phone and dialed the number. After several rings, an automated voicemail picked up. If this was an emergency call 9-1-1.

Jesus, that was dark.

His shit was nowhere near that serious. He could figure this out on his own. His finger hovered over the disconnect button. No. He had a kid on the way. He didn't have time to figure it out on his own.

The automated voice said for Dr. Lindley, press 2. Brandon pressed 2. Finally the answering machine clicked to leave a message. "Hi this is Brandon Sims. Cal Schneider from the San Diego Hawks gave me your number. I was hoping to schedule an appointment." He quickly left his number and hung up.

Brandon dropped his head against the sofa. Good lord, all he'd done was leave a message to schedule an appointment and he felt exhausted.

He absently rubbed Leo's back. All the work and training had been worth it for Leo. He was like a different dog. Maybe it would have the same effect on him. He sure as hell hoped so. And if it didn't at least he'd know.

Thinking of Annie, he picked up his phone.

Hi Annie. Just wanted you to know I made an appointment to talk to someone.

Good

Can I see you?

Have you changed your mind about the baby?

Had he? He didn't have a clue. All he knew was he couldn't imagine not having Annie in his life. The idea of being a dad terrified him, but so did the thought of not having Annie. For her, he was willing to try to figure his shit out. That was about all he knew right now.

I don't know.

You don't know?

Not really no. All I know is I love you and I'm trying to figure this shit out.

I love you too.

So can I see you?

I don't think that's a good idea.

Why not?

> Because if you decide you don't want to be
> a dad it will just hurt more

As much as her answer hurt, he understood where she was coming from.

> So no communication till I figure my shit
> out?

> I think that's for the best

> Brandon, don't do this for me.

> What do you mean? Of course I'm doing it for
> you.

> I need you to do it for yourself.

For himself, right. If he was doing it for himself, he would keep doing what he'd been doing and avoid thinking about his past altogether. Thinking about it, digging into this shit was way too painful and in his experience, nothing good ever came out of dragging up the past. Nope, the only reason he'd lay himself bare was for her. But he didn't think she wanted to hear that.

> Sure.

I really hope you get what you need from this Brandon.

Me too.

His stomach knotted. He chucked his phone on the end table to stop himself from picking it back up. He wasn't sure if he wanted to call Annie or call the doctor's office to cancel. Either way, it was a bad idea. He clenched his fists, then shook out his hands. Then gave his arms a shake like Annie had showed him. With an exhale, some of the tension eased. What would he do without her?

Fuck. All this better work.

CHAPTER TWENTY-NINE

A nnie stood at the stove and stirred the bolognese sauce she'd made for dinner. Glancing at the clock, she calculated about two more minutes on the noodles and they'd be ready. Her stomach fluttered and she placed her palm on her belly.

"Hi baby," she said. "Are you hungry too?"

The little flutter happened again and she smiled. She'd just started to feel the baby move the past couple of days and every time she felt the movement, it stopped her in her tracks. She'd heard the heartbeat at each appointment, but feeling the baby move was something completely different. Special, just hers and the baby's.

The timer on the stove beeped. Annie pulled a noodle out of the pot and gave it a taste. Perfect. She grabbed the pot and drained the water. She scooped penne noodles into a bowl, then added a generous serving of sauce on top.

At the sound of the doorbell, she pulled up short. Gah, she was not in the mood to talk to someone trying to sell something. She wished she was one of those people who could just pretend she wasn't home but she always felt too guilty.

She set the pasta on the counter and made her way to the front door. Annie pulled open the door and gasped. "Brandon, what are you doing here?"

"Uh hi." He gave a little wave as he spoke. Then his eyes widened and he took a step back. "Wow. You're —" He pointed at her stomach. "I didn't really expect you to look so different already."

Annie placed a hand on her belly. She'd outgrown most of her clothes a couple of weeks ago. "It's been six weeks since I saw you, Brandon."

"I know. I just...I didn't realize it would all happen so fast. I guess I should have. I mean, I know, but seeing it is different." He raked his hand through his hair. "Can I come in?"

Annie stepped back and gestured for him to enter. Her heart raced. What was he doing here? And why did he have to look so amazing?

As he stepped past her, he brushed against her arm and goosebumps danced on her skin. Stupid pregnancy hormones. The things had a mind of their own.

"It smells great in here," Brandon said. He peeked toward the kitchen. "Did I interrupt your dinner?"

Her stomach growled loudly, and Brandon laughed.

"Yeah, I was just about to eat." And her stupid manners dictated she offer him some. "Did you want some?"

His head cocked to the side as he looked at her, and she instantly sank into his rich brown eyes. She'd always been such a sucker for his eyes. The rest of him was so hard to read, but his eyes had always been so expressive. And damn him, they still were. The attraction between them was still very much alive and well.

The corner of Brandon's mouth curved up like he knew she wasn't immune to him. "I wouldn't say no," Brandon replied.

He wouldn't say no to what? She racked her brain for what he was talking about. Dinner, right.

"Come on," she said and walked toward the kitchen. She pulled a bowl from the cupboard and handed it to him. "Help yourself." She pointed at the strainer filled with pasta in the sink. "Sauce is on the stove."

Brandon filled his bowl. "Thanks, Doc."

Her throat clogged with emotion. She placed a hand on her belly. As much as she wanted to be with him, it was about more than just her now. She had this baby to think of. "Why are you here, Brandon?"

He gestured to the table. "Why don't we eat and then we can talk? From everything I've read, it's important for you to eat properly."

"From everything you've read?"

His cheeks turned pink and he ducked his head. "Yeah, umm. I've been reading up on things and the books all say how important it is for you to properly fuel your body for both you and the baby."

Annie pushed her bowl away from her. How was she supposed to eat now? "What are you doing, Brandon? You're reading books now?"

He winced. "Sorry. I'm sorry. I'll shut up. Eat, please."

She watched him. What was he doing here? Had he done the work? Was he ready to be a dad?

"Doc, please, eat." He pointedly stared at her.

With a grumble, she picked up her fork and took a bite, then gave him a fake smile. "Happy?" she mumbled around a mouthful of food.

"Yeah." He stuck his fork in his bowl and took a bite. "Wow, this is amazing." He gestured to her bowl with his fork. "Eat."

"Fine," she growled. She stabbed her fork into her bowl and took another bite.

"I've never seen anyone scowl and chew at the same time," Brandon said.

Annie raised her eyebrows at him. "I really don't think we're at the place where we tease each other over a meal. Do you?"

Brandon dropped his head. "No."

Annie took a couple more bites of her meal, then pushed the bowl away. Enough of this. "Okay talk. Why are you here?"

Brandon set his fork down and wiped his face with his napkin, almost like he was buying himself more time.

"Talk, Brandon," she demanded.

He closed his eyes and took a breath, then nodded his head slowly. Finally, he opened his eyes and squared his shoulders and her stomach knotted. Oh shit, what was he going to say?

"I'm sorry, Doc."

Tears burned in her eyes. Damn it, she'd really thought he'd come around. She placed a hand on her belly. "It's okay, Brandon. You don't have to say anything."

"Oh shit, no, Doc." His eyes widened and he jumped up from the table and rushed over, dropping to his knees beside her. "I'm not saying I don't want to do this."

"What?"

"I panicked and I fucked up."

Annie blinked as the pregnancy fog in her brain tried to compute what he was saying. "Okay? What does that mean?"

Brandon sat back on his heels. "I'm saying if you'll have me. I want to try to do this."

"You want to try to do this?"

"Yeah." He nodded.

"There is no try, Brandon. You're either all in or you're all out. I'm not having you be some half-ass dad."

"I don't want to be a half-ass dad. That was never the problem."

"No, the problem was you didn't want to be a dad at all."

"Yeah." Brandon dragged his hand over his jaw. "I didn't. I honestly never saw that in the cards for me."

"Right."

"But I never saw you in the cards for me either and—" He grabbed her hand. "I can't imagine my life without you."

"I can't imagine my life without you either," she said. "But there's a baby here, Brandon, and it deserves everything."

"I agree. 100%." He rolled his lips together. "I honestly didn't believe I could give him that." Tears glistened in his eyes. "I'm still not sure I can, but I want to try."

"Brandon, I have never met a better man than you."

He laughed without humor. "That's a pretty sad statement, Doc."

"No, it's not."

"Yeah, it is, but I want to get there. I want to be that guy and I sure as hell don't want to be my dad and my counselor says that's half the battle so—" He shrugged.

"You're still doing the counseling?"

"Yep, twice a week for the rest of my life at the rate I'm going," he grumbled.

She couldn't help but laugh. "I'm pretty sure you aren't going to need to be a lifer."

"God, I hope not." His thumb rubbed against the side of her hand. "I'm trying to figure my shit out and I guess if I would rather die than hurt my dog. I have to believe I'd be the same with my own kid."

"That's what I told you," she said.

"I know." He blew out a breath. "It just took me a while to get there."

"And now you're there?"

"Yeah." He shifted closer so his chest was touching her knees. "Look, Doc, I don't know if I'm ever gonna be able to get to where our kid deserves me to be, but I'm going to give it everything I've got."

"Brandon, no one is perfect. Every parent makes mistakes. All I need from you is a promise that you will never lay hands on our kid in anger."

Brandon shuddered. "I would cut off my own arm before I would ever do to anyone what my dad did to me. So yeah, I can promise you that."

"That's all I need. The rest we can figure out." She cupped the side of his face. "Do you think I'm not terrified about being a mom? I am."

He smiled sadly and tilted his head into her hand. "Yeah, but we both know you're going to be great at it."

"So will you."

"Fuck, I hope so." Brandon's beautiful brown eyes clouded with emotion as he looked at her. "I love you, Doc, so goddamn much it scares me."

She shifted in her seat so she could face him fully. "I love you too, Brandon. There is nothing to be scared of."

"But there is." He smiled sadly. "My counselor thinks that might have been part of why I was such an asshole when you told me about the baby."

"What do you mean?"

"The timing, with Carter and everything." He shrugged. "His injury rocked me."

Annie smiled sadly. "I know it did" She couldn't imagine how it must have been for him to have his best friend suffer a career-ending injury like that. How scary it would have been. How close to home it would have hit. "How is he doing?"

Brandon exhaled audibly. "Honestly? Not great. I mean, physically he's doing as well as can be expected. He's working with OT and PT, but mentally he's pretty fucked up about the whole thing. Understandably."

"I'm sorry."

"Me too." Brandon absently pressed his bottom lip between his fingers and sucked air between his teeth. "As shitty as it is to say, it wasn't just Carter getting hurt that fucked me up. Just being at the hospital brought everything with my mom back up again and made me think about what I would do if something happened to you."

He shook his head. "I couldn't handle that. Carter was bad enough, but if something happened to you? I couldn't..."

Brandon let out a deep breath. "Then when you told me about the baby, all I could think about was my dad and the monster he became after my mom died. And there was just no way I could do it. I freaked out."

She cupped his face in both of her hands and forced him to look at her. "Brandon, you aren't him. Even on your worst day you couldn't be like him."

He smiled tightly. "I'm starting to see that." His eyes glistened and he blinked rapidly like he was trying to stop them from falling. "It just all freaked me out. And you were right. I needed some help to work through some shit."

She wanted to wrap her arms around him and take all of his pain away, but she couldn't. "I'm glad you are getting help. I'm here if you ever want to talk about anything."

"Thanks." His head bobbed up and down. "My counselor wants to have you come to a session. She thought it might help."

"Anytime."

"Thanks." He licked his lips. "I'm sorry it took me so long to get my head out of my ass."

"All that matters is you did."

Brandon moved forward on his knees and wrapped his arms around her waist, resting his head against her belly. She stroked her fingers through his hair. The baby kicked to let her know it was there.

Brandon raised his head. "What was that?" he asked.

"That was your baby letting you know they're glad you're here, too."

Brandon's eyes widened. "That was the baby? You can feel him kick already?"

"Mmm-hmm, I'm nineteen weeks."

"Already? I missed half of your pregnancy." He pursed his mouth tightly. "I'm sorry I wasn't here for you."

"You're here now, and that's what matters."

Brandon sat up higher on his knees, putting him almost face height with her. "I promise I'm going to make it up to you."

"You better," she teased.

"Fuck, I missed you."

"I missed you too," she said.

Brandon smiled as he tucked a hair behind her ear, then cupped the back of her head and leaned in close.

"How about you let me start making it up to you?" he whispered.

His warm breath danced across her skin, and she shivered. Suddenly, he stood up and picked up her bowl. Annie blinked. "What are you doing?"

"Dishes?" He smirked at her. "What'd you think I meant?"

"Umm."

Brandon held the bowl in one hand as he leaned in and placed a soft kiss against her lips. "You've got me for the rest of your life, Doc. There're all kinds of ways I can show what you mean to me." He kissed her again, then stood up. "Starting with the dishes."

While it wasn't what she'd been expecting him to say, she wasn't going to argue. "Well, I'm not gonna say no to that."

Brandon chuckled. "Didn't figure you would."

Annie leaned back in her chair and rested her arm over her belly as she watched Brandon putter around the kitchen cleaning up. This was exactly what she'd always wanted.

EPILOGUE

B randon walked out of the locker room and scanned the hallway. Where was she?

He pulled his phone from his pocket and pulled up their text thread, and started typing as he walked down the hall toward the exit.

Where are you?

Still in my seat

What the hell? Why was she still in her seat and not down here like she normally was after the game? He punched the call button. The phone had barely rung when Annie picked up. "Why are you still in your seat? What's going on?"

He could hear Annie's breath, followed by a grunt.

"Annie?"

"I'm in labor."

"What?"

"Can you come get me? I'm scared to stand up."

Panic clenched his chest. Scared to stand up. What did that mean? Why was she scared to stand up? "Are you okay?"

"Not really," she whimpered.

"Fuck. On my way." He took off running. He threw open the door and raced up the stairs toward the main stadium seating area. He skidded to a stop to get his bearings. Shit, he should have gone the other way. Pushing past a couple of lingering fans, he ran toward the first baseline where Annie's seat was. She was the only person still sitting in the area. He flew down the stairs as fast as he could.

"Doc?" He called as he got to the end of her row.

Annie raised her head. A look of relief flashed across her face, quickly followed by a grimace. He sucked in a breath at the pain clearly etched on her face. He dropped to his knees beside her. "Talk to me, Doc. What's going on?"

"I'm in labor."

"What? That's impossible. You aren't due for another couple of weeks."

"Apparently this one has other ideas." She placed her hand on her belly.

"Why are you still here? You should have gone to the hospital."

"It's the World Series."

"Jesus, Doc, it's game one."

"I wanted to be here for you and—" She hissed out a breath as her hand clamped around his arm.

Finally, after what seemed like an eternity, her grip loosened. "It's our first baby. I thought labor would take longer, but after my water broke."

"Your water broke?" He looked down just now notic-ing the wet ground where he was kneeling. He wrinkled his nose. "Jesus, is there always this much?"

"No, I knocked over the guy beside me's beer because I didn't want him to know what happened. Then I didn't want to stand up because it would look like I peed my pants and the game was almost over anyway."

He shook his head and smiled at her. "You dumped a guy's beer instead of admitting your water broke?"

"I didn't want to freak him out."

He stroked a hand down the side of her face and cupped the back of her head before he leaned in and kissed her gently. "Well, you've certainly got me freaked out. Can you stand now?"

"I don't think so. This baby feels a whole lot closer to coming than I'd like."

"Fuck, okay, umm." He couldn't think. It was like his brain had completely short-circuited.

"There are paramedics on site, right?" Annie asked.

"Yeah," he mumbled.

"Can we maybe call them?"

He dimly heard what she said, but it wasn't registering.

"Brandon?"

He shook his head to try to get his brain back on line. "Sorry. Yeah." He pulled his phone out of his pocket and dialed the team doctor. "Come on, come on," he muttered when it rang a second time.

Finally, the call picked up. "Hello?"

As soon as he heard the team doctor speak, he blurt-ed, "Annie's in labor."

"Brandon?"

"Yeah." Annie gripped his arm again as another contraction hit. "I'm bringing her to you. Meet me in the treatment room." He told the man on the other end of the phone.

"What? Why are you bringing her to me? Take her to the hospital."

"No time. We're here and this kid is coming."

Dave grumbled something Brandon couldn't understand, then said, "Fine."

Brandon hung up and shoved his phone back in his pocket. He looked down at Annie. "Fuck this." He scooped her into his arms and carried her down the row. Instead of going back the way he'd come, he headed down the stairs toward the field.

"What are you doing?" she asked.

"Getting you to the doctor." He set her down at the railing, then hopped over.

"Hey, you, stop," a voice called out.

Brandon flicked a glance toward the security guard. Ignoring the guard running toward them, he reached over the railing, hoisted her into his arms again, and began walking toward the tunnel.

"I said stop!" the security guard yelled.

Brandon ignored him. The guard raced up to them and grabbed Brandon's arm. Brandon shrugged him off.

"You aren't allowed to be here," the guard said.

Brandon stopped walking when the guard pulled firmly on his shirt. He whipped around. "Are you fucking kidding me?" Brandon growled as he glared at the smaller man.

"You aren't allowed to be here. No fans on the field."

Jesus, this guy didn't have a clue who he was. "I'm Brandon Sims."

The guy stared at him blankly.

"I play for the fucking team," Brandon growled.

The guard looked him over and sneered. "Sure you do."

"Jesus, is this your first fucking day here?" he snapped.

Annie's body tensed in his arms. Concern for her gripped him tight. "Move out of my fucking way," Brandon snarled.

The guard grabbed his walkie and said, "I need backup on the field."

"Are you fucking kidding me? This woman's in fucking labor and you want to go toe-to-toe with me, asshole?"

"Maybe just show him your ID," Annie said calmly.

"I'll show him my fucking fist if he doesn't get out of the way and let me get you some help."

"Brandon." Annie placed her hand on his chest soothingly. Even in labor, she was the voice of reason. So much for all the techniques he'd learned in counseling because none of them were coming to mind right now.

He glared at the rent-a-cop, then looked at the four security guards running toward them. Hopefully, one of these fucking yahoos actually watched the team they were employed by and knew who he was or shit was about to get real ugly because he was all out of patience.

Annie whimpered and her entire body coiled tightly as a contraction ripped through her.

They needed a doctor now. He looked up from Annie and the security guard had moved and was now doing his best to block the entrance to the tunnel. This fucking guy had a death wish.

"Get out of my way or I will fucking end you," Brandon snarled. He would have already destroyed this guy if he wasn't so worried about protecting Annie.

"Brandon, I am not having my baby in the tunnel of the stadium. Move this asshole, plow right through him," Annie screamed.

Whoa, things were getting desperate if Annie was losing her cool.

"Everything okay, Brandon?" A voice called from the left. He glanced toward the tunnel. Thank god. "Mario, will you tell this asshole who I am please?"

The equipment manager jogged over to them. He eyed Brandon with Annie in his arms. "What's going on?"

"Annie's in labor and this dickhead won't let me get through."

The four backup security guards arrived at the entrance to the tunnel. "What's the problem?" one of them asked, eyeing the scene in front of him.

"This is Brandon Sims, right fielder for the team that employs you." Mario glared at the security guard blocking the tunnel.

"That's really who he is?" the guard asked.

"Yes. And even if he wasn't, this woman is clearly in labor, so you should have called for medical attention," Mario snapped.

"I didn't know for sure it was real."

"You didn't know it was real?" Brandon yelled. "Who the fuck fakes labor to get back to the locker room? "

"You'd be surprised," the guard responded.

"Jesus," Brandon muttered. Annie's body tensed and she moaned as another contraction hit.

"Move." Brandon ordered the guard. The man ducked his head and moved out of the way finally.

Shoving past him, Brandon glanced at the equipment manager. "Dr. Dave is meeting me in the treatment room. Can you be a runner and get anything he says he needs, please?"

"Done." Mario jogged away in search of the doctor.

"I don't want to have my baby in the locker room," Annie whined.

"I know, babe, but I don't think you have much choice at this point." Brandon pushed the door open to the locker room and made his way to the treatment room. It wasn't the warmest place, but he figured it at least had medical supplies and running water, so they should have everything they needed.

He set Annie down on the massage table. Was this thing even strong enough to support a woman in labor? Shit. "Let me go pull the couch in from the other room."

"I'm not having my baby on the locker room couch," Annie said.

"Doc, we don't have a ton of options."

Tears welled in Annie's eyes. "I know," she whispered. "I just had this whole birth plan." She sniffed.

Brandon heard voices in the main locker area a moment before Mario rushed in with the team doctor.

"Thank god," Brandon mumbled.

The doctor eyed Annie, then clapped his hands together. "I hear there's a baby who wants to be born."

"I know this isn't exactly in your normal job description, Dave," Brandon said.

Dr. Dave walked to the massage table. "Hi, I'm Dr. Błaszczykowski, but everyone calls me Dr. Dave. You must be Annie."

"I am. Sorry about this."

"Not a problem. I'm guessing this wasn't part of your birth plan," Dr. Dave said as he swept his arm out to encompass the room.

"Not even close." Annie's eyes watered again. "God, sorry, I don't know why I'm so emotional. This is stupid."

"Not a problem at all. It's perfectly normal. When my wife was in labor, she went from loving me and wanting cuddles to grabbing my balls and threatening to tear them off if I ever came near her again." Dr. Dave chuckled.

"You have kids?" Annie asked.

"I do. Four of them. All home births."

"Home births?" Brandon shook his head. They'd discussed it, but the idea terrified him. What if something went wrong? He'd been 'Team Hospital' all the way and now here they were, potentially delivering their baby in the locker room.

"I can only imagine how you're feeling, Annie, but let me put your mind at ease. My first two years in residency were in obstetrics before I switched to sports medicine. I delivered all four of my children at home with water births, so you're in good hands. I promise you."

"You did water births?"

"I did, yes."

Annie looked at Brandon. "That was on my birth plan."

"I know, but..."

Dr. Dave squeezed Annie's arm. "Why don't we see where things are at and we'll discuss options." He eyed

Annie's outfit, then looked around the room and sighed. "Brandon, do you have anything clean that Annie can put on?"

"Umm, yeah." He dashed to his locker, where he always kept a spare set of clean workout clothes. He grabbed his shirt and ran back.

"I'll leave you to change. Holler when you are ready," Dave said.

Brandon helped Annie peel off her clothing. He undid her bra and was momentarily distracted by the sight.

Annie slapped his arm. "Did you really just stare at my boobs?"

"Uh..." He cleared his throat. "Umm..." What could he say? Annie had a fantastic rack. There wasn't going to be a time when she flashed her boobs that he didn't look. He shrugged.

Annie rolled her eyes. "You're such a guy."

"Guilty." He leaned in and pressed a kiss to her shoulder. "If you didn't look so good, I wouldn't look."

She snorted. "Yeah right. I'm sure I look really hot, all sweaty and blotchy."

He pressed a kiss against her lips. "You look gorgeous."

He rested his head against her forehead. "You're having our baby, Doc. How could I think you're anything but amazing?"

"Thanks." Suddenly she winced. "Okay, let's get this going so we can get the doctor back in here."

Brandon pulled his t-shirt over her head and down her body so she was covered. He jogged to the cabinets where he knew they kept blankets and towels and pulled out several of each. He draped one over Annie's lap so she was covered, then opened the door and called the doctor back in.

"All right, Annie, let's see how far along you are. If we have time, we'll call the ambulance and get you to your doctor so you can still use that birth plan."

As the doctor took position at Annie's feet, Brandon made his way to the head of the table. There were certain things he didn't really need to see.

"Okay, then, looks like this little one wants to be born where Dad works," Dr. Dave said.

"What?" Brandon's head snapped up. "Like now?"

"Afraid so," Dave replied.

Annie's phone rang. "If that's Rayne, can you answer it?" Annie said.

"You want me to answer the phone and talk to Rayne now?"

"I texted her earlier when I was in labor to see if she had any breathing exercises I could do to slow things down and she said she'd come to the stadium."

Brandon answered the phone. "Hey, Rayne."

"Brandon, why are you answering Annie's phone? Is everything okay? Is she still in labor?"

"Definitely still in labor."

"Put her on speaker." Annie demanded.

He swiped the button to switch to speaker.

"Rayne, there's no time. I'm having this baby at the stadium. That's got to be some weird energy. Can you come and clear the room or do whatever you need to do? I'm not having my baby born hopped up on testosterone and competition."

Brandon rolled his eyes. "The baby is not going to be born like that. That's not a thing."

Annie glared at him. "Brandon, if you don't have something helpful to add to the conversation, then keep it zipped." She shook her finger. "Maybe if you'd kept something else zipped, we wouldn't be in this situation."

Oh boy. He pressed his lips together.

"I'm standing outside the gates trying to get in," Rayne said. "And there's an ambulance parked right out here."

"I'm not delivering my baby in the back of an ambulance. That's even worse energy than delivering it here," Annie cried.

"When the hell did you start caring about energy?" Brandon asked.

"When you suggested I go to Rayne for massages." Annie pushed up on the massage table. "No, if there is no time to drive to the hospital, then we are delivering this baby here where I can have some semblance of control. And I need Rayne to clear this room."

Brandon scrubbed his hands over his face. At prenatal classes, they'd told him to be prepared for Annie to have a range of emotions, but this was ridiculous. She couldn't deliver the baby until Rayne did an energy clearing?

"Brandon, I need you to go get Rayne," Annie told him.

"Me? Go get Rayne." He shook his head. "No chance I'm leaving you."

"Brandon, please." Annie winced and rubbed her lower back.

"Fine, I will get someone to go grab her." He pushed open the door to the treatment room and spotted Mario pacing in the corner. Brandon stalked toward him when the team owner walked in. "Mr. Hoffman, uh, hi," Brandon said.

"Brandon." The owner looked toward the treatment room. "I got a call that your partner was in labor."

"She is, yes."

"Why aren't you in there with her?"

"Umm, I need Mario to go grab our friend Rayne and bring her back here."

"Rayne? The woman I saw you with at the park?"

"Yes, sir. She's waiting at the back gate, but security won't let her in."

"I'll go get her," Mr. Hoffman said.

"You'll get her?" Why would the owner of the team go get his friend and bring her back here? Why was he down here at all?

Annie's groan echoed through the door. At this point, he didn't care as long as someone went and grabbed Rayne. "Thank you, boss."

"Your baby is being born in my locker room, Brandon. I think you can probably call me Matthias at this point."

"Right." He eyed the treatment room. "I need to get back to Annie."

Matthias clapped him on the shoulder. "I'll go grab Rayne."

Brandon hustled back into the room. Annie's flushed face turned toward him. "Where's Rayne?"

"She's coming."

When Annie doubled over, he rushed back to her.

A minute later, Rayne burst into the room. "I'm here."

"Thank god," Annie said, then groaned. "Oh god,"

Rayne rushed over to the table. "What do you need me to do?"

Panting, Annie closed her eyes. He'd never felt so helpless as he stood and watched pain rip through Annie's body.

Fuck, he wished he could do something.

Rayne placed her hands on Annie's abdomen. After a few moments, Annie's breathing relaxed.

Annie opened her eyes. "Thanks," she told Rayne. Her eyes filled with tears. "I'm not supposed to have my baby in a locker room."

Brandon swept his thumb across Annie's cheek to brush away the tears. "I'm sorry, Doc, if you hadn't been trying to support me, you wouldn't be here."

"Stop it," she growled. "I was staying for the game. It's not that." Annie looked around the room. "It's just—"

"I'll clear the room." Rayne squeezed her arms. "But honey, your love is more than enough good energy to cancel out any negativity that might be floating around."

"I'm just scared. I don't want to mess anything up." Annie sniffled.

Brandon's chest tightened as he watched the woman he loved battle her fears about delivering their baby. If she needed some weird energy clearing thing done to help her feel more in control, then he was all for it. Hell, he'd sweep the room himself if it would help.

Not that he had the first clue how to do that kind of thing, but he'd try. He would do anything to help.

"You won't, honey. Everything is going to be great." Rayne glanced at the Dr. "You look like you are in good hands."

"You are," Dr. Dave said.

"I know," Annie whispered. "It's just, we had a plan."

"Plans change, Doc. No one knows that better than us." Brandon rested his forehead against hers. "I'm right here, baby, I got you."

"I love you," she said, then sucked in a breath. "Holy shit," she grunted. When she looked at him, her eyes were wide with pain and a little fear.

"You okay?"

"Not really." She winced. "This baby is coming now."

"Clear quickly," Brandon growled at Rayne as Annie's nails dug into his arm.

"I got you covered," Rayne said and squeezed Annie's arm. "When I'm done, I'll just stand over there and send you Reiki and hold space."

He didn't have a clue what that all meant, but Annie seemed to appreciate it.

"Thank you," Annie said through gritted teeth.

"All right, Annie, I think this baby is ready to make its way into the world," Dr. Dave told her.

Annie looked at Brandon and he gave her what he hoped was a reassuring smile. "You got this, Doc."

She nodded.

"Time to push, Annie," Dr. Dave told her.

Brandon sucked in a breath as a wave of fear crashed through him. She was ready to push already? This was all happening too fast. What if something went wrong?

"Brandon," Annie groaned and reached out her hand to him.

As terrified as he was, he needed to focus on Annie right now. Not himself.

"Brandon, maybe you could get behind Annie and hold her up so she has some support at her back," Dr. Dave said.

He eyed the massage table. There was no way this thing was holding them both. He pulled his chair closer and moved his body so he could support her with his arms. It was awkward as hell, but nothing compared to what Annie was going through. He braced himself as she pushed her weight against him.

He was dimly aware of Rayne as she moved around the room doing god knows what. Honestly, he was too focused on Annie to care.

"I need you to focus and push, Annie," Dr. Dave said.

Annie's body went rigid as she pushed. And pushed. And seemed to push again. Brandon's arms burned from holding Annie in place as she continued to bear down, but there was no way he was letting her go.

She dropped her head against his shoulder. "I can't," she gasped.

"You're doing great, Doc. I'm so proud of you, you're so strong," he reassured her. She was so amazing.

"I'm not," she cried.

He kissed her temple. "You are. You got this. One more." He shifted his body so he could push her more upright. "Push."

Finally, the baby's head popped out, quickly followed by its body. After a moment, the unmistakable sound of a baby crying filled the air.

Tears burned in the back of his throat. Holy shit.

Dr. Dave put the baby on Annie's chest and held out a pair of scissors toward him. "You want to cut the cord?"

Brandon blinked at the other man. Did he? He looked at the helpless baby on Annie's chest.

Dave pressed the scissors toward him. "Cut the cord, Brandon, between the two clamps."

On autopilot, he did what he was told.

"Oh my god, he's perfect, Brandon," Annie cried.

Reality crashed in like a mac truck. Any semblance of calm vacated his body as every fear and insecurity rushed to the forefront. He stumbled back. He couldn't do this. What if Annie was wrong and his dad's jeans were stronger than they thought?

Annie touched his arm. "Doctor, can Brandon please hold him?"

What the hell was she saying? Terrified, he looked down at her. Annie smiled. "Trust me. Hold him, Brandon."

Brandon took the baby from the doctor. The second they placed the baby in his arms, his fears disappeared as a wave of love so strong it nearly knocked him on his ass crashed into him.

No, Annie had been right. He was not his dad. As he looked down at his child's face, he knew he was nothing like his father. He'd die before he ever raised a hand to his kid. And he'd kill anyone who even thought about hurting his son.

He dragged the back of his hand across his cheek to wipe the tears that were streaming down his face.

Holy shit, he was a dad.

With a laugh, he bent down and kissed Annie on the mouth. "You're incredible."

"Thanks." Annie smiled.

He placed the baby back on Annie's chest and crouched down beside her to stare in wonder at his son.

"Sorry to interrupt. I'm going to step out and give you two some time alone. Once you're ready, we'll have the paramedics take you to the hospital to get checked out." Dr. Dave said.

"Is everything okay?" Brandon asked.

"Absolutely. Just routine given the circumstances."

"Thank you, Doctor," Annie said.

As the doctor walked out of the room, Annie's eyes widened. "Oh my god, are you seeing what I'm seeing?" she asked. "I think Rayne is out there flirting with your boss!"

Brandon flicked a glance at the door and saw Rayne and Matthias talking. With a shrug, he turned back to Annie and his son. "Honestly, I don't really care about anything but this. Look at him, Doc, he's perfect."

"Yeah, he is."

Brandon gently rubbed his hand over the baby's head. "I'm thinking since he was born in the locker room, we should revisit the name discussion. Maybe call him Hawk instead of Liam."

"There is not a chance in hell I'm naming my son after a baseball team."

"We'll talk." He kissed her on the cheek.

"No Brandon," she chuckled.

"We'll see," he teased.

Annie pressed a kiss on the baby's head. "Your Daddy is a goofball, you know that?"

Hearing Annie call him Daddy took the air out of his lungs. Daddy. Never in a million years did he imagine this would be his life. Now as he looked at the woman he loved and his son, he realized nothing could have been more perfect.

I hope you enjoyed Catching the Fly. If you want more Brandon and Annie click below for a free Bonus Scene that takes place 5 years in the future.

https://www.laurenfraser.com/catching-the-fly-bonus-scene

The next stand-alone book in the Playing for Keeps Series is Carter's story. Sleighing the Game is a grumpy sunshine holiday novella about a small town girl and the wounded baseball player who moved in next door.

This year there's not much holiday cheer for a grumpy ex-ball-player, but maybe he's stumbled onto the small town—and Christmas angel—who will turn his life around.

Carter Daye has always known exactly who he is. A ball player. Until an accident took his lower leg and his dreams along with it. Now he doesn't have a clue where he belongs. Hiding out in a small town in the middle of no where feels like the perfect place to figure it out.

Diner owner, Kelsey Danvers loves her small town, all things Christmas and believes there are very few things that can't be made better with a smile.Unfortunately, her grumpy neighbor disagrees.

But Kelsey has never met a Scrooge who didn't eventually appreciate a little holiday cheer.

Carter stopped believing in the magic of Christmas long before he lost his leg. But his sunshiny neighbor seems to have made it her holiday mission to help him see that life is what you make it. If only that were true. Kelsey's pulling out all the stops to make him see there's a whole world beyond the diamond.

PICK UP YOUR COPY: books2read.com/sleighin gthegame

To stay up to date on news, releases and sales from Lauren, sign up for her newsletter here. **www.lauren fraser.com/newsletter**

ABOUT LAUREN FRASER

Lauren Fraser resides in British Columbia, Canada with husband. They have two children and the requisite dog.

When she's not busy writing, Lauren loves to spend time with her family outside: camping, hiking and kayaking.

Lauren writes about love and relationships in many different forms, but in the end she's a sucker for a happy ending. She is multi-published and loves to hear from her readers. For the latest updates, visit her website: https://www.laurenfraser.com

For all the latest updates, contests and other fun little goodies sign up for the newsletter. https://www.lauren fraser.com/newsletter

*Reviews help other readers find books. If you could please take a moment to review this book I'd really appreciate it.

ALSO BY LAUREN FRASER

Playing for Keeps
Too Far   Prequel- not sports romance
Protecting the Plate – Book 0.5 novella
Everything to Me   Book 1
Throwing the Curve   Book 2
Sliding into Home Book 3
Hitting the Gap Book 4
Catching the Fly Book 5
Sleighing the Game – Book 6 Christmas

Cowboy Code
Rode Hard Book 1 Cowboy Code Series
Rough Stock Book 2 Cowboy Code Series
Round Up Book 3 Cowboy Code Series

Best Things are Three Series

Longing for Kayla
Dani's Duo

Flirty Forties Series
Sun, Sin and Surf
Aged to Perfection

Standalone Books
The Geek Next Door
Letting Go
Too Hot
Yielding for Him